MERCY

Prism

Book 1

LOVE BELVIN

MKT Publishing, LLC

mercy

the prism series : one.

ISBN: 978-1-950014-55-2 (Paperback)
ISBN: 978-1-950014-51-4 (eBook)

MKT Publishing, LLC
First print edition 2021 in U.S.A.

Cover design by **Visual Luxe**

Part I

16 Years Ago

Time for a new manicure…

I held my left hand in the air against the beaming sun.

I wonder if Amanda will let me drive this time…

My housekeeper knew I wanted to drive each time I could since I'd gotten my permit a few months ago.

"Shi," Becky called over to me. Her naturally red-stained lips puckered in a gesture, driving my attention toward Shizu. "You think she's gonna do it?" she asked while flapping her arms and legs beneath the water to keep afloat.

"Do what?"

"Keep up!" Becky hissed. "Make out with the new guy. How do you pronounce his name again, Shizu? You guys all have those difficult names." She giggled, looking my way to have her back.

Not this shit so early on…

The summer had begun, and we were three days fresh out of *Bishop John Yancey Christian Academy*. I invited my friends over for a dip in the pool, not a clowning session over names. I rolled my eyes.

"First of all, Re*bec*ca," Shizu carefully enunciated. "My parents are from Mori, which is within the vicinity of a place called Shizuoka. Hence my Japanese name, Re*bec*ca. The guy you speak of is Aisake. He's Polynesian. Grab a fucking map before we start eleventh grade, why don't you?"

When a hard snicker escaped my tight throat, Becky smacked my float, almost knocking me into the water. Laughing, I tried explaining, "She's got a point, Becky!"

"No, she doesn't." Becky's face turned red and tightened. "Shizu, you're always trying to belittle everyone. Isn't that a lonely place?"

"No, Becky. I just call you on your bullshit and sound good doing it. Maybe Shi-Shi should do it more often, but nooooo," Shizu intoned, rolling her eyes over her low-hanging heart-shaped sunglasses.

"So not true!" I laughed impossibly harder as Becky turned apple-red.

"Even your mom says so, Shi," she grumbled, then her attention drew to Becky. "I'd question this one if I were you."

I gasped, still unable to stop laughing.

"I think you've blown the whole conversation out of proportion," Becky argued. "What does you making out with the new guy have to do with you lowkey calling me racist?"

I rolled my eyes. "Oh, god!"

Shizu sat up on her floatie, getting near Becky. "Maybe the fact that you assume I have an interest in a guy in school just because you think we're the same—"

"What the hell?" Becky yawped from her throat as her eyes grew wide.

Following her line of sight, I peeped my dad with four young guys. My Dad kept it stylish in khakis and a polo shirt with boat shoes. Sadly, the guys with him were in button-down dress shirts, dress pants, and shoes. One towered my father while two were his height—give or take an inch or two—and the other was shorter.

"Who are they?" Becky demanded.

"Interns." I could tell by the way they were dressed alone. The bright sun obstructed my vision as they trailed after Daddy along the veranda of the back of the house. They must have been reporting to our home today.

"Mr. Witherspoon sure knows how to keep with diversity," Shizu observed out loud.

Of the four guys, one was white, one Indian, another of Asian lineage, and the shorter one Black.

"That orange head is so fucking hot," Becky groaned beneath her breath.

Shizu and I both turned to her.

"Shocker!" Shizu whispered mockingly, and I knew why.

Becky had a head of beautiful red curls with lips to match. When I was having a lazy hair day or wanted an edgy look, we'd walk the halls of *Bishop John Yancey Christian Academy* with my voluminous, moisturized bouncy fro and her red curls. My mom showed me how to express my rich ass Black pride in a predominately white school.

"Fuck you, Shizu. I'm not racist," Becky's tone was low now that the guys were within earshot.

"It's my job to keep you from it." Shizu lifted her sunglasses. "I spy two hunky ass fellas I wouldn't mind wrapping my legs around and tonguing down," she growled like an animal.

Becky giggled at her as I locked eyes with the Black guy. He was the shortest of the bunch. His shirt was oversized and belted pants hung lower than anyone else in the group.

Oh, my god…

Those were sneakers. The kid wore a fresh pair of *Concord Air Jordans* beneath the loose khakis. My heartrate spiked, body suddenly dialed up to a scorching temperature as I inched up the floatie.

jas

"Sinclair."

I heard the warning, but couldn't look away.

She had long legs and wild, dark hair with sunglasses keeping it from her deep-bronzed face. Even from a distance, I could see the twinkling gold bracelet on her ankle. I ain't never see a white, Black, and Chinese girl in close proximity, unless in a store at the mall or something. The Chinese chick was pouting her lips my way. The white girl tried hiding her smile like she was shy or something. But the Black one? She just stared at me. Maybe she was mean as hell. She damn sure was corny with wack ass 80s pop music bumping from the speakers.

Damn!

A grown lady came out of nowhere into the lounge area of the pool. She dumped her robe on a lounger, leaving her in a sexy ass bikini. I watched as she sat on the ledge of the pool without flinching from the cold water then grabbed the Black girl from behind her floatie and smiled with affection painted on her beautiful face. Her every move, from kissing ol' girl on the head to whispering something in her ear, felt like… love.

Is that what that shit look like?

It looked cool and foreign to me at the same time. It was something I never had and didn't feel like I needed until this very moment. I wanted that. I wanted safety and touching and belonging *and* power—

"Sinclair?"

Bobby, another intern for this stupid ass summer program, tapped me on the arm. I turned to Mr. Witherspoon, the builder my guidance counselor had hooked me up with. I swiped my nose with my thumb, a little embarrassed from having all eyes on me. Mr. Witherspoon's face was balled tight as hell.

"Maybe one of these days—in the distant future and by way of a rare miracle—you can have what you *apparently* like watching over there. Until then, why don't you focus on learning something today to possibly better your circumstances, because I can guarantee you none of those girls out there *or* my wife want the likes of what you're turning into."

I swallowed hard, jaw tightening.

This nigga…

I ain't need this shit. I knew I should've stayed on the block with Man and Juggy. Could've made some dough lifting cars or playing stickup. *But no...* I had to pacify my father's attempts at "raising me right." Raising? Shit. I'd been a man for years now. A man I could show this corny ass, fat ass, punk ass, wanna-be boss, Witherspoon.

"And what am I, *sir*?"

He took a step closer to me. "A lucky son-of-a-bitch to be on my roster this summer after the seedy shit you did during your school year. A smart kid with a world of opportunities at his feet, but wants to be a street nigger. You give us a bad name, Sinclair. I know this—knew this—but still tried giving you a chance. So, the least you can do is act like you fucking belong here, *even though you don't.*"

My throat went dry. The nigga tried to play me. On a normal day, I'd tap his chin and knock his big ass out in front of his interns and old lady. But for some reason, his words hit harder than anyone's before them trying to break me down.

"Yeah," he grunted, shaking his head. "Let's go."

Two of the dweebs with us shook their heads as we all turned to walk off. My heart was banging in my chest and my head spun as I widened my nose to breathe.

But I said nothing. I promised Ms. Greene, my guidance counselor, I wouldn't blow this opportunity after the shit I found myself in last school year. So, yup. I just ate it. And that shit burned like fucking acid.

One day, I'd show him. I didn't know when, but I'd show niggas like Witherspoon and my father I could play their straight-laced, corny ass, legit game and win my own fucking way.

"You're excited," my mom whispered near my ear.

"Am not," I ground out, deeply annoyed.

"Your nipples are hard, baby." *I'm gonna die!* I gasped, quickly folding my arms over my chest. "Is it the shorter one with the baggy clothes?"

"It's no one." I was seething. "What are they even doing here?"

"Your dad's showing them the addition to the side of the house," she answered sweetly, as she always did when amused by my torture.

I didn't think about that. "Why does he have to bring his work home?" He had plenty of projects in development.

"I don't mind." Shizu winked. "They can stay for lunch if they want."

My mom's breathy teeter annoyed me. Why was she entertaining Shizu? "Which one would you sit next to, sweetie?"

"The one with the dark, silky fade." Shizu rubbed her hands together.

I wanted to laugh, but was still confused by what I saw and felt at the sight of the guy in *Air Jordans*, and embarrassed by my mom's observation.

"The Japanese guy!" Becky blurted. "Okay. Then what's wrong with me thinking the red-head is hot?"

"The fact that you think the guy I find hot is Japanese. Girl…" Shizu rolled her eyes and picked up the magazine she'd been reading.

That made my mom *and* me laugh.

"There's nothing wrong with being attracted to a man with the same features as you, ladies. In fact, I'd find it strange if you weren't. Beauty comes in all colors and features. I tell my Shi-Shi here to just be sure her heart beats for the color and features of her daddy, granddads, and uncles *especially*. If that ain't happening, we have a problem." She squeezed me around the floatie, forcing me to draw in her flowery scent that I loved.

"See, Shizu!" Becky's arms swung into the air. "That's all I've been saying about the Japanese guy—"

"*POLYNESIAN!*" Shizu and I shouted at the same time.

About 1 & 1/2 Years Later

The distinct volume of the pigeons' coos, police sirens in the distance, and the animated exchange between the fish market owners a block down in their native Mandarin Chinese tongue brought comforts of an early morning in Harlem. Sitting on a cement foundation framing the property of a corner house, I took in a deep breath then went back to writing my list.

-*finish Club Sin*

-give F down payment for apartment building
-cop boat—
Nah...

I ripped the sheet of paper from the wire ring of the notebook and burned it with my lighter. When the flame reached my index finger and thumb, I dropped what was left of the paper to the ground and stomped out the small fire with my boot.

After taking a sip of my hot tea through the plastic lid, I tried again.

-cop mom a crib
-put up the $ to invest in Divine's rec center in Cali
-finish Club Sin—

"Will this be the day you join us inside?"

I snorted then glanced up, knowing who had approached me from behind with that deep ass, raspy voice. *The new church guy.* He took a seat next to me on the cement, not saying much at all. He'd done this before, a time or two. The nigga ain't want shit. A weirdo, kinda, but cool. Smart as hell. He'd been coming around here for a couple of months. All I knew was his name and that he went to this church.

Sitting across from the back of a big ass building just outside the gates of its parking lot, I mindlessly read the name attached to the stucco siding.

Redeeming Souls for Abundant Living in Christ Family Worship Center

The spot had been around forever. When my grandmother used to walk past here on her way to do her shopping, she'd up the speed of our stroll, squeeze my little hand tight as hell, and always perform the sign of the cross. I thought it was normal until I got older and learned a little bit about religious practices. Not a church-goer herself, she respected the idea of God and His Sundays. She wouldn't use His name in vain, so no *goddamn, thank God* (unless you really were), or swearing to Him either. And on Sundays, she didn't gamble, fight, or put my mother out—if she'd been let back in since her last drug-induced infraction. I knew as early as nine years old grandma feared God.

After she died when I was sixteen, there were two things I knew for sure. One was I would fear no man. There had been many in my circle with a higher ranking than me, and I respected them, but never from a place of fear. The second thing I knew was I would treat God the same way. I'd acknowledge Him, but only from a place of respect. I could never fear any *thing* or being the way my grandma—

"The fear of the Lord is the beginning of knowledge, but the morally deficient despise wisdom and instruction," the guy next to me murmured.

I glanced his way, noticing his phone out with words filling its screen and a leather portfolio opened on his left thigh. *Left-handed...* He was writing something down, attention fixed to his work. That's when I realized I'd been so caught up in my head about this church and memories of my grandmother that I hadn't realized he'd set up shop next to me.

See...

Strange ass.

It was the dead of winter and the man appeared out of nowhere —again—and pulled out his writing tools.

I laughed quietly, to myself. Then I read over the last list I'd made.

-cop mom a crib
-put up the $ to invest in Divine's rec lot in Cali
-finish Club Sin

Instead of picking up where I left off, I quickly decided against it. After ripping the paper from the notebook, I grabbed the lighter.

"I dreamt of you last night," he rasped, head still low.

Now frozen, slowly, my head swiveled his way. "Pardon?"

He nodded, still scribbling. "Unimaginable irony for you; normal whimsicality for me," his tone bitter.

Confused, I ain't have shit to say. We'd exchanged a few words in the past, but I'd chalked it up to him doing what the *real* good church folks did; being friendly, especially on Sundays. I sparked a flame, lit fire to the paper, and lazily watched it quickly dissipate into the air. I came here—as I always did—to have quiet time alone. This morning, I was running out of time. I had to get to Jersey to meet with Double E, some shit I couldn't be late for. He hit me with the 9-1-1, which wasn't his normal play.

"Finish up with whatever you've been developing, and secure even the long-term, high-risk investments available to you."

I scoffed. "Why would I do that?"

How did the nigga even know what I was doing out here? He must've read my writing.

"Because *Shammah*'s about to show you mercy."

My head whipped to peer around me. "Who?"

He looked at me, eyes tight. "The Lord *who is here*." His eyes circled the air. Then he grabbed up his things before suddenly glancing my way again. "Invest in yourself and for yourself, not for other people."

I dabbed my nose, laughing again. "Is that what your 'dream' told you?"

I knew I should have been concerned about the dude being 5-0, but there was something in his aura telling me since the first day I met him that his suspect behavior came from the walls of the building across the street from us and not organized law enforcement.

"Perhaps." He nodded. "In the dream, you were alone in isolation, restrained." He shook his head, eyes closing to a tight squeeze. "The serial of visions is hard to explain, but the Lord also showed me you are a prism. There are two ways about you that are identical: the way you meet people and the way you're affected by them are the same. You have only one face and just one tongue. Although your actions are of a member of the dark underbelly of society"—*Damn!*—"your essence is not. Light comes through you one way, but because of how you were uniquely and wonderfully designed on the inside at His hand, that light—the energy—leaves you multiplied, and spectrally. You reflect dispersive light, sir." He stepped off toward the street.

Scoffing again, I turned away. "Light…"

Shit sounded weird, but didn't feel off.

"You don't even know," he questioned, more or less in shock as he took a step toward me. Dude whipped back around, glancing at the back of the church then my way again. "*Christ…*" he whispered in frustration. "You're still in darkness. That's why—the isolation." His eyelids closed again, the balls behind them rolling around. I could even see the clenching of his jaw on his clean-shaven face. With his nostrils spread, he began, "Hebrews twelve and eleven—I doubt if you read the Word yet, but do not doubt you will in due time—speaks about chastising," he whispered, no eye contact involved.

"'*No discipline seems pleasant at the time, but painful. Later on, however, it produces a harvest of righteousness and peace for those who have been trained by it.*' I know you're thinking I'm two shades past insane, but on most levels I assure you, I am not. Nonetheless, your life is going to course in a manner that will be immoral and illegal."

Man, you're years too late on that guess…

Still, I didn't blow him off. Church people were nice on Sundays.

"And again, *Shammah* is going to show you mercy. Not only that, He's going to change how you reflect His light to the world. Through you, good will multiply and you'll be given grace."

"Yo, E!" My eyes landed on a short cat across the street. He waved, going to the trunk of his car. "I got the new microphones with me this morning!"

"I'll be with you momentarily, Dwayne," he shouted in return. "Just finishing up with my pal, Jas, here!"

He remembered…

"Yo, man—"

He cut my words. "That prism in you is going to be what you'll need to get to the promise."

"What promise?"

His brows shot up as fast as his shoulders. "I have no idea of that. I am not God." His nod was a way of ending the conversation. "But Jehovah-Shammah does." Then dude stepped off.

"Where are you even from, yo?" I scoffed to his back. "Who are you?"

I'd been coming here for about four to five years, but only started seeing him a few months ago.

He turned around, smirk lifting on his face. "I told you when we met: Ezra Carmichael. I'm a man like you, but in covenant with Christ. You'll get here, though. Of that, I am confident."

"Nah." I shook my head, studying his face. "I mean what do you do at this church?"

His neck twisted and he tossed a quick gaze at the building. "Keeping with my end of the bargain. My parents pastor this tabernacle."

I didn't know what that meant. "I just started seeing you here not too long ago."

"I'm not sure how long you've been around. I returned to the States this year." He began backing away. "I'm not sure how long it will be, but I look forward to seeing you again, Jas. Take care of yourself and guard your internal prism." With a nod, he was off.

Mind-fucked and with a queasy ass stomach, I watched him cross the street and meet up with the little dude waiting on him. They exchanged a few words before Ezra helped him take equipment into the back of the church. Minutes after they disappeared, I snapped out of the zone his strange ass, cryptic words got me into. Then I glanced down at the clean sheet of paper in the notebook and jotted down *mercy*, *grace*, and *promise*. I found my head lifting toward the sky, catching the golden cross atop the building. That's when I thought to write out *prism*.

A sharp ass snort pushed through my nose as I realized I let that weirdo nigga get into my head. I ripped the page from the notebook then rolled the spark-wheel of the lighter and began to burn the paper as those four words did the same in my brain.

When the metal door of the warehouse ascended, O.G. Iban Ellis stood with his hands behind his back in a typical expensive ass suit. It was the Ellis uniform. His face was hard as stone, body rocking on the balls of his feet as he waited. As usual, Ellis' soldiers were planted inside the warehouse and throughout the parking lot with guns present and in position. I'd been used to this aggressive guarding of the Ellis fortress.

I'd known the Ellises since I was thirteen, spending summers here in Jersey with my father, but had heard urban legends about them since I could remember, growing up in Harlem, New York. Double E was a ruthless kingpin, slaying anyone getting in the way of his reign and money. He not only ruled by fear of life and the quality of it, but also by rewarding loyalty and respect. As a kid, his name scared the shit out of me. I never thought our lives would have intersected, with me being a trusted affiliate of his.

Iban tossed his chin my way as I stood alone. "He waiting on you."

When he turned to walk off, I followed. A few of the armed soldiers trailed behind. Before we made it to an interior door, I was patted down, checked for wires and weapons. Again, I was accustomed to these security measures: it was nothing personal. Once cleared, Iban led me inside. The moment I stepped through the door jamb, the distinct scent of raw coke filled my nostrils. That was the first odor. We'd pass the crack and weed segments, thankfully missing other production areas like opioids.

As we continued toward the offices, Iban murmured, "For what he 'bout to put you D on, if you need back up, I got you."

Shit...

Work. I was here to put in work.

But of what kind? Iban was his father's top executioner. His work far exceeded mine.

The next thing I knew, a door was being opened just before Iban crossed through. I was on his heels, telling myself to be patient; I'd know what this was about soon. Double E, whose real name was Earl Ellis, had just ended a call before we stopped in front of his desk. After handing the phone over to a cat standing over him, Double E nodded my way.

"Young O.G.," he greeted, standing from his desk.

I pounded my chest. "Much appreciated. Good to see you, sir."

We shook hands. "Have a seat."

I obeyed, backing into an available chair. A few of his guys left the office, leaving just the Ellis men and me.

"Say, Sin," Double E began. "I've been made aware of an opportunity, something that would bring me to the role of broker." I nodded my attentiveness when he paused for a reaction. "Paulie Rizzo, the brother of Salvatore Rizzo—you know that cat. He runs the port." I nodded again. "Then you may know his brother, Paulie. Got a construction company—" He snapped his fingers to propel his memory. "—it's not *just* construction. It'll come to me in a minute. But anyway, he's in need of a—" He cleared his throat. "—exterminator. Seems he's got a beef with a Polish family over near the Iron Bound section of Newark. He move a little arms."

Polish… Iron Bound… Guns…

"The Bartnickis?"

"You know how to pronounce that shit?" Iban snorted from behind me. "Good, too!"

Ignoring him, Double E's attention dropped back to me. "From what I heard from Rizzo himself and a few heads from around the way, Bartnicki's son fucked Rizzo's daughter up real bad at one of them white kids' parties. He was drunk and showing out for his stupid ass little friends and got rough with her. The little muthafucka took it too far and wound up raping her." *Damn…* Double E cut out a lot of details because I didn't see that rape shit coming in the story. "Rizzo called up Bartnicki to try to handle it on the street…Bartnicki been giving him the run around for weeks. Then Rizzo finds out the young fuck, Bartnicki's son, done fucked another little girl a few days ago."

"Nah, Pops," Iban interrupted. "He raped that little Spanish bitch."

Double E's head seesawed left to right, expressing his indifference to the detail. "All I know is Rizzo wants the Bartnickis out. He wants it clean and unconnected to him. They ain't involve 5-0 from the jump, so there's no police report or paper trail that could lead them back to Rizzo."

I would have thought having Double E get a Black kid to do it could possibly draw the distance Rizzo needed to the job. But if you knew Double E, you knew he could have outsourced to any race and got the job done, and right. And to think, he'd come to me. Guns was my occupation, not bodies. But money was a common motivation for cats in our game.

"Building." Double E suddenly snapped his fingers again. "That's right! He a property builder. Been for at least thirty something years. I think he had that shit going when I had my second son, Deek." His brows met as his face tightened in deep thought.

"You said Rizzo's a builder?" I asked, chin dropping for clarity.

"Yeah," he mumbled, still trying to recall. Then his head lifted and Double E Bags waved it off. "Don't matter no way. Just wanted to show he got the dough to pay for this shit. Just name ya price, Young O.G. If it's reasonable, I'll make it happen."

Property builder…

That's when I recalled who Bartnicki was. He was a butcher with three meat markets between Newark and East Orange. He also sold guns, but wasn't a major player. He sold just under enough to keep the top dog arms dealer in the tri-state, Popov, off his ass.

I also recalled the Rizzo brother, more specifically, the logos on his utility trucks. He built a few houses near my father's place after a blaze burned them down to their weak bones. I observed their work every day I was with him that summer as the crew cleared out, dug, and built new houses. It was one of the most fascinating things I'd ever seen. The prospect of doing this hit began to thrill me more than a potential dollar amount.

"I know this ain't your…usual M.O., but know you're clean about your shit, too. If you want it, the job'll be paid six months after. My fee'll come off the top—"

I shook my head, standing for the door. "I'll take it."

"What's ya price?" he asked to my back.

I turned to face him. "Half a M in case I get jammed up. My lawyers gotta eat."

His head bucked back. "Only a half?"

"Nah." I rubbed my chin. "I want his business."

"The building business."

"One hundred percent, no questions asked. Paperwork'll be drawn up and signed before I make the play."

"How do I make that happen?"

"I'll get the paperwork to you, then you can get it to Rizzo. Lemme kick it with the lawyers first."

I had lawyers I knew only because of a mentor, not because I was legit in any formal occupation. It was because of him and Double E here that I'd been low key sitting on a fortune at this point in my life. If this shit went right—which I was confident it would—having Rizzo's company could be the legitimizing agent I needed to come from out the gutter.

I lifted my hand out of respect. Double E reciprocated, shaking firmly.

Then I turned to Iban whose eyes were wild and expectant. The nigga was practically salivating. I respected the O.G., but he was a wild one. Iban killed niggas for sport. That wasn't my play. I couldn't risk getting caught or having the job turn into a massacre instead of a clean execution. Shaking my head, I had to be clear on my decision to not include him on this. He'd get over it. Iban was a known bully. He'd fuck up, and with some of the weak Ellis soldiers as well as affiliates. In that moment with my eyes, I explained I would not tolerate it. Within seconds, he opened the door. Passing through it, I began to flex my fists. If Iban wanted to see me, I'd do what I had to do.

But he didn't. Iban opened the door, but stayed behind with his pops. His wisdom served in my favor.

Good.

I had a job to put into play.

6 Months Later

There is a suspect of interest for the Bartnicki massacre.

"Can I get you something?" I glanced up from the newspaper at the thick Dominican accent to find a leggy, wigged red-head with tortilla skin.

I checked my wrist for the time.

"You got tea?"

"Sure." Her plastic-looking pale lips pouted as she flipped a page of her small memo notebook. "What kind?"

"Green?"

"Sure," she repeated before spinning around to head behind the counter.

My attention went back to the article in *The Record* newspaper. My name or any part of my identity were not mentioned, but it was me being reported on. Shit was real, but still felt distant.

I made the play. Rolling up on Bartnicki, his brother, brother-in-law, and his son outside of Bartnicki's main meat store in Newark was an easy and clean execution. My assignment was just the father, but luck would have it for Rizzo that Bartnicki's son had pulled up unexpectedly for a chat. And I wiped them out. My getaway wasn't as clean. Newark PD worked fast and smart, finding traces of the plates from the stolen car I used that night. I didn't know just yet how they connected me to the car, but they did. According to the news reports, there was a witness, but nothing more.

Whatever the fuck that means...

I'd already been in the system from being locked up back in high school. Using my moms' given address on my record, Newark PD headed straight to Harlem and pulled up to the projects two days ago. The fuckers spotted my real car, broke in, and found two of my clean ARs in the trunk. They shouldn't have been there. Fucking Juggy didn't drop them off to the buyer that morning. But, of course, it was my jam-up. That got NPD riled up enough to go bust my mother's door down, only to find I wasn't there. I hadn't lived in my mother's apartment in years, though it was still my legal address.

Glancing back down at the paper, I saw the shooting was a headliner. Soon, my name would be attached to it.

...and according to a spokeswoman from the Essex County Prosecutor's Office, there is a person of interest. We hope an arrest is imminent—

"Sorry for the holdup," Double E murmured, unbuttoning his suit jacket before lowering himself into the seat across from me at the booth. I closed the paper, stowing it to the side of the table near the window. He noticed. "That's the bullshit," he grumbled. "Iban's on the 'eye witness' as we speak. The shit'll be deaded before I close my eyes tonight." His gaze locked upon me.

"Appreciated." I nodded. "They'll need more than him."

"Glad to hear. Just know, they ain't got him."

I wanted to assure how clean my work was. They'd never find the gun. But that wasn't something I'd waste my time assuring. Not only was it useless in this instance, it would've been the weak route. I did my job. The fall was on me.

He nodded toward the window where a silver minivan had turned the corner, passing the diner. "That's your payment."

I nodded in response as I watched it turn into the diner's parking lot.

It was his men with my payment. Juggy and Man were awaiting them in the back for the drop.

"I included another quarter for your trouble."

I shook my head just as the waitress had returned with a mug and two tea bags then poured steaming water inside.

"Thanks," I murmured to her.

"Anything for you, Mr. Ellis?"

"My usual, sweetie. Tell Richie back there to use some salt in my oats and to fry that fuckin' bacon hard for me."

She winked while snorting, "I'll make sure today." Then she took off again.

I sat up in my seat, grabbing the teabags. "You can keep the money." Double E froze. "I was actually going to give you a half a M."

His brows met. "For what?"

I understood his gift of a quarter of a million dollars to me was an incentive for my silence when I'd finally have to turn myself in or be apprehended—the latter was some shit I wouldn't let go down. But it wasn't necessary.

"For my security."

His face opened in shock and confusion. "You know I hold mines down, kid."

I pulled the bags from the steaming mug. "For the Bartnicki work."

"Your compensation is the half a M and their business."

"And I need them to know after I deal with the charge, I'll be collecting on it no matter how long it takes me to clear this shit up." I tossed my chin toward the folded newspaper. "I'm not sure how long it'll take. Don't know what they'll try to stick on my ass, but I do know it won't be the bodies. I need that Rizzo nigga to know they'll have to adhere to the agreement: their company."

He nodded his understanding as the waitress arrived and poured him coffee. Then Double E laughed softly. "Son, what're you gonna do with a damn construction company? Rizzo was confused as hell when I told him that was a part of your payment. I can't front, that shit threw my ass, too."

I wouldn't explain that to my O.G. At least, I wouldn't now. Right now, I had to face Newark PD and the fucking Essex County prosecutor's office. My dreams would have to wait, as well as me sharing them.

"Don't matter right now. All the Rizzo family needs to know is the Bartnickis ain't a problem for them and they owe me more than the money being dropped in the back of this diner right now. And the only person I trust to make sure they do is you. So, that quarter you're giving me will go back to you double the amount to be sure of that."

Double E got quiet, going about preparing the mug of coffee

to his liking. I didn't interrupt him with pleas or assurances of grandeur. That was a fucking no-no in the game. I'd just have to expect him to trust I wouldn't get cuffed and start singing to police about who had been behind the Bartnickis' demise. As soon as I accepted the job, it was my work alone as well as my sword to fall on. I'd fight whatever lay ahead the same way I did the job: alone.

"I don't know why I got this strange ass trust and respect for you, Young O.G.," he murmured, pouring multiple packs of sugar into his coffee at once. "Nah. I know why. It's because of that time mad years ago when my son, Deek, peeped your work with moving those guns and handling the Westside Latin Kings when they tried cutting into my territories. You handled that shit before I had to think of my first strike. My son told me you wasn't like them other kids I had on my payroll. You was a leader. Smart and a fore-thinker…" His eyes met mine, expressing his seriousness. "something like Sadik. He said that—my son. Ain't a soul on this sweet earth I trust more than that kid." Double E sat back in his seat, fingers reaching up to pinch his lips as he gazed out of the window into the Paterson traffic.

And I waited. I'd already mentally written my plan—several, not knowing which way the wind would blow on this shit. Either way, my anemometer would catch it and I'd be prepared. Committing crimes and catching charges were the cicadas of the underworld. I knew it and so did my O.G., Earl Ellis.

"I don't need a quarter from you. If you dead set on giving me back the quarter, I'll hold onto it until we see how this shit blow over. You beat it, it's yours. You eat a charge and bid it out, it's yours."

Relieved, I pushed my palm over the table. I was grateful for his trust alone. I was no snitch, neither was I sloppy with anything I did. Double E met my shake of trust and respect. That was all I needed, so I left for the door.

"Say, Young O.G.," he called behind me. I glanced over my shoulder. "I don't visit, can't write, but your commissary'll never run dry."

Pulling in a deep breath, I turned to leave, braving myself for yet another battle.

FAST FORWARD 11 YEARS
(*2 Years Ago*)

The buzzer sounded and the two dozen of us waiting began to move. The doors opened outward and we filed outside, gliding into the beautiful ass bright spring sun. It graced my tight face, bringing along with it a warmth I'd never take for granted again. The excited screams of children could be heard as I glanced around the yard in search of my visitor. He'd come every year since I'd begun my bid, even when I started in a low-security facility for a year before being qualified and transferred to this minimum one.

When I spotted him, his gaze was already set on me. It didn't take long for me to make my way to the table he'd picked for us today. A smile widened his face as I was en route.

"My last fucking visit to Montgomery, Alabama."

We embraced in a dap.

"My guy," I greeted. Taking a seat, I returned his declaration with, "This town is better than Littleton. They were disrespectful with shipping my ass."

He chuckled, rubbing his nose. "Indeed. But Colorado's only a couple of hours away from my crib. What am I going to do in Montgomery? Visit the first White House of the fucking confederacy?"

I twisted my neck, lifting my lips. "Hank Williams was poppin' in Montgomery." I joked.

He took a deep breath, eyes sweeping the yard. "We're at the end of a journey, bruh."

"That we are."

His eyes narrowed as he gazed into the air contemplatively. "Last New Year's Eve, me, the wife and kids hit up a morning "watch night" service at our church——" I couldn't help my sudden cackle. "What?"

"You, man. You got a whole wife and kids and going to church." My brows shot up. "A Christian. My nigga?" I shook my head. "Shit is just insane."

He chuckled, pushing his tongue into his molars as I recalled of him. "Indeed." He nodded. "And so are you."

I nodded, too. "I am. But you were Islam."

"And I still respect the faith," he made clear. "But anyway. We went in, did the service, then hopped on a plane for the East Coast. We had a party to attend and stayed up till damn near four in the morning." He scratched his chin. "The bizarre thing about the event was that I woke up at six-thirty on the dot with an eerie feeling. A minute later, the baby woke up. I took him into the kitchen for a bottle, trying to figure the hell out why was I up so soon." He motioned the act with his hands. "I pulled the fridge door open, found the bottle, warmed it over the stove—even started to feed lil' man, all the while trying to figure this shit out. When baby boy's eyes fluttered, mine popped open wide. I registered the year. This year. That's when it hit me: you're coming home, Sin."

I nodded, processing the weight of it. "True story."

"What does it feel like? It's been a decade."

"Over ten since I turned myself in," I corrected. I'd been chained since then. "But we don't count days: we count push-ups or books read." I snorted. "It's been crazy."

"This isn't anything like the first one." His eyes continued to roam as though it was his first time here, which wasn't true. He'd been my only consistent visitor.

Being a federal inmate makes it likely that you're incarcerated out of state. Not always, but often. The *Bureau of Prison* claim you'll be housed within five hundred miles of your residence, but double fucked me. Both prisons I'd been in were more than triple the distance, reducing the likelihood of any visitors. Except this one.

"Nah. Less restrictions here."

"Indeed. More whites with their white-collar crimes."

I nodded. He was right.

"Can't complain much."

The Essex County Prosecutor's Office charged me with the Bartnicki murders, but only because of technology. The police department ran the footage of all the city cameras in the vicinity of the restaurant, like an ATM across the way. My face and body were picked up faintly on two. And for someone like me with a record, my information was in their system, which was how they were able to pull up to my mother's crib in Harlem.

They were also able to catch a portion of the license plate number on the car I'd jacked for it. But it was really the parking lot I'd dumped the car at that got me jammed up. That building had been abandoned for over fifteen years. Until that night. The place had been purchased and began functioning that very day at noon, manned with security. The security guard saw me leaving out. My clothes matched the same from the vague camera recordings near the shooting.

So, of course, the prosecutors thought they had a solid case. Maybe for some bum ass, low-level street kid without quality representation. My lawyers ate them up about the missing search warrant when they broke into my car and found the two ARs Juggy left in my trunk. Dumb asses thought it was their lucky day, not considering it was an illegal search. They said probable cause, but didn't have a search warrant for my moms' apartment or my ride the day of the search. So, my victory took place in the case of the *"Bartnicki's massacre."*

But after sitting in the county jail for close to a year and a half, fighting my case during the trial, I still got hit. The *FED*s picked up the case for the ARs. They were waiting in the wings to get their hands on my ass, likely thought I'd get life for the four bodies. Since Newark couldn't do life with the bodies, the *FED*s did a twenty-year sentence for the weapons unrelated to the murders. Each gun was a charge to run concurrent, leaving me with ten years.

So, yeah. I recalled each day of this "journey." I crisply recalled being transferred into the custody of the *Bureau of Prisons*. The first meeting with my caseworkers, having to do the paper-party shit with the inmates awaiting my fresh-blooded ass, even remembered having to knock a Vice Lord out cold before I was a week in. But that was in the low-security facility in Colorado. About a year and a half in, I qualified to transfer to a minimum security, which landed me here. This was dormitory-style and laid back, which was why I couldn't complain. I'd made my presence known within the first month. Had a reputation of *do not fuck with*, and had been left to my thoughts. My post-release agenda.

"Some years slow as hell. Some not so much, but they were all long and delaying my progress."

"Progress?"

"Post-release plan. The agenda for the rest of my life. I've been left back about eleven times in the academic realm of life. I got so many leaps to make to play catchup."

"Which will be the energy of my visit today." He leaned toward the table, planting his elbows.

"Spit."

"Like you said, since turning yourself in, you've been locked down for about eleven years. Your money upon release is the first thing we need to address. The bag needs to be secured so you have a launching pad. I know you're sitting on something that the COs and the damn warden could only dream of, but you've outgrown what you stashed. What's your portfolio looking like?"

I took a deep breath. "*Club Sin*'s been in motion almost since I've been away. I've dabbled in a lil' real estate…flipping a few houses, made investments—most of which you've thrown my way. Non-liquid assets? Close to seven this year. Liquid?" I rocked my head left to right to quickly count. "I can easily count…two."

He was loosely familiar with my money. Almost each visit, he'd ask about it. I'd been sitting on money since eighteen years old because of this guy and Double E Bags. He kept my commissary stacked by way of a random chick from East Orange. He even made sure I had allies in both prisons upon my arrival. But it was this guy here who made the visits and kept extending my business while I'd been away.

"Seven *M*s is way behind what you've lost by being in here. You'll have more time and need to do more."

"What do you have?" Because I knew that was his angle.

Dude printed money, that's how much of it he'd made over the years.

"*Château Blevin*." I was already an investor. "There's gonna be quite a bit of shares available in the next few months."

I already owned seven percent of the company. "How much?"

"Enough to take you to forty."

My brows shot up. "You're at sixty?" He shook his head. "Fifty?"

"Thirty."

Shit...

"Divine—"

"I can't do more than thirty right now. The new casino in Vegas that ain't so new still needs my close eye on it. I got a few more start-ups in the works now. Lots of tech moves." He rolled his neck. "*Mauve*'s still blowing up and making moves in all markets. The shit takes work, not to mention all my other ventures and my growing family."

"Congrats on the new baby, man."

When he visited last, his wife had recently delivered.

He gave a neck bow. "Appreciate it. He's gorgeous. Perfect."

"Bless up."

"Indeed." He scoffed dryly. "And I'm back in my industry bag."

"Music?"

Divine shook his head. "Hollywood. A track, no less."

Damn. Azmir Jacobs had made a fortune in Hollywood and was a force to be reckoned with. He moved everything in that industry—powder, pills, uppers, downers, West Coast security for rappers, and had even brokered countless career deals. The nigga was arguably one of the most influential people in entertainment, who the average consumer never knew existed. And not just Black Hollywood: A.D.J. was the plug for old money and new in white Hollywood.

He gave it all up to go legit. Even met and married a good woman and had kids. At this point in my life, I was convinced that once a man put aside the bullshit and focused on the bag and building an empire, good things would follow. This was why I'd been yielding to a lot of Divine's mentorship since being locked down.

"How that happen?" My first few years in the pen, he'd told me he was leaving the game for good, which included the entertainment industry.

"My sister-in-law dated— or did some shit—with a kid from Milwaukee coming up in the ranks. He's good, I must admit. She's playing talent agent for him. Got him doing the Tyler Perry circuit."

When he closed his eyes and shook his head, I laughed. "What the hell that mean?"

"It's good shit, I guess. But when she had me kick it with him about his endeavors, he's talking Don Cheadle, Danny Glover, Sam Jackson—"

I snorted, "Denzel shit."

"Exactly. And for that track, he's gotta come out of that TP chokehold. So, I'm plugging him into my people in the theater world. He's gonna need to get his stage chops up in that circuit." Divine shrugged, fingering his chin. "I think he can pull it off and chart his own path."

I nodded. "That's what's up."

"Anyway." He waved off the previous topic, switching lanes. "Another prospect I have for you is a cigar outfit."

I squinted. "A company?"

"Yup."

I scoffed, "I don't know shit about cigars unless we're talking about the *Dutch*es I used to roll that Dro with."

Divine shook his head. "You don't need to be conversant with smoking cigars for this venture just yet. A relatively new company a friend of mine owns is looking to revamp its brand. He's recently partnered with the *Château Blevin Estate* for land-share and profit split. He's looking for investors, primarily for mostly marketing needs, but would rather a partner. For all intents and purposes, they're building a conglomerate. Sixty/forty split is on the table for you. You'll have plenty of time to catch up on your knowledge of fermented tobacco leaves, starting today."

"How much is he asking for?"

"Three?"

"I just told you I've got about two," I snorted.

He cocked his head to the side. "What's underneath your mattress?" *Ahhhh…* "Whatever you're short on there, I got you on a loan. He's looking at a two-year plan for profit. This outfit is no different from mine with *Mauve*. I was a funder initially until I saw my way to the head of the table."

I nodded, the idea becoming crisper in my mind. "Have him forward the logistics to my lawyers. I'll consider it."

Of course, I had legal representation while incarcerated, and not just criminal. I'd been running businesses and flipping houses for years behind bars. It was Divine who helped aid me in finding good ones who wouldn't drain the small bag I'd had.

"That brings me to my next topic of discussion." I tossed my chin toward him in acknowledgment. "Your mental."

"What about it?"

"It needs to be adjusted. You've been locked up for over a decade; your brain isn't prepared for where your money's about to take you. You need help sorting."

"What do you mean?"

"Therapy."

My head bounced back, face tightened. "Come again?"

I was trying to decide not to be offended. I'd always been a solid guy: never easily roused, not temperamental, and well-read. Even being locked down, I'd been a leader most cats came to for guidance, no matter the age. What the fuck did I need with a therapist?

I sat up, clearing my throat. "O.G., you're one of a short list of people I trust. I know you've got my best interest at heart. You've held me down since I was a pup. But I can't front: I'm a little insulted by you thinking I'm a nut job just because I've been locked down."

"And you know you shouldn't be. This is coming from me. Prison ain't the real world. Your currency is about to change from sardines and stamps to cash, credit, and shares. Your interpersonal skills, as is, have been conditioned by the regulations of the *BOP*. You ain't had no pussy since you were in your twenties. My nigga, you're gonna need help." His eyes were hard on me.

I had my agenda set; a company to arrogate. There'd be no damn time to be engaging a fucking head doctor. Nonetheless, I forced myself to yield to logic. I never challenged Divine. Pushing and urging only happened from one direction in our friendship since we met. Shit never got out of pocket with us. He had no reason to flex on me. Similar to Double E, Divine had taken me under his wing and groomed me into a man. The difference between the two men was one had retired from the illegal trade game, and the other had pledged his death to it. Azmir Divine Jacobs had shown us coming up behind him how to flip that dough. He never steered me wrong, so I wouldn't insult him with my doubts now.

I twisted my mouth before asking. "Where am I gonna find a goofy ass shrink?"

He cracked a smile, rightfully sensing my brewing agitation. "You ain't got to. I'll give you mine. One last thing." I reclined from the table, my forehead lifting. "Pussy."

"What about it?"

"It ain't a woman."

The hell?

I angled my head. "What's the difference?"

"Pussy is a temporary companion."

"And?"

"And a woman—the right woman—can be a long-term partner. A man of your grooming will be suitable for a partner: a woman who can help stretch his dollar and dream. Pussy'll get your ass jammed up if you don't know the difference."

And there he was again.

Ten fucking steps ahead of me.

"Y'all niggas thinks it's sweet…
Industry niggas be weak.
Too scared to stand on ya on feet…
Y'all niggas with the wave…
Ha! The agenda.
Nah, chill. I'mma behave.
Let a bunch of empty-melanin suits tell you how to move…
They tell ya what to say, what to do…just be smooth.
Fuck that. I got my Ms standing on the industry neck…
Pop my shit then run my mafuckin' check.
Raised by the streets with real block soldiers…
Cut that coke, jack that rope, pay cash for them motors.
Real hustlers, big hammers, salty baby mothers.
Y'all look up to skirt-wearing men…
I pay homage to that gangsta, properly named SIN.
Took out them Polack niggas…
Missed the charges then ate the FED's pen.
Sat quiet, never a rat.
Nigga 'bout to hit the streets.
Ran the cellies…now ready to spin the block…
Fuck y'all niggas, jerkin industry cock."
~Young Lord

Chapter One

Part II
February | Present Day

ashira

I NEED TO DO THIS MORE OFTEN...

I expelled a lung full of air in total contentment. As I lay over the table, the mild breeze showered my bare back, arms, and legs. The friendly sun-kissed the back of me, and the roiling ocean along with the seagulls serenaded my spirit. This was everything I needed and had been long overdue. My massage was sadly coming to an end, making me regretful.

Back to work I go...

Though my face was buried in the donut of the massage bed,

and even over the music of nature, I could hear the girls were done. I'd gotten started after them, thanks to work. So it made sense that I'd be the last to finish.

After she performed the final trailing of her fingertips around my body, I lifted hesitantly and managed a smile on my sleepy face. "Thanks so much."

The masseuse acknowledged me with a bow before packing her things up. I reached into the pocket of my table for her tip and my sunglasses.

"She's up, y'all," Corinne announced to the small group, spread out over massage tables on the coast. "You enjoyed it, Shi-Shi?"

Smiling goofily, I nodded. "Mmmhmm!"

"I hope I can afford the tip," Kema commented so unnecessarily.

I rolled my eyes, then attempted to assuage it with a soft smile. "I told you, I got you covered."

Reaching back, I gathered my bikini top to tie behind my neck, and regrettably left the table.

"And we're off," Peach singsonged, dropping her feet to the sand, following after me.

I headed down the beach, closer to the water where there were chairs lined up, facing the gorgeous ocean.

"God is magnificent," Peach whispered breathlessly before taking to a seat.

That was her thing. Acknowledging God in everything. It was a quirk I'd always known her to have as a preacher's kid.

Corinne whistled for the attention of the beachside waiter while Kema stretched out in the chair next to Peach. I pulled out my laptop, getting back to my duties.

"I feel so bad you're working while I'm enjoying myself out here." Kema pouted.

I smiled, signing into my company's system.

"Kema," Peach scoffed at her friend. "It's all good."

"I'm sorry." Kema fake cried. "It's just that this is *Karsyn Cove*. *Karsyn Cove*! I'm getting married in a few months and we could *never* afford *Karsyn Cove*. This is huge! I kind of feel guilty about experiencing all of this beauty without Jeff."

The chick was becoming annoying at this point. It was the curse of being fortunate enough to invite someone to a vacation. Last week, I decided I needed to get away and wanted to do it with my girls. It was last minute, so most couldn't make it happen. Corinne said yes. Peach said she wished she could, but had promised her friend at church, Kema, a day trip to give her a break from the stressors of planning her wedding. Really wanting Peach with me, I offered to pay for her friend. I'd been around Kema a few times over the years, but didn't know her enough to want to vacation with her. I'd just hoped she'd make these few days bearable by just relaxing.

And shutting the hell up...

Corinne asked, "Where will you guys be honeymooning?"

With a wry smirk, Kema murmured, "We're booked in *Macen Beach*."

"That's amazing. Shi-Shi's considering buying a vacation property down there," Corinne provided.

"Oh, nice," Kema cried. "With Austin?"

My regard swung from the laptop to her. "No." I shook my head. "Just me."

"What exactly are you working on, Shi?" Peach asked just as the waiter approached for an order.

"Dirty Lemon, Shi-Shi?" Corinne asked to confirm my order.

"Yup."

Corinne flicked her thumb into the air. "That'll be two, and two virgins, please."

"Pay increase reports," I finally answered Peach.

In jest, Corinne shouted, "Who getting a raise?"

"Now, I see why you're working on vacation," Peach noted. "Can't play with folks' money."

"Your father builds houses," Kema amended, "Right?"

"Shi-Shi builds houses," Corinne slickly explained. "Her father just owns the company."

Peach and I laughed at that.

"Ain't that the truth," I breathed out loud. "I'm so damn tired, y'all," I grunted, sitting back in the lounge chair. "I feel like I'm aging prematurely. It's like, I'm more valuable at this man's company than he is."

"You needed this." Corinne nodded with pouted lips.

"I need more of it. I'm vacationing all year," I declared. "I've already told my father and the staff. If they need me, it'll have to be remote."

"We have *Saint Justin* booked later this year," Corinne reminded me.

For a while, the conversation quieted, my attention caught up in the raucous waves. This was a complete contrast to the scenery I'd left back in wintery New Jersey. Most of my trips had already been booked for the year. I just needed to add a few. I'd miss the dance studio but would, at least, reclaim my damn youth.

Before I knew it, Corinne was excitedly sitting up in her chair. The waiter had returned. I received my cocktail as the waiter passed them out.

Peach stirred her drink, "Is that an all-girls trip?"

"Which one?"

"*Saint Justin.*"

Before I could answer, Corinne advised, "You and Austin can use some time together."

She was right. I'd hardly seen my boyfriend this year. It was only February, but still a sad fact. I took a long sip of my drink before answering, "I don't know. He's been pretty busy preparing for a new project."

"The movie he has coming with Brielle?" Corinne asked.

I nodded.

Peach lifted her sunglasses. "Does she know you're dating him?"

"You know Brielle?"

"Not really," I answered Kema.

"Ashira danced for her on her "*Forbidden Love*" tour," Peach explained.

Kema gasped. "I forgot you were a dancer! How do you fit it all in?"

I shook my head, emptying my lungs. "I don't. That tour was four years ago. I was invited back for the next album tour, but had to turn them down."

"The company's sales dropped." Corinne's face tightened behind her sunglasses. "I forgot all about that shit. You were pissed."

"I was. I busted my ass and not only got us into the black, but within fourteen months, we were in the green. I had no life."

"That was before you met Austin?" Kema asked.

I hated questions about him from strangers. At only twenty-seven, Austin Seers was up and coming Hollywood royalty—and not just in Black Hollywood. He'd surpassed that barrier when acting alongside Kate Winslet and Meryl Streep in a blockbuster some said saved the movie theater industry last year. Four years ago after leaving Brielle's dance troupe, I'd fallen from my dreams of dancing as he rose to meteoric fame. And the guy wanted me. Me. The girl who couldn't come from beneath her father's shadow as a home builder, something so far from my real passion. But we'd been dating publicly, which was how I couldn't believe Brielle didn't know. Paparazzi had been making sure the world knew for years.

I read through three more employee evaluation reports before slamming my laptop closed. "I need something to do." I swallowed back a bit of my drink.

"Like what?" Kema asked.

I wanted to roll my eyes. It had been hard being so transparent with my girls while having an interloper around.

Shrugging, I thought out loud, "Get some plants for my place… get a damn pet. Something."

"Like the dog you said you'd get last year?" Corinne reminded me.

"I *am* getting a dog." I pouted. "I live in a high rise. A dog needs a big backyard to run and roll in."

"My fiancé wants one," Kema added.

Corinne snapped her fingers to a fictitious beat. "I'm getting one this year. A French bulldog."

"How cute." The muscles in my face squeezed into a moue. "I

can't wait. Until then, I may settle on a plant." I busted out laughing with Corinne following me.

"Big difference." Kema howled herself.

"Start with the plant," Peach's voice was soft yet authoritative, sobering me. "Eventually, move on to life form, and eventually, you'll get to what your heart truly wants." She winked, sipping her drink through a straw like it was spiked.

When she spoke like this—like she knew shit about me I didn't —I listened. Always. Peach had superpowers.

"And on that note," Corinne chirped, leaving her chair. "I'm going to the water. I gotta pee."

"Ewwww!" Kema stretched her lips in disgust as she stood. "I'm following, but gonna keep my distance."

"Do as you may!" Corinne sang on her way to the water.

We watched them until their ankles were subdued, then I turned to Peach squinting. "Are you advising me or"—my voice dropped an octave—"advising me."

"What's the difference?"

"One comes from a loving best friend and the other a fore-boding necromancer." I bit my lip then flicked my chin toward the water. "Did she get the sorcery treatment, too?"

Peach glanced down at the water toward her parishioner then she slowly turned onto her back, pacing up the lounge chair. "Is that what you think I am? A witch, Shi-Shi?"

I rolled my eyes, annoyed by the accusation. Since we were kids, I always defended her eclectic behavior. It had always been me to accept Peach even when I didn't understand her. It was offensive for her to accuse me of mislabeling or dehumanizing her. She was a preacher and church kid turned assistant pastor. Peach was short for preacher, a dig turned into a nickname. We all accepted Peach for who she was. She had weird superpowers and I'd come to accept it since we were kids.

"I think you're an amazing weirdo made for me. Look who saved me from getting engaged to a financial bloodsucker right out of college."

She nodded, gazing toward the water. "Similar to the way I'm telling this one that Jeff ain't ready for marriage. He's too busy following behind his cousin, posing as a photographer's assistant when he's really filming dancers in strip clubs throughout the tri-state area." My eyes burst wide and jaw dropped as I peered down at Kema kicking her feet in the water.

"Shit," I murmured. "Did you tell her that?"

Peach stretched her arms overhead and yawned, "I did one better."

"What?"

"I told them both that and more." She shrugged with her face. "But of course, no one listens to the prophetess." Peach cringed. "Ewwwww! Did I really just give myself that title?"

I chuckled. Although she'd been turning into exactly that, Peach never wanted to be her father.

Then, I didn't quite recall her father's spiritual title other than pastor and bishop. Although I'd done my formal schooling at *Bishop John Yancey Christian Academy* and was taught the five-fold ministry, I never really appreciated it because my parents weren't churchgoers outside of what we had to do for school.

I sighed, closing my eyes then rolling them beneath the lids. "Peach, I'd love your insightful thoughts on my future. I'm so fucking frustrated I could lock myself in my apartment and hide for months. I love being a big help to my dad and the family. *Shit.* I even love to see the employees grow—buying their own homes, sending their kids off to great colleges, paying for their weddings, and even vacationing. We do that at *Witherspoon Homes.* But I feel like the last eleven years of my life have only been dedicated to helping other people fulfill their dreams."

She scoffed, "Welcome to my life. That's ministry, Shi-Shi."

"Yeah, but it's not exactly me. I want to do what makes me feel good and fulfilled. I want a deeper connection to my being. I want to express the talents I have. When we were growing up, I never said I wanted to build homes. This is my father's work; his dreams." My gaze rolled over to her. "What do your Spidey senses tell you about me?"

Her chin burrowed into her chest. "Is that why you invited me out here? To play fortune-teller, Shi?"

My eyes ballooned and I sucked in a breath. "No!" Even I knew that was the wrong move to make with her. "Hell no, Peach! Come on!"

She shook her head, annoyed as she looked toward the perfectly blue sky.

"Peach! You're my best friend—"

"Since we fantasized about getting our periods and needing training bras."

"Exactly! So, when I'm so lost in my dark orbit, I have every right to call on my resources. Peach, you are that for me," I exclaimed so uncharacteristically dramatic, yet sincere. " I'm just exhausted. Period. Do you know I'm entertaining a merger?"

Her brows shot heavenward. "A merger?" I nodded in the affirmative. "Mr. Witherspoon's gonna kill you, girl!"

"I've told him, Peach. He's not working. He lost interest years ago. It's been me running this firm since I graduated college—technically, mid-undergrad years. I'm tired. There's this longstanding builder and developer in Jersey, *Just Homes*, who's been fishing around for a partnership. Now, I know their true attempt is to acquire, but their business proposal is moderate and details a time-line I can agree to, to slowly merge to alleviate so many of my responsibilities. I think it's what I need to do."

For a while, Peach said nothing. Her lips were upturned and attention to the whipping waves and glaring sun. "Be anxious for nothing, Ashira." Her chin dipped. "But let your requests be made known to God in everything by prayer and supplication, with thanksgiving. And the peace of God, which surpasses *all* under-standing, will guard your heart and mind through Christ Jesus." Her gaze rolled over to me. "You remember scriptures, right?"

I rolled my eyes, turning away embarrassed. I hadn't remem-bered them. Forever, I'd been the leader of the pack. The one with all the knowledge and guts. But today, at the start of a new year, I was the comprised party who needed support and refused to feel weak for asking for it.

Kema trekked our way, first through water then the sand. Immediately—and unusually—I felt sorry for her. I'd been on the other side of Peach's foreboding before. And I, too, had dismissed her warning, erring on the possibility of her getting it wrong that particular time. The difference between Kema and me was that I ignored Peach on matters other than my impending engagement. *That* was the time I'd listened.

"So, where's the wedding?" I asked Kema, applying a smile.

Her shoulders lifted in excitement and she all but squealed before taking her seat. "At an Elks Lodge." Her grin was wry. "My coworker's getting married the week before me and mentioned renting a house to do an all-in-oner. She was looking all over Bergen County."

"For random houses?" I asked.

Kema nodded. "There's a house along *Lake Sha'ron*. You know that exclusive row of big houses?" I recalled the neighborhood from talks of the real estate value there years ago. I couldn't recall the conversation to memory in that moment. "Well, her crazy idea was to squat the house for a day."

"What does that mean?" Peach's face tightened.

I snorted. "It's when you know a luxury property is vacant and use it for your event, free of charge."

"Oh!" Peach's eyes blew wide like saucers. "That's bold. Is it legal?"

"Well, no!" Kema laughed. "But I've read about weddings like that. This house on *Lake Sha'Ron* had been vacant for years. None of the houses in that neighborhood make it to a listing—"

I nodded, knowing that bit of trivia to be true. "Because they're sold the second the owner decides to go."

"Yes!" Kema's head bounced over her shoulders as she sipped her drink. "Me being a scary cat, I warned her to at least be sure no one had bought it because if you're not in that ritzy lifestyle, you really don't have a pulse on the status of the house. Good thing she shared her 'bright' idea with me before securing the party planner. Because, girl, she looked up that place on our lunch one day and we saw it was sold. An internet search led to a name, but she still didn't believe it. Homegirl had been plotting on this house for years—it had been *allegedly* vacant that long. So, we drove all the way there one day and saw this old, white lady with jet black hair pulling up weeds in the front yard." She snapped her fingers. "You know who she favored?"

"Who?" Peach inquired.

"The old, short white woman from that old movie, '*She-Devil.*'"

After a spell, I asked, "Rosanne?"

"No." She shook her head. "The old white lady. Short…with the 'Matilda' blunt cut bob with the bang?"

"Oh!" I chirped. "The old woman from *Kindergarten Cop!*" Then *I* began slapping my bare thigh, begging the name to memory."

"Linda Hunt," Peach's voice was calm and heavy. "All you had to do was say the lil' old lady from *NCIS – Los Angeles.*"

"Oh." Kema's expression fell.

"You guys are calling movies out from the eighties, and junk." Peach shook her head.

I sighed, dramatically heaving my body up from the chair. I backed away rhythmically from the chairs and twirled in the sand. "I'm about to open a tab at the bar and have a few more drinks to get me through these reports." I kicked up sand doing a somersault.

"Yes, hunty!" Kema performed the NeNe Leakes finger snap. "You better work that dancer's bawdy!"

I gave a cute curtsy. "Then I'm calling my boyfriend and seeing if I can talk him into one of my many impending vacations this year." Wiping the sand from my oiled skin, I winked. "This bitch finna be outside all year!"

As I twirled off, I caught Kema spit-laugh then try covering her mouth. Peach shook her head grinning. They were Christian churchgoers and while I respected that, they had to respect my need to let loose out here on this lovely island.

"Are you shitting me?" I shot to my feet, pressing the phone to the side of my face as though I could hear something more palatable than what she'd said.

"No." Her one-word answer decidedly curt.

I charged over to the window of the waiting room. "He said he'd get back to me in a day or two?"

"That's what I said," my assistant maintained her deceptively low and colorless volume, almost sounding bored with the conversation.

My chin dipped. "Marge-Jean, we only have four roofing contractors. *Wegman and Sons* is the most tenured with our firm and with the work. I mean…they've been around since… Since—"

"Since before your hind was old enough to play boss around here, Ms. Witherspoon; I know."

I rolled my eyes, ignoring that snide remark. "How can he turn his back on us, and at a time when we need them for this big ass job?"

"He said he's been requesting a renegotiation of pay for two years now. His staff has increased."

"Yet the speed at which the jobs are completed has not!"

"He also said you've been promising to meet with him in as many years, but to no avail."

"Because there's nothing of substance to fucking talk about." I snatched my tense body from the window, remembering I was at someone else's place of business, waiting to be seen. Heading back to my seat in the waiting room where my temporary office setup was spread all about, I sighed in frustration. Even at my therapist's office, I had to work. "He has mentioned a word about a twenty percent contract raise to my father, but wants to come to me with his faulty math? Jim Wegman hired his son's loser ass friends and thinks we're supposed to pay them not to booze off during the job?"

"Ms. Witherspoon, Mr. Wegman didn't mention a word about if he's expressed anything to Mr. Witherspoon. Neither did he speak about his son's drunken friends. I actually don't give a shit about either of those things. What I need to know is how we will get the goddamn Peterson project completed if our biggest contractor is pulling the hell out, child!"

That was Marge-Jean. The pint-sized seventy-one year-old, white-haired, Irish-American office assistant I'd inherited from my father.

I dropped my face into my palm and shook my head. "Why do I deal with this?" I whispered rhetorically.

The door to my therapist's office clicked to open just as Marge-Jean retorted, "I honestly don't give a shit about that either. If you don't want to work, then damn it, quit. Because I want to work—no, I need to work. So I don't just show the hell up to this place bitching all day—"

"You do!" I quipped, packing my things to prepare for my session.

"I do not, Ms. Witherspoon. That is reserved for you fuckin' millennial brats. The people of my generation find solutions to our problems, we don't whine over them."

I slipped my laptop into my tote along with my portfolio report. "There aren't many of you, Jesus Christ's peers, around so how would you know?"

Just as she gasped audibly into the phone, my neck snapped up at the sound of a masculine rumble.

My therapist smiled at a dude with warm hazelnut skin, a thick beard, dark grey thermal shirt and black bubble vest with stained blue jeans, and tattered construction *Timberland* boots. "Thanks for your time today, Mr.—"

"Did you hear me, Ms. Witherspoon?" Marge-Jean demanded in my ear over my therapist's parting words.

I couldn't answer her. My gawk wouldn't leave the guy.

"I'll address this when I get back to the office, Marge-Jean," I snapped, disconnecting the call before she could reply.

As I continued to pack up, his presence swelled the room. The awkwardness from my curiosity didn't help at all. Like...functional *Timbs*. That was a novelty. But so was an apparent thug being at my therapist's office in nowhere New Jersey. Was he a relative? I bit the inside of my rolling lips.

"Yeah," his thick vocals vibrated. Chancing a glance, I saw he was holding a cellphone. "Coming down."

Shit...

My head shot down after catching sight of his ass. His jeans sagged.

I knew it!

A thug. A real thug-a-boo in here of all places. *The oddity of it all.*

I took another gander, observing the space between his thighs caped in wide-leg jeans. There was a confidence to him, an air of something. When the elevator tolled, I was *just* able to remove my eyes from him. I sat back in my seat and allowed my eyes to roam in the opposite direction. My therapist stood there, gaping directly at me with her brows hiked.

Oh, noooo...

I cringed internally.

She cleared her throat. "Ashira."

My spine straightened in the chair. "*Ya*—yes."

"I'll be with you in twenty minutes. I have to make a call after using the restroom. There's a fire I need to put out then I'll be ready."

I was here early, so in no rush. Usually when this early, I'd camp out at the coffee shop across the street. Today, I brought my coffee with me and decided to do a little work here while I waited. I would have explained that but for my nosey ass being compelled back to the opposite side where I caught eyes with the thug as the elevator doors were closing. The thug whose name I didn't catch, thanks to Marge-Jean's aggy-ass ass.

Maybe I should start hanging out here before my sessions to catch more interesting characters?

The sound of her clearing her throat again had me turning back to my therapist. Finally, able to acknowledge her, I shrugged. "I'm early anyway. I can wait."

jas

When the foreman's air palm-pump stopped and raised higher into the air, he barked, "Got it."

I switched gears, putting the lift in reverse then backing away from the pallet. Once at a distance, I turned the lift and parked it away from the traffic. Jumping off the forklift, I thought to check on the other units before hopping on a conference call. Passing by the guys on the site, it was good to see some pepper mixed in the salt. It wasn't enough, but I'd been working on it.

The next single-family unit over was a five-bedroom Dutch colonial. The roof was being applied and electrical work installed. I peeped a couple of my hires putting in work, including Lamont running lines for the main panel. I was just grateful as hell for cooperating weather. The temperatures and snow in February could be unpredictable. We'd had no rain or snow for the past five or so days, which meant no delays—so far. I mentally knocked on wood.

As I approached the next unit, right away, I noticed Jamal, a dude I hired straight from the halfway house seven months ago, edging a border of a paver walkway. He'd learned much of what he knew of brick-laying since being employed here and had even mastered using the tile saw, it seemed. Tamir, observing him, caught my presence and greeted with a smile, nod, and thumbs up. I saluted him before moving along to the next house. Rolling my neck, I recalled how fucked up my sleep was last night. It had been the third night in a row. But nothing energized me more than work. The progression of these projects brought unbelievable satisfaction.

Scrubbing my face with my hands, I kept trekking down the freshly paved street. The fourth and final unit was the one closest to complete for this new development in Flanders, New Jersey. The owner bought the property from concept proposal. We were at the interior phase of the job, installing floors, garage doors and a few other things. My eyes squinted when I saw Steve, one of the woodworks men, unloading the vinyl flooring planks. That wasn't right.

"Yo, Michael-Angelo!" I called over to the head woodworks trade.

His little five-foot five-inch frame backed up, looking around Bart, part of the electric trade, and squinted. "What?"

I hated that one word out here. Yeah, we were all construction heads, but out here that word carried crazy derogatory energy when spoken to me. This building firm was run by and, by and large, had employed Italians. That was until I came along. Ever since, the tension on job sites had been thick as hell.

I pointed to the vinyl being carried into the house. "This is a premium property."

"And?" he barked.

I blinked, but kept my cool. "Ain't no vinyl in premiums."

"Let me do my job and you go find yours to do, buddy."

"This is all of our jobs, Michael-Angelo."

Dumbass with a long, dumbass name...

"Well, that ain't on my spec sheet." He shrugged. "So, it won't be my fuck up."

"I'm sure it's there. Positive. Check the file."

His eyes swept around, a grin playing at his cheeks. "I don't see no file around here, Jas."

I rubbed the back of my head, praying for patience. "Michael, it's electronic now—"

"It's fucking Michael-Angelo." He walked closer to me, but was still at a distance. "I don't alter my identification to create street names, *Jas*."

A couple of snickers rang out and I sensed Juggy at my side. He knew it was fucking unnecessary. I told him it only added to the static on the site. And I especially ain't need assistance with this little ass nigga.

"Charles!" I called out to the project foreman.

Sighs of anger rang out. These cats were pussies for sure. Generally, I didn't believe in snitching, but when it came to the job, I ain't fuck around. Reputation meant everything, and I wouldn't risk it on these lowkey racists fucks.

"Yeah, Jas!" Charles shouted from the second-floor open window frame. "What flooring are we installing today?"

He dropped down and returned to the frame with his work tablet.

"Don't worry about it, Charles," Michael-Angelo pumped his hands in the air. "If there's a problem, it can always be corrected."

"And cost time, money, unnecessary manpower, and an unsatisfactory experience for the buyer," I warned him.

"You know what, Jas." He stepped even closer, leading with his index finger. "I'm sick of your ass walking around these sites like you run shit. You're a fucking worker like everybody else. In fact, I don't even know what you do, you be over every trade's job, micromanaging without a title. And I bet you make pennies on the dollar compared to us head trades. I thought you people were done working for free." My brows shot up.

Charles shouted with a shaken delivery, "Damn it, Michael-Angelo! I'm coming right down!"

"So what you got a few of your friends hired." Michael-Angelo's hands shot up and he shrugged. "I never knew of Rizzo having *BLM* branded on his heart, but God bless him. But I draw the line at fucks like you trying to boss me around. I've been a carpenter for close to thirty years. I don't have to take shit from you!"

Taking a deep breath, I felt my face tightening. "All I asked was for you to crosscheck the order."

"Fuck you, ass twat!" He turned to walk back to his little cypher as Charles gusted out of the house with his tablet leading the way.

"We don't have to be hostile, Michael-Angelo! Here." His fat fingers punched the device. "I think I do remember a special order —*ahhhh!* Here. Yes. Italian mosaic tiling."

My gaze went to Michael-Angelo's petite ass as he whipped his body around. His tiny lips were white and tight. The dude was seething.

But I knew it. The buyer asked for expensive ass Italian marble floors she offered to purchase directly and have them shipped to our warehouse months ago for today's installation. I didn't give a shit about the racism and lack of acceptance of Black men at the firm, but I didn't like for my knowledge about the work to be doubted.

Paulie—because there were at least a dozen Paulies attached to this family—one of the guys working on the deck in the back approached Michael-Angelo. I was sure he didn't disagree with his sentiments, but Paulie also knew what time it was as he mumbled words of caution to him.

"Yes!" bubbled from Charles' gut. "Please talk to him, Paulie." Then he approached me. "Jas—"

I shook my head. "It's all good, Charlie."

"He's a good guy," he shared expressively, walking alongside me.

"Yeah. A good pain in my ass." I tossed my chin, silently dismissing Juggy to go finish his work. "All good, though."

"Listen, you did the right thing by calling me, Jas. I'm here to work with you and everybody. We're doing stellar work here at *Rizzo's Custom Homes…*"

And there was the bullshit. Charles knew what time it was, trying to save as many jobs as possible. It was our dance. Had been for over a year now. As he went on and on, I zoned him out to mentally prepare for this conference call I had to have my *A* game ready for.

Chapter Two

FEBRUARY | PRESENT DAY

jaz

IT WAS HER. THE CHICK FROM EARLIER THIS WEEK AT THE therapist's office. She breezed inside the coffee shop, rocking a long, black bubble goose with a fur hoodie bouncing behind. Her head was low, attention seemed to be in her phone, but her eyes swung. When she used her available hand to flip her long, thick hair from one side of her face to another, I realized I'd been eye-whoring her too much and turned my attention away. The kid brought my drink to the counter and I checked the time. Still having a few minutes before my appointment, I paid and grabbed a seat near the window.

I was able to peer out into the street. Juggy's weird ass was a block away. I could see him behind the wheel in the van, marking in his crossword book. Scoffing, I pulled out my phone, recalling the unfinished conversation I'd been having with the manager at *Club Sin*.

"Mr. Sin," he answered on the second ring.

I tested the heat of my tea before returning, "Yeah."

"I'm thinking if we add more security and give them longer hours we should be—"

"That's the problem right there."

"*Wha*—I'm sorry?" his voice shaky although the incident was two days ago.

"Your muscle. Somebody gave them the dime on the security at the club. They know about the surveillance, when cash comes in and out, and where it's stored."

"Ah…"

She noticed me. The girl from the therapist's office.

Her eyes tightened and chin dropped a bit when she did. I tripped for a minute, but got my shit together and looked away, out of the window. "Aye, man."

"Yes, sir."

"I'm going to make a few calls, talk to the team about switching up some things regarding the money drops and security. You'll have someone with you before you open on Thursday."

"Thank you, Mr. Sin. Thank you!"

"A'ight." I disconnected the call.

The moment I pulled it from my ear and glanced down to go into my contacts, I smelled her perfume and *damn*, was she right next to me, standing at the other end of the small ass, round bar table.

"I guess since we have the same—" She cleared her throat as I browsed up from my phone, doing a double-take. "—practitioner, I should introduce myself to the new kid on the block. Don't want you sitting at the lunch table alone."

Her smile was fucking life.

Vulnerable, flawless, full lips, white ass teeth, and goddamn worldly eyes. Her bold and unexpected presence said to me right away she was bright, too damn forward and cultured for my liking.

And like a dickhead, I laughed at her. Too long. I tried stopping, but my damn diaphragm wouldn't let up. Then her happy expression faded, sobering me enough to slow.

Shaking my head, I explained, "I'm fuckin' with you."

The muscles in her pretty face spasmed as she tried to decide if I was clowning her or not. "And I wasn't a member of the welcoming committee in school either." She screwed half her face. "I was more of the tormentor."

I snorted, face set. "Then it's the karma for me." This time, I didn't laugh; I'd gotten my shit together.

Her eyes bounced likely at the speed of her brain. She was trying to figure me out again. She squinted then blinked. "Santana —City Girls, right," she murmured.

Who?

She pinched her lips together. "Seriously. Do you mind if I have a seat?"

I shrugged. "It's free and doesn't belong to me."

As she strapped her purse on the back of the chair, those deep eyes slitted again. "You look familiar, but I don't think I've seen you before. Does that make sense?"

"Maybe it's because I'm not the new kid on the block." My chin was low as I finished texting the manager. "I can say the same about you."

"What? That I'm the new kid?"

"That, and you look familiar." I placed my phone away in my pocket.

"Oh!" Her mouth froze in position of that word, eyes rolled around. The girl was off her game.

Good...

I wasn't beat. I was never beat, *until I was.*

"Well," She picked up her mug, blowing into it, "let's start with names. I'm Ashira. Ashira Witherspoon." I nodded, studying her face. She scoffed. "You're not going to tell me your name?"

My head reared, realizing her expectation. *Oh...* "Jas."

She did that quirky feminine thing again. Her brows drew together and lips pouted a little. "Just...Jas?"

"Mr. Jas, if that'll make you feel more comfortable." I took a swig of my tea then sat back, staring her straight in the eyes.

Women approaching me had been a regular occurrence, especially since being home. The problem was most were with the shits. But they were unlimited—Black, white, old, too-fucking-young, hood-out-the-ass, and even butch. Typically, I smiled and kept it moving, especially when the scent of bullshit was louder than their perfume. I'd been moving a lot since landing home. Today, in this small ass quaint, never heard of town, I had time.

This time, *Ashira* squinted with a little bite in her demeanor. "Where are you from, Jas."

"Harlem."

Her head swung back and brows shot into the air. "Harlem?"

"Is that a surprise or a revelation, or you know why I look familiar?" I took another sip, waiting on her.

"Maybe surprise. You're a long way from Harlem, out here in Jersey."

"And where are you from?"

"Jersey." She rubbed her lightly glossed lips together. "I live in Edgewater."

"Not exactly around the corner."

The Witherspoon chick snapped her neck, b-girl style. "But not as far as Harlem."

I snorted, taking the bait. "I work out here."

"Oh, really? Where?"

"All over Jersey, mostly northern."

My phone vibrated in my pocket with a text as she asked, "Would I get clowned again if I asked what you do for a living?"

She asked for it. Another round of silent laughter bubbled from my fucking belly. This *Ashira* was used to being queen bitch I could tell, sounding like a demanding white, middle-aged woman interviewing me for housing.

Until now...

The text was from across the street. My therapist was ready for me.

Dumping my phone back into my pocket, I stood from the table and grabbed my drink. "Construction." Then I shook my head and walked off.

"A builder," she spoke loud enough to my back to catch my attention.

I glanced over my shoulder and Ashira was facing ahead, her back to me. "Pardon?"

She then turned around, a half a grin pinned to her pretty face. "What I do for a living. I'm a builder."

"Oh. Say less." I shook my head. "I 'on't need a job," I wanted to make clear.

She tossed her head back, busting out laughing. Then *Ashira* stretched her neck to see more of me. "And I'm in no need of help." She winked. "Enjoy your session, Jas."

When she turned away, her long, thick wavy hair cascaded in the air before landing on her small shoulders. I continued to the door with one dumb ass question bouncing in my head.

Have I ever seen a Black woman with hair that long, natural, and—quite honestly—fucking adorable?

ashira

"So, Thursday of that week?" I peered into the phone, observing the exaggerated movements of his lengthy frame as he lay lazily against the wall.

Austin yawned on our *FaceTime* call, "Yup."

"Okay." I power-walked down the corridor of my father's house. "I'll be sure to clear my schedule for those two days."

"You miss me?" His cheeks curled into a sly smirk.

Adorable.

I giggled on my way to the dining room. "*Mmmmmm...*" My nose lifted and eyes squinted as I applied my baby voice. "Not so much with your hydrating mask."

Austin spit out laughter. "You're the one who told me to try this shit."

"I know, and it should help. But seeing it is not making for the most moisturizing event down below." I winked, entering the grand dining room. "Look. Gotta go. I'm about to scarf down dinner with my dad and baby sis. I'll try you when I get in tonight."

He blew a kiss that never failed to make my heart flip in my chest. "Love you, babe."

"Not more than I want you to wash the mask off, sugah plum." After air kissing the screen, I disconnected the call and took to my seat.

"Was that Austin?" The beam on her face was impossible.

"Awwww," my father sighed playfully. "Do you have a crush on your big sister's boyfriend, honey?"

Continuing with his teasing, I forced a smile, mimicking an old lady and wiggling my shoulders stiffly in the chair. "I have to share my affection for him with a gazillion other girls; why not with my baby sis, too?"

Daddy snickered harder. "Oh brother, Noelle. You're gonna steal your sister's movie-star boyfriend from her?"

"No!" Noelle declared firmly. "He said he'd get me tickets to the Dale concert. Lil Leval is opening for him. I really wanna go." She pouted.

"Oh." I sobered up. "I can get you tickets to that——"

"Austin said he could get backstage passes."

"If you'd let me finish..." I rolled my eyes dramatically. It may have annoyed my sister, but she knew the silliness I brought to these dinners when I attended. About five years ago, I told my father he had to spend more time with her. The standard one weekend a month and three holidays a year wasn't cutting it. Since I begged him to pick up more time and effort with Noelle, Daddy had been consistent with having dinner with her at least twice a week. Unless he was away or had an obligation with his favorite charities, my father had kept his word. I made sure to pop in every once in a while to check in and steal time with them, too. "I would have told you Austin gave me three passes, but I can't go. You think your mom can take you?"

Noelle rolled her eyes. "Nope."

"And I'm not going to see no pissy tail Dale or nappy headed Lil Decal, so don't even ask." My father flipped his palm in the air, dismissing her prematurely.

"His name is Lil Leval, Daddy, and I wasn't going to ask you." She shook her head, mindlessly twirling a straw in her glass. "You'd be weird."

"What about your aunt, Brenda, or your cousin, Lisa?"

Noelle shrugged. "Maybe Lisa. I'll ask her." Her mood perceptively deflated.

The door swung open and I began my drumroll on the edge of the table. "Thanks be to Lucky Leon, Basil. I'm starving and gotsta go!"

"Here you are, Shi-Shi." Basil, my dad's cook, served me first.

"Baked salmon, sauteed asparagus, and sliced sweet potatoes!" I yelped, "Yum!"

I checked my chirping phone as everyone else was served. A text from Austin with a cleaned face.

Me: OH THERE HE IS. MOISTURIZATION DOWN BELOW HAS BEEN ACTIVATED.

I snickered while placing the phone down, preparing to chow down.

"I want a new *Asè Garb* book bag, Daddy," Noelle announced, her head leaning into her palm, still twirling the straw.

A reverberating guffaw left his belly at the top of the decorated table for eight. "*Asè Garb*? You hear that, Shi-Shi? When you were twelve, you never asked for an *Asè Garb* book bag."

Weirdly, he found that funny.

"The makers of *Asè Garb* are around my age. I'm pretty sure the brand hadn't been conceived at the time." Craning my neck, my gaze was directly ahead on my sister. "And I'm positive I asked for *Louis Vuitton*." Then I winked.

Noelle giggled, knowing I had no qualms ruffling our father's feathers for her.

"That was your mother's work. She bought you shit you couldn't pronounce."

My gaze reached up the metallic embossed wall to the poster-size portrait of my dad, mom, and me dressed to the nines in formalwear. Then it traveled to the adjacent wall where there was another, the same size and theme, hanging of Dad, Noelle, and me. Another push I had to make to include her.

I cleared my throat. "Language, Daddy."

"I'm sorry, Noelle." His apology sounded so dry.

"So, Daddy." I fed myself a stalk of asparagus. "Have you given more thought to my suggestion of taking a meeting with *Just Homes*?"

"Have you?" he asked while cutting into his chicken.

"Oh, you know I have. I've looked over their proposal three times now and even read over it with David."

"You had our legal team take time out of their day to look over a simple proposal?"

Chewing, I stared him straight in the eyes and nodded. "Yup." I waited until I swallowed my food before I reminded him, "I have to check everything. I'm on my own and before I bothered you with it, I had to be sure."

"And what is he asking for?"

"A merger."

"A merger?" my dad repeated as though I hadn't shared that with him the first time I told him about the proposal.

"Yup."

"Do you not realize my firm is the largest Black-owned of its kind here in the NY-Tristate area and all of New Jersey?" His head fell to the side. "You think I'm sharing my company with that man? Then just hand him over the keys?"

My lips pushed out and face tightened as I considered his words. "I don't think that's what he's proposing. You'll merge, but you'd retain a significant percentage of ownership for a period after the agreement."

"And what about the Witherspoon name?"

"It's something I think you can have answered by Dan Lewinski at *Just Homes*. He's made it clear he's a fan of your work."

"As he should be. I've persevered over the years. Seen many come and even more go. My firm is strong and my legacy is proof of that."

"But, Daddy—"

"What's so hard about being my partner, Shi-Shi?" He scoffed cynically, "Is being over a multi-million dollar company such a significant thing to cry about?"

I gulped down my, now, tasteless food. "It is when that very thing delays and sometimes derails your dreams for your own life—"

His spine straightened and my father's nostrils flared. "What dreams, Ashira?"

My head bounced over my neck as I stared blindly at the wall across from me. He knew. I'd been telling him for years. My father knew damn well what my failing dreams were.

Finally, I faced him again. "As you know, I'd like to put more time into my dance company. I want to open a club, too."

"Ashira," his tone dismissive. "You're young. You have years beyond you to conquer the world. I'm just trying to keep you on a path of generational wealth. You'll have time to pursue frivolous hobbies soon enough. I mean…look at me. I've been able to have a real life, all before the age of sixty. My real job now is to take requests for *Asè Garb* from a teenager."

"And on that note." I lifted my glass of water. "I'm out." My body tremored with anger as I gulped it back.

"Wait. You're done?" Noelle's head craned around the center-pieces to look at my plate.

"That was really fast, Shi-Shi," my father lamented.

"I asked Basil to keep it light for me tonight." I would be dancing and didn't need the heaviness from a robust meal.

Dumping the dinner napkin into the plate, I amended, "I guess he's a man who listens to my concerns and takes them into serious consideration. What a *wise* man."

I lifted from my chair and tossed a wink to Noelle.

"Can I hang out with you tonight?"

"I'm dancing. Sorry." Once in the doorway of the dining room, I turned and winked at her pouting face again. "Text me the *Asè Garb* book bag. You'll have it by first period on Monday."

The last I saw was my sister's face brighten like a Christmas tree and my dad's accomplished smile as though he contributed to it.

Ugh...

jaz

"So, happiness is unimportant to you?"

"I mis-spoke. Happiness isn't prioritized."

She nodded, undecidedly. "Over contentment."

"Correct. I prefer contentment."

"Interesting," she hummed, going down to her tablet to jot down notes. "Can you define the difference and tell me why?"

"For me, happiness is the state of joy in the absence of problems. It's an impossible destination—deceptively allowing you to let down your guard, and impedes survival skills. With contentment, I have control. Problems may not be at an all-time high, but still exist. Shit," I scoffed. "Problems can be kicking my ass, but mentally and emotionally, I realize I'm healthy enough to take them on. To be content is to exist comfortably with adversity. I'm very comfortable here."

Gazing toward the floor, she nodded again. "And how was this philosophy developed? Certainly, your parents didn't pass it down."

I shook my head. "My mother's instilled a lot unintentionally. My father was intentional with being a dickheaded poser."

She eyed me closely. "His influence did some good."

I shrugged. "Got me out of Harlem a lil' bit...went to college. Barely a couple of years at *NYU*." I chuckled. "We can hold the cigars."

"Do you know what their admittance rate is reported to be? I looked it up a few months ago when you told me about your experience there." I shrugged with my lips, never having given it thought. "About sixteen percent." When I didn't have a reaction, she continued, "I know our time is up for today, but I'm hoping next week, we can start a discussion on your external influences."

External influences?

"Why is that?"

"Because I have a feeling they're very limited. I think you're a leader, Jas. Your control comes from within. Your sight reaches farther than most. And you're innovative and influential. Again, a leader. But being a good leader also takes embracing the discernment of those around you. You have to 'read the room,' as well as be able to take wise counsel from people you trust. I only know of two—maybe three—so far from what you've shared. Your external influence may be compromised."

"You're an external influence," I tried, half sincere.

Standing to end the session, she shook her head while grinning. "If that's true, I'm confident my influence, so far, has been very limited."

I trailed behind her, chewing on "external influences." She opened the door and smiled. "Next week."

"Next week. Thanks for today."

She offered to my back, "You're very welcome."

After sorting my schedule for next week with the receptionist, I made my way across the street to the coffee shop while texting a few guys on the job site and hitting back my partners at *Por el Amor del Amor*, the cigar estate. When I spotted Juggy in the van, I acknowledged him with a nod then continued my way to the door of the café. I decided to try this place one morning a few weeks ago when arriving at my therapy session too early, and recently realized I was hooked. The place was hectic, the morning crowd zipping around for their edible morning aids.

"A large mint, lemon please. Just a drop of agave."

"Sure thing, sir." The metal mouth young dude tapped away at the register.

I handed him a five spot. "Keep it."

"Thanks. We'll have that right out for you."

I moved toward the back of the counter to give room for the next in line as a text came through from Roberto, my partner at *Por el Amor del Amor*.

Roberto Perez: *Can we meet next month here on my ranch?*

Damn…

One of the disadvantages of being an entrepreneur for a convict was not having total liberty. *Probation*. I couldn't travel freely, and the places I could go, I'd need permission before planning. Hiding my custody of the federal *BOP* was typically unnecessary. I didn't give a shit about what people thought of me. There was nothing but confidence and gratitude in my walk now. I'd defied the odds and turned my life around while in prison and had been reaping the rewards of much of what I manifested while there.

But this…

Damn.

Me: *You're gonna have to come up. I'm swamped for the next few months but can be more accessible on US soil.*

"Here you are, sir." A young girl handed over my order.

I nodded, accepting it. As soon as I was about to take a final look at my phone, I saw her. The girl from three days ago. Witherspoon was first to memory. *Ashira*. She was rummaging through her big ass purse while walking to the counter. I couldn't recall what I was doing before seeing her. Didn't give a single fuck. I just needed to get the hell out of dodge.

I threaded through a few unsuspecting and preoccupied name- less bodies until I reached the door. The sight of snow coming down was a lesser evil than having to kick it with her again.

ashira

A ghost-like feather swiped across my neck and had my atten- tion go to my left. There he was, outside the coffee shop pulling his hood through the back of his vest to cover his head. Then I realized I must have just missed him.

Oh…

"How can I help you?"

My head bounced ahead and eyes blinked at the guy who looked to be in his early twenties with braces. Then my phone chimed. A notification that my therapist was ready for me. That snapped me into action.

"French toast latte with coconut milk." Suddenly, I felt flustered.

It was enough that I'd been running late because of practicing this morning and losing track of time. I was able to avoid a collision on the way here by inches. *And now…* I didn't understand why I felt so unstable.

"Should we add whip cream to that?"

Blinking successively, I nodded. "*Ye*—yeah. Just a bit."

It took less than five minutes for me to pay, wait for my drink, and be out the door. A sheet of snow covered the streets and sidewalks as I click-clacked vigilantly in my four-inch barbie doll boots. It was clear I had not been prepared for the day. Everything seemed weird.

I walked inside the building and was immediately hit with the cozy warmth of the place. After signing in with security, I took the escalator to the open second level where her assistant was waiting for me with her hands clasped at her pelvis.

"Morning, Ms. Witherspoon." Her smile was kind.

"Good morning, Ms. Seal." I exhaled. "You're a sight for sore eyes."

Her beam brightened. "She'll be right with you...just taking a call down the hall. I'll walk you to her office and get you started." I followed her as she began down the hall. "Now, you've begun a two-day a week course recently." She glanced back at me and I supplied a nod of acknowledgment. "So for clients like you, she has them filling out a mood chart—*Ut!*" She stalled for a few seconds. "Looks like she didn't erase this after her last appointment."

She scuttered to the far end of the office and began erasing handwritten answers from the dry erase marker board. I froze, observing before removing my things. I caught the neat, curvy writing that caused me to wonder if it had belonged to him. He wrote in straight lines, words evenly spaced. It was similar to Amber Stalling's in seventh grade.

Ms. Seal's hand and arm moved fast, but I caught two things. The first was his answer to the question, *Who was the last person to upset you and how did you resolve it?* The answer was, *"A colleague. It happens often. In no rush to the inevitable resolution."* My hungry regard jumped to the name *just* before her eraser did.

Jas...

Was that his real, real name? Just Jas? The guy, I knew already, was a pompous ass. His aura was off and I had a distinct inclination that he knew he was good-looking and had gotten away with having a dry ass personality.

"Hey, Ms. Ashira!" my therapist breezed inside. "Did Ms. Seal explain the assignment?"

31

"I assume I have to answer the questions inside the bubbles?" I placed my latte down and began to unlayer.

"Yes. It helps with conversation for those I see more than once a week." She sat behind her desk. "For clients, conversations can run dry or they may feel they're overwhelming with what they perceive to be 'grievances.' If you share a few updates with me, our conversation will flow seamlessly. Answer as many as you'd like."

"Don't forget to include your name on there. She'll take a picture for future references." Ms. Seal handed me a marker before excusing herself.

I sidled up to the board wearily. Which ones would I answer?

"Well, I guess it doesn't matter which ones," I muttered to myself. "At least, I'm open enough to write my full name."

"Huhn?" my therapist chirped from behind me. I shook my head. With a grin, she pushed, "Who isn't open enough to give their name?"

As I began to spiritlessly write on the board, I murmured, "Mr. Thugged Out-I'm too cool to be seeing a therapist-so why am I seeing one-Jas."

"Jas? What do you mean?"

Rolling my eyes with my back to her, I shared, "I know you can't confirm because of client/patient confidentiality, but that guy seems full of himself. Mr. Untouchable."

She snorted as though confused, "Jas?"

I swung my head over my shoulder to see her. "Whatever he goes by, wearing those construction *Timbs*."

My therapist's warped face expressed confusion. "He's fine."

I scoffed, "Yeah, but that's where his story ends."

"Ms. Witherspoon!" she laughed. "I meant his personality and ability to get open is just fine. His story is just fine. Just like whatever has you on this mood trip: when we're done exploring it this morning, you'll be just fine."

Then dramatically, she dropped into her seat with her *iPad* and waited for me to finish filling out the stupid bubbles on the board.

Just fine my fat ass…

Nice arches, but where's the wow factor?

I spoke into the microphone, "Thanks, Mandy." After nodding over to Leah at the stereo, I requested, "Michie."

Clearly practiced. Her kicks are passive. She's not being aggressive. Same arch routine as Mandy.

After a minute or two more, I transitioned again. "Thanks, Michie." Motioning for the track to change, I called on another. "Shawn."

Nice energy. Quick transitions—ooh! Deep backward dips. I told her to work on those harsh facial expressions. And—oop... The same arch sequences as Mandy and Michie!

Moving along...

I leaned into the microphone. "Thanks, Shawn. Ronmesha." I motioned Leah and the track changed from Cardi B's *"I Like It"* to the remix of Sego's *"Mystery Lady."*

Seconds into her freestyle, and I'm bored. Her transitions are so damn slow tonight. Are her joints tight? Can't be! Sore! Oh, god! What did she do between Wednesday and an hour ago? And—ugh! The same arch sequence as Mandy, Michie, and Shawn! And got the nerve to be stiff as hell!

Rushing toward the standing mic, I requested, "Toya, please. Thanks, Ronmesha." Leah cut the track as Toya laughed and skipped her way to the center of the studio. Ty Dolla Sign's *"By Yourself"* featuring Jhené Aiko began.

You're still giggling?

Oh, now you don't know how to start?

It was unbelievable. They knew the drill. We were in the middle of a veiled showcase, which meant there were any number of people on the other side of the one-way mirror, floor-to-ceiling glass.

This was my "passion" life. Owning a freelance dance studio had been one of the most rewarding agencies in my world. An art form passed down from my mother, I reveled in dancing before I was developed enough to possess rhythm. There was a long stretch of my life where I was morbidly shy until middle school—unless it involved dancing. The ability to lose myself through physical musical expression aided in me creating another facet of my otherwise dry personality. Dancing generated my confidence, making way to a sense of humor. I used that trait sparingly, but it was there.

Not tonight. These bitches were playing in my face!

"Cut the music please," I abruptly demanded.

"Shi," Ronmesha tried. "My shoes. I don't have the flats I need for an uptempo—"

The sight of my shaking head halted her weak excuses. "This is more a midtempo, but it should never matter." My attention went to Leah. "Something mid to up."

While she searched the playlists, we waited with whispers and sighs of anxiousness. Again, this was a showcase, something we put on several times a year. Video directors, theater scouts, and reps for all types of musical artists among others were beyond the wall observing. My crew knew this. Typically, these events were successful and benefit everyone, including my heart from providing the opportunity.

The series of African drums shot from the speakers and it didn't take long for me to recognize Whizkid's "*Essence*." And *that's* when I understood the assignment and got to it right away by pushing the tabletop microphone over. I gyrated while climbing aboard the rectangular desk occupied by my team. Standing in my heels, I snaked my body to my full height then laid out on the table to seductively roll to the floor to my feet.

The crowd made room for me when I forced them to with high rhythmic kicks. I transitioned into a variation of a *Rosalinda*-style waist gyration. The artists on the track, I noted, were Nigerian, so I wanted to incorporate as many homeland techniques as possible. My next transition was to the *ShakuShaku*, but then I had to hit with the *CatDaddy* and a seductive *Dougie* my four-inch *Loubs* would allow.

I grooved, lost myself in my expression; the artistic abilities of my body. It's what I did. The single most pleasurable thing for me over the years. Freestyling was my shit. So when I recognized the song coming to an end, I executed the *Pilolo*, a Ghanaian dance style, before kicking into a leg swing and landing on one hand behind my legs.

When I lifted my torso from the half wheel pose, the whole room went up in applause, shouts, and whistles. That didn't surprise me. I may not have been the best, but—and again—dancing was one area where my confidence soared. However, my eyes widened at the sight of a larger crowd. The group behind the glass was now in the studio.

As I meandered through the crowd of dancers reciprocating hi-fives, my heart shot up to my throat at the sight of Rayna Jacobs. My knees wobbled when her husband, Azmir, came into view taking her side.

Thee. Fucking. Azmir. Jacobs.

Rayna had been a member of the dancing circuit for years. Like me, she never pursued it full time, but couldn't stay away from the art form. She didn't have a studio, but had a huge one attached to her home where she got busy and had been shooting routines from her *YouTube* channel.

"Oh, my!" I shrilled while Rayna and I embraced each other. "What are y'all doing here?"

Smiling expressively with low eyes, Rayna was beaming at me. "I told you I'd come see the studio! I wanted to surprise you."

"Hey, Shi-Shi," Azmir greeted me and with it came a one-arm hug.

High key excited yet uneasy on the low, my emotions were all over the place.

"So I guess this winter is blessed with a Jacobs' visit to the East Coast?"

"Azmir's mother, Yazmine, is seeing a specialist out here," Rayna explained. "We flew in this morning and are leaving the day after tomorrow. The kids are with us."

"Awwwww! Really? The little people?"

They chuckled.

How did I know the Jacobs? My boyfriend. The craziest of connections, Austin used to date Rayna's sister, Chyna, in grad school. She helped him break into the movie industry. Eventually, she enlisted the assistance of her ever-connected brother-in-law— enter Azmir Jacobs. *Thee. Fucking. Azmir. Jacobs.* The one who I later learned, was more decorated than most of your favorite singers and actors because he'd had a hand in so many of their careers. Contrary to their success, he was not famous. The average person didn't know who Azmir was. I would have thought Austin's explanation of him was exaggerated until I visited them in California and attended his birthday party at their Rancho Palos Verdes residence last summer. There, *I*—little old me—was in the room with his caliber of friends, had even seen pictures of them together in the galleries of their home.

What made it weird was Austin having dated Chyna. She claimed he cheated on her, something I found hard to believe. Still, because at the time of their split, Austin was in bed with Azmir's little black book, the Jacobs embraced me. They'd been respectful each time I'd seen them. It also helped Rayna and I had the same passion. We choreographed together in her studio last Thanksgiving holiday weekend. It was life. I wondered how Chyna felt about her accepting me, but never had the heart to ask.

"Pardon me." Azmir pivoted away with his phone to his ear, not going far at all.

"I'm glad you're here." And I was. It was truly an honor. "We should do the Lit Twin Cities. Show them that RayChoppa flavor." I winked. Her eyes lit in excitement, apparently recalling one of our choreographed numbers we created at her place. "Will Azmir kill you?"

Rayna rolled her eyes. "Girl, please. He owes me my time. Always got me zipping all over the place when we touch down. I don't have a lot of time. We're meeting Stenton and his wife for drinks."

"That's cool because I was about to wrap this showcase up anyway. I'm dancing at *Sin* tonight." I flashed my tongue and did an air twerk, hopping in a circle with one knee and arm in the air.

As Rayna laughed at my silliness, Azmir had returned to her side, attention fixed on me, which killed my humor. "When we pulled up, my security peeped a pap squatting in a van in the back of the parking lot. Austin hasn't arranged some type of security for you?"

My father had expressed a similar concern to me a few times over the years.

I shook my head, waving off the notion. "I know who you're talking about. There's about three of them who park back there, hoping to catch something picture-worthy. Like…maybe Austin coming in or out. They're wasting their time. He never comes here. Only once or twice. Plus, these paparazzi are passive, nothing like the ones in NYC, L.A., or Miami. These guys are coming out here to Jersey from the City just in case my life is that consumed with celebrities other than Austin."

"What about when you go into the City, like tonight, to dance?" Rayna wanted to know.

"I haven't been bothered or harassed. They get their shots, but no biggie. When and if they start showing at my job or apartment, I'll hire someone."

"Austin should've had someone already." Azmir posed in a way you couldn't provide a rebuttal.

I wouldn't ask Austin to do it. Something I'd learned about my boyfriend of three years was he did what he wanted to do. The guy wasn't big on improvement, leaving me no expectations of him. I didn't need Austin for money or clout. And in his own way, he showed that was something he appreciated.

When Rayna could read that Azmir's comment left me on "stuck," she tried changing the subject. "Hey, A.D. I'm going to do a number with Shi-Shi. It'll be quick—"

"With those heels—" His face was hard as stone.

"*And* when we're done," she spoke over him, continuing her first thought, "you and I can go meet up with Zo and StentRo."

The great Azmir Jacobs' expression turned placid. "Don't forget we're stopping by a club after."

"I haven't." She reached up and kissed his lips.

And he let her. He didn't rush to pull back. He didn't punish her for her assertion. He…took what she gave with…patience.

When Rayna left her husband's mouth, she turned to me and chirped, "Let's go!"

Thee Azmir Jacobs remained in place, gawking at his wife through low, hungry eyes. It was weird to me as she pulled me away to bust a move.

Romantic, cute, and…a little weird.

That is thee *fucking Azmir Jacobs…*

Chapter Three

jas

"AND HERE, IN THIS COLUMN, IS WHERE THE STAFF TURNOVER IS calculated. And if you click on it." The screen changed and more columns populated. "You'll see the breakdown of employee type—"

The sound of the office door opening had Man and me looking up from the computer screen. The club's manager craned his neck inside.

"Those bar chairs have been delivered. They're setting them up now." He waved the clipboard, requesting a signature.

"Sin's here today, Sergio," Man reminded him, mumbling while still clicking in the spreadsheet. "Let the boss man sign. Get his shit wet."

Sergio stepped in and grabbed the pen in the cup on Man's

desk. When Sergio handed me the paperwork, I glanced over the details. "So this is to replace all the bar chairs?"

"Yes, sir."

"And the rest of the lounge chairs are coming when?"

"Next Tuesday, I think…" Man answered.

Sergio corrected his supervisor. "Monday morning, actually." Man looked over at him. "I paid for expedited shipping to guarantee the guys'll have enough time to put them together." An uneasy smile pushed up on his face.

"Who's putting them together?" I asked while signing.

"Tito from *Tilton Homes* and his crew."

Oh, yeah. "He started his moving company last year or something," I recalled.

"Around the time you got home," Man answered. "So a little longer than that."

"That's what's up." I handed the clipboard to Sergio, a brown-skinned, boney kid with silky, wavy hair to the bottom of his neck.

Funny looking to me, but since I'd been home, I had been to *Club Sin* just a handful of times. It had been a gradual act of resuming the responsibility of all my businesses, *Club Sin* being one of them. When I got locked up, Man and I agreed that he'd run the club and I'd provide whatever support I could through my resource, and when I was released, I'd eventually take over. Well, since I'd been back on the streets and getting caught up, it had become very clear to me that Man had dedicated himself to the business. *Club Sin* had become a piece of his identity. He ran the place with closed eyes, which was why I'd been taking my time.

In the three or four times I'd been here to check out the new upgrades live and in color, I'd seen Sergio. He was a suave nigga. Last summer, he was draped in loose Bermuda sets with the tops matching the bottoms and boat shoes. In cooler temps, I'd seen him in velour sweat suits and *Wallabees*, like today. Country as hell, but he'd obviously been a good club manager because he'd been here with Man for a few years.

I tossed my chin his way. "You with the security lineup?"

"Yeah." Sergio took a quick peek over his shoulder. "These cats look strapped." He laughed nervously.

Man didn't. Neither did I. "They are."

The humor melted from his face. "Damn." His eyes blinked away. "Uhhhh…"

"Yeah, my nigga," Man chimed in. "I had you call Sin to give him your account of the shit that went down because, as the owner, you need to get used to reporting shit like that directly to him, too. At the end of the day, it's him who figures out the solutions and shit."

Sergio's hands shot into the air. "So long as one of you sign my checks…" His goofy ass laughed again.

And again, we didn't.

My forehead wrinkled. "You never been in a room with two niggas as real as us at the same time, have you?"

His shoulders dropped and his mouth twisted. "No."

"And it shows. You gotta relax," I advised, fighting being irritated by his undeniable telling of his weakness. In prison, you only had seconds to read niggas. It was the single most important skill of survival. Misreading or not attempting to size up anyone—prisoner or staff—could mean your life or livelihood in lockdown. "Let's start there."

Before I finished my last sentence, Sergio was nodding.

"Got it?" Man asked.

"Got it."

"Cool." I eyed him closely, absorbing all the vibes. "I'mma finish up on the books and then you can take me around downstairs to catch me up."

"You got it." Sergio headed for the door. "I'll check in with the bar chairs."

Before the door closed, I turned to Man. "This ya mans?"

He snickered, still clicking to change the pages on the screen. "Sergio's a good face for this place. He may not have the combat boots for East Harlem, but the nigga definitely got the face to run a nightclub on Lennox Ave."

Laughing, we went back to the books.

I hate clubs…

As I peered over the balcony, attempting to count over two hundred bodies appearing as ants, I felt like I'd aged beyond my years. Was it prison that did it to me? Couldn't have been. I wasn't in the club when I was running the streets. A more accurate assessment would have been me robbing niggas coming out of an upscale club similar to…mine. This shit was crazy. I owned this. *Club Sin* had been up and running—*and growing*—since it opened the year of my arrest.

I recalled sitting on a cemented block debating if I'd put the money behind this as advised. Man and Juggy hyped me up after we kicked it with a few known party promoters from around the way at the time. I blindly threw the money at it under the condition that not only would it always be mine, but mine in name, too. Those two stipulations remained over the years, although management and staff did not. Man was always supposed to be my eyes and ears here, but him being a day to day manager wasn't in the cards. He was a street nigga. But three years into the club's success, we saw the bullshit.

Snakes always left their shed skin behind and we built our reputation on finding it. The promoters were stealing money and risking the liquor license. Once, we were shut down for a month over some inspection bullshit that could've been avoided. So, I had Man step up and revamp the business. It was a challenge for him—and a blessing in my opinion—because it matured him. Running *Club Sin* even with a manager like Sergio and the two before him legitimized Man, providing a skill, bi-weekly paychecks, and a W-2 form each year.

And peering down on this hyped crowd below, including those seated in the various VIP sections across the main floor, I had no desire to take over this responsibility, though I'd do what I had to do.

I sensed someone coming near. Man strolled over and sidled up beside me as I leaned over the balcony.

"And this is just a Thursday night…"

"Tomorrow into Sunday will almost double this." *Damn…* "We have to turn so many people away Friday through Sunday that we extended hours on Thursdays."

Sergio appeared holding a tray of filled tumblers. Man took a glass and I shook my head, declining.

"We brought out our reserve of *Mauve* since Mr. Brandy himself is in the building. He's asking for you down there," Sergio announced. "You sure you don't want one?"

Man snickered, which was hilarious to me, though I didn't laugh. I shook my head as I pushed from the ledge. "Nah, bruh. I'm good."

"Okaaay…" he sang in a warning manner while taking off.

Man laughed this time and I chuckled.

"Lemme go holla at him."

"Like that," Man bade, staying behind.

I took the winding stairs down to the lower floor and passed through security at the bottom. The energy was electrifying even for my lackluster desire to be here. I had to be up before five in the morning to prepare for my main job. My time here was coming to an end, but I needed to be present for this leg of my enterprise.

"Sin!" Divine greeted over the music and we fell into a dap.

His wife, Rayna, next to him, held a glass of their signature drink as she bobbed her head and sea-watched the crowd.

"Mrs. Jacobs," I greeted.

Her smile was big, sincere. "Nice to see you again, Sin!" She hugged me, making sure I heard, "This place is so nice! So glad I came."

After releasing her, I offered a neck bow and patted my chest. "Appreciated. Glad y'all were able to make it and on a night I was here."

Divine had been to *Club Sin* more times than I had over the years. It was his way of keeping an eye on it for me. He was the one who provided the idea of pushing Man to step up instead of relying on "outside vendors." It was also Divine who inspired me to get into the nightclub business. I'd seen what he'd done with his two out in Cali and thought to add it to my portfolio.

"Where's your drink, Sir *Château Blevin?*" Rayna asked.

Azmir supplied her with an answer. "The nigga don't drink."

"Don't drink?" she giggled. "You're smarter than the drug dealers in the eighties and nineties." She sang, "Never get high on your own supply."

The music lowered just a bit and the deejay shouted, *"Club Sin."* He scratched the record. "Let me help y'all get ya asses on the dance floor." He scratched again. "But first, make room." Then he began a new track.

The crowd got hyped and the dance floor below us seemed to shift. A small gang of chicks appeared, gyrating toward the dance-floor. A few of them even somersaulted to their destination. And as soon as Mooski's sang, "She's a runner. She's a track star," they all jumped into a choreographed dance, shifting so one was in the center of a circle.

The chick in the middle dropped to the floor and moved sensually and with crazy agility to her full height like a snake. She wore black leather combat boots and dark baggy pants hanging low enough to expose the almond of her hips in a yellow bodysuit. Her body—even with her legs covered in baggy cargo pants—was fucking wicked.

"Oh, my god!" Divine's wife screamed, but I couldn't tear my eyes from her. "That's Shi!"

"Who?" he asked over the music behind me.

"Shi-Shi! The one we just left in Jersey...before the Rogers?!"

I didn't hear more from them because when shortie flipped her hair from her face while doing a Michael Jackson style of groin grab and pelvis thrust, I noticed her face. It was the Black "Karen" from the coffee shop. The one who saw my therapist, too.

Oh, shit...

She looked nothing like a builder while busting her ass wide open on the dance floor. She was fucking weightless and flexible... energetic and expressive. Did she lie?

I did tell her I worked in construction…

Did I give her a live bait to, in turn, tell me a lie? But why would she say a builder out of all things?

Because what the fuck is construction?

More often than not, the purpose of construction is to build in most people's minds.

But "home" building is a specific industry…

See.

Snakes shedding their skin…

I started to regain my breath, but the adrenaline still pumped in my blood as I hi-fived Melody, one of the dancers with me tonight.

"Amazing!" she tried shouting over the music.

"Right?" I trilled, so high from the performance.

A hot hand grabbed me at the side of my waist and as I turned, Sergio's low eyes came into view. He was carrying a drink.

"For me?"

He leaned in to speak in my ear. "Only for you."

I smiled, sipping the cocktail through the straw. "Oh, my god. This is soooo good!" I droned.

Still with that lustful gleam in his eye, he spoke into my ear, "Just break up with the motherfucker. Be with me and open your club like you've been wanting to. I can help you; you know that."

My eyes circled over and around him. "You forget you work here?"

"I'll quit. I'm over this place anyway. The owner's been back on the scene. This place's been turning a little hood'ish recently. I can make your dreams a reality, *Shi*—"

Cash being swiftly handed over had me taking a few steps back from Sergio. I glanced up from the rolled cash to its grantor and stumbled.

"Shit!" I tried covering my drink to prevent it from spilling.

"You looked good out there," his velvet chords spoke over the music as he stretched his arm, offering me cash.

I almost didn't recognize him. He wore actual clothes. A black sweater topped by a thick gold link chain. It was conspicuous, yet not an ostentatious display of ghetto wealth. Tasteful. His jeans were fitted yet not tight. He was the same man, but a completely different being. Damn, he looked edible. It didn't help that he was surrounded by men struggling to keep their hungry eyes off me. That was strange considering his reception to me seemed patently indifferent.

When one of the guys with him broke a snicker and tried looking away, I knew what time it was. But Sergio spoke before I managed to.

"Oh, no." He chuckled. "She's not an erotic entertainer. She's a member of the dance company that—"

"Fuck you!" I hurled over Sergio to Jas and took off into the sea of people resuming the dancefloor.

"That'll be six-eighty two, sir."

I had no idea why the sound of that communication, out of all the exchanges happening in the coffee shop, caught my attention. My eyes swung from my laptop to the other end of the store, at the counter. Sure enough, *Mr. Construction* was there, paying for his morning beverage. The young girl at the register beamed too hard and her eyes were slit lines, she was so enamored by him. And apparently, so was the girl behind her at the tea machine, and the one packing the pastry orders. They all failed to hide their fixed attention and attraction to him, something I noticed the last time I'd seen him in here.

Rolling my eyes, I went back to the contract I'd been going over from a potential roofing trade company before sending them over to our legal team. I arrived at my therapy appointment early to get in some work before I made it to the office this morning. The agreement, so far, ran smooth and was the typical legal jargon I'd been accustomed to, but still needed a preview.

That was until I got to a line stating my firm would have to pay the roofing company an exuberant amount of money if its installation start time has been delayed. It was unprecedented and an abuse of my firm's success. So, I fired off an email to express just that. I was sure the word was out about us losing *Wegman and Sons* and now those who should have been neutral were preying on our weakness.

Or so they think...

By the time I was done with the email, I'd lost control of my breath. I'd also forgotten where I was. My eyes brushed around the buzzing coffee shop, taking a three hundred-sixty tour until I peeped him at eleven o'clock—mere feet away.

I sighed, "Well, if it isn't the big tipper." Jas glanced over to me, paying a second of eye time before scoffing with a mild smirk and returning to his drink and phone. "I hope you were more generous than that twenty-dollar bill last night. The hard-working baristas actually need it."

"Well, if it ain't Ms. *Builder*," he half-heartedly greeted without his eyes.

My face wrinkled. "What the fuck does that mean?"

Jas took his time answering and even giving me the respect of his attention. Finally, he looked at me again and my stupid body shivered.

"Only that you're either clever or a struggling builder in Jersey, moonlighting as a dancer at night in the City."

"Are you calling me a liar?"

He looked my way again and blinked successively. "I don't believe I've used that word once during this lil' exchange."

Little?

"Good, because you'd be foolish and would look as dumb as you did last night 'tipping' me twenty bucks."

He wouldn't give me consistent eye contact. On the one hand, I was grateful for it because his attention was heady. The flip side to it was it was rude. An act of disregard. No one dismissed or disregarded Ashira Witherspoon. No one.

"How do you figure I'm foolish for not believing you're a builder, or a successful one at that…" His eyes circled the air.

Did this dude forget my name?

"Ashira," I tested out my theory.

The fucker snapped his finger as though relieved. "Yeah. Ashira. What makes me foolish?"

"Your unfounded assumptions. I'm a studied dancer. Got a bachelor's in fine arts from *BSU* and a master's at *Steinhardt, NYU.* And not only am I a reputable builder in this state, I'm the largest Black-owned in Northern Jersey."

"Really?" he all but hummed while reading something on his phone.

One of the coffee shop girls strolled past his table stealing two glances. That made me roll my eyes again. What these young girls saw in his type, I didn't know. There was nothing appealing to me about being in line to be the subsequent baby's mother of a guy no less prepared to become a partner than their own father.

"Yeah. And that's a lot more than I'm sure you can say as a 'construction' worker."

Damn you, Jim Wegman!

Then Jas turned to me with a smirk I wanted to slap from his face. "Maybe you're right, Ashira." He almost turned ninety degrees to face me. "But more than anything, you've explained why you're seeing a shrink."

What?!

Appalled, I pulled in a deep breath.

48

"Then explain how can *you* afford said therapist? I know her rates and they aren't feasible for 'construction workers.'"

"Wow." He nodded. "It's sick as hell that, that's all you see when you see me. Say less."

Say less?

"Nope. I'll say more. I see what you present."

"Which is?"

With touted lips, I nodded. "Like a typical hood dude."

"What, to you, defines hood?"

"In your case? Someone who values time on their block or any illegal hustle more than they do an honest, hardworking living. How soon are you willing to quit your job? As soon as you find an *OSHA* violation or the moment you're past the point of qualifying for unemployment? And trust me, I know; I employ your type when child support or probation is on your ass."

What in the hell am I doing?

Where had these twittering hate-filled, judgmental words come from?

He snickered in his "cool guy" way. "I've been employed for seventeen months." Then he pretended to shiver. "God, I hope we ain't got no violations. That ain't good for paper—I mean, business. You know?"

My brows hiked. "With whom are you employed, Mr....Jas?"

Damn.

I cringed inside. Did I not sound like my aunt, Kimberly?

"Well, uhhhh, Missus, I reckon I do work for Master Rizzo over der' on the *Rizzo Custom Homes & Developers*"—*Paulie Rizzo?*— "plantation—"

I couldn't take a mental breather from his heavy energy.

"Fuck you!"

His head tossed back in a silent chortle before blowing softly into the opening of the lid of his drink while looking ahead. "You've threatened that already, Ms. Ashira. Let's get more original. Spice it up or say less." Then he took a careful sip of the hot beverage.

"Say less." I scoffed, hating the phrase. "But am I wrong?"

After a considerable pause, he answered, "I ain't hugged the block since…I was thirteen…sixteen years old, maybe?" He then peered my way. "I love what I do. I enjoy building," his tone soft, not offended in the least.

Confused, I turned to my neglected latte. "Interesting."

"Very."

"What?"

"That once again, I can see how you need help from a therapist with your personality."

"How?"

"It seems we're getting out of pocket with assumptions here. Have you ever heard the aphorism to 'never judge a book by its cover'?"

I scoffed, snapping my head forward. "Miss me with the 'J' word. Judgment is a tool we've all used since we were toddlers and continue to for survival. It's not limited to people's character traits or lifestyles. It can be as primitive as deciding to follow a man asking you to help an injured friend down the alley, or interviewing a parolee who has never filled out an employment application prior to his conviction and imprisonment."

"Interesting…"

"Why the hell is everything I say so damn interesting this morning?"

"Ashira, I think you are an interesting…person," he mumbled, returning to his buzzing phone.

"How?"

Another pause. "That's for the good ol' therapist across the street to diagnose."

Wa—what?

"Has she told you how to let go of the Colombian connect?"

He chuckled again. At this point, I was feeling like the bratty little sister. My mood had definitely turned irrevocably sour since reading that stupid ass bootleg contract.

"Why don't you ask me about my life instead of embarrassing yourself with assumptions—not that I owe you a single answer."

"How much do you make an hour over there at *Rizzo's*?"

He looked my way again. "Say less. That's not your business, but you really have to work on your erroneous assumptions, yo, because who said I'm paid on an hourly basis?'

"Because in construction, by and large, that's how trades are paid."

"But not exclusively. Next question," he instructed as his phone vibrated loudly. "That's my five-minute check-in text from across the street."

I thought for a minute. What else did I want to know about someone I didn't give a shit about?

"Which trade are you?"

"A few. I've done diggin', concrete, brick-laying, tiling, roofing, framing, plastering, a bit of carpentry, structural iron and steel… even some landscaping, but I try not to fuck with it much. I've done some electrical work and plumbing, but not as much as everything else."

"And which of those trades have you actually been formally trained in?"

He let out a heavy breath. "Certifications in HVAC, operation engineer—*trucks*—"

"Oh, I know what an operation engineer is." I rolled my eyes, scoffing. "Knew before they put a fancy spin on construction truck operators."

"Okay," was all he said before continuing. "I plan on finishing up electrical and plumbing soon, which is why I said I don't fuck with them too heavy. Gotta be certified for those."

"I know that, too. I run *Witherspoon Homes*." I lifted a brow and took a sip from my drink.

"So, you guys get a lot of felons over there at *Witherspoon Homes*?"

"Of course. But I don't hire too many. Those are easy trades, certification-wise, but not a lot with experience or tenacity. Back to you. Why do you feel it necessary to take courses for trades you should simply know from on-the-job experience?"

"I wouldn't say that. There's a lot to be learned in school that you don't have the benefit of knowing until you've worked the trade for ten/twenty years and experienced disasters yourself. I actually dig the classes, even if they take up so much of my damn time."

"Why are you taking so many? You can't possibly do all those jobs at a firm. Are you doing it for job assurance?"

He shook his head, appearing at ease as though I'd not been popping shit to him since he sat down. "Nah." He scoffed while turning to me. "I told you, I like building. Wanna head a firm of my own one day."

There was a compelling pull in his eyes. Something unable to hide the audacity of his truth.

"Why are you asking about who I hire?" That question came, honestly, without attitude.

"Because I work with an organization assisting Black and Latinos with trade jobs in building. Just wanted to know if you had an interest in employing on the basis of second chances."

"Does Paulie Rizzo?"

Jas scoffed, "Only on paper and in action. His heart is something he's gotta answer for. You know?"

"Well, I'm an equal opportunity employer with an impeccable bullshit detector."

He nodded without rebuttal. "Well, I've answered everything."

He was closing up. For some reason, I didn't want that.

"Except how much you make an hour, but I'm not dwelling on that." I rolled my eyes internally, thinking of how to redirect this conversation. "Who's your favorite rapper?"

He snorted before taking a drink. "Who's yours?"

"Young Lord most days."

He nodded, eyes ahead.

Away from me…

"Mine, too." He tapped with his thumbs into his phone. "I fucks with Nas, too. Old school heads, too."

"What's your favorite book?"

What am I doing here?

He peered up from his phone, eyes squinting. "Now?"

"Duh…"

"I'm feeling Dr. Twanece Edmondson's shit. I read a few of her books since the summer. I'm on '*Tending to the Man Who Governs the Masses: How to Protect What He Values Most.*' Good shit."

My forehead wrinkled and I blurted, "Are you gay?"

Jas smiled into his phone then shun his beam my way. "You really are interesting, ain't you?"

"I'm sorry." I turned to gaze blindly out of the window. "I shouldn't have asked that. You can't in today's climate."

"You think?"

I needed to rebound. Here I was, losing my attention to a conversation with a thug I didn't know, but had been standing in the gateway of his essence.

Weird as fuck, but true…

"Nah," his voice broke my musing, "but I actually like the book you quoted earlier about judgment, even though you quoted it wrong. Ezra Carmichael?"

I brushed the back of my neck, turning away from him. "I don't remember the author."

Am I embarrassed?

It was a self-help book Peach gave me three or four years ago. It took a few months for me to crack it open and ended up being a hard read, causing me to self-analyze.

"A'ight." He exhaled. "That's my time. I got this…thing across the street." Jas stood from the table, leaving me feeling some kind of way.

"What's your favorite television show?" I asked as he slipped into his bubbled vest.

Jas snickered, swiping his nose. "When I can watch," he added a disclaimer. "*Taking Tips from Tynisha*'s my shit." Then he headed toward the door, appearing completely unbothered by abandoning our strange conversation.

What?

That was my favorite show. No way this completely confident and well-read thug could get through forty-five minutes of my favorite reality show.

Right?

I couldn't ponder it. My attention had to return to work. I had site visits today, leaving me no time for my office work, hence me showing here so early.

"Taking Tips from Tynisha."

No damn way...

Two days later, I pulled onto the block of my therapist's office building. The rain had been coming down hard since the crack of dawn. Once again, I arrived early with the hopes of getting a head start on work. I had a mountain of reports to get through, and the "almost hangover" poking at my skull was sure to make my mood irritable.

Just after spotting a parking spot across the street on the side of the coffee shop, I saw a lengthy figure with a heather gray hoodie and a blue vest power walking down the block. It was him. It *had* to be him. I was pretty sure there were no other men with the Black man-swag walk like Jas in this area and possibly town.

I pushed down on the accelerator to move past the delivery truck directly in front of me. Why had he parked so far? Did he have a car? Did I have time to drop him off? We were in a pretty secluded town.

This nigga had better have had a car. But he kept walking past empty parking spaces. These blocks weren't filled with vehicles this time of the morning. The best action on this block was the coffee shop, and this was a walker's town, minimizing motorized traffic.

I tried beeping the horn to get his attention, but Jas turned the corner. By the time I made it to the light and looked both ways before making a right, I'd lost him. The only thing I saw moving was a white cargo van pulling off.

A beat-up one at that...

My phone rang, frustrating me. The rain was relentless and something as simple as tapping for Bluetooth connection was too much of a feat.

"Ashira Witherspoon," I answered without identifying the caller.

"Ms. Witherspoon, I have the pile of roofing trades applications you requested. What should I do with them?"

"Email them to me, Marge-Jean." A thought struck as I turned the corner. "Can you make a few calls to find out where their sites are this morning? If this rain can let up, I'll make a few stops to see them in action."

"I'll try in earnest, Ms. Witherspoon," her pledge drily and without promise.

Rolling my eyes, I bade, "Bye, Marge-Jean."

Chapter Four

FEBRUARY | PRESENT DAY

ashira

By the time I was done with my therapy session, the rain had graciously relented. I'd driven by several abandoned construction sites, which I was sure was due to the weather. One thing I knew for certain: those from my firm had better had their asses out the second the rain cleared.

Nonetheless, I was now a block away from popping up on a small roofing company who'd applied for a subcontract for my father's firm. At the time, we weren't in need and if we were, I didn't have faith that *Brown Roofing* was a large enough outfit for us. Today, just out of curiosity, I wanted to give their work a look. Sneaking up on a trade's worksite wasn't always ideal. I braved it because I knew we had the work they could use to stay afloat.

The moment I rolled up to the site on the resident block, I was pleasantly surprised to not find it abandoned due to the weather. Looked like Kareem Brown's guys were doing what they could in the aftermath of the downpour. *Hmmmm…* Maybe this fifty-five had been a good idea? I had no hopes of my visit being fruitful, but I'd been compelled to try for two days now.

Oh. Shit…

I didn't expect to see him here. Zebedee Baker of *McKinnon & Baker* was on the site. How did he know Brown, a convict with an outfit of maybe three men, which included himself? I didn't want to see Zeb, my former mentor. I hadn't spoken to him in over a year. After countless ignored calls and emails and no-show luncheons, I'd been too much of a coward to explain myself. This would be so awkward, I thought as I pulled into a park and killed the engine.

While closing the door to my pickup, I brightened my face mildly. This was not what I expected when planning to prove myself right about Brown's work ethic today. But I was here and wouldn't scurry back into my truck and cower from a potential nonplussed situation, especially one I caused.

Fuck…

I stumbled, quickly catching my stride. The guy, Jas. He stood next to Zeb, chatting with Brown. What in the hell was he doing here? This wasn't a Rizzo job. Or was it? Was Brown subcontracting for *Rizzo's Custom Homes?*

"Well, look it here," Zeb began with the most gorgeous beam ever. He was such a good-looking man for his age, always had been since I'd known him. "If it ain't the baddest, most talented female-builder in the damn state!"

When I reached him, we greeted with a friendly hug. "I mean no disrespect, Mr. Baker, but I've been taught by a wise man to never take a title hyphenated with female. My balls don't hang but they're big enough to be seen. I do believe I am the best builder in my lane. Full stop."

With a firm nod, he confirmed my assertion. "It was a test I'm proud you can still pass, young lady."

The sincerity in his voice gave me pause. It brought back

the warmth I'd feel from his validation. Zebedee Baker was a rare find in this male-dominated industry. He was a nurturing beast. When my father basically threw me into his office the week I returned from *BSU* after graduating, he taught me the books, how to build a beautiful home, and the company's philosophy. But it was Zeb here who taught me how to swim with sharks. Who were the sharks? All the men I encountered with dicks, the handful of lesbians guaranteeing to turn me out, and finally, the pick-me women accepting misogyny every day on the job.

He'd spent countless years coaching me on how to step into a room, take a meeting, negotiate contracts, and more often than not, not to cry when my emotions flared. Zeb taught me how to remove the emotion of my disappointment and anger and to pour that passion into governing and maintaining a solid reputation for my father's firm, and being the best builder on the planet. I owed him more than missed calls and canceled meetings. Only I was too immature to find the words to articulate why.

"It's great seeing you, Witherspoon," the caramel, gray-haired man murmured.

I found myself pulling him into a hug again, silently thanking him for never objectifying me and making my youth and features the focus of his attention. He was sincere in toughening me up, never creating a gross experience of inappropriateness. Zeb had two daughters he raised: one older than me and the other younger. He was far more attentive and encouraging to them than my dad had been to me in years past.

Feeling my emotions swell, I quickly turned my attention to Jas. "Funny how we didn't know each other existed two weeks ago. Right?" I smiled more than I felt in the moment, trying to calm myself.

I didn't want to mention where we'd been seeing each other to maintain our privacy.

Jas' eyes were low, body stock-still with his hands in the pockets of his jeans. "I never said I didn't know you existed."

My face folded in confusion. "Come again?"

"I knew of Ashira Witherspoon, the builder. I just didn't know you were her in the coffee shop."

That was an unexpected boost to my confidence.

"Well," My spine straightened. "that's good to know." I turned my attention to Brown, initiated a hand-shake. "Kareem."

"What's good, Witherspoon?"

I glanced over to the roof of the house his men were working on. "Thanks for seeing me."

"I was shocked as hell when I got the call. So the Wegman rumor is true?"

I shrugged with my neck. "So it is."

"You good with replacing his outfit?"

"Just stopping through to count my options." I pushed out an impressive whistle. "That slate?"

"The fake shit, but it's what the wife wanted. Husband said she biting off her sister in Ohio."

We all shared a chuckle. "Yeah," I snorted. "Aren't we all familiar with that story?"

"Boss!" one of Brown's guys called for him.

"Give me a minute, Witherspoon." He excused himself and took off.

I nodded then turned to Zeb in the predictably awkward moment. "So, how do you two know each other?"

"Oh." Zeb's brows shot up. "For about a year now, Jas and I have been working on an initiative to get more Black and Brown men and women into building."

"I've never heard of this."

"You were the first I hit up when he came to me with the concept," Zeb answered, clearing his throat.

Quickly, my eyes darted away. I felt like shit.

Trying to rebound, I inquired, "Does it have a name?"

"It's in the works," Jas' thick chords vibrated. "I guess it's one of those machines that have legs before it gets a name."

Zeb cosigned, my heart programmed to heed to his instruction. "It's definitely been functioning."

Hmmmmm…

This guy worked for Rizzo, was friends with the likes of Kareem Brown, and had been partnering with my mentor.

A phone sounded and Zeb dug into his pocket, pulling his out. "I need to take this. Jas, we'll kick it soon." Then he neared me, quickly pulling me into his chest for a brief hug and kiss on the head. The man was adorable. In so many ways, he nurtured me. "I'm always here," he whispered before taking off. "Yeah, Ted," he finally answered.

I turned to watch him take off along the side of the house. Zeb tended to his call as my chest was shearing. Before I could think, I began jogging, power-legging it after him.

"Baker..." I kept my voice down, remembering I was on the job, in the vicinity of the sharks. "Baker!"

He turned to find me. "Hang on a sec, Ted."

"Listen." Suddenly, I was breathless. "I'm really sorry. I never meant to... You know you've always been good to me. I just..." My words failed me.

But Zeb caught on, half of his face lifting in a forlorn smile. "Your heart ain't in it." *What?* I didn't quite understand those words. "Building has burned you out. You tried, but it's never been what Ashira chose." His eyes incredibly soft. "And I don't blame you for it, sweetheart. I blame that damn Noel for not paying attention to you after dumping the firm on your shoulders. Don't worry about me being mad at you, honey. Your disappearance hasn't been personal, I know that. But I'll tell you like I tell my girls: if ever you need me, I leave the porch light on every night."

My eyes welled with tears. I was melting, and fast.

Zeb took a step forward into my personal space, towering. "Don't you even think about shedding a solitary damn tear on this site, young lady—"

Heaving in a breath, I murmured, "I know! I know!" I was trying to convince myself, not him. "I won't. I just feel like shit and don't want you to think it's reflective of my heart. I miss our talks. My life lessons. It's just that I...I..." My mouth hung open.

"You're burnt out and need to follow your dreams, Wither-spoon. Hurry up." He clenched his cell phone to his chest inside his

Carhartt Duck coat. "I'm waiting to cheer you on over there, too." He winked then turned to leave again.

It took me a few seconds to get my emotions in check, but I did. Then I turned and sauntered back toward Jas, who was on a call now himself. He ended it just as I met his side. Jas' expressed attention was on me, demonstrating and confirming what I'd discovered a couple of days ago in the coffee shop. The guy was damn good-looking. His features were a cross between artful and rugged.

My face dropped into my hand, belly upending an unexpected snort. My head shot up and I sighed, "*Ahhhhh...*" I shook my head softly. "I don't know if it's a result of my lingering hangover this morning or waking up on the wrong side of the bed"—*it was actually the conversation we had the other day about being intentional with hiring Black and Brown men and women that sparked it*—"but I find myself feeling generous and so, so, so apologetic today."

"What does that have to do with me?"

"The shit I said to you at the coffee shop was cruel and antagonistic and highbrow and...very bigoted. I'd just learned some upsetting news that shouldn't have been all that *upsetting* and took it out on you." Out of nowhere, a revelation hit me. "And you just taking it and not telling me to eat my own shit fueled my rampage."

A faint grin grew on his face. "So, it's my fault you're an asshole?"

My head bobbed up and down before the words formed. "Yes. Yes! It's absolutely your fault." I found myself laughing and Jas must have found humor in my pathetic avoidance of accountability, too. "I'm no angel. I mean, I've got my shit with me, but I'm not what you saw the other day."

His forehead stretched. "Well, you did say the welcoming committee back in school wasn't your kind of hype."

I rolled my eyes. "Touché, Jas. Touché." I found myself nodding and internally laughing at myself more. "You remember that, huhn?" The question was rhetorical as I turned away, tucking my hair behind my ear.

"There's very little I forget, Witherspoon." He pulled in a

breath. "Look... I gotta bounce. Don't wanna be late for this appointment. It was good seeing you in a better light today."

My voice upraised in a rush as he stepped off. "Hey... If you're up for it, I'd like to hear more about your efforts with job placement. And I have a boyfriend, so you don't have to be worried about me trying to come on to you like the girls in the coffee shop." His face lit beautifully from a silent chuckle. My palms shot into the air. "I'm happy in my situation. I promise, I'm not *that* pathetic."

His lips pushed out and Jas nodded. "Yeah. We can do that. I'm sure we'll bump heads again at the coffee shop. Looks like we've been on the early morning shift lately."

"Let's be more intentional with it. How about tonight? Dinner at *DiFillippo's*—completely my treat."

Am I that desperate to hit the restart button with a stranger?

Apparently.

"I'm in Harlem. By dinner time, I'll be across the bridge. Besides, it's all good. We straight."

"Maybe at *Club Sin?*" *Ashira, have some dignity!* "I see you know the place."

Jas turned up his nose. "My boy run that club. I was doing my obligatory pop-up to you know...appear interested. The club scene ain't never been my thing."

"Sergio?"

"The one he reports to."

Oh...

My eyes fell as I struggled with one: trying to figure out who Sergio answered to. And two: accepting Jas' apparent rejection.

"You dancing tonight?"

I shook my head. "No. Just meeting friends there."

"There's a tea shop two blocks away from the club. I can bum a ride there and meet up before you club."

I squinted at him. "Are you an early bird, Mr. Jas?"

He croaked out, laughing as he turned to leave, "Oh, please believe. And I gots no shame."

Remembering why I was here, I turned and found Brown to no avail. Then, somehow, my attention went back to Jas. A van had pulled up as he approached the street. A white bummed out van. The exact one I'd seen around the corner from the therapist's office a few hours ago. Jas quickly jumped in on the passenger side and they pulled off with the roar of an aged engine.

jas

The moment we pulled off, my phones began chirping off the damn chain. A few notifications were from the site managers about having to report in with muddy conditions, my lawyer about trademark shit, and Renee.

Renee...

As I tried keeping up with the notifications, Juggy shared, "Damn. She look better without all the makeup, but she look like a mean bitch, too."

I fired off text messages to my crew at a site in Parsippany. "Who?"

"The one you was just choppin' it up with."

I looked his way. "You know her?"

"Who don't? You 'on't know her?" Then he snorted. "I forgot who the fuck I'm talking to. Yo ass don't keep up with shit but work."

"What you mean?"

"She be everywhere. On *E!*...all over the *Gram*, and shit."

My head drew up and I asked, "This chick?"

"Yeah. She the one that fuck with ol' boy." He snapped his

fingers. "The one that was in that movie with the old head nigga." I laughed to myself, thinking that could be a gazillion goddamn people. "Jack Nicholson! That nigga. You know who I'm talking about. He was in that *Starz* shit with 50." When I didn't give him the verbal recollection he needed, Juggy grunted. "Shit, man. Anyway, she fuck wit' him. They be on red carpets and shit. Young Nicky at the job love him some Black pussy. Be showing me mad pictures of her and them City Girls all the damn time. Young ass." He shook his head.

"Man, I've got no damn clue what you're talking abou—"

"Austin!" he damn near shouted. "Austin Seers. That lil' muthafucka alright, too."

I nodded, half into the conversation at this point. The chick, Witherspoon, said she had a man. She never said it was a famous actor.

"She was at *uhhh...*" I stalled, typing a text to my lawyer. "*Club Sin* the other night."

"Yeah. Man told me a while back how she and her crew like to come there and dance a lot."

My head swung up again. "As in on the payroll?"

"Nah. It's just what they like to do. It gets the crowd hyped. The deejays like that shit and the crowd be going mad in that bitch. I saw them there a few times. Paparazzi be out there sometimes, tryna catch her. Damn security be giving them hell, too."

Finally, my gaze lifted to the oncoming traffic ahead.

Paparazzi?

That speed and popularity seemed to fit her energy. Witherspoon was a full-packaged woman for real. Smart, sexy as hell, assertive—able to be humble—and a leader. Giving thought to things that didn't further my goals or nourish my soul wasn't a habit for me at all. In fact, I couldn't process my feelings about seeing her so much over the past few days, but again, frivolous things as such never got much mental play from me.

God, bless Witherspoon and her boyfriend.

But I 'on't give a shit...

I hopped up the stairs and straight up to the metal detectors manned by armed officers to clear my pockets. I was annoyed. The nuisance of having to stop my day or plan my schedule around these visits. It was a waste of time and a reminder of the compromise of my integrity. In here, I still belonged to them. In these walls, I still walked the way they taught me to and only spoke when spoken to. In these four walls, I was reminded of the scent of Black male fear, the most degrading yet common emotion in this country.

After my pat-down, clearance, and collecting my personal belongings, I made my way to the office of my reporting. Then I remembered to silence my phones.

The old, pudgy Asian woman didn't even look up at me from behind the plexiglass when she demanded, "Name?"

"Sinclair."

"Your reason for being here, Sinclair."

"Check in."

"With whom, Mr. Sinclair?"

"Reed."

"Sign here and have a seat."

After giving my John Hancock, I found a seat against the wall. The waiting area was mostly crowded. So many low and lower energies in one space. Dudes were pacing, scared as shit, likely because they knew they'd fucked up. Some were hopeless in post-lives, struggling to grasp on to fleeting opportunities.

"Roberson!" An officer appeared, barking across the room. "I just hung up with *Dunkin Donuts*. Yo ass ain't clocked in, in four days—"

"That's what I was tryna explain," one of the pacers pleaded.

"Fuck that!" the officer swung his arm in the air. "Your dumb ass going back to DRC. Come get ya paperwork."

Roberson sighed, eyes closing as he moped toward his P.O. "Fuck me, bro!" he hissed beneath his breath.

Then I waited and waited. Overhearing petitions over the phone for extra work time, niggas bumming rides, even one inquiring about juices for clean urine. The shit killed my vibe. But I waited.

"Sinclair!" I was gratefully called and buzzed in. Back here, the heat of anxiety was edged up a few notches. Surrounding the officers' cubes were traditional office-sized rooms that were holding cells. When you made it in there and were shackled, you knew you'd fucked up.

"If you violate today, I'm fuckin' you up," a hard feminine voice had me looking to my right.

Instinctively, I smiled, recognizing her. An officer who flirted her ass off with me since my first day out when I showed up here to check in. I didn't respond. I never did. It was an absolute no-no. I wasn't trying to get caught up with no damn officer.

"My man!" Mr. Reed greeted once he saw me turn down a walkway, near his cube. He removed his reading glasses. "Finally, a break in my fucking shitty workload. Have a seat."

I obliged. "How are you, Mr. Reed?"

"That's my job to discover about you, Sinclair." He plucked my file from a stack. "Still employed by *Rizzo's Custom Homes & Developers?*"

"I am."

"Pay stub available?"

I silently pulled out a couple of folded, printed pay stubs.

"Hmmmm!" he breathed out while reading over them. "I swear you're a lucky son-of-a-bitch, Sinclair. I'm damn near twice your age with a degree and over twenty years on the job, and have yet to bring these numbers home to my old lady."

"Rizzo's got openings."

"And I'd have to put in sometimes sixteen-hour shifts? Fuck no! I'm too old for that shit, too." Going back to my file, he muttered, "I got two adult boys; I don't even cut the lawn or take out the trash anymore." *Damn…* The visual in having a family. It was something I craved. Here, though, wasn't the time to dwell on it. "You're gonna have to piss here today. I see you haven't been screened in a while.

Let's do that and I'll swab your mouth. I see I take it too easy on you."

"No problem at all."

"Have you been around unlawful weapons such as firearms... guns, rifles and such?"

"No, sir."

"Have you entered your hot zones like the Iron Bound section of Newark?"

He wasn't supposed to ask that. My conviction had nothing to do with the Iron Bound section of Newark. The *FED*s were funny. They were still riding my ass about the Bartnicki murders. I'd asked for my forgiveness for those transgressions. I wouldn't let an agency such as this keep me in condemnation.

"I haven't had the pleasure," I answered. "No."

"And how are those sessions with your therapist?"

"Expensive as hell."

He laughed hard, neck turning red. "But you're still going regularly. Correct?"

Sighing, I sat back, sweeping the top of my head. "Yes, sir." *Twice a week now.*

Chapter Five

FEBRUARY | PRESENT DAY

ashira

I scuttered behind the little white woman with a stark silver bob and blunt bang toward the front of the small restaurant.

"Thank you," I offered, winded, heels clacking against the weathered hexagon mosaic tiles.

I hated being late. And when Jas came into view, alone, sitting with inexplicable solemn energy, I loathed it. That and the bizarre angst stirring in my belly. He wore casual clothing. A denim button-up shirt beneath an off-white shawl cardigan sweater framed his torso, rolled up at the lower arms. Jas' hairline was sharper than I'd last seen as he sat with his elbows on the table and one hand cupping the other.

"I'm late and you're falling asleep," I breathed while dancing out of my coat.

Jas turned to me, and I swore his dark brown irises sparkled. Why was he…cute tonight, under soft lighting?

"Damn," he murmured, sitting up. "I ain't think you were coming."

"I couldn't find these booties. Had to search three closets twice and enlist help to do it." I twisted out of my coat. "My boyfriend's in Sudan, just getting settled in. We haven't spoken since the night before he boarded. I didn't want to rush him off the phone when it was time to leave out. The guy talked my ear off about nothing. Then I had to find this spot and figure out how to come in through the back."

"Why the back?"

"You smell amazing." I slid onto the small bench across from him, immediately submerged in his scent. "I'm feeling this aromatic aura." With my palms flashing open and closed, I rocked my body back and forth, earning a grin from him. Then my attention went to the tattered menu off to the side, near the window. "I never knew this place existed. Tea—*and food!*" My stomach growled. "Thank god. I'm starving," I muttered while perusing the limited options. "Paparazzi, to answer your question. They know where I moonlight as a teenaged beat-bopper."

I heard and felt the fragranced blow of his snicker from his nostrils, we were that close.

"This place's been here since I was a kid. Low key and simple."

My head lifted. "Would you say that resonates with who you are as a person?"

Quickly, his eyes narrowed and lips pursed. "Is this an interview?"

Ignoring that, I sat up and searched for the lone woman, ready to order. "What are you having?"

"Tea."

"That's it? Don't make me eat alone."

"It's after ten."

"And I'm about to hit the club. I woke up this morning with a hangover because I skipped dinner last night." I turned up my nose. "Have you had their tacos?"

"Yeah."

The woman was finally making her way to the front of the restaurant.

"Any good?" I whispered.

"Yeah."

"Good." I turned to the little woman with fine lips and circular framed glasses without lenses. "Can I have five of your supreme tacos—even though it's sketchy to have tacos from a tea shop."

She laughed. "I know you. My neighbor's granddaughter is crazy about your boyfriend."

I rolled my eyes, smiling. "Ma'am, everyone seems to be crazy about the guy. I just hope it continues to translate into ticket sales. Momma needs a new pair of shoes," I jeered.

She laughed, shoulders lifted, as she covered her mouth. The crow's feet aside her narrowed eyes were endearing. "Is he doing that movie with Brielle?" I couldn't pick up her accent.

Irish?

"That's the plan."

"Well, good luck to them both. But my neighbor's granddaughter would say Austin doesn't need it." She winked. "I'll get those tacos started. And what about you?" she asked Jas.

He shook his head, dismissing the offer. "I ate already."

I sucked in a breath, hella dramatic. "So, you make me eat alone? Tacos?" I wiggled my fingers for emphasis. "With sauce and lettuce falling down my chin?"

He snorted, perhaps not exactly moved. This guy was wound so tight. "A slice of peach pie."

"Vanilla bean ice cream with it." When Jas' brows met, I amended, "I can't feel like I'm eating alone."

"I'll get right to it." The miniature woman took off.

"Anyway, I'm here. Let's talk." He brought a thick binder from beneath the table. "What's this?"

"It's what I've been working on." He opened it and began flipping through pages. "Compiled profiles of men and women we've been able to place in jobs or trade training."

"Tell me about them."

He shrugged coolly. "Everybody's got a story, some more unique than others. Right? Some we can pull from the streets with zero skills—*legal*, that is. Some recently released from jail and prison."

"Aren't you a laborer in school yourself? How do you have time to do all of this?"

He nodded. "By not moonlighting at *Club Sin*...or eating after eight at night."

This time, my eyes narrowed. "There's something about you. You've got a story." I crossed my arms over one another and leaned into the table. "Who are you?"

His head bounced back softly in a shrug. "Jas."

"Are you married?"

"Nah."

"What's your real name?"

He snorted again, "I'm Jas. I told you."

"Jas what?"

"Jas Jas. And yeah, everybody got a story."

"And yours is just going to school to learn each trade available in building?"

He shook his head, eyes peering into me in earnest. "Ain't it obvious? I wanna be a builder."

"You've said this, but you don't need to waste your time in trade school for that. I mean...formal training in one of the bigger trades is cool, but just build your contracting team and get registered in Jersey or... Didn't you say you live here in Harlem?" He just stared emptily at me as though it was a dumb question. *Okay...* "The process isn't much different here. I think they specifically do a child support clearance, though. You in arrears?" I joshed.

"What do you mean?"

"Arrears. Do you owe child support?"

"Oh, I know what in arrears means. But I told you I wasn't married."

Huhn?

71

"Wait." I snickered. "Now, *I'm* confused."

"Why?"

"Because I asked about you having kids."

"I understood that, too."

My palms flipped upward. "Then what're we talking about here?"

"You asked if I was married and I told you no."

"Okay..."

"Then how could I have kids if I'm not married?"

I snorted, "How old are you?"

"Thirty-two."

"You're only a year older than me. Most of our peers have kids before they even think about being married."

"Is that what you did?"

Smacking my lips, I was offended. "I don't have kids. What makes you think that?"

"I can assume the same reason you asked if I was in arrears. Insulting. Right?"

Twisting my mouth and nodding, I admitted, "This is true." It really was. It was also something I wasn't used to hearing from men my age. "*How*—was this something you purposed since being a kid?"

He shook his head, using his fingers to pinch his full lower lip. It seemed like Jas was thinking. Or uncomfortable.

"Nah. I ain't think past each day's agenda as a kid. I was *a kid.*"

"Then where did this discipline come from?"

There was a delay before Jas' eyes landed on me and he shared, "From being a man. It's how I've decided to live. Each day is with purpose and intention. I look forward to having kids. But I'm more excited about building with their momma first."

A lump formed in my throat. *That's so sweet...* "Does she know that?"

He chuckled, forehead wrinkling. "I don't know her. I think that's where we'll start."

Wha— "Wait! You don't have a girlfriend? *Girlfriends?*"

"That's personal, Witherspoon. I thought we were getting together to talk about my initiative."

I blinked a few times, stung by his rejection.

Again...

"I'm sorry. *I*...I don't even know how this train jumped the rails." I really didn't. What had gotten into me? *Again.* Feeling a little embarrassed, I shared, "Apologizing to you twice in one day. Oh my." My humor dry.

"I like to think you've expressed your humility twice. Nothing wrong with that."

"It's not true if no one else has witnessed it. My word against yours."

"Oh, so you won't cop to it?" The sight of the teeth behind his canines and hiked cheeks made my stomach somersault.

"I need a drink." My neck twisted, head swinging in search of the elf lady. "Is tea all they sell here?"

He pulled back. Jas sat up farther in his chair, visibly withdrawing. I switched moves too quickly for him, I knew it. I also knew I wasn't comfortable around him. I didn't trust myself not to say something stupid. Never did I get so out of sorts around people.

"I'm used to people being unsettled in my presence and, for some reason, I'm feeling like that in yours."

"And you're trying to take me down the road with you." Jas blew out a breath. "I'm feeling like I'm on a job interview. I think it's your tone. You tend to speak down and not laterally."

I cupped the front of my neck. "And where did that come from?"

"Therapy." The cheap smirk on his face couldn't be confused for anything but.

It made me hoot in laughter. "She has a way of calling those loud yet invisible things out." I smacked the table. "Oh, my word! Why would she say that about you?"

He shrugged, looking away with a sincere grin. "I guess after me sharing a few scenarios of my interaction with people on the job."

My jaw dropped. "Is that why you're seeing her?"

His chin fell in the same manner. "Here you go again, Nubian Karen, asking personal questions."

From the corner of my eye, I caught the little white woman gaiting our way with a tray of food.

"Wow. That was fast."

"I guess that works out for you," Jas observed. "You going to the club and all."

"Right, but I've got plenty of time for that." My eyes grew at the sight of the tacos being placed in the center of the table.

They looked like home, no garnishments other than lime slices. And that meant they'd be good at best.

"You got spirits back there?" Jas' inquiry excited me.

"Ah, let's see." She tapped the frame of her glasses. "I've got beer, wine, and whisky."

Jas looked to me for my selection.

"A dry red?" I posed to him, and he looked her way for the answer.

"Pinot Noir and *ummm…*" she hesitated, thinking. "Merlot and a blend."

Facing Jas again, I asked, "The blend?"

Again, he faced her. She winked, understanding the order and went back behind the counter.

I reached for my purse to get hand sanitizer. "A tea shop that serves tacos, pie, and liquor." Then I wiggled my brows.

"This is Harlem, man. We're multifaceted and know how to woo our tourists."

"Interesting." After making an act of rubbing my hands together, I went to dig in.

"You don't bless your food."

That shit had my arms suspended over the table. "Shit," I muttered before mentally saying grace.

When I opened my eyes and continued to my first taco, he asked, "Do you have a specific prayer for your food?"

"What do you mean? Are you asking if I know how to say grace?"

"Yeah."

I bit into the taco then chewed. "Of course, I do. Went to Christian school all my formative years."

"Oh." His eyes sparked up like the damn sky on Fourth of July. "So you know the Word?"

"Like the Bible?" I didn't know if I should be talking with a mouthful around Mr. Mysterious, but he kept me engaged as though I'd known him for some time.

"Yeah." He finally cut into his pie.

I took another bite, deciding I liked the tacos. "Like…sixty-six books—thirty-nine Old…twenty-seven New? Moses authored Genesis through Deuteronomy." I twisted my mouth, thinking. "The shortest verse is 'Jesus wept' in the book of John. The longest is…I think…is in Esther. Maybe in chapter eight somewhere. And let's see… *Ah!*" Something came to mind. "The longest word in the Bible I cannot only spell, but I'm pretty decent at pronouncing, which is Mahershalalhashbaz. I break it up in my head to spell. Maher, shalal, and hashbaz."

Okay, now I'm nerding out…

He studied my face. "Nah. Like know God through His Word. Like having a relationship with Him."

"I mean…" I took another bite and chewed. "I know He's up there. He knows my fuck ups, but He also knows how He wired me. So, we tête-à-tête every now and then."

With a hard expression, Jas slowly nodded then returned to his pie, ignoring the ice cream. "Interesting."

What in the hell did that mean?

Why do I care?

"Do you know Him?"

He nodded again, attention on his pie. It made me crazy insecure and wonder if he was busy judging me. Again, why did I care? Who was this guy to judge me on anything?

He's a laborer…

Jas was right; this could have been an interview. I'd interviewed "Jases" more times than I cared to recount. They were hardly impressive—at least, not to the point of feeling inferior to.

"Oh. So, you *know* Him?" Regardless of how it was delivered, my question was glib.

Jas' eyes appeared again. "Sure, I do." His spine straightened. "I received Him as my personal Friend and Savior seven years ago."

My face tightened. "How?"

"In prison."

I dropped the taco. *And there it was...* I knew there was something with this dude. Still, I was in an utter stupor. *Floored* by this news.

My lashes smacked several times as I mustered the ability to speak again. "Seven years ago? How long have you been out?"

His eyes were stapled to me when answering softly, "A little more than a year and a half."

"A year and a half?"

His smooth and sudden smile was cunning. "You like to play parrot."

"I'm trying to gather my bearings here. I wasn't expecting this." Studying his face, I found no inconsistencies. "Are you kidding me?"

His head shook faintly. "I would never."

"If this happened seven years ago and you've been home for less than two years, how long were you incarcerated?"

"From arrest to release, I did a little over ten."

"You're serious."

Jas went for his tea. "Is that a problem for you?"

"Why would it be a *prob*—what were you locked up for?"

"Are we on an interview again?"

My head fell to the side. "Don't give me that shit. I can ask and have every right to. What if you're a murderer? Shouldn't I know who I'm spending time with?"

"We're not dating, nor do we have any real relationship. Just a 'trade' and a builder, chopping it up about an initiative to help employ people who have crazy circumstances like I faced coming home."

"Where were you locked up at? And fair warning: if you say Avenel, I'm hightailing my stuck on stupid ass right on out of here."

He snickered. "I wasn't locked up in the state. My violation wasn't with the state. I did most of my bid in Montgomery, Alabama."

My eyes grew wide. "You did federal time."

He nodded, eyes pinned to me. "I did."

What the fuck!

I'd been tricked. I couldn't believe I'd been choked up and giving extra headspace to a convict. A federal convict. I'd been slipping. What the fuck was I thinking? I'm Ashira Witherspoon, not some helpless, hopeless, un-spirited, broke, uncultured chickenhead from the block who was so thirsty for the attention and affection of a man that I'd allow one nowhere near my pedigree to intimidate me or make me second-guess my position and/or actions.

"You never answered my question."

"What's that?" He sat back in the booth. There was something substantial in his body language. I felt Jas was prepared to be open with me.

"What did you go to prison for? And please don't say you don't want to answer because you may one day apply for a job at *Witherspoon Homes* because if you were to, I wouldn't be *bias*—"

"I will never apply for a job at you and ya pops' firm, Witherspoon. Let's start there. I don't have a problem sharing with you about my time away. I just need you to understand, for you, it's privileged information. I'm not obligated to share anything with you. I'm telling you simply because I'm good with you knowing."

That stung, but no way would I let him know. No more of him making me feel less than a Witherspoon. Done. *Finito!*

"Are you done? Because first, I want to know why you wouldn't consider working at my firm. Why narrow your options that way?"

Jas laughed breathily. Like…a full-on chortle in that cute "Jas laugh" way again.

"Because, man." He shook his head while peering at me dead on. "I don't need you as an option. Y'all good over there. I've only heard good things about your business model and employee treatment, but I didn't need you for employment last week. And if I see you again after tonight, I don't want you to think I need anything from you then either. I'm good. Making my way, you know."

I tried studying him again. I didn't understand Jas. Was he an arrogant asshole? A bit of one, yeah. Was he trying to antagonize me? I couldn't say for sure he was.

So, I nodded. "Okay. Right. One trade class at a time until you feel confident enough to go apply for your business license." I picked up my half-eaten taco, though my appetite had faded.

He took a deep breath, picking up his spoon again for more pie. "Gun charges."

"Huhn?" I hummed, biting into the taco.

"My charges. Possession of firearms."

I asked around the food in my mouth. "What kind?"

"ARs. You know about guns?"

I shook my head. "Why did you have one?"

"I sold them."

My jaw collapsed with a mouth full of food and closed lips. I caught myself and tried chewing again then swallowed. "Oh." I took another tasteless bite as I processed this information. "How many guns did you get caught with."

His eyes widened as he peered up from his plate.

Why was this weirdo so cute? He had really great features I discovered the more I spoke to him.

"Two were in a vehicle registered to me. I wasn't there."

"Who was?"

"No one."

"Why would you leave illegal weapons in your car?"

"I didn't. One of my boys did. They were supposed to be sold hours before but wasn't." He shrugged. "Cops broke into my ride and found it."

My head popped back. "Broke in as in illegally searched?" He nodded. "Then shouldn't that have been thrown out of court or something?"

He smiled, licking an escaped piece of crust from his upper lip. "You watch a lot of crime shows?"

I felt silly and smiled. "Maybe, but that doesn't sound just."

"It was illegal and concessions were made. Charges ran concurrent. I did the crime then did my time. No biggie."

"Losing more than ten years of your life is a huge biggie."

"I don't focus on that anymore. I did what I did and faced the circumstances. Still, the Lord saw fit to introduce Himself to me behind bars, something no man's worthy of, especially one like me. He saw value in me. We've made our peace together and now that I have my freedom again, I've got the opportunity to hit the restart button on life. I'm out and free, and pursuing my passion—*even as slow as you've been bustin' my balls about*—and I get to help others find theirs or, at least, learn a trade and do honest work until they find it."

"I respect that." Another unexpected nugget of insight on this enigmatic guy. *He's religious.* "Can I ask you a question?" Jas, by lifting his forehead, granted me permission. "If you don't have a girlfriend or wife, why are you reading Twanece Edmondson?"

Recognition washed over his face. "Oh, right. That's what made you ask if I was gay the other day. You sure come with them."

I dropped my head to the back of the bench. "I don't represent myself well around you, do I?"

"S'all good. I'm a confident man. No, I'm not gay—despite being incarcerated for so long. And the reason I fucks with Edmonson like that is because I dig her teaching. She's trying to instruct young women living in what's turning into a feminist society of anti-men—note I'm not referring to feminism ideologically. I'm into teachers who nurture communities for family and promote equality on some level. She does that in her books."

"You think men and women are equal?"

"I think men and women are equally important...needed. I don't think we're the same and I'm good with that."

"What's different about us?"

"It depends on the context. Are we talking physical abilities, emotional, or intellectual ones? If so, that's a hard call for me to make. I'd have to defer that to empirical studies. They're very individualistic."

"Let's talk about where you see the striation or striae."

"Well, I'm speaking in the context of relationships. Men and women don't have to compete. Roles should be assigned—" His voice hiked to clarify, "in the relationship I'm in. I don't need to be the breadwinner, neither do I need for her to have a big bag. Earning can be both our responsibilities or I can take the lead easily. In my mind, it's about roles and responsibilities—" He shook his head. "You know what… I'm not getting into that. Say less."

My eyes ballooned. "What?"

His head shook softly and Jas murmured. "It's inappropriate. Besides, you invited me out to talk shop. Let's do that."

No!

I didn't want to do that. I wanted more time getting to know this very peculiar guy. A guy I had no interest in yet was highly interested in getting to know. Yes, it was strange, but oh so palpable.

"What's wrong with getting to know one another?"

He scratched his chin. "Maybe the fact that this ain't a date or a personal meeting. That and you gotta man, and I wanna respect that by not getting so personal."

"There's nothing you can say here that would make me want you in that way, so what's the big deal?"

The muscles in his face fell into a relaxed state and Jas stared at me.

There was an odd delay before he murmured, "Witherspoon."

"What?"

"You wanna politic about the project or not?"

"Well, when you put it that way, I guess I'm forced to either talk about that or forget about finishing my tacos and get kicked the hell out of here."

"Nobody said all that."

I took another bite into the cold food. "That's what it feels like." Sighing, Jas' attention went toward the window. "Okay." I rolled my eyes, though he couldn't see. "Let's hear about your initiative. I'm not in the market for laborers, but I'm really interested in seeing what Zebedee Baker sees in you."

Without eye contact, Jas went back to his booklet, opening it up and pointing to the profile on the first page. "The first successful placement was me. When I was released, I applied to three…maybe four builders, and only one hit me back: *Luxury Building* out in Lodi."

"You mean two builders: *Luxury* and *Rizzo*."

His eyes blinked and Jas shook his head as though frustrated with his error. "Right. Two. But anyway, them niggas wanted to pay minimum wage, so I moved on. But more important than that, let's get into their interview process…"

As Jas spoke passionately, my focus was on his picture. He didn't photograph well at all. In the picture against a white wall, his facial features were decent, at best. Then I wondered what his mug shot looked like. Did he scowl in it? Was he bruised and battered? I'd seen some of those. Had Jas been apprehended violently for the gun charge?

Who is this guy?

"Oh, shit," I mumbled when I caught the time.

"What?" She didn't even look up from the booklet.

"It's a quarter to twelve. You gotta get around the corner."

Witherspoon went for her phone, eyes tight from exhaustion, it looked. "Do I really?" she asked, I was sure rhetorically, being cheeky as hell.

It was what she did from time to time, I noticed tonight.

"You gotta meet ya girls, don't you?"

She dropped her hand holding her cell to her lap and her head to the back of the bench. "Damn!" she breathed. "I just skipped galaxies. My phone was on mute from a *Zoom* meeting I took from my apartment before Austin called." She yawned with an open mouth so distastefully, but crazy enough, I wasn't offended by it. Witherspoon was pretty as hell, which was why I was happy for this discussion to be over with. I ain't have time to waste on her type. "I'm so damn tired." Taking a deep breath, Witherspoon scooted out of the single booth.

"You gonna be good getting to the club?"

She fingered her long, brown wavy hair into the air, sprucing it up. "I should go now. I've gotta put on some lipstick and find a park." Witherspoon rolled her eyes. "I'm gonna be late."

"Anything I can do to help?"

I wanted to offer her to let Juggy drop her off at *Club Sin* in her car, park it, and bring her keys inside. Or I could have dropped her off in her car, parked it, then had Juggy bring the keys inside. But she didn't know us from shit. I would've been mad at her for trusting strangers, so all I could do was ask her that dumb question.

"Go hang out with my peeps for me at the club." She smiled. I snorted at her humor. "Good night, Jas." She started digging into her purse. "I almost forgot my bill."

"Nah. You're good."

"No. I offered. I'm paying." She walked a fifty-dollar bill back to the booth. "That should be enough, right?"

"Witherspoon, it's a'ight. Not that deep." I handed her the money. "I can pay."

She snatched the crisp bill from me and slammed it back on the table. "I insist, Jas. You're right. It's no big deal at all." She tapped me on the arm, closing the argument.

Then I watched her strut away in a thick ass three-quarter length shearling coat and brown boots with a high, gold stiletto. It reminded me of how classy she was. That simple and subjective word was a new revelation for me. Witherspoon was a classy chick. How that nigga let her prance around unprotected was beyond me.

When I turned and pulled out my phone to text Juggy, she called, "Hey…"

I looked her way over my right shoulder. "Whaddup?"

"Did you watch last night's episode of *Taking Tips from Tynisha?*"

I thought for a second. "When Alton's trifling ass pulled up on her in *Saint Justin* to apologize again?"

Retired professional basketball player, Alton Alston, was married to a high-profile fashion influencer, Tynisha Lang. They'd been married for mad years and he'd been cheating on her the same amount of time. It was a shit show, but a culture I was familiar with before going to prison, so I didn't shun it. In last night's episode, Tynisha packed up their family and made an impromptu trip to the Caribbean, needing to get away from the media swarming around Alton's latest baby by another woman. Alton, claiming to feel guilty as hell, showed up announced, holding his dick in one hand and heart in the other, saying he wanted to give them both to Tynisha to control.

It was stupid. *Again*, my guilty pleasure.

Witherspoon nodded. "Did you catch when they talked on the porch while the sun was setting? Alton asked Ty if she could have any superpower what would it be. She said she would have the power of healing so Alton's mother wouldn't have died. Remember when Ty said she believes that's when she lost Alton—*two months after they got married?*"

"Yeah."

"He told her if he had a superpower, it would be the ability to go back to the day they met so he could see the light in her eyes again that Alton burned out." I nodded, recalling his pathetic attempt at a save for getting caught again. "If I had a superpower, I'd go back to young Jas before he was seduced by the streets and felt the need to involve himself with guns. Maybe we could've been friends...I could've been an annoying younger sister who dragged you to house parties in Franklin Lakes and summer weekend trips to Ocean City, New Jersey." Her smile turned helpless when I didn't respond right away.

"You should go, Witherspoon. They're waiting on you."

She nodded and turned to walk off. I went back to the text to Juggy. After hitting send, I took a deep breath while looking out the bay window into the dark street.

I would have never been your brother, Witherspoon.

That *has been* my *superpower…*

Chapter Six

FEBRUARY | PRESENT DAY

ashira

"Thanks for this, Dan!" my dad boisterously shared with a hard shake of Lewinski's hand. "I appreciate what you and your team did today. And to express that, please accept this on behalf of the *Witherspoon Homes* family. These are my latest cravings." He handed a small gift bag with *Por el Amor del Amor* samples. It was me who'd put him onto the relatively new brand.

"Well, Noel, I appreciate your generosity!" Lewinski accepted the bag.

My father then gazed around the party consisting of a few of our folks at *Witherspoon Homes* and Dan Lewinski's from *Just Homes*. "You young people came in and seduced us this morning!" Another gut-pushed rowdy guffaw.

I rolled my eyes internally. They came with donuts, coffee, and a presentation for a standard offer based on what they believed our firm was worth.

"Well, Noel, we aim to please." Lewinski gave a neck bow. "These youngsters help with the technology, but you and I know it took years to develop the heart of the machine."

"That's right, Dan!" my father agreed, leading him to the door. "That's right. Look! You wonderful people have a great day. You've given us lots to go over and consider."

"Don't forget those fall and winter projects," I reminded him loud and clear as I stood behind the group preparing to leave.

Lewinski smiled. "Oh, we won't, sweetheart—"

"Ms. Witherspoon." A tight counterfeit beam spread on my face. "Or Ashira, or just Witherspoon would work."

Lewinski eyed my father then rushed a smile back to me. "You got it."

As they filed out of the room, I spun on my heels, going for the carafe on the food buffet to pour myself water. I needed to pop a couple of ibuprofens to kill the cramps popping off in my belly. Mother nature's visit began this morning and she kicked the damn door open.

"That was wonderful!" my father declared behind me just before the door slammed.

I turned to find him with his hands in the air. "You look like you've accomplished something."

"Dan Lewinski has always thought himself to be a step above the rest. Always brown-nosing at conferences, stealing high-level management from firms—remember Ted Bush, the former sales manager here?"

"I do." I nodded, rolling my eyes. "But what did you think of Lewinski's proposal today?"

He shrugged, taking a seat at the table. Seeing the simple act reminded me of how little my father visited the office. It was now strange seeing him here, in the place he built with his own sweat, passion, and ingenuity. Today's conversation wouldn't exist if he'd retained the passion component.

"I think he sees what's been built here." His sausage fingers drummed the conference room table. "But I'm pretty sure he's low-balling me. And low-balling won't be tolerated for the low percentage of interest he's offering. It doesn't matter that he's handling all of the contracts, including trades."

"And keep in mind, this isn't a merger, Dad. Not in the big bowtie way his team tried to frame it during their presentation. It will be a buyout with a two-year transition. Max. That means your name and letterhead are removed and will be added to a footnote at the end of *Just Homes'* contracts. That seventy-five percent starts when you sign off the company and ends in two years. Then you'll be at three percent of *Just Homes*, who swallowed *Witherspoon Homes* into its very wealthy and powerful conglomerate."

"Hmmmmm…" He grunted. Face tight like it was when matters weighed on his heart. This was the man I missed. The one who gave a damn about this firm. "I see. *Just Homes* will be like *Amazon*."

"Taking over the world. But *Just Homes* will be monopolizing the North Jersey building industry one firm at a time."

His eyes remained low, though swinging left and right. I hoped he was adding up all the wins and losses. I had. I needed my freedom. But in spite of my needs, I'd never let my father lose his life's work. If I could only figure out a way to accomplish both.

"Hmmmmm…" he verbalized his cognitive processes again.

jas

"And what's the percentage of your control during the transition?" I asked.

Rizzo, at the far end of the table, cleared his throat, hand at his tight mouth.

The young representative from Dan Lewinski's *Just Homes* building firm glanced down at his folder. "Uhhh… That'll just be twenty-two percent."

"Over how long?" was my next question.

Dan's eyes fell on Rizzo, who sat at the head of the table while I was closer to the *Just Homes* crew on the opposite end. The power structure for *Rizzo's Custom Homes & Developers* was set strategically with Paulie Rizzo being at the head. His president, Marion Lucci, was next to him. After was one of the lawyers Rizzo used. Then a rep from *Rizzo's Custom Homes'* accounting team. Next to him was an administrator. Then there was one of my attorneys, Briar, and then me. I appeared to be the lowest on the totem pole. It was by my sole design.

When potential partners or associates came to *Rizzo's Custom Homes & Developers* to pitch or negotiate, I'd always have Rizzo's team—all white faces—sit near Rizzo, leaving me at the farthest distance from the "boss." It annoyed the hell out Rizzo when I spoke business publicly as his name was still on the letterhead, but I couldn't wait until after this was done to get clarity. Dan Lewinski may have had a sharp vision of regionally dominating the building industry, but I saw more in his monopoly plan than he wanted us to.

"Is it okay for us to ask how many firms you have shopped this to?"

Dan's rep's eyes swung from me to Dan. Then Dan's attention went to Paulie Rizzo.

I had no idea what their exchange was, but eventually Dan cleared his throat. "I've never had anyone ask me that question…?"

"Jas."

"Jas," he repeated, tone dry. "Approximately eight is the answer. The expansion is my son's idea. I'm grooming him to take over when I retire."

"You're retiring, Dan?" Lucci inquired sharply.

"Yeah..." he breathed out, standing to pull the waist of his pants above his big ass pear-shaped belly. "I promised my Marjorie that if she beat that cancer, I'd spend the rest of my days spoiling her. All she wants is to be underneath me. Can't do that when I'm always on a job or in the office, ya know?"

"And how old is Dan Jr. now? Late twenties?"

"No. That kid is almost forty, Lucci. It's either now or never for him. He's been working on this for about two years now. I'm proud of him. Thought to include you because you're no spring chicken either."

"No," Paulie Rizzo sighed hard. "I'm not, Dan. I've got some shit in the works myself to land me."

His lawyer looked my way. The muscles around his eyes tightened before turning away. I was unruffled, knowing what time it was.

"Alright. I believe that sums up the pitch," Lewinski's guy announced to the room. "Any more questions?"

"Anything else from this end?" Paulie Rizzo asked me without looking my way.

I spoke up while quickly scanning the packet handed out today by *Just Homes*. "I think it'll be interesting for you to see *Just Homes'* sales predictions."

"Why?" Lucci demanded to know.

I couldn't hide my grin while closing the information packet. "Because you don't sell your business to a company that could fold right after folding you."

"That's not the plan, by the way, Paulie." Lewinski held one panicked hand in the air. "Now, Paulie, this may be my son's idea, but I'm giving respect and pitching guys like you and me who are at retirement age. We deserve a deal like this. You'd be getting a lump sum and residuals for the duration of the firm."

"That part," I pointed out, "is in the report. Those projections are not." I stood from the table. "If it's all good with you, Rizzo, I need to get back to that Oakland site."

Rizzo gave the fake approval before I exited the room, leaving my esquire behind for the afterparty.

"I wonder if they serve Arnold Palmer…" she mused out loud.

As we waited in line, I peeped the place. High ass ceiling, cranberry walls, thick, red paisley carpeting, and burgundy plaid curtains. It was my first time in a Broadway theater, and only one person could drag my ass here.

"Alcohol-free, of course." Chelsea twisted her mouth. "Because I'm going to have an apple martini."

"Your favorite," I murmured, amused.

"And you know this."

I pulled out my phones to see the countless notifications.

"I can't believe we're here. I love her work— *Holy crap*," she whispered in a way that had me scanning the concession area.

"What?"

"I'm trying not to stare, but I think…" Chelsea hesitated. "I think—*oh, god!*" she whispered. "She's looking our way. I think she caught me." She squealed. "Yup. It's her."

My eyes shot all over, but all I saw were stiff ass people dressed to the nines, waiting in lines for drinks just like us. There were so many—more Blacks than whites, but a little of everybody was here to see the show.

"Who?"

"A girl I follow on *Instagram*. Austin Seers' girlfriend."

The name rang familiar, but, "*Who?*"

"Shi-Shi, the dancer," she whispered, now facing me with huge doe eyes.

"Who the hell is…" But then, I caught the growing crowd at the other end of the lobby. I could also see cameras flashing and even a couple of dudes who looked like security. "Damn. This play's attracting celebs? Who's the writer again?"

"Christina C. Jones. Remember, I told you it's actually an adaptation of her book, *Wonder?*" Oh… Didn't ring a bell when she invited me and still didn't. "Is she still coming?"

"Coming?" I glanced over her head. "They got her locked in a corner over there. At least, that's where the crowd is." My vibrating phone had my head dropping to check it.

"I'm gonna look again," Chelsea whispered again.

Without thinking, I glanced over her head again.

Damn...

There was a prowess squint in her eyes as Witherspoon approached us. I caught the dart of her little tongue swiping the lower inside of her orangey-red lip.

"I thought that was you." Her tone was spiritless, but eyes expressive as hell.

Chelsea, in between us, turned to face her.

"Oh," she breathed. "Hi."

Ashira Witherspoon's dark lined eyes traveled down to Chelsea and a faint smile lit on her blushed cheeks. It was the makeup, I knew, but... *Damn.* Her hair was up in a ponytail wrapped loosely at the top of her head. The red tube gown she wore fit like a damn glove, exposing ample cleavage. Her earrings were small, classic in size. Faint enhancements. And even the small gold clutch at her pelvis line reminded me of her level of class.

"Hi." Witherspoon's eyes swept back up to me. "I thought it was you."

Chelsea turned to face me with big eyes then looked at Witherspoon again. "You two..." She pointed between us. "You know him?"

"Whaddup, Witherspoon." I pushed my hands into my pockets.

For the most part, I ignored the hell out of Witherspoon, and now realized why. The girl was so fucking easy to look at.

"Nothing. I didn't know you were into fantasy." Her eyes brushed against me from head to toe. "Or Christina C. Jones' books."

I was in a suit and had to admit I looked damn good when getting dressed earlier. I hadn't worn a formal suit much in my life, but liked the way I looked in them. Not to mention my fresh cut and clean, hard-bottom derbies.

"He's not," Chelsea blurted, nervousness lacing her tone.

"He'd never heard of her until I dragged him here. You probably know he has no life. Just work, work, work." She turned to me, laughing with a high ass level of anxiety. She mouthed, "You know her?"

Smiling with closed lips, my attention went back to Witherspoon.

Her lashes clapped, face set in an emotionless expression. Something was off. "You're not going to introduce us?"

That's when Chelsea turned back toward Witherspoon. "My apologies—our apologies." A nervous chuckle escaped her again. "I'm Chelsea, Jas' cousin. His mother and my father are siblings."

The relaxing muscles opened on Witherspoon's face when she processed Chelsea's words. "Oh!" Her eyes bounced between the two of us. "Oh, wow!"

"Yeah." Chelsea beamed proudly.

"He's just so…"

"Enigmatic? Strange? Off-putting?" Chelsea rambled as we moved up in the line again.

"All of the above." Witherspoon laughed with her.

"He's always been that way. Well, to most people. He's really a sweetie pie. Even though I had to drag him out here. He deserves to be out and enjoying cultured events like this. He's smart, the best-read man I know. High aptitude for learning. Our grandmother said on her sick bed, Jas was the best-mannered of her children and grandchildren."

"Oh, wow! I'd have never have guessed that."

Chelsea's eyes popped wide as she turned to me. "Maybe it's because he ain't jail-broken yet," she whispered admonishingly while popping me on the arm. I laughed quietly when Witherspoon snickered, partially covering her mouth, turning away. Chelsea's mouth dropped. "Did she catch that?" she thought she whispered again. When I nodded, she mouthed, "Sorry."

Finding it cute, I shook my head. "S'all good. Witherspoon's a builder. We met…around the way. You know."

"Oh. That's how you two know each other. Through work!" Chelsea beamed Witherspoon's way.

My cousin knew I was seeing a therapist and why. I just thought it would be rude to share Witherspoon had been, too.

I tossed my chin her way as we moved up the line. Just one more guy was ahead of us. "What're you doing here?"

"Oh, with Austin," Ashira explained.

Chelsea sucked in another heap of air. "Austin Seers is here? You two are the baddest couple! Like in the world!"

"Thank you." Witherspoon performed a humble neck bow and an innocent blink of the eyes. I was sure she was used to receiving compliments like that. Her eyes roved back up to me then she pointed over her shoulder. "Would you like a pic?"

I thought Chelsea's ass was having an asthma attack, her lungs worked so loudly. "Could you?" When Witherspoon nodded, agreeing to it, Chelsea turned to me. "You mind taking a picture of Shi-Shi and me?" Her head whipped back. "Oh, my god! Do you mind?"

"It'll be my pleasure." When Witherspoon looked over her shoulder, she waited until she caught eyes with one of the beefy guys I'd seen earlier and waved him over.

That's when it dawned on me how I saw at least two security guards, but none followed her over here. What type of protection set was in place for Witherspoon seeing that she was with a high-profiled dude?

We were next in line for the bar and had to order.

"Hi. Can I have an apple martini?" Chelsea ordered.

"Sure." The bartender waited for more.

"And please tell me you make Arnold Palmers."

"We can do that for you. What alcohol do you want with it?"

Chelsea shook her head, eyes closing. "He doesn't drink. Virgin, please." She glanced back at Ashira, who I realized was looking at me before swinging her gaze over to her boyfriend trying to make his way to her. "Anything for you, Shi-Shi?"

"Oh!" Witherspoon chirped when she caught on. "I'll take a glass of Cab. House is fine." She went to open her purse as Chelsea turned for the bar to give her order.

Before the bartender could take off, Ashira had slapped a fifty-dollar bill in front of him. "No. That won't be necessary," Chelsea proudly announced. "Tonight's my treat. I had to get him to agree to it. I can't fight with you, too."

Dismissively, and maybe because Witherspoon's boyfriend was mere feet away in his approach to us, she waved her off. "No worries. The intermission will be over soon."

Witherspoon then rushed to meet her boyfriend. She whispered something to him while swiping lint from his brow with her thumb. And it was in that moment I knew I couldn't trust myself around her. I knew I needed to distance myself from Ashira Witherspoon, because I determined in my mind in that quick second I didn't like that nigga.

Her man's eyes whipped between a twittering Chelsea and me. He nodded, agreeing to whatever Witherspoon said, but never smiled.

"Okay." Witherspoon returned to us. Chelsea, meet Austin Seers. Austin, Chelsea is my newfound ally against her cousin, Jas here. Jas, Austin." We shook hands, his grip was weak as hell.

"You two know each other?" he asked.

One of his bodyguards eyed me too closely. I shifted my body just enough to signal back I wasn't the smoke he wanted.

"Yeah. Jas has been in building for some time. He's looking to open a new firm."

Austin laughed. "Maybe he can take over yours."

Witherspoon rolled her eyes. "If only it were that simple, I would've signed over the keys to him yester-year."

I didn't understand that comment. Her framing of my professional experience was a bit embellished, too. But it was nothing I felt compelled to clarify. I didn't know these people and didn't want to either.

The drinks were finally made and when Chelsea handed hers to me, Witherspoon hurried this little meeting along.

"Come on, y'all. I don't want to miss a moment of the second act."

"Me either," my cousin agreed. "I've been waiting forever to see her work on stage! Have you read her paranormals?"

"Girl, all of them!" Witherspoon turned around and asked me, "What's taking you so long?"

"Oh." I moved toward them. "You want me to take the pic?"

"No, silly." She giggled. "You want in on the picture with Austin?"

The fuck?

"Oh, nah. I'm good." I backed away.

"He's not into Hollywood," Chelsea came in for the save.

Not that I needed it.

The fuck I look like taking a groupie pic with Austin Seers? I am not that nigga, Witherspoon. Maybe your nigga is that type, but not Sin, baby girl…

As I waited for them to finish with the flicks then Chelsea getting dude's autograph, the lights blinked.

"Shit," Witherspoon swore. "We've got to go. It was really nice meeting you, Chelsea!" Her smile was warm. Sincere.

It was an entirely different vibe than the one she approached us with. And that, to me, meant one thing: Witherspoon was good once she learned Chels was my cousin and not my lady. The chick was funny. *Beautiful and funny.* And she was also the type I planned to stay away from while looking for the right woman for me.

Chelsea, grinning from ear to ear, began toward me with Witherspoon on her heel.

"I've been meaning to give you this." She handed me a business card I quickly pushed into the pocket of my suit jacket. "You haven't been at the coffee shop this week."

I bade her a farewell with a salute swipe from the forehead. Witherspoon dashed behind to catch up with her man and his security. Chelsea and I headed in the opposite direction where I grabbed the door for her to head back inside the theater.

"I wonder where they're sitting." She squealed. "I can't wait to post these pics! I'm sending them everywhere. The *Gram*, *Facebook*, *Twitter*, *TikTok*—everywhere!"

"You on *TikTok*?" I asked as we made it to our row.

"I will be after the show ends."

I had to laugh at that. Chelsea was dead ass serious, I knew. "You're nuts."

The lights began dimming and the talk around us lowered to a progressive hush.

"You know," Chels whispered, "bringing you here tonight doesn't chip away at the insurmountable deeds you've done in my life. Grad school was one thing, but you paying for my doctorate is still unfathomable." She blew out a breath. "I can't believe I'm wrapping up my doctoral program. I still have to find a suit I need to defend my dissertation next week. I'm thinking pants. All because of you believing in me."

I was stuck, reading the card made of thick ass stationary and bold colored fonts. When I wondered why she'd give me a business card when I could look her up through *Witherspoon Homes*, I noticed that logo wasn't on here. Neither was her business mentioned.

"S'all good, Chels." I tossed her a wink and grin. "We Kearneys got big brains we need to shape and share with the world. It's nothing. You know that."

Witherspoon's home address was on the "business" card. It had to be based on the noted apartment number. Her home and cell numbers were there, too, and so were all of her social media and email addresses. The shit was weird. Who had cards made for their personal lives?

Someone you ain't got no business spending unnecessary time with.

"Nah!" Chelsea's insistence snapped me out of my thoughts. "You pretty much bought me a house by paying for those degrees. That's huge. How many people can say their cousin bought them houses free and clear?"

A hard snort pushed from my nose. "Who said it ain't come with a price? You know what you got to do."

She nodded. "I'm getting it done, too. Just filed for the incorporation. Next is the 501(c) (3)." She winked.

"That's my girl. Medical research for health issues commonly found in the Black community. Breakthrough studies, alternative medicine. It's necessary."

"And you know it." She raised her hand for a fist-bump.

My marred knuckles met hers in agreement.

At just after seven at night, I was grateful to be turning in after a fourteen-hour day of hard labor. I didn't have class today or therapy, which left my itinerary open to work three sites between land-leveling, cementing, and window installation. Tired as hell was an understatement.

Still, I pushed myself to strip and hit the shower. I made myself a sandwich then opened and organized my mail. As I trailed off to my bedroom, I remembered telling myself this morning to change the battery in the smoke detector. That wouldn't be happening tonight. I barely had the energy to feed myself.

That aside, I looked forward to my wind down time in prayer. It was a must. My time with God was my true therapy where I could say whatever I wanted. I could reveal my heart without worry of judgment or mishandling. It was when and where I flushed and refueled.

I dropped to my knees and immediately began to praise Him, for He had done great things. Then I warmed up with my plea: Mercy. "*Have mercy on me, God. Please blot out my transgressions. Wash away all my iniquity and cleanse me from my sin. Lord, I know my transgressions—all of them—and sin always seduces me. I know I've sinned and done what is evil in Your sight. Your verdict is correct and judgment is justified, God.*

"*Cleanse me, God, and I will be clean. Wash me, and I will be whiter than snow. Let me hear joy and gladness in Your delight of me. Let the bones You have crushed rejoice. Please hide Your face from my sins and blot out all my iniquity, God. Create in me a pure heart, God, and renew a righteous spirit within me. Do not cast me from Your promises. Lord, please don't take your Holy Spirit from me.*" I moved on to convey my fears, then my desires. Finally, I took my time to express my gratitude for His friendship: His grace. And lastly, I acknowledged the promise we'd made to each other.

When I stood from my knees to peel back the comforter of my bed, I verbalized a weakness of mine, a habit I couldn't shake.

"God, forgive me for my filthy mouth. I'm gonna do better; I swear."

My bed was cold. For the first time in my life, I hated the shit. I longed for the day it would be filled with feminine aroma…and babies. That was the promise. In the meantime, I had to be patient and behave.

And stay away from fucking distractions…

"Good morning, Witherspoon." The thick masculine vocals had my head shooting up from my laptop. Jas was taking a seat across from me at the small table. I didn't know why this felt unexpected, knowing we'd been seeing each other here for three weeks in a row now.

My face wrinkled. "Good morning to you, too, Jas. Just Jas."

He laughed, eyes dropping. "Yeah. That's me," he murmured. "How was your weekend?"

"Ummm…" I thought for a minute about how fast it flew by. "Accelerated and filled with being arm candy." I shrugged, going back to my laptop to send the email I'd been working on. "I'm used to it."

"Being arm candy?"

My head lifted and I could read the sincerity on his face. "Yeah —no. Well, not in a conceited way. My boyfriend has a high-profile lifestyle and sometimes, with my hectic schedule, the only time we manage to get together is when he's working local to me. Like doing events out this way or filming."

Jas nodded. I went back to my laptop, not knowing how brief this conversation would be, the guy had been so strange to me. Hot and cold.

"I heard about you hiring Kareem Brown's outfit for your firm. That's what's up."

"Hi." The young waitress who was shamelessly smitten by Jas' dark features appeared at the table. "Can I get you something?"

Caught off guard by her forwardness, Jas' eyes swept the room as he sat up. "Uhhh…" He snorted at the girl's dreamy gleamy expression. "I'll take a large mint tea."

"No sugar and no honey, but a drop of agave," she seemed to be confirming with him.

"*Uhhh…*" He chuckled again. "Right."

"Coming right up."

When she turned to take off, I called to her. "Excuse me." She returned to the table. "Can I have a warmed banana muffin with butter on the side?"

"Sure. That all?"

With my attention on Jas, I answered, "Yeah. I guess so." When she left, I went back to my computer. Something was different about his energy today. His aura still affected me, but I didn't want to come off as needy or thirsty with Jas. He was cool in my head, but guys like him…thug niggas were too cool for school sometimes. In my teens and early twenties, I dated a few, going through a thug-a-boo phase. At least, that's what my mom called it. They treated me like I was dumb and/or insignificant. As though I wasn't enough to hold their attention no matter how many proverbial headstands I performed to keep them engaged. I was too old to go down that rabbit hole, especially for a guy I had no interest in dating. "I wanted to talk to you about that."

"About what?"

"When I gave you my number on Thursday, I wanted to talk to you about a roofer."

"Oh." His brows met. "Your business card."

"It had my personal information on it."

"Yeah. I saw. I must've left it in the pocket of that tux jacket."

"Do you want another one?" I moved for my purse.

"Nah. I know where it is." More rejection. *See! I'm done...* "It's all good. But what did you want to kick it about?"

"*Witherspoon Homes* was in a pickle. Our main roofing outfit bailed on me when we had so many projects in progress. I scrambled to find someone good and reputable. Was wondering if you had any recommendations."

"You were gonna ask *me* that?"

I shrugged. "Like I said, I was in a pickle. If you believe your second-chance folks are having their talent overlooked because of their records, I'm willing to give at least one person a try. Someone who has experience, though. I don't have time to train or pay for them to get trained."

"But you got Kareem, though."

"I need more, which is what I'm here with my laptop way earlier than my session again. I need a few more in my repertoire. I can't be in this situation again. The old roofing outfit had been with us for years then switched up at the most damn inopportune time."

"You guys don't have in-house trades?"

"No. We contract out."

"Hmmm…" He scratched his cheek. "Didn't know that."

"It's common."

"Maybe."

"Rizzo does it."

"Not anymore." He sat back, sighing. "We have each outfit now, except for landscaping. I think they're working on that now."

"Shit." I blinked. "I didn't know."

"Recent change. Don't sweat it. I gotta few I can check in with before throwing them your way."

I continued to type away. "So, no alcohol?"

"Come again."

"Chelsea—who's adorable, by the way—said you don't drink."

"Oh, that." He scratched his head. "Nah. I don't drink."

"Is it because of your religious beliefs?"

"You mean my spiritual ones? Nah. Christ loved wine." He chuckled. "I've been focused on building, don't want any distractions or anything blocking me from being able to see my goals."

"Becoming a builder."

He nodded. "That's one."

"Oh. There's more. Good. Because I don't think abstaining from alcohol would impede on that."

"Yeah. I want more. But it's more about the sacrifice than the being consumed by it. I abstain from a lot of shit, even keep just few people in my company."

Shit...

My head dropped to the side. "That explains it."

"What?"

"Why you can be so asocial with me."

His smile grew wide and my spine straightened at the sight of its beauty. Jas was alarmingly handsome. And when he whipped out an unbridled smile, it could catch an unsuspecting girl's lungs. Like the waitress delivering his drink.

"Here you go." She placed it in front of him. "And this is for you." My muffin lay next to my coffee.

"Thanks." Jas reached for his back pocket.

But I'd already had cash out for my muffin before he came. I was waiting to finish the emails before eating.

"Is this for the both of you?" the girl asked Jas while holding my twenty-dollar bill.

"Yes," I replied. "Thanks."

"It's all good, Witherspoon. I got it."

"I won't hear anything more about it. It's just stupid tea, Jas." I motioned to the swooning girl dancing on one leg at a time while gazing at Jas with my eyes, dismissing her. Thankfully, she got the memo and left.

"It's not personal."

"What?"

"Me being cold or not so talkative with you. It's actually out of respect for myself and your relationship."

"I don't get it. It's my job to protect my relationship, and ain't

101

nobody but these little girls in here checking for you." I rolled my eyes as he laughed.

"I 'on't mean it that way."

"What other way could you mean it? I respect my relationship and because of that single fact, it will be protected. That's my responsibility."

"I respect that. I guess you know now why I see a therapist." He opened the flap of the tea lid.

"*Wha*—Why?"

Jas shrugged casually. "Being in prison for so long and in my mid to late-twenties and early thirties, my social development is skewed." My mouth dropped. I would have never thought of that. "Now, it ain't that bad, but since I've been seeing her, I get it now."

"How does that relate to you being so icy to me?"

He shrugged again, eyes going out the window. "I'm a narrowly focused man. When I was released, I had a solid checklist of how I planned to rebuild my life. Like…how I'm going to make good of the time I have against the years I lost. My financial goals, businesses, and finding a wife are all on that list. A mentor of mine," he tossed his head toward the window, "been recommending I come see her for over a year, riding my ass. I had to make time because I wanna be right when I do find her."

"Again—*and I'm not trying to be sarcastic here*—what does that have to do with me?"

"It's a mental discipline. I don't engage with anything or anyone unrelated to that checklist."

I got it. Although it was a narrowed view, I understood where Jas was coming from. So, I nodded, processing it. "Yeah, but you can also use friends or associates around to help socialize you."

His forehead stretched and eyes furrowed playfully. Or I had hoped. "You qualify to help socialize me?"

"I can for sure loosen you up, but in the most appropriate way. I don't want you, Jas; these junior baristas in here do. Maybe you can ask them out on a Valentine's Day date."

"Women *really* like Valentine's Day?"

Sipping my coffee, I hummed, "*Mmmmhmmm.*" I swallowed, then amended, "Lots do."

"What about you? What're your demands this year?"

"To simply see my boyfriend in the flesh. He's doing a round of interviews for his latest release and won't have time for much but sleep while on that tour. That's no fun for me. I promised myself last New Year's Eve I'll begin to act my age again and travel. I'll be in Jamaica on Valentine's Day."

"Without your man?"

I tossed my head in a shrug and began to butter my muffin. "I've given everyone fair warning. That includes my father for the company, Austin, and my girlfriends. I ain't trying to hear they're broke and can't go on at least one of my getaways with me."

"I think your pops can run the ship while you let your hair down."

I spit out a laugh. "Yeah, right. My saving grace is technology. My team's pretty solid, so hopefully my absence will be uneventful."

A van pulled up, appearing in the window. It was the same one I'd seen last week when trying to offer Jas a ride.

"I gotta go." Jas stood. "I 'on't know about me needing a friend for socializing. I'mma ask the therapist about that one, though. Enjoy your Valentine's Day, Witherspoon."

Wait—what?

That was a lot of rejection in one sentence. Way too much to process so quickly, but he had to go. When I managed a smile in return, Jas left with his tea. My attention went to the van I suspected was awaiting him. The guy was strange and I wondered why I even tried after telling myself I wouldn't.

Indeed, Jas stalked across the street, disappearing in the passenger side of the van where I couldn't see him. My vibrating phone snapped my mind into the here and now.

Unknown: *I FORGOT TO SAY THANKS FOR THE TEA*

My head whipped to the window just as the van pulled off.

Chapter Seven

FEBRUARY | PRESENT DAY

"*And if you need me, babaay…*
Just call and bring another ladaaay!"

We fell into laughter in the booth after reciting two of our favorite stupid lines from the rapper, Wally's, last single. We were turned up at *Sugar Factory* in the City—and on a school night.

"That joint be on speed, yo!" Brandy, my sister, Noelle's, friend shouted.

That made me laugh even harder, because I wondered if that's what my suburban girlfriends and I sounded like when we were coming up, trying so hard to be tough. These girls were that on steroids. I loved hanging out with them. They made me drop the CEO persona and pick up the one that tried to prove I was still relevant. At twelve and thirteen, these girls knew who was hot and what was not, something I used to be in knowledge of myself. Spending time with Noelle was priceless, I just wished my father could see the value in it.

"Alright." Noelle tried gaining the reins of the conversation. "Alright! Who's the better rapper?"

"Out of who?"

"Between who?"

Brandy and I laughed when asking the same thing.

"Well, we all know, Lil Leval is bae!" She blinked successively with her hands in the air. When my little sister's tongue flapped out, I almost lost it. Noelle was something else and I loved it. "But I'm not going to let y'all vote on my man."

"*Nahhhhh!* Bullshit!" I croaked as Brandy and I cracked the hell up.

"Okay! Okay!" Noelle sat up in her seat. "Well, between Wally and…Young Lord. Who's the best?"

"*I pay homage to that gangsta, properly named SIN.*
Took out them Polack niggas…
Missed the charges then ate the FED's pen." Brandy rapped.

And on cue, Noelle followed up with, "*Sat quiet, never a rat.*
Nigga 'bout to hit the streets.
Ran the cellies…now ready to spin the block…
Fuck y'all niggas, jerkin industry cock."

My eyes burst wild as I whipped my torso her way. The girls laughed and I had to join in.

"Young all day!" Brandy declared with a wrinkled face and her palms in the air as though begging her pardon.

"Who do you think, Shi-Shi?" Noelle asked me.

"C'mon, son! Everybody knows Lord is the top dawg emcee right now. *BUT!*" I cautioned them when they began to hoot in agreement. I rolled and popped my spine seductively, yet playfully appropriate for their tender ages. "I like a little ruggedness in 'em, and that Wally is a wild bull!"

The girls cracked up. "Okay! On Mr. Seers' arm," Brandy cracked, saying my Austin was far from the thug I claimed to like.

It was hilarious. I was sprawled in the corner of the booth, knowing we were roisterous.

"But Lord is!" Brandy agreed with wide eyes. "Oh, my cousin sent me that *Spilling That Hot Tea* post the other day about him peeing outside in public! Did you see that, Noelle?"

"Yup. And the one with him sticking his tongue out while giving his middle fingers to the cops…"

My phone flashing on the table stole my attention. The muscles in my face felt permanently stretched from laughing so hard with these girls. I didn't need alcohol to loosen up when hanging out with them.

My tight face dropped. *Shit.* This was the last call I expected to get and especially from this recipient.

"Give me a second to take this," I told the ladies before stepping away.

Between our high-spirited conversation and the music, there was no way I could hear a phone call.

"Hey…" I answered, threading around a small group being seated.

"Whaddup, Witherspoon. Now a good time?"

"Yeah. What's going on?"

"I got a few guys with roofing experience. They come as an outfit."

I sucked in a breath. "Damn. That was fast."

"You asked. I delivered. How soon do you wanna move on them? I can show you their profiles and resumes."

"Resumes?" As I asked, I heard a loud ass chirp in the background on his end.

"Yeah. I tell everybody coming in to try and have pictures, addresses, and even written testimonials, if possible. The shits gotta be legit, though. So, if a potential builder wanna check it out, they can ride past a house to see a roof or windows and shit."

Ahhhh…

"I see." In my mind, I quickly rolodexed my crazy schedule for the current week. "How about Thursday at seven? Too late for you?"

"Nah." *Another chirp.* "I can make that work."

"Harlem?"

"Doesn't have to be."

I remembered his penchant for early hours. "The tea shop is cool."

"It's a bet."

"Cool." That felt awkward. *Jas* was awkward. After a beat, I followed up with a mild, "Okay."

Chirp. "A'ight."

When I knew for sure the call had ended, I returned to the girls and tried jumping back into the conversation, but that quickly felt off.

"Young Lord's a little nasty, though," Brandy noted, pushing her teeth past her lips expressively.

"Something you girls'll appreciate in a few years. Nothing wrong with that," I added before sipping my Carmel Sugar Daddy Cheesecake milkshake.

"Yo, Jas!" White boy Tony called me from the outside of the house we'd been framing. I leaned out of the open window. "Some folks're here for you!"

I dropped the drill in the corner and headed for the staircase. We were working in Wayne, near *Willowbrook Mall*, and it was freezing today. When I stepped outside and walked to the front of the house, I saw the pair.

Shit…

I smiled approaching them. Holding my hand out, I observed out loud, "Your little ass is gonna be taller than me soon."

Nicholas smiled, meeting my palm in the air before I wrapped him in a hug. "I'm the same height as Dad."

"That's an easy feat," I teased my pops standing behind him before shaking his hand next. "How are you, sir?"

"I'm good." My father made a show of glancing around the property we demolished then rebuilt. "Nicholas mentioned you were near the mall this week. He needed some sneakers, so I figured we'd come check you out before dinner."

I turned to my little brother, a mixed kid with a dark wild fade cut, glasses, and braces and smiled. "That's what's up."

"How long are you gonna be here?"

"Why?" I ruffled his thick, wavy hair. "You want me to take you to hack this shit off?"

"No!" Nicholas made clear. Then he shrugged, lacking confidence. "Just wanted to hang out—maybe—before dinner."

My father and his family lived in Totowa, a two-family home his wife got when her parents died mad years ago. A few years before I got locked up, they had my brother. While I was in prison, my father married Nicholas' mother. In spite of my shaky relationship with my pops, I tried opening myself to one with the kid. He showed a strong interest in me when I came home and visited them for the first time.

"I'll be here for a bit then got a meeting later this evening." I faked jabbed him, to which Nicholas slowly reacted. My brother couldn't fight for shit. I'd be happy to teach him how to handle himself in battle and start with him putting on some damn weight. *Witcha light-skinned ass…* I saw men violated in the pen just for having the same pretty boy features without the weight and ability to defend themselves. "But don't sweat it. There'll be other opportunities. How's school?"

"Meeting?" My father interjected. "Like job-related?"

"Work-related, yeah."

"At night?"

I scoffed, "Yeah, man. Like a working dinner."

"About…" He glanced around, "construction?"

"For sure."

He was doing it again. Since I could remember, my father never provided praise, always criticism. Mark Lamont Sinclair complained about me not playing sports; about me wanting to live in the projects in Harlem with my mother instead of here in Jersey with him; about my run-ins with the cops as a kid; about me not dating enough girls for him; about me wanting to stick by my mother's side despite her addiction; my eight-month juvie sentence in my early teens; my dropping out of college; about me spending money on a talented legal team instead of getting a public defender to appear poor and therefore less guilty; and about me being my own man and making the best of my circumstances.

Pops was the type to blame a pedestrian for getting hit by a car at a red light. Yes, much of his beef with me coming up was that I was a knucklehead in love with the streets. But my problem with him was he never showed love, only critiqued. And the nigga loved to make you think his life was without fault. He bragged for the purpose of tearing me down. And I wasn't Lamont's only target for this coward shit. My mother was often brought up only to throw jabs at, even when he thought his attempts were clandestine.

"Oh…" he murmured, looking away. "Well, Nicholas, if you can maintain that three-point-nine grade point average, you can have these men build you a home out this way. Ain't that right, Jas?"

I pulled in a breath and my brows pushed up at that jab. "Yup. That is true. And you'd get a quality home, too." Then a thought occurred. "Did you give any thought to the landscaping business I put you D on a few months ago? If my plan is carried out to the T, I'm sure you can be pocketing three to four hundred dollars a week. Easy."

"What landscaping business?" my father demanded to know.

Nicholas' eyes fell and I knew the emotion. It was irritation. Our pops could be a real dick.

"A summer landscaping business I started last year. It's good for the young kids to learn the trade and earn some cash when they're out of school."

"Last summer?" He chuckled. "You was just out of prison last summer. How you start a business?" He shook his head, dismissing the fucking notion. "I can get Nicholas a great paying job with less risk at my company. We've already discussed it."

My eyes remained on little Nick. I knew he wanted more time with me, but I struggled with that being a good idea seeing our pops didn't respect me. He thought his job as a manager of a telemarketing company was better work than what I did with my hands.

A text came through, the chirp cutting my attention.

Unknown: *SIN MAN THIS IS DANNY LEWINSKI. HOLY SHIT ! WE CROSSING PATHS AGAIN. SURE MAN LETS MEET UP. TONIGHTS THE BEST SHOT.*

The little shit typed the same way he presented himself.

"Shit…" I whispered.

"Everything okay?" My father's tone was suspicious. "Break over?"

"Nah," I answered as I texted my response.

Me: COOL. LET ME KNOW WHEN AND WHERE.

"Then what is it?"

I pushed my phone back into the pocket of my sweats. "Just a switch-up in my meeting tonight." I didn't want to blow the meeting with Witherspoon, which could mean employment opportunities for the men and women I was recommending to her. But this chat with Danny was an even bigger opportunity for me. "No sweat. I need to finish up so I can be prepared, though. I have to go home and clean up before. Nick, you got my number. You know how to tap me." I offered him some dap.

As he readily received it, my father noted, "Oh, back to Harlem. And how's Charmagne?"

Here we go with the bullshit…

"Mom dukes is good." I couldn't even look at him when I answered.

"I hope she's staying out of trouble. She used to be a smart girl—"

"Nick!" I shouted out the kid while giving them my back, returning to my work.

ashira

I exhaled, leaning back on my headrest as I stared out into the empty parking lot. "So, I have to wait damn near a week after Valentine's Day to celebrate Valentine's Day with my boyfriend."

He cooed, "Come on, babe. I feel bad about it as it is, and now you want to overexaggerate the number of days."

"So you do admit it's days later?"

"Shi-Shi," he whined like a big baby. "Instead of celebrating on Sunday, we'll be doing it on Friday."

"Yeah. A whole five days later." I rolled my eyes.

Yes. I was being a bratty girlfriend. At times, I took the liberty considering how much I had sacrificed in the name of Austin's career. I totally understood what I was getting myself into when I decided to date him after he chased me without relent for four whole months. Back then, he had the time; Austin's career hadn't exactly taken off. Now, time was a sour word for me because he rarely had it. What was worse was I wasn't a needy girlfriend. In fact, I preferred my time to be with the girls, work, and especially dancing. But these past ten months had been brutal for me. I'd mostly see my boyfriend when doing red carpet or press events. I was simply arm candy, something I didn't relish.

"Alright, alright, alright." I stuck out my tongue as though he could see me. "You're flying in on Friday morning. We'll hang out until your podcast interview that night."

"That's my girl."

"And I've gotta go. This meeting's about to start."

"Okay. Tell Noelle I got her on those tickets."

"Then you'll have at least one Witherspoon lady delighted." My eyes rolled again. *Yup.* I was being a brat, likely because I'd been feeling really lonely in the companion department.

"Shi-Shi," he cried again. "Have fun at the wedding."

"I'll try."

"And tell Jarvis thanks for not marrying the most beautiful girl to ever enroll at *BSU*: my girl."

Petulantly, I rolled my eyes again and balled my mouth. "Whatever, Aus. I gotta go."

"Bye, big baby. I love and adore you."

"You better be prepared to show it next Friday. Bye."

When he hung up the phone, I shot a text to Corinne about dropping by her adult shop next week. As I was about to leave my car to go inside, I received a text.

Jas: *WITHERSPOON I KNOW YOU'RE OUT IN THE PARKING LOT. UNFORTUNATELY I GOT CALLED INTO AN EMERGENCY MTG FOR THE JOB. MY PARTNER JUGGY'S INSIDE WAITING ON YOU WITH THE PROFILES. HE CAN ANSWER ANY QUESTIONS YOU MAY HAVE. SAVE WHAT HE CAN'T FOR ME. YOU'RE TOTALLY SAFE WITH HIM. HE'S NO FELON. LMAO BUT I'VE GOT A STRONG SUSPICION HE'S GOING TO ASK YOU TO HOOK HIM UP WITH ONE OF YOUR GIRLS. TELL HIM TO KISS YOUR ASS AND HE'LL BACK OFF. HE TOLD ME YOU PULLED UP SO YES I COULD HAVE CANCELED. BUT I AIN'T WANT TO. I OWE YOU FOR THIS IF YOU DON'T PULL OFF.*

My suspicious eyes lifted to the back of the tea shop in Harlem where I'd just met Jas about a week ago. Could I trust this? Jas seemed really cool and I still wasn't decided on his truth about having been incarcerated. He didn't fit that type other than his occupation. And he was weird as fuck. Jas was strange, too mysterious. I had yet to learn his real name.

Still, I bravely left my truck and hiked it to the back door that was unlocked again. Inside, the old white woman was behind the counter. She smiled and nodded as I walked past. When my eyes met a man appearing vaguely familiar, I slowed.

He dropped the crossword puzzle book he'd clearly been working on. "Yeah. I'm Juggy." He pointed to the same table at the window facing the street that Jas and I sat at last week. "That's the file. You could look through 'em. He said it's like eight profiles in there. You got any questions, I can help you with 'em."

I had to decide my safety course again. Juggy was a lanky man, russet brown skin with droopy eyes and a long ass hook nose. There was a darkness to his aura, similar to Jas, but different. Jas was dangerously unknowable. Juggy looked like a simpleton with a secret. Weird, but true. I figured I'd look over whatever Jas left for a few minutes then leave. Instead of explaining that, I began toward the booth.

"A glass of wine, dear?" the gremlin-looking white woman asked.

"I'm fine. Thanks."

I didn't remove my coat, only unhooked my bag from my shoulder, dropping it on the bench before joining it. I opened the thick file and found more than I bargained for. Jas showed me profiles last week, but these roofing candidates had lengthy entries. There were cover letters and testimonials from instructors, former customers, and a few from parole officers.

"Does he—*Jas*—know these people personally?" I asked Juggy, who stood across from the counter, watching a sports channel from a posted television above the register while working in the crossword puzzle book.

"Oh, nah. I think one or two."

"Like who?"

"I think JuJu in there." He snapped his finger, realization hit. "*Ummm...* Jason. Jason Hughes. We came up together at *Renaissance* as pups." Juggy's eyes crept back up to the screen, pencil still positioned in the book. "He did the whole block of roofs over in Jersey."

I went back to find Jason Hughes' file, and sure enough, there was note of an entire block of residential homes that had roofing repairs and replacements. There were also a few pictures of the jobs. He wasn't hard to find in the binder; it was in alphabetical order. The content and organization was superb and nothing I'd ever seen. Admittedly, I hadn't interviewed or hired in years. It was a task our human resource's two-man team took care of.

But this…

What was planned as a quick five-minute stay turned into thirty when my head drew up from the binder. I'd just read the last profile and my mind was churning with the possibilities. These men and women were humanized in this makeshift booklet unlike I'd ever seen on a simple application. Were they angels and everything represented in their profiles? No. But they were people like me, just with a more colorful story.

"Are they all ready for hire?" Juggy's attention was into his phone and he didn't hear me. I cleared my throat. "Are they all ready to work, Juggy?"

His head shot up from the book and he blinked. "Like tomorrow? I 'on't know about that, but like after a job or some shit, maybe."

"Can I keep this?"

He shrugged. "I think Si—Jas said they gotta apply the usual way."

I nodded, wondering about the official answer. "Okay." I closed the binder then grabbed my bag. "I'm going to keep this. I'm willing to have my staff interview them all except for the two released at the end of last year."

He stood. "You leaving?"

"Yeah."

"He told me to ask if you wanted me to drop you off at *Club Sin* and park ya car for you close to the entrance. I can bring the keys inside. I 'on't steal. My word." He held his arms and palms in the air, pencil intertwined in his long fingers.

The memory of me stressing out over a parking space last week came to mind. An unbidden smile lifted on my face. "No thanks. I'm not dancing tonight. I appreciate the offer, though."

He nodded, patting his chest. "A'ight."

"Thanks for this." I turned and headed to the back of the restaurant with one thought in mind.

Arrogant or not, what could be more important to a laborer than meeting with a reputable builder about multiple employment opportunities?

Jug: *PULLING OFF*

As I waited in the lobby, my eyes rolled up, processing that Witherspoon stayed long enough to read through potential applicants. I hoped she had an open mind. It could mean good and long-term eating for good brothers and sisters.

Me: Copy

The skinny kid with a lip ring, nasal chain, nostril chain, and brow piercing appeared at the top of the steps in the restaurant and waved us back. "This way."

We followed him down three steps and into one of the dining

rooms. I took in the empty but smoky place. I'd guessed they closed early on Thursdays because the only action was where we were going. Immediately, his crew, all at one table smoking cigarettes and drinking, came into view and he stood, anticipating me.

"Sin, my brother!"

I met him in an intentional shake, but he grabbed me into a hug. It was aggressively expressive, but that was exactly what I'd recalled of the guy.

"Stand up, motherfuckers, and greet a true fucking boss!" he ordered the men at his table.

"Pleasure." One nodded.

Another saluted. "Good to meet you. Ricci," he introduced himself.

There were six in total, all greeting in some form. I was only three deep with myself, Man, and Bullet from the Bronx.

When the introductions were over and silence settled over the smoke, I studied his excited persona for a few seconds before I greeted, "Ol' boy, Danny Lew."

His smile widened and he shouted to his guys. "See! I told you that's what they called me in the pen!"

"Danny Lew," one tried it out as they cracked the hell up.

"Everyone had a nickname in there! I kept mine close to the real one!" Danny explained to his guys boastfully. "Fucking Danny Lew in that bitch."

I snorted. That wasn't exactly the truth. In lockdown, everyone was given a name. Your moniker either followed you in from the streets and continued in the pen, or you were a nobody who got into a fucked up situation due to your lack of criminal skills and were assigned one based on how you presented inside.

Daniel Lewinski Jr., also known as Danny Lew, was a dumb ass party druggie from the suburbs who belonged to a crew of equally corny, dumb ass white kids trying to hit a lick. They attempted to rob a local pharmacy in their neighborhood unsuccessfully. The crew popped pills while in action and couldn't run from the cops when they arrived if they tried to.

In jail and prison, similar to the streets, everyone had what's referred to as a face card. It was your reputation or lack thereof. Your face card determined how you'd been treated. Danny Lew's face card was his pops' money. Those white boys' fathers paid top notch attorneys, allowing them to evade any serious prison time. I'd run into Danny Lew while in lockup during my trial. We were bunkies, and ironically, he was undergoing his as well. The problem was his face card was weak, which meant Danny Lew needed protection.

When the Brim Bloods out of Passaic were trying to extort him for money, Danny Lew had no protection, and no one to wipe his ass after shitting his pants. I knew the niggas trying to snatch his pockets and helped him out. Truthfully, it wasn't because of any benevolence on my part. People got taken in lockdown all the time. I decided the second time the fucker pissed his cot above me. I knew the kid was out of his league, and he didn't fuck with anybody. So, I cut a deal with Scarface, a lieutenant in the organization, who just so happened to be in lockup with us. I had to cut a deal with him because deals were currency, too, when locked down. It was an easy arrangement for me, just a pair of *GLOCKS* to be implemented on the streets.

I had no intention of riding Danny Lew who, after, thought he'd been initiated into a gang by the way he moved with his chest pushed out. I'd honestly thought we'd never cross paths again, understanding the consequences hanging over my head. But still, having made that arrangement meant he owed me, something he verbalized with passion in there when I explained his new freedom. Eventually, Danny Lew walked out with just probation and I'd gotten snatched by the FEDs, never thinking of him again. That was until a few days ago in a business meeting.

"What can I do for you, Sin?" Danny asked while inviting us to sit down. "I've got pills, credit cards, and even foreign bitches. Anything for you, Sin. We're still brothers on the outside, huhn?" He slapped the side of my arm. "Oh!" His wide eyes shot over to his guy. "And I've got a few prize fighters. Yo, Sin if you're trying to get back in the game, I've got for sure bets for a starter fund."

I chuckled quietly. "Nah, man. I'm straight and easy now."

"Oh, yeah?" His face sobered and Danny leaned into the table. "What are you into?"

My eyes narrowed and cheeks spread slowly. "I'm a builder. Home builder, Danny Lew."

Every muscle in Danny's face fell and he blinked. "That's my father's line of work."

"And from what I hear, will soon be yours, Lewinski." I drummed the table with my fingers as his brain switched lanes from criminal to legitimate businessman.

Thursday 4:05 PM

Me: ARE YOU GOING TO ASK ME ABOUT THE CANDIDATES?

Thursday 5:57 PM

Jas: *MY BAD. BEEN BUSY ON THREE NEW PROJECTS. YOU AIN'T NEVER TEXT BACK THAT NIGHT. THOUGHT ABOUT THAT WHEN I GOT UP THIS MORNING FOR WORK AND FIGURED YOU PASSED ON THEM.*

Me: THAT'S NOT HOW THIS WORKS. I'M THE EMPLOYER WITH THE OPPORTUNITY. YOU SHOULD HAVE FOLLOWED UP.

Jas: *BUT I THOUGHT YOU WERE SHORT ON LABORERS AND NEEDED PEOPLE ASAP*

Me: AGAIN THAT'S NOT HOW THIS WORKS. YOU ALSO STOOD ME UP AT THE LAST MINUTE WITHOUT EXPLANATION. YOU'RE NOT A VERY GOOD BROKER.

Jas: *AGAIN MY BAD. HOW CAN WE MOVE PAST THIS?*

Me: I THINK WE NEED A FOLLOW UP MTG. THAT'S HOW THIS WORKS.

Jas: *OKAY. I'M KINDA TIED UP NOW. TOMORROW TOO. AIN'T YOU LEAVING THIS WEEKEND?*

Me: I AM BECAUSE I'M BUSY TOO. YOU SAID YOU OWE ME FOR STAYING AND READING THE PROFILES.

Thursday 6:29 PM

Jas: *I'M A MAN OF MY WORD. NAME YA PRICE*

Me: I HAVE LOADS OF ERRANDS BETWEEN NOW AND TOMORROW NIGHT. IF YOU'RE AVAILABLE TO DISCUSS WORK YOU CAN STOP BY MY PLACE SO WE CAN DISCUSS AVAILABILITY AND BACKGROUND CHECKS. WE USE **BRADON.** JUST WANT TO BE TRANSPARENT.

Friday 5:02 AM

Jas: *ALL GOOD. WHAT TIME?*

Me: IS SEBEN TO LATE?

Me: *IS SEVEN TOO LATE

Me: MY APOLOGIES. IT'S TOO DAMN EARLY TO BE AWAKE. I REMBE YOU SAID YOU TURNDOWN EARLY AT NITE. YOU CLEARLY HAVE NO LIFE.

Me: *I REMEMBER YOU SAID YOU TURN DOWN EARLY

Jas: *LMAO DON'T SWEAT IT. I'LL NAP ON MY BREAK TO BE READY. HAVE A BLESSED DAY WITHERSPOON*

Chapter Eight

FEBRUARY | PRESENT DAY

Jaz

THE SHIT WAS LACED AS HELL...

I walked slowly from the elevator to the end of the hallway for apartment 7D of a luxury apartment building in Edgewater, New Jersey. The security in the lobby explained why Witherspoon could be so comfortable giving out her address. Not only did they confirm I was an expected guest, they required my ID to be permitted inside. And they were armed. I had a thing about being in the presence of authority with guns. It was some shit I had to deal with each parole visit. Being lorded over made my skin crawl.

I took a deep breath, swallowing back the question screaming in my head all day: *Why am I here?*

I'd been crossing paths with her for about two weeks now, and too many times I thought it was the last time, only for there to be one more time.

The door pulled open and immediately, I was enclosed by a rushing wave of a cranberry and floral mixture. The scent was dominant, but not offensive. It added to her strong aura. She looked different—good as usual, but different. Witherspoon had a phone wedged between her face and shoulder and one hand on the doorknob. The other hand held some type of clothing with tags on it. I wasn't expecting to see so much of her skin in just a fitted black tank and matching biker shorts stopping mid-thigh. Her body was athletic and posture, even though slouched, was so…damn femininely graceful. I forced my attention to her face.

Or I, at least, thought I did.

"Alright, Daddy. I've gotta go. I have a visitor," her tone flat. "Alright, bye." She took a deep breath in the same unenthused manner. "You like my watch, Jas?"

That's when I realized my focus had been on her wrist.

My lips pushed out as I gave it a last once-over. "Yeah. That's pretty dope. Hunter rubber with a blacked out, rectangular face. That's the new *Apple*?"

She shook her head. "It's the new Ambrose McNeil design for *Moments & Measures*. Dope, right?"

"The truth."

"Come in." Witherspoon turned to take off and that's when I realized she had a head of fresh box braids falling down her back and flapping in the air with each step she took.

I hesitated. "You sure you're prepared to have company?" For some reason, I bit my tongue, not saying what I really meant.

"Not really, but I've gotta do what I've gotta do." She left me behind to follow her into a small sitting room before passing through a large vestibule and into a hallway before spinning around to me. "Now, I know this is business, but I'm also packing, hence me asking you to come over—"

"If you want to reschedule this, I'm good with—"

"No." Damn. "That's not what I'm saying. If you'd just let me finish, Jas," she laughed uncomfortably. Her eyes rolled to the side. "I knew this wouldn't be a good idea," she almost whispered.

"Again, Witherspoon." My body swayed backward, motioning the entryway. "I ain't with putting you at risk for no weirdo shit." I had Juggy waiting for me down in the parking lot anyway.

"Could you just stop?" She pumped her palms. "I don't think you're a weirdo, Jas. Strange, hell yes. But weirdo, no. I haven't picked up those vibes. You just make everything so awkward. If I felt you were dangerous, I damn sure wouldn't have given you my card, and certainly wouldn't have you in my home."

"Okay, so—"

"And if I didn't think you were straight up, I wouldn't have entertained your organization. Would you relax and let me simply be friendly?"

"Okay, so the whole cutting me off shit, that ain't friendly."

"No, Jas." Her hands went to her hips. "The tough guy shit is what's not friendly. I suggest you take it up with your therapist during your next session."

My head flew back and eyes went low. "I'll do that when you kick it with her about your aggressiveness."

"Now, you're making me the weirdo."

I dropped my face. Arguing was not an activity I took part in. I could always articulate myself well to express my thoughts to another man, and even I had limitations with that. With women, there was one simple rule: no back and forth. With men, I limited my tries of expressing my argument because in prison, fighting led to harsh consequences. It didn't matter that I didn't lose. I'd always felt a man lost as soon as the argument began with a woman. Their stamina was usually stronger and at the end of the day, you could lift a finger to settle it.

So, when I realized there had been too many useless words exchanged between Witherspoon and me, I jumped off the ride.

My head drew up and I asked, "What would you like to discuss about the profiles I shared with you, Witherspoon?"

"If you would give me a minute, I could explain I know you came out of your way to accommodate me. I know you live in

Harlem and turn down early. I imagine this is your dinner time, so I have something here for you."

Dinner?

"How long do you think I'll be here?"

Dramatically, her eyes closed and she collapsed her shoulder into the wall, covering her face with both palms, one clutched with the tagged clothing. "I don't need this."

I wanted to say fuck it about the initiative. No way *I* needed this bullshit. But I took a minute to consider what was happening. Witherspoon wasn't bad, boss bitch in this short moment. I could peep her break from aggression.

"What don't you need?"

It took a few seconds, but her head finally drew up. "This stupid ass life of mine."

"That sound crazy as hell. Life is a gift and add freedom to it, and it's beautiful."

"No." She sniffled. "I don't mean it in a fuck my life way. It's just that I've been stressed out with a lifestyle I didn't choose. Instead of settling in my own dreams, I'm dealing with shit that honestly, fucking bores me at this point."

"What's your dream?"

She twisted around from her shoulder on the wall to her back. Then Witherspoon snickered. "This is so not how I expected this visit to go." She shook her head, looking away.

I stood in the middle of her hallway, not feeling awkward, but definitely out of place. "Neither did I. But I'm here and you're not playing corporate bitch, so, tell me what your dreams are."

Witherspoon looked at me without turning her head, one brow plucked. "I want to ask if it's the Christian in you who cares, but your language speaks to the contrary."

"I'm working on it, but you're one to talk." Her eyes skirted away. "No disrespect, Witherspoon, but I ain't got all day. Tell me."

"How can you expect me to be so transparent with intimate information when you don't seem to want to be here?"

My head bounced back again and I smiled to keep from laughing. "I 'on't think you got a problem being transparent when you give out your address and phone numbers on business cards."

"You were locked up for over ten years and just got home; how are you to know that's strange?"

I sighed, "Alright. You win. We can kick it about the roofing gig next week when we run into each other at *Brown Baristas*." I turned to walk off.

"You're such a fucking thug, you know that?" I turned back to see her arms crossed beneath her tits, the piece of clothing dangling from the fold. "And I don't just mean in your work clothes, I'm talking about your lack of emotional development."

For some reason that didn't offend me. "I told you why I see a shrink. But I'm also that nigga who was just asking about your dreams." I winked. "The bread I'm paying her must be worth it. Right?"

For a while, she just stared at me. More than it was intimidating, it was annoying. I had better places to be, like my bed.

"You know I dance," she damn near whispered.

Ahhhhh...

How could I forget? Witherspoon was pretty good at it, too. I'd seen her work at *Club Sin*.

"But that's what you wanna be doing instead of building?" She nodded. I didn't understand the problem. "Then do it."

Witherspoon rolled her eyes. "It's not that simple. I've got people depending on me, namely my father. But he's not my biggest concern; the people who've given decades of their lives to the firm...those who rely on us to feed their families and pay tuition, they need me there."

"Why?"

"Because my father doesn't give a shit."

"He wants to walk away?"

She spit a laugh. "That would be a lot more simple for me. No. He wants me to run it and be happy. That's basically how it's been since my college summers, and when I moved back home, going to grad school locally, my fate was cemented." Her face spread in a smile unlike the spirit of her conversation. "Year by year, he appeared less in the office. And by my twenty-fifth birthday, I'd been given the lofty title of COO." She shook her head, lashes meeting. "He's been having his cake and eating it, too. I'm his sleeping aid at night. But enough is enough." She swiveled on her shoulder to flip her body back my way. "I'm at the end of my rope. Sooooo at the end of my rope." She emphasized with big eyes. "It's all confidential, but I'm preparing for an M&A."

Merger and acquisition…

"M and A?"

"I know you're a laborer and all, but please don't say it's above your paygrade as a trade. Merger and acquisition. This would be more of a merger, for the most part, since my father doesn't want involvement in the day to day transactions. It's coming with an acquisition in a couple of years. By then, I'd be free and clear of my work with *Witherspoon Homes*, leaving my father with the reality of his official retirement."

"And you to live out your purpose."

Her attention fell toward the floor and forehead stretched. "Purpose."

"Dancing, I'm sure you know, is an art form. One that involves the body." I shrugged, flashing my hands. "You use your body for art."

Her eyes grew wide. "After your little tipping attempt last week, I never expected to hear this from you. Yes. I do!"

I nodded. "Yeah. So, do it. Go live your life. Be happy. That shit can be fleeting. If you're healthy and got your freedom, go live your purpose."

"Are you living yours?"

I nodded as I answered, "I am. Every day I get up, praise God, then go about my day worshipping Him by making the most of this shit. I'm healthy and free—on many levels—which means I have opportunity."

"You're really spiritual." Her tone was soft, processing. "When and why?"

I took a deep breath, fucked up because this wasn't my reason for stopping by. This was supposed to be twenty minutes, tops, about hiring Black and Brown trades. Witherspoon must have sensed my hesitation. I didn't want to be rude; it was just that I didn't have a reason to be here and that made me uneasy.

She pulled in a breath. "Jas…" She hesitated then turned on her heel. "Follow me for a second."

I didn't feel easy about that shit either, but I obeyed. It wasn't my safety I was concerned about. I could hold my own. It was walking into the unknown that I was uncomfortable with. I didn't know Witherspoon but understood her type and wanted no parts of it.

The closer we walked into her home, my stomach began to talk. The unease from being here allowed me to ignore it. Then we turned into her dining room; high brown matte walls with posted gold and silver frames boasting fine art. The chairs were high wing-back, enough for eight people. Flower arrangements were at the far end of the table, at the other was a setup for two.

Witherspoon turned my way and must have read my expression. Her eyes grew wide. "It's not a romantic setup, I swear. Like I said, I know you're an early bird and I needed to finish packing. Look." Her ass flapped a little as she carried the tagged clothing over to the head of the table to show me the binder I put together for her the other day. "All business, Jas. Nothing weird."

Two things happened at the same damn time: I felt bad as hell for brushing her off. It made me look like a bitch. The second thing was the rolling of my stomach turned into growls. The smell of the food enhanced it.

"*Shit…*" I mumbled, pulling out my phone.

"It shouldn't take long," Witherspoon continued to plea.

"Nah. It's just that I gotta tell my ride downstairs that I'll be longer than I thought. We were gonna pick up *B-Way Burger* when we left here, before me going home."

I texted Juggy to go get his food without me. He had to be hungry as hell, too. We busted our asses today, skipping lunch.

A woman with golden caramel skin and a blonde Caesar cut walked into the room carrying a tray of food for the table.

"I think her branzino can do you better than any *B-Way* burger," Witherspoon popped her shit. "My roommate's skills are unmatched." Roommate? "She's being offered a head cook's position at *DiFillippo's* in Hackensack."

The woman—apparently older—rolled her eyes. "Roommates split the bills. Cut your shit, Shi-Shi. I'm here bill-free. Just enjoy the food." The woman arranged the table then left as Witherspoon bit her lip in possible shame.

I fought laughing, shifting away with my fist to my mouth.

"She's sweet in real life," Ashira grumbled. When I looked her way again, she shifted weight on her legs and popped a fist on her hip. "Now, can you spare the little dignity I have left and eat?"

"Aren't you packing?"

"Yup. And can get back to it once we're done. Besides, I'm only taking one suitcase. I don't have a lot to do. It's MoBay, not Finland." She scoffed, rolling her eyes with humor.

Shit...

"What's for dinner?"

Her eyes combed the table. "The grilled fish, white beans, and..." She lifted a lid of a bowl. "...rapini."

"I 'on't know what rapini is. I'll pass on that."

"It's a green vegetable."

I widened my stance, clasping my hands behind my back. "I'm good. Where can I wash my hands?"

Witherspoon shook her head. "No adult—and barely children—is allowed to eat at my table without vegetables. That's a hard limit for me, Jas."

And there was that boss bitch persona coming out. I couldn't lie: the shit worked.

I sucked in a breath and turned toward the door. "Where's the bathroom, Witherspoon?"

An accomplished smile burst on her little face and Witherspoon spun in the air. "I can show you on my way to put this shirt away!"

127

ashira

As I poured myself another glass of *Château Blevin*, I peered over the profile of a woman having been released three years ago from a sixteen-year sentence.

"I wonder what her story is," I murmured, observing the scar on her left cheek.

"What do you mean?" Jas spoke with a mouth full of food. He was on his second serving of fish and third of rapini.

That one observation made me feel oddly triumphant.

"Her scars…the lost years…her interest in construction. Like, what happened to her?"

"Patty'll rather you get to know her. She gets off talking about the dozens of free cakes she bake every fourth Friday of the month and especially on holidays for the elderly and youngins with crack-head parents in her hood. You should see the line when she set up her tables." He scooped up more of the fish so rapidly, my heart clenched at the sight of a virile man eating at my table, ravishing the food I arranged. I didn't think I'd ever seen it before. It was…hot. "Or how she fix cars in her hood for single mothers. Sometimes, Patty pays for the parts." He chuckled to himself. "I think she be chasing pussy sometimes, but she's always had a helpful heart."

Oh…

I went back to eating and reading a new profile.

"This is good. You cook?"

While looking over Leon Cook's profile, I answered, "Yeah. Not like this, though." Then a question occurred. "How do you know these people? The guy, Juggy, said you don't know them all personally. But how do you recruit for this program?"

"It started from me identifying people I knew and could trust. I sat with them about the idea and gave them a little booklet for conduct code. Most of them had training and skills." He shrugged, wiping his mouth. "From there, they were recruited. I had about twenty-two people within the first four months."

"And you place them with builders?"

"That's the purpose. Either getting them trained to be employed or just employed. But also, making sure they're sustainable."

"Have you had any issues?"

"A few." He was back to his plate. "Of course, you're gonna have a knucklehead or two. What I found with the ones that caused the headache was they suffered from mental health shit. With those, it's hard to hold them to the code of conduct."

"And that's it? You just get these people with miscreant pasts and tell them to obey your code of conduct on the job you help them get and, for the most part, they do?" I found that hard to believe.

"Precisely." He licked his fingers while looking me square in the eyes.

"How?"

"Because I'm Jas, Witherspoon, the most heretical of them all," his voice soft and confident.

I spit, "Bullshit. You can't—couldn't have been that nefarious."

"How do you know?"

I shrugged, nerved by the question. "Because I know. I've been around an array of characters in my lifetime. Even in my line of work as a builder, I could spot a bullshitter a mile away. I'm rarely wrong."

"And neither am I." Our eyes stapled and, for seconds long, I was in sight of a distinct and palpable aggression I could smell on Jas, but tried hard fighting against it.

He's a laborer, nothing for you to be concerned about…

All things being true, there was something behind those chocolate irises, a huge metal gate guarding a maelstrom of passion. Of what kind, though? I was curious, but honestly didn't care enough. Jas left a lot to be desired in the personality department. If it weren't for our therapist and *Brown Barista*, I could check out a few of his cohort of libertines and never hear from him again.

"Do it," his deep vocals woke me from my thoughts.

I blinked, clearing my throat as I readjusted myself in the chair. "Do what?"

"Dance. Grow your studio. Open more in the state—around the country. Young Black girls need exposure to your type. Give them that. At the same time, you'll fulfill your purpose, waking up every day with a full heart and the stamina to inject it into everybody you encounter. Go, dance."

"I never thought about it that way. Other than to my little sister, I've never thought about role modeling."

"We got to. The focus has to be on the community around us and the one coming after. Our gifts and passions ain't just for us. It ain't only our parents' job to influence us. Sometimes, parents can't touch the minds of their kids. That's where a responsible community comes into play."

"Have you always thought this way?"

Jas shook his head. "Not before giving my heart and life to Christ. Before that, I ain't see much past the latest scheme my brain cooked up." I had no idea why I found that so funny, but I did, and Jas did, too. "Nah. In the Good Book, Matthew chapter eleven says, '*Come to me, all you who are weary and burdened and I'll give you rest.*' That was me. I'd been in the *FED*s for only a few months, and bustin' down niggas to solidify my place. It was hard as hell, but I did it. Once it was over—no more fighting, being put in the hole, or walking with eyes in the back of my head—I wasn't satisfied. I was just..." He shrugged. "...tired."

"Physically and emotionally, I bet."

"Spiritually, too. I was in a high-level security federal prison, looking at ten years on top of what I'd already put in waiting and walking through my trial. How would I occupy my time? How would I keep my mind? I was states away from my family, so they couldn't visit. Plus, I had just sat through over a year waiting on my trial to start and then going through the trial. The fighting my first few months in the *FED*s actually helped get out a lot of pent up energy. But when that shit was done, I was..."

I swallowed. "Tired." He nodded, eyes on his empty plate.

"Yup. Going back to your question about the way I think: So a few days after feeling low like that, this old head introduced himself to me on the yard. Once I could see he wasn't on no funny shit, we started to kick it and I found out he was a Christian, saved himself. He hooked me up with a Bible, put me on to Bible classes, and helped lead me to Christ. After I gave my life to Him, I needed to rework my way of thinking. The Bible also says, 'As a man thinks in his heart, so is he.' I knew I had lots of work to do on me. Romans twelve, verse two speaks about being transformed by the renewing of our minds. That was a big work for me—or maybe my presentation is. I'm still working on my language."

I laughed hard as hell. "You are a fellow-potty mouth."

He snorted, half tortured, half amused by that truth. "I swear, I pray about that every day."

Laughing, I explained, "Well, who am I to judge? I know the Bible, been taught it book by book, but totally lack application. The second verse about what the heart thinketh is from Proverbs, chapter twenty-three." He nodded, and of course, Jas knew that. "It's refreshing to see a peer do it. Inspiring." I lifted one cheek.

He checked the time on his phone again. "So, you fed me and we've talked about the candidates and your background check process, and my selection process. We've also kicked it about your dream to open dance schools—"

"I didn't say that. You actually dropped that idea in my head, though."

"So, all you have to do is retire from *Witherspoon Homes* and you're good?"

I shook my head, immediately feeling vulnerable. "I want to open a nightclub."

"Word? Where?"

I shrugged. "I've looked into Hoboken, Greenwich Village, Atlanta, Baltimore…Miami." I shrugged again. "But I don't want to move to do it, so somewhere in the Tri-state area."

"There're lots of clubs. What would be unique about yours?"

I winked, masking my nervousness. "And there's the magic question. It wouldn't be a lounge type of vibe like most of the clubs around. This would be a dance-themed architect. The seating would be conducive to seeing the dancefloor. There'd be troops performing choreographed dancing every night, just about the whole time the club is open. The dancers would be the entertainers, but the patrons could still do their own thing in designated areas if they chose."

"How would you get ya mack on if the dancing is the main event?"

I laughed. "People have been known to find a way in just about every institution. I'm sure you've seen your lot of prohibited sex while away—probably had a female C.O. or two—"

"Or three," he quickly corrected. Then a smile broke out on his face. "Nah. I'm just fuckin' with you, Witherspoon."

I had no idea why I found his unexpected humor so funny, but I howled. "Oh, my god, man!" He grinned innocently, but now I wondered if he *was* fucking with me about being with a corrections officer or three. I didn't want to ask because Jas would, no doubt, shut me down if I asked anything related to his dating history, past or present. But I wondered. I'd also decided Jas couldn't have had a girlfriend; he was too uptight for that. "Anyway, as I was saying: people would find their way to get their mack on. The music wouldn't be any louder than it is at a regular club. The difference would be the clientele. People enjoy watching dancers. Dancers enjoy watching peers. I truly do believe there's a market for this, and for those unfamiliar with the vibe. If they came just one time, they'd get it."

"Well, I'm unfamiliar and ain't ever been to nothing like what you just described, and I get it."

My eyes went wild. "You do?"

Before he gulped down water, he confirmed, "I do."

"Yaaay!" I faked cheered in my baby voice to not demonstrate how happy I really felt about his acceptance of my vision.

He's only a laborer...

My phone rang on the table. I noticed Austin's name automatically and stood from my chair. "Would you excuse me for a second?

I've gotta take this. Boyfriend." Before I could catch Jas' response, I answered, "Hey cutie-wootie."

"Hey, babe…"

I took the call into my bedroom.

I asked myself how long I'd wait. Ashira Witherspoon seemed like the type of chick who'd be inconsiderate of others' time, especially for her boyfriend. I hated to admit, chilling with her wasn't bad at all. Dinner was delicious, and I ran through the rapini. Didn't have much of a funkiness to the taste. The fish I'd never had before either, and that was tasty, too. This was fine dining tonight.

Of course, my G: it's Ashira Witherspoon!

I shook off that thought, thinking it was okay if the night was over instead. We kicked it about a lot of shit, but business seemed to be complete. At this point, if she was interested in any of my people, the ball was in her court.

The older woman with the blonde hair came back into the dining room. "You two finished?"

I checked the entryway like an idiot for Witherspoon. "Uhh-hhh… Yeah. I think so." My phone rang in my pocket. When I saw her name on the face I cringed, knowing this was not a good time, but also not a call I could delay. "I'm gonna take this outside in the hall."

"You can just go out on the terrace," she remarked without eye contact.

"Terrace?"

"Ummmhmmm." She pointed. "Walk out to your left, not your right and it's on the right side. Shouldn't be hard to unlock. Just cold out there tonight."

I was on my way. "Thanks," I offered over my shoulder. Cold was right. It was the middle of February, beyond brick. And I didn't wear my coat up here, leaving it in the toasty truck we drove here instead. "Hey…" I answered.

"Jas?"

"Yeah." I managed to unlock and open one of the French doors and walk out onto the terrace. The night air bit my ass right away. I was sure to close the door behind me. "I'm here. Sorry about that. I'm glad you called back."

"Yeah." Her voice was small and we both knew why. "I was running around today with my grandma. I knew I had to call you. Figured it was no rush."

"Why, Renee?" That was bullshit coated by sympathy.

"You know why, Jas." I did. "You said you'd make your decision two days ago. I heard it all in your message that night, and all you said was to call you back."

That fast, the phone was too cold to hold up to my ear, so I put the call on speaker while tensing from the frigid ass breeze.

"Renee, I knew this wouldn't be easy. But please tell me I've been honest."

I'd hoped so. The last thing I ever wanted to do was mislead or hurt a woman. That was counterproductive to what I needed.

"Yeah," she sighed. "You've been honest, but…" There was a delay before she admitted. "I'm just confused. What do I need to do to be better."

I blinked. "Better at what?"

"Better at getting someone to want me."

"There's nothing wrong with you. Ain't nothing wrong with you at all."

"Must be because you don't want me. You want her."

I wouldn't say all that...

Cynthia was another chick I'd been considering, but she was no guarantee for me.

"I haven't said that."

"But you said all this time, it's been just two of us."

What I'd actually said was I wouldn't date more than two women at a time in this process, and I wanted to be honest about that. And I had.

"That doesn't mean she's my choice, Renee."

"Then what does it mean, Jas?"

I took a deep breath. "It just means I've decided not to waste your time. I wouldn't disrespect you by having you in this shit, using up potential time on me. That ain't fair to you."

"But the..."

"The what?"

"The rejection of it all. Jas, you men, especially good-looking and fit ones like you with no kids, will never understand what it's like for women out here. You got two women trying to date you. You were the first guy I've been interested in dating in two years. The game is imbalanced." Feeling less chilled all of a sudden, I shook my head, agreeing. "So, when you, as a woman, finally get the attention of a good man and he calls it off, it stings like rejection. That is why I'm asking what I could do better. What did I do wrong, Jas?"

The soft scent of coffee and cinnamon had me wondering if Ashira's neighbor had just opened a window.

Lord, give me the words to put her heart at ease...

"You did nothing wrong, Renee. You're a good woman of faith, taking care of your family. You're responsible and handle your bills independently. Plus, you're a good cook and homemaker. You're..." The odor, now, smelled more nutty and obviously smoky. I turned back for her apartment and Witherspoon was on the sofa, wrapped in a thick ass plaid coat. Her leg crossed over the other, hiking a sheepskin bootie in the air. She crossed one arm over the other, holding a burning cigar. Her eyes were dead on me without apology for obviously eavesdropping. "...upper crust," I lied to Renee while staring Witherspoon dead in her face.

Then I turned away, face pinched. "Renee, I'm sorry. I'm not by myself anymore. I have to go." Then I thought, "If you wanna kick it again, I'll make myself available to you whenever you need."

After a few beats, she calmly dismissed me. "Bye, Jas."

The call was over and I dropped the phone. My eyes squeezed closed and I prayed I didn't hurt that girl. This part of the game wasn't fun.

"How long were you two together?"

Witherspoon...

In the short time since joining me on the terrace, she confirmed what I'd been feeling about her. Her bad bitch status was real. The invisible crown not so indiscernible.

Why was I here?

I took a deep breath before turning her way. She had a heating lamp on, creating a harmless glow in the sitting area.

"We weren't together."

"Not by the sight of you and the sound of her."

I walked over to the couch and sat a seat away from her. "It's not like that."

"Do you mind?" She lifted the cigar. I noticed the watch again, peeking from the cuff of her big coat. Witherspoon's eyes followed mine to her tiny wrist with a boss ass timepiece. "You really like this, huhn—*no!*" She shook her head. "I can't believe what I just saw and have to stay focused. I know all you're going to do is shut me down in your coldish, thug ass way, but the least you could do is humor me; I did feed you." Her brows met. "Dude, did you just break up with your girlfriend on my balcony?"

I made a quick decision to share a little about it with her. She was right: it was the least I could do for her generosity. That, plus, in the moment, I could use a point of view from a contemporary woman.

"We weren't together: just dating, man." I scrubbed my face with my hands. "This shit ain't supposed to be so hard."

"Okay. So, she wasn't your girlfriend, but you broke it off with her? Make it make sense, thug-a-boo."

I scoffed, not feeling the least bit offended. Part of the reason why, I was sure, was because I didn't think she meant for me to.

"I know I shouldn't get this personal with you, but..." Using my thumb, I pointed behind me. "I told you last week about my checklist. I've always been a list guy. I need to see the plan itemized. I've got a few things on there, like my career and my wife." Damn, I hated sounding so fucking corny. "I told myself to give it a year before I carried out the plan."

"Which was?"

"Damn." I laughed at her impatience. "Let me finish." *Am I that different to you?* Ashira's eyes fell away and she smoked on the stick. "I needed to pace myself. When you're behind in life from doing a bid, your focus gotta be narrow. Even with the list, priority is a must. So, a few months ago, I started actively seeking out women I thought I could see as a wife. I made a few rules for myself. I would tell them everything about my time away and when I was released, and all I'm doing is dating. That and the fact that there's another woman I'm considering, too, but there'll only be two at a time."

"Two?" she breathed out in disbelief.

"Yeah. Dating is expensive, which is why I only give it two months—tops—before deciding if I want to continue to get to know them or stop wasting their time. What you just ear-hustled was me telling a cool girl I won't waste her time anymore."

"What's wrong with her?"

"Now you sound like her." I asked, being realer than real, "Why does something have to be wrong?"

"Because romance novels exist. Everybody wants their romance novel-worthy love. If you're coming in the picture talking marriage, women—" She blinked. "—are we talking the rainbow, color-wise?"

I wasn't sure of her question. "As in race?"

"Yeah."

"Nah. I like 'em Black. Maybe a dark Dominican—*maybe*."

"Oh, then, hell yeah! Black women, specifically, who still believe in romance will think there's something wrong with them when they're cut off before getting to the 'and they lived happily ever after' part. It's rejection."

"That's what she just said," I groaned into my hands. "I don't get this shit."

"Did you…" When she hesitated, I lifted my head to look at her. "Did you—*are you*—fucking them?"

My face fell. "Say less. That's personal as hell, Witherspoon."

I wasn't discussing that shit with her. It was bad enough I was in her crib with Juggy's ass downstairs waiting on me, *and* sharing all the shit I typically didn't in the first place.

"There's nothing wrong with being nice, you know." I caught her eyeroll.

"And nothing wrong with you minding your business, too. I ain't ask you nothing about ya man. Say less, Witherspoon."

"But I'd answer."

"Until I asked about your sex life."

She seesawed her head from side to side. "Fair point. Anyway." Witherspoon took a quick pull from her cigar. "Tell me, why did she get eliminated. Was she fat? Ugly? Unintelligent?"

"Nah." I found that funny. "She's a cute girl, decent body… smart. Got a bachelor's degree in African American History."

"What in the hell is she doing with that?"

"Teaching. She's about to go to theology school."

"Oh." The drop in her tone had my gaze swinging her way. Witherspoon's eyes were toward my waist as she wiggled her fingers. "Let me see a pic of her?"

"Hell no!" I laughed, too hard. I'd been doing a lot of that tonight.

"Why not?"

"For one, I don't have any. And two, that shit's weird, Witherspoon."

"You're shitting me, right?"

"I don't lie."

She balled her mouth. Witherspoon didn't believe me. "You don't have any pix of the girls you're dating?"

I thought for a minute. Then pulled out one of my phones. After tapping a few times, I found a picture of Maria, a woman I met last week. "I'm thinking about asking for her time." I handed over my phone.

Witherspoon studied the image, but gave no reaction. Then she gave it back. "Her brows are nice."

"Brows?"

"Yeah." Her face tightened as she quickly navigated the conversation. "What are you looking for in a woman?"

"I'm not just looking for a woman, I need a wife. I want somebody old school with old values. No clubbing, no kids, no non-Believer, domesticated, and can communicate and understand what her role is in my life."

"Which would be?"

"To support me while I build an empire. To have my babies and help raise them to be superstars in whatever lane they choose." I shrugged. "Not to have a focus bigger than us. And I'll, no doubt, support her in all her endeavors, too."

"And what about the one you just broke it off with wouldn't fit into that narrative?"

"She won't be able to "leave and cleave.'"

"Come again?"

I pinched the bridge of my nose, not believing I was talking about this shit. "She's got a big family. They depend on her: grandparents, two aunts, three little brothers, two nieces and four nephews. And more than half of them are living in the house she rents. There's no way I can remove her from that situation…uproot her from her place where so many live, and bring her to a home for just the two of us to have a family. Devoted women don't work that way. Yeah, she could be a mean mother to my kids, but we would never get started on building shit of our own with her reaching back to take care of all of them."

"The Bible." When my gaze found Witherspoon, she was nodding toward the ground with pouted lips. "Genesis. Adam and Eve. 'Leave and cleave.'"

"Yeah. In the second chapter, but in Matthew, too."

"You're really a Bible head, aren't you?"

I shrugged, sitting up and bringing my elbows to my knees. "I'm narrowly focused, Witherspoon.

"You make demands on life." She expressed it like a deep revelation.

"Which is why I can tell you with no reservation at all to dance, Witherspoon." I stood from the couch, needing to leave. "You said you're about a year younger than me? If that's the case, we ain't pups no more. Our visions for our lives should be clear at this point. If we can live out the next forty—*fifty*—years of our lives, what would we do and who will be there with us?" When she didn't speak, only stared into the night air, I asked, "You gonna walk me out?"

"*Ye*—yeah." She rushed to place her stick into an exaggerated groove of an astray."

"You like cigars?"

"Love them." She laughed softly, swinging the blanket from her legs.

"Oh, yeah?" I tried keeping the conversation light as she led me inside. "What's your favorite?"

"A few, but my latest obsession is *Por el Amor del Amor*. I even got my dad hooked." *Oh*... "There's nothing like lighting up one of those babies with a velvety glass of *Château Blevin*." She glanced at me from over her shoulder while removing her coat now that we were inside.

Her body...

Maybe it was me feeling hungry as a man with no warm body to eat from or feed at night, or maybe Witherspoon was just that oblivious to how powerfully feminine her build was, but she held no regard to be underdressed in my presence. It shouldn't have mattered that we were in her home. I was a stranger to her. Seemed pretty reckless to me. *But hey*... That was her risk and her man's problem; not mine.

She smiled as she opened the door for me. "Thanks for entertaining my requests. All of them."

I shook my head, smiling. "Enjoy your time away, Witherspoon."

"Maybe I will. I'll be witnessing another girl having her romance novel played out." I turned toward her confused. Her pretty smile deepened. "I'm going to a wedding."

"One of your girl's getting married?"

She shook her head. "Guy friend. One of my besties from *Blakewood*."

My eyes went low when my forehead wrinkled. "You going with your girls?"

"No. By myself."

"Ya man good with that?"

Witherspoon cocked her head to the side. "That ain't none of ya business, Jas. Say less!"

I turned back for the elevator, laughing my ass off.

Chapter Nine

Jas

SHIT!

It's dark and I can't breathe. My stinging, tearing eyes are squeezed closed and my throat is on fucking fire. The biting is in my eyes, nose, mouth, throat— shit, I feel it in my lungs, too. Not enough air sloughing through. It's the worst peppery taste and reaction ever. I know; this is one of several methods the C.O.s use to herd us. I wish just one day, they fought without props. Man to man. I'd beat the shit out of all of these bitches.

But first I gotta breathe. And I can't. I need oxygen, but without this stinging pepper. Fuck! How much longer before this shit'll stop burning? My chest and abs are working overtime without progress. I can't fucking breathe and the shit is painful—

My body leaped in the air, landing on the balls of my feet. My fists were tight and in the air, eyes wide and wild, and body drenched in sweat. My sight was back, adrenaline dancing on every cell in my body, dick pounding, and I was ready. On fucking go.

Heaving in plenty of air, legs and feet locked in the southpaw position, I was ready to discharge on the first in sight. My wild eyes were in search, tense knuckles ready.

But it smelled different. No pissy odor, pepper, or turmoil engulfing me. Instead, the shit smelled of pine and apples. The floor beneath my feet was padded, long wool sheepskin. And the air around me was free-flowing, not stale or restricted.

My shoulders dropped, even though my heart raced like a meth'ed up horse.

I'm home…

The strain of my fists eased and I closed my eyes in relief and frustration.

Another fucking nightmare…

"I wonder if the pizza's any good?"

Looking over the menu, I replied, "I 'on't think you can get a grilled chicken sandwich wrong."

She leaned into me with a nudge. "You're so wise. I'mma have the same thing. I do wanna try their onion rings, though."

"Then get them."

"Yup. And the red velvet cake is calling out to my soul!" She squeezed her eyes dramatically.

I was sure church folks wouldn't get cake wrong. They had better not.

Tonight, on a rare Thursday where I wasn't working or in class, I was on a date with Cynthia. Her church was having a fundraiser for their singles ministry's annual cruise. I didn't get it, but there were lots of things I didn't get about the foundations of church, but respected her commitment to the religion.

I'd just hung out with Cynthia on last Sunday for Valentine's Day. Tonight, she wanted to support her church's efforts, and I wanted to get to know more about her, so I didn't mind participating tonight. We were outdoors in an enclosed tent behind their church. I could easily count close to forty heads in here and the place was reasonably warm with our coats still on, so I guessed that was a success. Afterward, I'd go home and rest up for tomorrow's site visits. It would be a long Friday.

"So, how has your week been going?"

I exhaled, brushing my face with my hands, exhausted at the thought of it. "Busy. Never-ending."

"You work too hard." Her eyes were soft, but full lips twisted.

More than Cynthia was being comforting, she was expressing her dislike of my schedule.

"I've got a lot to make up for." I gazed deep into her eyes. She didn't hold back as much as she thought. "I also have an empire to build."

"How much longer, though? My dad asked about grandkids two days ago." Then her eyes fell. "Two more of my girlfriends announced their pregnancies this week. One is my soror, and the other's from my church."

I nodded, examining her. "Congrats to them."

"My little cousin, KeKe, got engaged on Valentine's Day. Did I tell you this already?" I shook my head. "Oh, I thought I did. She's like twenty-four. Her fiancé works for waste management. Her ring is so cute. Kind of big, too—"

"Hey there, kids!" A leggy woman in a brown ski suit with a belted waist and oversized hoodie stood over our table with pen and pad. Though her head was low, I could peep her matching ski mask. "What can we get ya tonight?"

"We'll take two grilled chicken sandwiches with the works," I began. "One fry and one order of onion rings. I'll take water…" Then I looked to Cynthia for her answer.

"*Diet Coke.*"

"And a slice of the red velvet cake."

My phone vibrated just as I finished. It was Man. Quickly

glancing over his text, I understood there had been no progression on learning who'd been threatening to rob the club. It was something I'd have to deal with once I left here, but I hated that my theory on the club's security vulnerability was correct.

"Okay," the woman taking our order spoke up. "So, I have two grilled chickens all the way, one fry, one onion ring, water, *Diet Coke*, red velvet cake, and finally, a bowl of rapini."

Rapi—

My head flew up, eyes squinting.

"What's rapini?" Cynthia asked confused. "He didn't order that." Her perplexed eyes swung over to me. "We didn't order that."

The waitress tapped her pad with the tip of her pen, and that's when I peeped the watch.

Almost at the same damn time, Witherspoon busted out laughing and pulled her fur-trimmed hoodie off. I snorted, shaking my head. The coincidence of her being here hadn't settled in yet: her humor had, though.

"Hey, Jas," she greeted, no longer laughing, but still fighting it.

"How you?"

"I'm good! Gotcha!" She laughed again, not as hard, but had removed her mask. The flattening in her plump lips against her gums didn't escape my attention. Witherspoon was so fucking cute, constantly reminding me of that when it was the last thing I wanted to think about. "Lucky for you, they ran out of your favorite green veggie."

"Cynthia, this is—"

"I know Shi-Shi." Cynthia's face didn't register that, though.

"Oh, cool." Witherspoon's eyes brightened. "Well, I guess I know your name now. It's good to officially meet you." She extended her hand for a shake.

Cynthia met it nervously. I was confused.

"How do you know her, but she don't know you?"

Cynthia's giggle was consistent with her reaction to Witherspoon. "Well, she's friends with my assistant pastor. They've been cool forever. I see her at the church every now and then." Witherspoon's grin was goofy. Was this her polished persona? "And duh! She's only Austin Seers' gorgeous girlfriend, too."

Oh. Him...

I'd forgotten that fact. I could never forget Witherspoon had a boyfriend, but what never stuck was the fact of him being a celebrity. I didn't watch too much television other than *Taking Tips from Tynisha* and the news. And not a lot of my time with women was spent in movie theaters, so the next great Black hype was lost on me.

Cynthia's eyes fell again, but her shy smile remained. When I glanced over at Witherspoon again, I started at her lengthy thighs with a two-inch gap. Even in the puffy one-piece, her posture was elegant, waist small, and tits prominent. By the time my perusal made it to her face, Witherspoon's narrowed eyes were on me.

"I know." She smiled thickly, bringing her arm into view. "It's the watch. I love it, too." Then her attention went to Cynthia, her expression opening more. "I'll get that right out to you." She was out.

"You know her?"

I had to measure how I'd answer that. Witherspoon laid the foundation for the answer to be yes, but that was untrue. I didn't really know her, and I didn't want to lie to Cynthia, someone who was clearly fan-girling Witherspoon.

"She runs a building firm similar to the one I work for."

"Oh. Like what you're trying to do?" I nodded. "So, you've run into her...on job sites?"

"One or two." I put my phone in the breast pocket of my coat. "Crazy seeing her here at your church, though."

"There she is." Cynthia pointed to a woman at another table with a black wool swing coat. "They've been friends forever. I'm not surprised Shi-Shi is here. She's a supportive friend. What I am surprised about is that Austin ain't proposed to her yet. Have you met him?"

"Once maybe. Why're you surprised?"

"Because she's no spring chicken. No kids, beautiful, successful with about a half a million followers on *Instagram*, and she's smart.

She's got her own life, had it before Austin. Got her own money, too. That makes me wonder why they aren't married or, at least, engaged."

I didn't want to ask, but had to know.

"Why do you think it's time for all of that?"

She turned to me and whispered, "Because, like I said, she's in her thirties. They've been dating for about three years. Even you said you wouldn't go beyond two months before knowing if I had wife tendencies. I respect that."

ashira

"Alright. I'll get that right out for you!" I tapped my pen on the check pad then took off.

"Thanks, Shi-Shi!" they shouted cheerily behind me and with familiarity.

Peering over my shoulder, I snickered and winked. Inside the church's kitchen where about a dozen people were busy working various roles, I put in the order. Down at the other end was Peach, waiting on food for her tables.

"Hey, girlie." I sauntered over to her, skipping in the air a few times for her amusement.

"How's it going?"

"Cool," I answered before stepping closer to practically whisper in her ear. "You know the Cynthia girl who sings in your choir?"

"What about her?"

"How long has she been dating him?"

Peach hit me with the maternal glare. I rolled my eyes then flashed them wide, urging her.

"I'm not exactly sure," she whispered, "A month maybe."

"She into him like that?"

"If she can remove her focus from everybody else, I bet she could be." She collected a salad and sandwich for her tray.

"What does that mean?"

Peach shrugged with her mouth. "Always been a good girl," she continued to whisper. "Just too into comparing lives and social statuses. Her family joined when we were in high school. I thought she would have grown out of that by now. Other than that, she's cool—"

"Dry."

Peach's head fell to the side as more food was being made available. I took two sandwiches belonging to her order and added them to her tray.

"Shi, that's subjective."

"I don't know. I may be right about this one. She's the one who works for a thrift shop, right?"

"Her mother owned one. Father is a barber. They were able to send her and her brothers to decent schools here in Jersey."

"Dryness isn't about class," I murmured, chewing on my lips. I couldn't shake what I'd discerned from her—*from them*—in those brief minutes of taking their order. "It's about self-pride and expression." I shrugged. "That can all be interpreted in your presentation."

"So what if she is, Shi-Shi? What's it to you?"

My lips protracted and I shrugged with my head. "Nothing. Just gotta be compatible with your guy."

"And how do you know she isn't? Do you know him?"

"Kinda." My eyes rolled over to her. "Met him a few weeks ago."

"So, you don't know him."

"I know he's more worldly than she is in a sensuous and cultural way." Or was he? Truthfully, I didn't know who the hell Jas was beneath his tough veneer. But it was a feeling. Just like the picture he showed me of the chick he was looking to date soon. She was rather thick with new growth taking over her cornrows, semi-dry lips, and a horrible girdle with an attempt at a compelling pose. *But I bet she loves the Lord…* And if that was all Jas was into, who was I to make a big deal out of his quasi-girlfriend, Cynthia? "Or I could be wrong. Come on. Let me help you with this. My orders are up next."

I lifted the wide ass tray and followed Peach to the two tables to serve. When we were finished, the order was done for one of my tables, and I served Cynthia and Jas.

"And here you go, love birds."

"Thanks, Shi-Shi," Cynthia offered while rearranging the food so they could share.

"How adorable," I thought was only grumbled in my head.

That was until Jas' dark eyes were over Cynthia's bowed head and on me. Blindly, he took a fry and placed it in his mouth. That shit caused an unfair stir in my damn groin.

"Witherspoon," he called just as I was turning to get to my next table's order. I pivoted back with a bright smile. "Cynthia and I were saying how dope it is for you to volunteer to work this event tonight."

I shrugged. "Not too much of a leap. This is for the singles ministry and last I checked, I'm legally single."

"Why is that, exactly?" Cynthia's head came up at her man's scholarly mien rearing. Her eyes desperately curious. "I mean. You've been with ya man for a few years now. Right?" Then the academic persona disappeared. Peach approached us at the table. "How long is too long to date, as a Christian?"

Okay…

Peach's eyes blew the hell up, too, at the odd question. As innocuous as it may have seemed on the surface, I knew it was not. The inquiry was coming from the steel fort of a man himself: Jas. He didn't discuss such personal matters, had shut me down each time I tried. He couldn't care less about Austin, that was made clear at the *Wonder* play when he declined the picture. What in the hell was this about?

149

I placed the tray beneath my arm as I switched the weight on my hips.

"I think that's subjective." I scratched my nose. "It's a decision to be decided between you, your significant other and, possibly, with the guidance of a spiritual leader."

"You think age is a determining factor?" Jas pushed.

"What do you mean?"

"Well, like Cynthia and me. We're both in our early-thirties with no children. Do you think dating for years before deciding if we'll marry is healthy?"

I understood it. Either way I answered would reveal my personal decision with Austin. I had been beyond annoyed with his fans and people I'd come across asking why we hadn't married or had any children. It was rude and judgmental. Now, Jas, the king of privacy and coldness himself, was doing it.

"Is this a general question, Jas? Or are you asking about me personally?" Cynthia's desperate eyes jumped to me.

Jas shrugged with his lips while grabbing an onion ring. He tossed it in his mouth so fast, chewed, then used his tongue to swipe the side of his mouth. I'd had a meal with this guy—drank coffee with him several times—and didn't recall that sensual move.

"Okay. Well, I think I gave the general answer. So my personal answer is I'm still being made whole."

In my periphery, Peach's head bounced back in shock.

"Whole? How old are you, Witherspoon?"

I swallowed hard. "A year younger than you."

"And you aren't whole?"

I shook my head. "I'm not complete on my own."

"Maybe it's because it's time for you to join your life with a man and be fruitful by having a family," Cynthia suggested.

I shook my head, irritated by the limited counsel. "Being married and having children is cool, but it's not a top three on my list."

"Then what is—*if you don't mind?*" Cynthia's jaw stretched with humility.

"Wholeness," I answered again. Then my gaze traveled over to her flummoxing ass boyfriend. "I had an encouraging conversation with my *best* friend last Thursday night at my place over dinner. He made the revelation very clear to me: I need to live out my purpose. There's this thing I now feel I've been purposed to do, and I can't let it come before someone else's dreams for me. It's unacceptable for me to allow society to deem the order of my life's work. I've been given good health and the freedom to do it, and that's what I plan to do. Marriage and kids are not as attractive as being made whole." I forced my million-dollar smile. "Well, unless I can get you two cuties anything else, I need to get my next table served before I clock out and cash out my tips for the night." My inspection swung over to Peach, who stood tense with big eyes.

Before struggling to figure out what it could mean from her, I took off while I still had my dignity intact. Back in the kitchen, I said my goodbyes to the cooks I knew. I'd served my last table and was preparing to go.

Then I headed over to the register. "Hey, Nema. This is for table six." I handed her fifty bucks, knowing that exceeded Cynthia and Jas' bill. But, this was a fundraiser after all. "He said to keep the change."

"Thanks, Shi-Shi."

Just as I turned off to leave for the night, Peach, in her black cape coat, looking like a dark and very contemporary Mary Poppins, was approaching me. "How do you know him?"

"Who?"

"The guy with Cynthia?"

"Oh, you mean her boyfriend?"

She blinked. "Yes. Him."

I wouldn't lie to her. Peach could be told shit in confidence. "We share the same therapist."

"Oh." She blinked successively again with a stretched forehead. "How long have you known him?"

I shrugged, ready to go. "I told you. Just a few weeks."

"And you guys are sparring about marriage and fulfillment like that?"

I shrugged. "And?"

She shook her head, eyes falling away. "There was something weird in that exchange."

My face tightened. Other than Jas being weird, what else could it be? "Like what?"

Her attention returned to me. "Your chemistry."

"He's cool—*kind of* cool. I guess." I shook my head. "I really don't know. I don't really know him at all. Look..." It was my turn to blink deeply. I was growing tired from this really long day. Not only did I make my therapy session early this morning, but I had two site visits and meetings in my office before volunteering here at Peach's church tonight. Now, I had to go over to the dance studio to pick up files for my accountant and inspect one of the speakers for possible repair. "I need to get out of here before I can't go anymore."

She nodded, lips twisting and eyes drawn downward.

I kissed her cheek. "You're cold," I noted, sauntering off.

"I'm working!" she shouted behind me. "Thanks, Shi-Shi!"

"Anywhere, anytime, and anything for you, Peachie!"

Ten minutes later, as I was driving, Austin sent a text.

Au: *ARE YOU STILL VOLUNTEERING AT THE CHURCH?*

I'd forgotten I told him about that when he called this morning.

Before I could think to answer, the phone rang. The name on the caller I.D. was *Ritz Luxuriate*, the hotel Austin typically stayed at when in town.

"Hello…"

"Ms. Witherspoon."

"Hi, Doris. Everything okay?"

"I hope so. I'm calling to be sure I didn't schedule your arrangements in error. The date I have is tomorrow, February nineteenth. Was I incorrect?"

Last week, I called over to *Ritz Luxuriate* to have them prepare for our post-Valentine's Day visit this weekend with champagne, fruits, and candles. Austin would be in town tomorrow.

My lips pouted. "No. Tomorrow's the day. Sounds about right."

"Okay." Her relief sounded reserved. "Because his check-in was earlier today and I didn't want to ruin it with one of my silly blunders."

Earlier today?

Austin texted me again.

Au: *SHI-SHI?*

The goofiest smile burst on my face.

This guy…

"No. You're perfectly fine, Doris. He's texting me now. Looks like we're trying to surprise each other. Thanks so much for your careful eye."

This time, a real sigh of relief was expressed through the phone. "I'm happy to help. Good evening, Ms. Witherspoon."

"Bye!"

Then I punched the keypad on my dashboard and called the dance studio.

"Denise?" I called after she answered.

"Hey, Shi-Shi."

"You gonna be there for a while?"

"For a couple of hours. Yeah."

"Could you get that file off my desk and scan them to email to me before you go?"

"Sure. I'm doing a routine with Chrissy right now. I can do it once I'm done."

My grip on the wheel intensified. "Thanks so much. And tell Leah I'll be there tomorrow about the speaker."

"Let me hurry and tell her now before she leaves."

"Thanks!"

Perfect timing, too…

I'd just made it to the exit for *Ritz Luxuriate.*

jaz

As I fired back a text to Juggy, now having read Man's text, I caught the Pastor girl coming our way.

"Hi," I called to get her attention. "I think ol' girl left. Can we get the check please?"

"You guys did good tonight, Pastor," Cynthia complimented.

"Thanks, girl." She smiled. "Oh, and your check has been settled already."

Cynthia's curious inspection swept over to me as her phone rang. "We didn't pay…" She took the call. The pastor's eyes stayed on me curiously, but not in a sexual manner; I knew those. I'd been the recipient of thirst gazes and approaches more than people would believe since my release. Even Juggy, who practically shadowed me, had constantly laughed and grumbled at the expected reaction from women I encountered, even casually. Nah. This was something different. Deeper maybe. I had nothing to hide, so I allowed her. "Yeah, Mommy. Pastor's right here. She did a great job with the single's ministry tonight." Then she whispered to her assistant pastor, "Mommy said congrats for a great job as usual."

The pastor winked. "Thanks, Mother Pollard."

"You heard her, Mommy?" Cynthia went back to her call. "Yeah. I know…"

"I'm sure that's a mistake. Is there any way you can check?" I tried. "I would really like to pay."

The pastor smiled again, youth filled her features. She looked to be younger than me, but with Black women, you could easily get it wrong. "It's been settled. No worries." Then she leaned toward me just an inch more as Cynthia yapped it up on the phone. "That's what 'best friends' do for 'best friends.'"

Shit…

I swallowed hard, dumbfounded as fuck by her implication. *Witherspoon and her slick ass story time!*

ashira

"Excuse me, ma'am." Hotel security stopped me as I ambled through the service door at the back of the *Ritz Luxuriate*.

My face folded. "Excuse me?"

I'd never been stopped coming in here. It was the way Austin and I had been entering the hotel since we began dating. Paparazzi had followed celebrities here since the luxury hotel opened ten years ago. I blamed Stenton Rogers and Alton Alston for it. StentRo used to bring his conquests here during his wild, rock star days. Paparazzi would catch him coming and leaving through the front so damn wasted.

"Yo," Bruce, one of the security guys I knew, called from near a delivery truck on the dock. "She's cleared." He waved his arm, demonstrating my pass to go inside.

The new, extremely lengthy ponytail-wearing suit hesitated too long. "I've got somewhere to be," I hissed.

"She's the girlfriend!" Bruce shouted over. "All good."

"Thanks, Bruce!" With the greasiest grin I'd recently learned from Jas, I shouldered past him.

"Hey!" he warned from behind, but didn't pursue me.

"Yeah. Eat hay, horsie!" I laughed, skipping toward the elevator.

Lucky for me, I caught the door before it closed. This service elevator did not follow the same pathway of the others for guests. It didn't even stop on every floor. Austin stayed in the same suite when here. It was spacious and private, with a rearview of the woodlands, creating an earthy ambiance.

I knocked at the door of the suite, heart expanding by the second in anticipation of seeing him. I hated surprises unless they were of the romantic variety. My eyes brushed against the doorbell and I quickly thought to use it, considering the size of the place.

Seconds after, I heard feminine muffling behind the door. "I know this is Shonda, coming to get my ass. I told you I need to —" The door swung open. "—go," she muttered as the muscle's in her face fell. Brielle's eyes squinted as though registering my presence.

I couldn't help it. My regard fell below her neck to her slender bare shoulders and breasts and trunk covered by an oversized towel. She was barefoot and naked. My attention went behind her. Maybe I was at the wrong suite. This hotel was popular amongst celebrities visiting Jersey, wanting a distance from New York City.

No…

This was the right place. Doris had made that clear. It still made no sense to me. They hadn't begun shooting for the movie yet. Why would they be spending time together? I was sure it was a misunderstanding. If only I could calm down.

"Do I know you from somewhere?" her voice was cold, yet sincere.

Her eyes were glazed over, demonstrating just how much she didn't recognize me. Brielle had no idea who I was. *How?* Even if she didn't recall me from her tour four years ago, I'd been photographed with Austin a gazillion goddamn times.

Am I invisible?

But a familiar frame with a bare upper torso crossed into my view behind her. Austin. He, too, was in just a towel, the same goofy smile as hers now melting from his face.

My eyes fell as I cleared my throat. "I'm his girlfriend," my tone exceptionally soft as I lifted my arm to point to Austin, who was frozen behind her.

I didn't know what was more insulting: Brielle not recognizing me from her old dance troupe or from being photographed a *goddamn gazillion* times with Austin over the past three years. The latter cut deep. How more visible could I have been as his woman to be recognized?

"Sh-Shi…" He hung his head, scrubbing his face with his hands.

My eyes filled with tears when I asked him, "She doesn't know me, Au?"

His head flew up, rolling back over his shoulders. "We need to talk. It's not like how you think."

"You know you're invisible to her, too? She just asked if she knew me, Austin, and I believe her. She's not that great of an actress. How invisible are you to her, too?" my voice cracked and that prompted my exit.

Austin never chased me.

The phone rang, ending my dip into a restful space to finally sleep. "Yeah…"

I couldn't open my eyes, life seemed too heavy for that.

"Witherspoon." His chords were deeper, velvety at this hour.

Tricky.

"Yeah," I repeated, and heard the first of that annoying chirping he had going on at his place sounded.

My forehead squeezed. I really didn't have the capacity to do this.

"What was up with that?"

"With what?"

"Last night."

Really!

"What about last night?" It was a stretch in time I largely wanted to forget.

"You paying, Witherspoon. The shit wasn't necessary."

What?

My eyes rolled behind my lids.

"Say less. It won't happen again." Jas didn't speak for a spell, allowing for the sound of that stupid ass smoke detector. "I gotta go. Bye."

"Yo," his gentle urgent call had my arm retract. "Everything okay?"

Rolling my eyes again behind my lids, I rubbed my dry lips together. "*It will—*" I swallowed back a cry bubbling involuntarily. "I will be."

He didn't speak right away and that irritated me. "Am I gonna *see*—you got an appointment this morning with the therapist?"

"I canceled."

"Monday?"

"Canceled."

He slowed. "Tuesday?"

"I *can't*—I don't know." Then the stupid tears fell. The last thing I needed was for them to be heard in my voice.

"Witherspoon…"

"Yeah, Jas." *Please!*

"My meditation from this morning, I'm gonna text it to you."

"Bye."

Another pause.

And that damn chirping!

"A'ight."

I hung up the phone and rolled over, hoping to sleep this day away and grateful for my blacked out bedroom. Then my stupid ass cell vibrated. I wished I could have powered it off, but needed to be available for the office. Grunting, I reached for it in the dark of my bedroom.

Jas: *THE LORD BLESS YOU AND KEEP YOU. THE LORD MAKE*

HIS FACE SHINE ON YOU AND BE GRACIOUS TO YOU. THE LORD TURN HIS FACE TOWARD YOU AND GIVE YOU PEACE.

Another text came through before I could finish reading the first.

Jas: *YOU KNOW THE BOOK CHAPTER AND VERSE?*

I rolled my eyes again, tossing the phone across the bed.

"Congratulations to our winter electrical and plumbing trades accelerated class!" our head instructor announced to the tiny ass room packed with a small celebratory crowd.

There were only four of us in this program. Most took on programs focusing on just one trade. I didn't have the time for that shit. I had a plan to implement and wanted to be done with classes as soon as I could. Of course, that meant Juggy had to as well. He would be a part of my executive team soon.

We stood like two proud idiots, holding our certifications to our chests as Man's girl took flicks.

"Let us know if we could be of any assistance to you two." John Hatchet offered us a final shake before going over to the other two who completed the program.

"Damn, I'm so happy to be done with this bitch!" Juggy cried.

"This the last one. Right?" Man asked.

Juggy's big ass eyes shot over to me. "Should be."

I snorted at his complaint.

Man pulled his girl into his side, and she wrapped her arms around his waist. "So, what do two extra certified niggas do to celebrate?"

"Shiiiiiit!" Jug groaned. "After this crazy schedule we been on, I'm 'bout to celebrate between a pair of legs out this bitch."

We all laughed at his dry but very honest humor.

"Who?" Man's brows met. "Brina?"

"Whoever answer my call, nigga." Laughing, he turned to me. "You wanna pull up on Cynthia? You deserve a celebration, too, Sin."

Cynthia was out with her cousin, buying decorations for an aunt's retirement party. "Nah, man."

"Maria?" he asked. "There's gotta be some chick you wanna celebrate with, ock. Somebody to rub ya back and say how hard you worked on this shit, man."

"How 'bout we get out of here and ride by that Oakland site to see if the windows are up and sidewalk and driveway been poured. After that, you can dump me at the crib and turn up for the rest of the night." Jug shook his head, taking off and leaving Man and his girlfriend cracking up behind him.

Chapter Ten

FEBRUARY | PRESENT DAY

jaz

JUGGY HELD THE FLASHLIGHT AT AN ANGLE AS I CLOSELY INSPECTED the thoughtful design brushed into the concrete driveway.

"Yo, Nicky's broom game is meticulous as fuck," Juggy muttered. "You 'on't even see a break in them fuckin' waves."

"Been at this for close to eighteen years, which is why I have no plans to clip the unproblematic old heads. They're needed to teach the new ones coming in." I scratched the tip of my nose. "I hope Jamal was here watching. Dude's gotta steady hand, too. He just needs to learn technique."

"That's what the fuck you call them rainbows?" He referred to the arc designs etched into the concrete. I nodded, peeping the edging of the parameter. Jamal, a former burglar kid from ATL, had a steady hand in plastering. If he tried, he could do intricate designs like this, too. "Yo, man, Sin, I be forgetting how smart you was in school. 'Member your pops transferred you that time in junior high to that brainy zany ass school over here in Jersey?"

I snickered. *Ellis Academy's* honors program was top in the state and top five in the country. It wasn't easy for my pops to get me in. And it didn't help I was mad as hell when he did. He fucked up our powerplay on the streets when we called ourselves pushing dime bags of kush.

"That was some bullshit." The start of a journey for me, little did we all know.

"And when you went to college. That shit was fuckin' up money, you heard?" He shook his head, chuckling.

A phone chirped in my pocket. Patty from Passaic texted me thanks, saying she got a roofing trade gig at *Witherspoon Homes*. That reminded me of a text I got a few hours earlier while finishing up on my final assignment from Leon Cook from Paterson. He hit me up about getting hired there, too. There was no time to consider the text and I'd forgotten about it.

Damn…

I made a quick decision to call her and not because of the quick hiring play, but because when I called yesterday morning, she seemed off.

Damn…

I tapped her cell phone. The call went straight to voicemail. I tried again to get the same results.

"You good?" Juggy asked.

I nodded, then thought to call her house phone. After motioning to Juggy, we took off for the van. I only wanted to be sure the site had been progressed so we could invite prospective buyers to view it.

"Hello?"

This wasn't Witherspoon. The voice was gruff and less sharp.

"Is *Wither*—Ashira home?"

There was a pause before she demanded, "Who's calling?"

My eyes rolled to the passenger sideview mirror. "Jas."

Another pause. "Are you the beefy youngster over last week? "

Beefy?

Youngster?

"Yeah. I guess I am."

"Why don't you stop by?"

My forehead stretched. "I was just calling to—"

"She's not taking calls."

"A'ight. Then I'll wait till—"

"Stop by."

"You said she ain't taking calls."

"I know what I said, young man."

"Okay…" I tried understanding what the lady was saying. "She 'on't want no calls, but you're saying…"

"Stop by," she repeated.

"You think she wants company?"

"No. But stop by."

"I'm sorry." I scoffed, not wanting to be rude. "But this ain't making no sense."

"You ate up all of my rapini."

As Juggy turned on a yellow light, I thought for a minute. "The food was good."

"I'll make you more tonight. Stop by." She hung up the phone.

I took a deep breath and without rhyme, but with reason, my damn stomach growled.

"Hungry, yo?" Juggy asked. "I can stop by *B-Way Burger* on my way to drop you off wherever." He was ready for his personal time, I understood.

"Yo, bust a U'ee here and let's pull up on ol' girl in Edgewater."

"Oh, word?"

I nodded, not knowing what the fuck I was doing.

From the moment she opened the door, a whiff of cooked herbs blasted into the hallway. The woman looked the same: caramel skin, short beach blonde hair molded to her head, black sweater and pants covering her slender frame. Her shoulders curled a bit and she moved slower than a woman with her appealing build should. Unlike my first visit last week, the spacious apartment was dim. Even without the sitting room, vestibule, and living room being lit, the ambiance still reeked of upper-crust society. That had me questioning my reasons for being here again.

She stopped at the balcony doors. Looking through the open curtains, I peeped Ashira's small frame curled on the patio sofa. She was wrapped in a big ass coat with a hoodie while smoking a cigar. Next to her, on the coffee table, was a tall sexy stemware and bottle of wine. Old school R&B cracked the cold air. Brownstone's "*If You Love Me*" crooned from the speakers she clearly had out there.

"Your friend's here, Sh-Shi," the older woman announced. "Checking on ya."

Ashira blew out a puff of smoke, allowing it to expand in the cold still air and dance over her head. "Who?"

The woman looked at me from head to toe. Then she turned back to the open door pushing glacial air inside. "The one who don't like vegetables but love my rapini."

Ashira's body whipped around, the hood hiding half her face as she looked at me. "Over fifty dollars? It was only a nineteen-dollar bill. If it bothers you that much, 'Jas', just leave nineteen dollars and eighty-two cents and we'll be fine."

My head popped back, damn face went hard. "Witherspoon, I ain't come over here over no bill, and if you wanna shell out fifty bucks at a fundraiser for me and my shorty, that's on you."

"Then what are you here for?"

"He came to check in on you, child." The older woman stepped up for me.

But Witherspoon turned back, facing the open black sky, and puffed on her stick once more before blowing it out. "I'll be in when I'm done out here. Feel free not to wait, Mr. Petty. You're a long way from Harlem."

"Say less." I backed away, ready to leave.

"I'll take your coat." The woman stretched her arm to reach for it.

"Nah. It's all good. She ain't beat, and I'm not the one for pushing."

"Coat, young man," she insisted. "I told you to stop by. You have, and I've cooked. She damn sure ain't gonna eat it. Coat."

Taking a deep breath, I pulled out of my coat and handed it to her. Then I shot Juggy a text telling him to leave. I didn't know how long I'd be here, but there was no need to hold up his celebration. I'd figure out my transportation home.

I wiped my mouth while chewing as the older woman returned to the dining room. The same space I'd shared with Witherspoon last week. She placed a platter of biscuits in front of my plate.

"I know you're about through with your food, but I remembered I baked those yesterday and the poor girl won't likely eat them. No need for it to go to waste."

She hardly looked me in the eyes before turning for the door. "What's your name?"

The woman turned back. She made eye contact for a few seconds before they went to the floor. "Ines."

"Ines. Is that with a Z?"

She shook her head. "Sounds like it, but no. Momma wasn't that sophisticated." A phone rang over the table. "Which one is it?" She referred to my two phones.

I snorted before picking up my mother's call. "Ma."

"Hey, Sin."

"Whaddup?"

"Whatchu doin'?"

"Eating?"

"What?"

"Some beans, rice, greens, and fried chicken."

"Beans? Greens? What kinda beans?"

Before my attention could get back to Ines, she answered, "Field peas and okra."

"Field peas and okra," I repeated.

"And you like that slimy okra?" Slimy? I did taste something silky and stringy, but it was flavored so well, I didn't mind. "Damn! And what kinda greens?"

Ines answered again. "Turnip."

"These turnip?" I asked in disbelief.

Ines nodded, eyes low, then left the room.

"Boy, you eating peas and vegetables? That coochie must be good!" She laughed. "She only got you to eat it because you still kinda fresh out and still ain't used to pussy." My mother laughed her ass off.

"What you need, Charmagne?"

"Damn, boy!" she choked out, hardly able to breathe. "Let me stop. I need fifty dollars."

"For what?" I bit into the chicken.

"For some shoes."

"I'm sure you got lots of shoes."

"Damn! For Sunday. They throwing a jam at *The Pub*, and I wanna be right for it."

"It's not the first, Ma. And this is the shortest month of the year."

"The hell? Boy, I know what day it is…what month it is!"

Here she go…

I blinked. "Ma, you get a thousand dollars every month and you don't have to worry about one bill. It ain't crazy for me to clock you." Then something hit me. "You keeping ya nose clean, right?"

"Oh, we doing that now? Don't disrespect me, boy! You sounding like Mark Sinclair. That nigga think he better than me. Fuck you if you think you is, too. I ain't having that shit. I'm ya mother."

"Yes, you are. And now you're disrespecting me."

After a few beats, she muttered, "Sorry, Sin. But damn, can a bitch breathe?"

I was over the conversation. "I'll *Cash App* you fifty now, but this better stretch over nine days."

"A'ight, Sin. Damn!"

"Love you, Ma."

"Yeah."

She hung up. Breathing out the heap of toxicity she'd just thrown at me, I sent her the money. After I was done eating, I thought to go check on Witherspoon. She was in the same place with a new cigar. The bottle was damn near empty. It was after eight and my damn body was preparing to shut down. *"TeachMe"* by Musiq Soulchild was in rotation. I couldn't do this shit. I wasn't that kind of man, and damn sure wasn't hers. I wouldn't know where to begin. A part of me had hope the first Witherspoon I peeped when we first met would rise up and get her out of this funk.

Yeah...

That was it. I turned back for the dining room. Witherspoon would have to take a piss soon. I'd just wait. All she needed to resume her snappy, fire-spitting persona was to see me in her home.

My phone ringing had my head shooting up in the dark living room.

"Yeah?"

"I'm here, bruh."

"Coming down."

It was close to eleven at night and Witherspoon was still on her balcony. Just to be sure I didn't miss her going to bed, I did a check again. Ines, coming from the other end of the apartment, must have had the same agenda because she met me there. As Mary J. Blige's *"I Can Love You"* bumped from the speakers, Witherspoon was in the same position without a cigar and the wine was all gone. I wondered what had her fucked up like this. Did she do this often? It was still tripping me out that Ines insisted I come over. Either way, it was time to go now.

"My ride's downstairs," I announced my leaving in little words.

"I'll get your coat and lock up after you." She trailed behind me.

"I think she wanted to be alone so I didn't wanna not honor that—"

From behind me, she made so clear, "She knows you were here and for her."

"Is she gonna be alright?"

"Call me and I'll let you know."

She handed me my coat from a closet near the front door.

"Thanks for dinner," I offered from the doormat. "I appreciated it."

Without looking at me, she returned, "If you really did, I'll hear from you."

Not understanding what that meant, I turned for the elevator.

"*Haaaaaa…*" Cynthia sighed, gazing out to the water. "I will never get over this view."

Biting my cuticle, I agreed. "Gorgeous, right?"

She nodded with a soft smile and I cupped her shoulders, standing over her stocky build. I had no idea where this friendship would go, but my patience at being single was growing mad short. Cynthia was a good-looking girl, had an education, a career, and wanted children, which was all great. She was family-oriented and looked forward to being married and exchanging nuptials at her church, making a big deal of it. I could get with that. But there was still something I was unsure of and I couldn't quite call it yet.

Her ass meeting my resting cock had me backing away a few steps.

I shook my head behind her. "Come on. I got a call I need to make."

Cynthia followed me inside where my mother was seated. "That view!"

"Ain't it all that, girl!" my mother agreed with her, eyes bouncing between the two of us. "Y'all need some privacy to make some babies?"

I shook my head, walking past to leave the room.

Cynthia, giggling, sidled next to her on a barstool. "I follow this page on *IG*. It's called *Houses of the LBU*. Ms. Charmagne, it's got every type of luxury house you could dream of. That's what this place is giving me."

Pulling out my cell phone, I called Witherspoon's house number. "Hello?"

"It's Jas. How is she?"

"Still the same."

"The same?" When I called last night, Ines said instead of moping on the terrace, Witherspoon was eating in her bedroom. We agreed she was on the mend.

But the same?

"She's back out there with her *Por el Amor del Amor* and a fresh bottle of *Château Blevin*."

At two o'clock on a Sunday afternoon? Today was the best day to reset and refuel for the new week. The day to get the Word and apply it to your journey. The fuck was she thinking? Irritation abraded my damn veins. I didn't even know this chick, but felt she was wasting time on unnecessary emotions. Nothing was worth taking a pity break from life.

"A'ight. I'll be by in a couple of hours."

She sighed. "I'm whipping up something."

I didn't have the heart to tell her it wasn't necessary, and didn't even know if the food was for me, so I ended the call without mentioning it. I didn't even know who the lady was to Witherspoon.

"Yo, Sin." Juggy craned his neck inside the room. "I'mma head over the bridge to go fuck with Jos-Renee."

"You still fuckin' with her?"

"You know how it is." He scoffed. "Some shit don't make sense, but it still stay lit. Anyway, you good?"

"Nah. Take my moms. I'mma drop Cynthia off and then I gotta make a run to Edgewater."

His brows shot up. "Edgewater, Edgewater?" I nodded, feeling agitated, which wasn't my style—especially on a fucking Sunday and because of a broad I didn't even know if I particularly cared for. "What's up with that?" he asked about my relationship with Witherspoon.

I shook my head. "Some bullshit."

"A'ight. Let me go get Ms. Charmagne. I'll see you in the morning."

He was off for the kitchen, and I was a few steps behind him to collect Cynthia.

When Ines let me into the apartment without a word, I headed straight to the balcony. It was over an hour later and I was even more vexed than earlier, having to drop off Cynthia and not explain why it happened so early and suddenly. Now, *her* shit was affecting my life.

I pushed open one of the doors and before I could even see her face, I ripped into her ass. "Please tell me this ain't about ya nigga. I been feeling that in my gut on my way here. All this sulkin' shit is because of you and that lil' nigga arguing over what?" I pushed my hands into the pockets of my sweats and leaned down to get face-to-face level with her. "He's too busy? He works too much? Was his late Valentine's Day celebration not magical enough? Did he forget to name you in his last acceptance speech?"

With heavy eyes and a tight ass face, Witherspoon roared, "*No!*"

"Okay. Is it that he can't drop everything on a whim to join you on your next excursion?"

"Fuck you. You don't even know me!"

"You're right, Witherspoon; I don't. But I've learned enough to know this sullen shit ain't you."

"And what's that supposed to mean?"

I stood straight, shaking my head at the water view. "I 'on't know. Maybe I've been off with my perception of you these past few weeks."

"What perception?"

"That you were a boss madam—a bad bitch—who not only takes the world by storm, but does it on her own terms. The same boss bitch setting trends for wannabes who'll never be able to wipe your ass with their ten-dollar an hour pay. You just don't make the rules for others, but break them bitches to right the world for yourself as you see fit. The madam that makes dreams happen for people, but *is* the dream for any man so fuckin' lucky, which is why I can't buy this teenage girl first heartbreak shit. Whatever went down was not all that serious. Now, say the fuck less, act the fuck less, and get it *togeth*—"

"*He cheated on me!*" she screamed. "I walked in on him cheating on me. And not with a busted ass, broke, ten-dollar an hour bitch." She spit, "No. This one is arguably the baddest bitch on the planet. The one who makes my salary combined with my trust fund equal ten dollars an hour when compared to her wealth." Pain flashed in her eyes. "I guess…" Witherspoon hesitated. "I guess I know what it feels like to be basic. So fuck you for acting like you know a grown ass woman with a broken heart."

Shit…

She was right: I hadn't been expecting that.

I squatted, hands on my knees to get into her line of vision again. "Who could possibly be badder than—" I stood, her image immediately flashing in my mind. "Brielle's flawed, too."

Witherspoon's lips pouted and she rolled her eyes away. "How did you know it was her? Because she's the baddest bitch on the planet." She scoffed, "See!"

"Because that's who I heard people asking you about him doing the movie with." Plus, Cynthia wouldn't stop talking about the movie with her being the biggest Brielle fan. *His stupid, weak ass…* He had to be weak. A man unable to control his urges and wanting extra servings of cake to eat it too was, by all measures, weak. "Brielle's bad, but she ain't every man's dream."

Her head swung back. "What?"

I shrugged. "She ain't the only one on that bad bitch level. You got Pixie and Alana from England. Hell, even Ameerah's more up my alley than Brielle."

"How?"

I shrugged again, feeling weird as hell in this conversational space. "She's…earthy. Low key beauty. Humble, nerdy talent. She ain't on stage gyrating her ass. Her dopeness has a veil."

"That's what you look for in women?"

I thought for a minute. "I guess. My preference is for a woman who saves all her sexuality for me only."

There was an uncomfortable spell of silence as I thought over my words. My shit ain't have nothing to do with Witherspoon's. I didn't like her flipping questions on me.

"You're not helping." She shook her head. "Say less."

"Exactly, man," I exhaled. "It's freezing out here. You need to shake this shit off."

"Why?" she shouted.

"Because you're alive!" I barked back at her. "In ya right mind—"

"Oh!" She laughed, clowning me. "And free. Right? I'm alive, in my right mind, and free. How deep is that, Jas?"

"Nah. Ain't nothing deep about it. They're all facts, and that's all you need to reclaim today…tomorrow…next week!" Then I tried from a different perspective. "Lamentations three. *Through His mercies we're not consumed. Because His compassions don't fail. They are new every morning.* His mercy and grace are new every day. You're right: ain't nothing deep about that. The truth is simple."

Witherspoon blinked hard as her head bounced back. "The Bible. Really?" Her eyes narrowed tightly. "What's your real name?" When I didn't answer her past a hard ass glare, she sucked her teeth. "Go, Jas. Isn't your Juggy friend downstairs waiting on you?"

I shook it off, my temper still growing. "Go get showered, throw on some clothes, and grab ya keys." I went to open one of the balcony doors for her.

"For what?"

"We're going on a field trip. Somewhere to help you put shit into perspective."

She sucked in a breath. "To a prison? Church? I don't do them joints!"

"Say less, Witherspoon, before I get insulted and change my fuckin' mind."

It took her a few seconds, but finally Witherspoon stood, throwing the blanket on the sofa before marching underneath my extended arm, into the apartment.

love believe

ashira

Holding the screws and nuts while Jas worked on installing another ceiling lamp, I glanced around at the women and children on the monitors. They were either traveling the halls of the building, in the dining hall eating, or in what they called the theater, listening to a comedy show. We'd been here for close to an hour, touring the facility. Jas talked to the building manager about a few things needing to be tightened up as far as the new construction was concerned. He tightened a few doors in the bathroom stalls on the main floor, and now we were installing lamps in the security room. As he worked, I assisted by holding his tools while perusing the monitors.

We were twenty miles west of my apartment in a middle of a nowhere town. The original commercial building was rehabbed and had recently opened for residential stay. So many of the women and kids we passed by recognized me from social media. I didn't like that part. That recognition likely came from Austin. I'd always had public profiles on social media, but my numbers soared when word got out that we were dating. I tried not to change my posting style, feeling that my own lifestyle aside from being his girlfriend was interesting between dancing and the traveling I did. Today, I wished I never opened a social media account although they were before Mr. Seers.

"Alright," Jas grunted high on the ladder. "Hand me a screw."

As I extended my arm, reaching high to pass it to him, I thought out loud. "I've only seen...maybe three men in this building today, you being one."

My attention raced back to the monitors, confirming that theory before Jas could retrieve the screw. Yeah. There was a groundswell of women and children. That's who filled the dining hall when we first arrived.

"That's because the facility services only women and children."

I frowned at him. "Why? To what capacity?"

"It's a safe house, Witherspoon." He drilled the screw into the ceiling.

What?

"How are we in here then?" I'd thought this was a side project he'd taken on and was making final touches to finish his contract here.

"Because I had to do a few things before being done. I actually have another coat of paint I want added to the vanity room. But security starts tomorrow, which is why I'm installing the lamps in here now. When they start, everyone entering will have to be cleared in advance, something like your apartment building." He chuckled.

I rolled my eyes. "They didn't stop you from getting in there."

"Ines was my plug." He winked slickly, making me look away.

I saw the women and children watching the comedienne in the theater. Some laughed, some smiled, and others stared blankly.

Then the scars on a few of the women—hard faces and slumped postures—suddenly all became visible to me.

"Who runs this place?"

"A church out of Harlem. Hand me the last screw."

"They contracted *Rizzo's Custom Homes* to rehab this?"

"Nah. The pastor's wife hit me up. She's Harlem Pride. We go back. I ran into her when I first hit the pavement. Chopped it up with her and her new husband—well, they ain't newly married. Their marriage is new to me. When she told me about her goals of expanding outside of Harlem for the families who needed more of a distance, I told her what I was into and that I would see if we could make something happen."

"So, you made it happen," I murmured, glancing around the brand new security bunker.

"It took a minute, but yeah. They were closing on this property using a shell company for privacy the month I was released."

"How long before you got the job at Rizzo's?"

"Not long. Hand me the nut." As he screwed it on, Jas continued to talk, something I decided I liked right away. "When I got on his staff, I told him I could hand over this project to the firm. It took some back and forth, but eventually he signed on. Took about a year, but finally they're up and running, which is all good. Grab the globe for me, please."

I handed him the final piece for the last lamp. "And you're finally done."

"Nah. I'mma have Juggy come through this week for the painting and a couple other things." Jas began his way down the ladder, peering up at his handiwork.

I swallowed, having a sobering moment. "So you brought me here so I could see how good my life is compared to these women in here?" It had worked. Suddenly, I felt guilty and childish as shit.

"That, and so you could see what real hiding is."

"I wasn't hiding, Jas."

"You were home since Thursday. You mean to tell me you were gonna get up and go to work in the morning?" His expression wasn't convincing.

"I was going to take Monday off only."

"Yeah. Hiding. Cut that shit out. Look… I 'on't know dude, don't know nothing about your relationship—*shit*, I don't really know you—but I do know him or that relationship ain't the end of the world."

Damn, did I feel weak. It made me roll my eyes and turn away from his piercing gaze.

"I'm no damsel, Jas."

"Nah." He shook his head. "I ain't think you were. But we all slip up from time to time."

"Have you…" I bobbed my head to explain. "And don't tell me to say less either."

"Have I what?"

"Been hurt or betrayed?"

His head swung from side to side as his eyes were cast to the left before landing on me again. "Nah."

We laughed together. I thought he was going to share something personal. "You're such a bullshitter."

"I'm not. Deadass."

"Like you've never had a girlfriend—before prison?"

"I did. We were cool."

"Did she write and visit?"

He shook his head. "That wasn't a requirement."

"What do you mean?"

"We weren't that deep in. She was someone I was fuckin' with for a couple of years on and off. And when I knew my bid would be long, I knew no one would do that time with me and shouldn't be expected to."

"Did she at least try?"

"To what?"

"To write and visit?"

"I was in the *FED*s. They say they'll keep you at a specific distance from your home to make it feasible for friends and family to visit, but not for me. I was on two yards and neither was within reasonable distance for people from back home to check in."

"Not even Juggy?"

"Nah. We kept in touch, though. Jug held me down like a soldier. The visiting thing wasn't all that necessary."

"Have you seen her?"

"Who?"

"Your ex-girlfriend? Is she one of your audition girls for marriage?" I busted out laughing, unable to help myself.

Jas chuckled in good fun, too. "Nah. I see her around, but she ain't it."

"What's her name?"

"Shi-Shi."

I laughed and nudged his arm, not realizing how solid the man was. Another sign of his virility. "Stop playing."

"Samona."

"Samona? That's her name?" He nodded. "Do you see her?"

"Every now and again. She's best friends with my cousin. I run into her when chillin' with them."

"And you've never tried to rekindle? She's never?"

Jas shook his head. "I'm on a different journey now, Witherspoon. Shit that used to appeal to me, gives me pause now. *I'm*—"

When Jas noticed my attention had gone to the right of him, he turned to see a man as tall as him, in the doorway. His arms were crossed as he yanked at the ends of his thick, massive beard sporting a smirk.

"Ahhh, man…" Jas whispered, turning for him. "Ezra."

The two thick men met just inside the room for a shake then hug.

"I didn't know you'd be here today," the bearded man rasped markedly. "Alexis said your men were finished."

"Yeah. I wanted to pull up and see what the finished project looked like." Jas' dark, expressive eyes brushed over me quickly and almost shyly. "Glad I did, though. There're a couple of things we need to brush up. But it shouldn't take more than a few hours here. Tamara told me about security starting tomorrow."

The Ezra guy nodded. He looked stately…well postured and fashionable in an off-white cable-knit cardigan, dark trousers, and the same brown *Ferragamo* "Chelsea" boots I'd bought my father for

Christmas last year. His left wrist exposed enough of his *Longines Master Collection*. The man was cultured.

"Alexis isn't happy about the lapse in time. They dropped the ball on having their equipment installed before scheduling their men to actually secure the parameters."

"Oh, wow…" Jas' thick chords vibrated lowly as his eyes toured the room. "Well, at least they have the monitors working."

"Uhn…" Ezra tweeted. "I have a few members of the security from the church volunteering overnight when most of the staff leaves. But even that isn't ideal. This is an undisclosed facility."

I understood his reservations.

And before I could express my apologies for being there unauthorized, a tall woman—even taller than my five feet-eight inch frame—peered inside. Her eyes lit up at the sight of the two men. She sauntered inside, announcing her shapely, ever-feminine build. The woman wouldn't nearly qualify for BBW, but definitely solid, wearing an ivory cashmere sweater, brown trouser pants coating her thick and clearly toned thighs, and heels. I could tell with this one ensemble alone, the woman understood how to maximize her curvy, fit figure.

"Hey!" She smiled at Jas, but sidled to the man, Ezra's, side. "You're still here?"

"Pretty much done," Jas answered. "I peeped y'all on one of the monitors. What're you two doing here?"

"Running a little late for the first bed night. We had dinner with the residents and staff then snuck in for the comedy show. E says she's corny." She laughed. So did Jas, but not Ezra. "I'm sorry. I'm Lex." She extended her arm to me.

"Hi," My brain snapped into action and I met her palm. "Ashira Witherspoon. It's nice to meet you." I went for Ezra's hand next, hoping he'd offer a shake.

"My apologies." He reciprocated. "Ezra Carmichael. It's nice to meet you, Ashira, though Jas didn't make the introduction."

"Well, I'm curious as to who she is," Lex made clear, "so I made it happen. It's a Harlem thing. Haven't I taught you anything? This nigga here won't say ish if he has his way." She laughed in a friendly manner. You could tell there was chemistry here.

"Alexis," Ezra breathed, cupping his face.

Humor etched Jas' face in a way that warmed me.

"You all go to the same church?" I asked, remembering the church was located in Harlem.

Lex laughed even harder. Grinning, Jas shook his head. And Ezra's expression remained placid.

Trying to fight her laughter, Lex's lips turned up. "Permission to speak, Sin——"

Who?

"I'm sorry, Ms. Witherspoon," Ezra remembered my last name. "My wife and I are the shepherds of *Redeeming Souls of Abundant Living in Christ Family Worship Center.* He's our friend we wish would officially join our ministry."

Jas spit out a gut-wrenching guffaw. "Lex Dawg...shepherd with a ministry all right."

"*Fuck yo*——"

"Alexis!" Ezra growled.

Lex took a deep breath, humor still bouncing in her eyes. "I see what you're doing?"

"What am I doing?" Jas asked expressively.

"You're trying to avoid explaining who this cutie with a booty is by making me act a fool so I can get in trouble."

Scratching his brow, Jas chuckled quietly. "Public chastising is better than having it done in private."

"Says who? I prefer mine in private."

"Christ!" Ezra swore beneath his breath, pinching the bridge of his nose with closed eyes.

"I have no idea what that means." Jas' palm was splayed in the air. He turned to me. "Let me get you back home. This concludes your field trip."

"Wait!" Lex chirped. "Ashira, this ya boo?"

I was typically a quick-witted personality, but the chemistry bouncing between this trio was beyond even my court-holding talents. It moved too fast.

"Time to go, Witherspoon." Jas emphasized with a steady hand at the small of my back.

I smiled, not being the one without the last word: a Witherspoon trait. "To indirectly answer your question—keeping with the spirit of Jas—I am not his type." I gave a slight neck bow with a sturdy jaw. "But it was a treat meeting you two."

Ezra's face opened wide as Jas led me out of the room. Lex snickered when Jas called back, "Sorry about all of that, Carmichael. I'll hit you later."

Chapter Eleven

FEBRUARY | PRESENT DAY

Ashira

On my way down the hall, back to the living room, Ines was quietly on my heels. I was too preoccupied with my guest and the activities of my day to acknowledge it. Ambling into the living room, I saw Jas with two cell phones laid out in front of him on my coffee table, but his focus was on one. Had he always had two cell phones? This guy had been such an enigma, I couldn't start making sense of him. My mind had already been reeling with what he'd told me on our way back to my apartment from the safe house.

"I can't believe that was the author." I plopped down on the couch, my knee accidentally brushing against the side of his abs. Reactively, Jas scooted more toward the center of the sofa, demonstrating his preference for personal space. "My best friend, Peach, gotta bone for Carmichael!"

I caught Jas' shocked expression as his head tossed back. "A bone?"

I propped my elbow on my knee as I nodded. Ines cleared off the coffee table, forcing Jas to move the phone his attention was on to the end table on the other side of the sofa. She didn't speak as she sprayed the table down once it was empty.

"Not like that." I couldn't help my eye roll. "That girl respects the cloth *too* much. She's called Peach for a reason."

"What's her real name?"

We'd been back at my place for about fifteen minutes. I lit the fireplace to warm the chill in my bones then changed into my house clothes. The single most perfect addition to my evening would be a glass of wine. Jas not being a drinker had me slow to pour.

Initially, I thought nothing of his innocuous question, then a thought occurred.

I dropped my head to the side. "What's your real name?"

Jas mirrored my actions with his head cocked to the side and nostrils expanding just slightly.

Breaking the tension, Ines asked, "Shi-Shi, you ready to eat?"

"No," I answered rapidly, that quickly annoyed by Jas' abeyance that occurred every ten minutes in our conversation, or, more specifically, when I wanted to discuss anything about him. "But a glass of wine would be great."

She took off down the hall and Jas turned to me with humorous mischief curving his plump lips. "That's what it's like to have someone waiting on you?"

"She doesn't wait on me."

"Then who is she? Why does she cook for you?"

I leaned toward him, over my lap. "You don't get to ask me personal questions but give none of yourself. You're in my home, but I don't even know your name."

"Witherspoon, my name is Jas."

"Is that what your girlfriends call you?"

With a cool nod, he answered with confidence, "Of course."

"Is that what Juggy calls you?"

"No."

My eyes lit with new inspiration. Shock.

"What does he call you?"

Jas scratched his chin, eyes falling away, all the signs of unease. Exhaling deep, he sat back, stretching his arms across the back of the sofa and armrest, and I hoped that was a demonstration of him opening to me just a little.

"Sin."

The muscles around Jas' eyes relaxed, lids lowered, and a flash of a storm lit in his eyes. I saw seductive wickedness, arrogance, and unrepentant pride. DANGER. DANGER! My heart raced immediately. Mouth secreted unbelievably fast to the point of forcing me to swallow.

"*Wha*—" I swallowed again. "Why Sin?"

"Because that's what I was good at. It's what I deposited on the streets. It's what I was known for."

His eyes swept from mine to above my head. Ines had returned with a tray stacked with food and wine. Just as I was about to remind her I wasn't hungry, she mumbled, "Go wash your hands, hun," to Jas.

His expression flipped again. From Satan to saint as he obeyed her, leaving the sofa for the bathroom. Ines set up food on the table. Seafood gumbo, rice, and cornbread. She'd even whipped up her homemade iced tea.

"Just roll the red carpet from the kitchen into your bedroom," I jeered, grabbing the wine glass then bottle.

Ines lifted her piercing gray eyes to me. "Elle called twice. She needs to know how you want to handle this shit."

I poured a glass of my favorite dry red, feeling a sulk coming on. "I'll call her in the morning."

Public relations.

I'm no celebrity!

No more dating public figures for me. It was easy sharing the happiness of the relationship, and now I knew it would be hell exposing the failure of it.

Jas had returned as I'd taken the first sip. The robust aged grapes, nutty, and licorice combo danced on my tongue and raced down my esophagus, warming my belly.

"Damn," Jas thought he whispered. "She ain't have to do all this."

"Seems to me serving you comes natural to ol' Ines. I'm sure you're used to it." Jas replied with a snort. "Does Cynthia cook for you?"

"She has." He went about spooning rice on his bowl.

"How did you two meet?"

"At *Home Depot.*"

"Really?" That surprised me. "I thought it was at church. Thought that was a requirement to join your harem."

The serving spoon full of gumbo was suspended in the air as Jas turned to me, expression wry with his lips turned up. "What's up with your jokes about my dating life? Have I cracked one on yours —before the bullshit with him?"

I rolled my eyes away. He was right. Jas never pried. Never inquired about our chemistry. Hell, he hadn't even asked about what I saw last Thursday between Austin and Brielle. He simply didn't care—not that I exactly cared about Cynthia either. I was just curious…about him.

For the next few minutes, silence shrouded the living room, but peacefully. I enjoyed a couple of glasses of wine while powering on my phone. I'd had it off since waking up this morning to six missed calls from Austin, twelve from his assistant, a voice message and text from someone in Brielle's camp. And now, once the phone was powered on, missed notifications began pinging silently, and mostly from Austin's crew. I didn't want to deal with them. Instead, I took comfort in touring *Instagram*, agonizing over what will be.

The quiet before the storm…

Jas' phones vibrating successively snapped me out of my doleful-ness. He grabbed the alerting one, glanced at the screen, then placed it to the left of his plate. I was able to make out the name *Mom* before it disappeared.

He continued to eat, and damn me for being so nosy. I immediately found it fascinating. He was…*big mon!*, a phrase Corinne often used to describe meaty, masculine men. He was on his second plate, and blissfully ensconced in solitude, eating alone. It was almost as though I wasn't in the room with him, and I was okay with that. It allowed me time to study his profile. Jas' roasted chestnut skin, incredibly thick brows, round smooth lips with a slightly pronounced cupid's bow, and two-inch manicured beard all were what I imagined fascinated those silly women and girls. Again, I wondered about the image of his mug shot photo.

His phone vibrated again, this time with a call. Jas actually checked the caller's I.D. and answered while spooning a mountain of gumbo-stained rice into his mouth. "Ms. Cyn," he droned, garbling around his food.

How cute. Sin and his Cyn…

I mentally rolled my eyes, not missing a second of Jas' chew game. It was quite an event.

"Hey! What are you up to?"

"Eating with a friend."

My pulse raced at that confession. It was a lie. Jas was eating alone. Happily.

"Oh, good! That's one of the things I was worried about. Your mom cooked all that food and you said you'd eat later. Then you told me you had an emergency and we shot out of there so fast."

"My bad." He took a generous bite of cornbread without skipping a beat, and I wildly wondered if this was the sight of a famished Jas in prison. "I got a call. Needed to go see about a homie."

A homie?

Am I the homie?

"Oh." Cynthia didn't sound too satisfied with that answer. Lucky for her, I was no threat to whatever she and Jas had going on. "Okay. I was sitting here eating the strawberry cake Ms. Charmagne made and was thinking about all that. I know she was concerned, too." She softened her inquiry with a giggle. "Oh, and her potato salad is made for kings and queens, not peasants. Whew!"

"She just hit me up."

"About that smoke detector, I bet."

"I have no idea. I told her I'd get to it, though." Rapidly, he stuffed his mouth as she pushed out a feathery chortle. Jas snorted. "I know. It annoys everybody except me."

"I don't know how y'all live with that chirp."

Neither did I.

"Mind over matter." Jas took several quick gulps of his tea, and I was over-the-moon invested in the show of him eating.

It was mesmerizingly satisfying. It was *my* food he was devouring. Ines may have prepared it, but I'd earned the money needed to purchase everything from starch to herb.

"Alright." Cynthia sighed. "I'mma let you guys eat in peace. Call me before you turn in. I'll be up writing."

"A'ight, babe. I'll hit you."

"Bye…" her tone softer than her physical build.

Cynthia was not cute, neither did she have body. She was built like a linebacker. If that was Jas' type, I'd respect it, but I couldn't help but make the observation. The man before me now, inhaling food from my kitchen seemed worldly, youthful, tickled by good ol' millennial spoils. That's in foods, travel, cars, wealth, and top of the line women. Dime pieces.

And Cynthia ain't even a nickel bag…

So, he'd left his family's Sunday dinner, at which was his little girlfriend. That was heady. Jas had been a huge distraction for me today. I appreciated his aggression in getting me out of the house and his obvious humility expressed in sharing his work at the safe house. I may have been on the outside of his personal network, but the guy deemed me important enough to help me out of my slump. That had me thinking.

"What do you like to do for fun—and please don't say church."

While chewing the last of his second serving, Jas chuckled with his profile to me. He cleared his mouth, big fist hovering over his lips. "I don't know, Witherspoon. I like to read. Recently—thanks to Juggy—I've developed a nasty habit of scrolling on *IG*. Is that telling enough for you?"

I leaned over, intrigued. "You're on *IG*?"

"By profile only."

"What's your handle?" I tapped my way to the search box on the app. *Jas on the Gram?* "I'll follow you." He hesitated. "Don't start your privacy shit. You're in my home, eating my food for chrissakes!"

From his profile, I could make out the balls of his eyes rolling up toward the ceiling. "Sin back on the pavement. One word."

My hands couldn't move fast enough. SinBackOnThePavement was indeed an account. A scarce account, too. I quickly exited out, wanting to get back to the matter at hand.

"What do you like to do, as in a hobby? There's gotta be something outside of reading."

He shrugged as a smile broadened his face in a hint of tenderness. Jas then wiped his mouth, tossing the napkin into an empty bowl. "Boating."

"Boats." My face folded in shock-confusion. "You like boats?"

"I like boats, yeah." His head bounced softly, eye crinkled at its corner. "And I like boating."

Oh…

"How often do you boat? What kind of boat?"

"Powered." He smiled while speaking. "Motorboats."

"What makes them fascinating to you?"

Jas shrugged. "The energy of cutting through the wind. Motion of water. The adventure of the distance and location. The stern power drive gripped in your palms. I can ride for hours."

"Just hours?" He nodded. "Have you ever ridden a houseboat?"

Jas turned to me with inspired eyes. "You?"

I shook my head. "My friend, Madison, from school. Her family owned one and would take it out all the time in the spring and summer. They'd pick up relatives in Rhode Island and would coast up to Maine. She used to say it was the most fun."

"Nah. I haven't been on for more than half a day. I want to yacht out one day, but pilot it myself."

My head drew back, eyes blossomed wide. "Really?"

Who is this man?

Jas nodded. "Enough of that." He dismissed the conversation

with the wave of a big hand. "About earlier when I pulled up on you. I should've never rattled you with the bad bitch, madam shit."

"Why?"

"That's Tynisha Lang's mentality, and as funny as she is with it, it shouldn't be perpetuated."

"I don't understand."

"For the people on the show, an emphasis is put on how money, clothes, and the latest designer bags and shoes determine the value of women. And whether or not the man can provide those things to a chick determines his value. It's all bullshit. Bullshit I find entertaining, but not good for the culture. Women, especially, need to be redefined in terms of what they bring to the table."

"What do we bring?"

"I can't say what you bring. I don't know you like that."

"True. But you're a good-looking guy. I see how women look at you. You're kind of single, I guess, and you say you're looking to be married."

Jas shook his head, his eyes spearing me. "I said I'm looking for a wife. Together, we'd make a marriage." Then he cupped his chin, visibly thinking. "I can say I'd like to see women who are built from the inside out. They're more solid that way. If a woman starts her approach to me with what she's wearing, I'm not impressed. We can all have pride in our presentation by dressing it up. But if her conversation is about designer this or that, or she has lofty plans for kicking off her own business without having already put it into motion, I'm turned off."

"What's wrong with a woman wanting to become her own boss?"

"Nothing. But I'm not into young chicks. And if you're twenty-eight and older and haven't begun putting that plan into motion yet, I'm less inclined to believe you."

"But people have extenuating circumstances. What about women with children from previous relationships? Raising just one child can derail career goals."

"I've never been opposed to women with children. But even with that, their mind and lifestyle's gotta reflect a nurturing provider.

Where are her values? On what she's pouring into her kids or what she's wearing?"

"And what about women recently released from prison? Does that ring a bell?"

"It does, and I'm not sure if I could be with a woman after doing hard time."

"That's a tablespoon of judgment dripped with a gallon of hypocrisy."

Calmly, Jas shook his head. "It's being real. I have my mental and emotional scars and handicaps from long-term incarceration. Having two of me interferes with my vision for my life. Is it possible? Yeah. But not for me, no more than me requiring my future wife to have a degree or a damn Olympic medal." A hard laugh cracked my throat. "Do you see how ridiculous it sounds to want qualifications in someone you, yourself haven't achieved?"

I sobered when asking, "Do the women you date know about your felony and time away?"

"It's not something I kick off the conversation with, but if I see potential in the relationship, I share, for sure. I'm not ashamed of who I am. I recognized my lawlessness, did the time, and now I'm moving on."

"Wow..." I breathed. "That's one to live by."

"Something you need to adopt, lil' homie," he returned right away. "I'm not going to ask what you're going to do about your relationship...I don't even have an opinion on it. But whatever decision you make, go into it with the confidence of knowing who you are, owning your actions, and know what you want versus what you need versus what you deserve."

I nodded, absorbing each word of his counsel without blinking. Maybe it was because I was so raw from learning about Austin's shit. Raw and vulnerable. But I was stupidly curious, too.

Licking my lips, I just went with it. "So what do you see when you look at me?"

Jas' face screwed as though I'd offended him. His nose and lips lifted and eyes tightened as he leaned away from me. "Say less,

Witherspoon. I ain't never look at you." *Shit, Shi-Shi!* "That's my time. I need to get to bed."

When he left the couch, I tried snapping out of my feelings. "Oh!" I chirped. "Juggy's downstairs." I offered a smile I didn't feel. "You've got to get back to Harlem."

It was weird to me that Jas didn't drive. How did that work with his employment? Juggy couldn't cart him around from site to site.

And that busted ass creepy white van...

Jas turned to me with an expression of empathy. "I hope I made some sense here to you. Sulking over anybody you think don't give a shit about your feelings is a waste of your time and God's grace and mercies for that day. And the day after. The day after that. And the day—you get the picture." He chuckled.

Say more...

Jas' unusual—*and beautiful*—humor distracted me from the burning question of if I should feel the same about him. Should I not be offended when he rejects my feelings over and over about simply wanting to know more about him? Or had he been keeping me at a 'lil' homie' level? Why did I even care? He was a laborer. And more than that, all men were the enemy to me until further notice. That included my dad.

I offered another smile I didn't feel. "Let me walk you out."

"Can I clean this up?"

I held my palm in the air. "It's the least I can do. I know Ines conspired with you to get through to me. How else would you be allowed in the building? My security's about that life."

Jas scratched his head, pulling in a deep breath. "I'mma plead the fifth on that." Then he headed to the door.

"Night, Jas," I bade, holding the door open for him. "Thanks for today."

"Be good to yourself," were his parting words.

As I locked the door behind him, Ines was headed my way, carrying the cordless.

"It's Elle again."

Taking it from her, I exhaled, "Hey, girl..."

"I just need to know if we're going to make the announcement before my staff clears for the night."

My eyes narrowed. "You guys work Sundays?"

"When our clients need us. This weekend was one from hell over here. I'm ready to go home and soak for a few hours with a martini while relaxing to Marvin Gaye. Alas, I've got diapers to change and bottles to make, and a big back to rub as I whisper sweet nothings in his ear."

Elle Jarreau-Hunter, public relations extraordinaire, and I had been friends for close to five years. We met at an NYC marathon after-party. Elle finished and I did not. But we met at a bar in Brooklyn where mutual acquaintances were hanging out. Elle and I didn't become fast friends. She was a bit closed off for a year or so. Then she met her now-husband, Jackson, and he consumed so much of her attention including work.

Nonetheless, we'd been reliable confidants, and the moment I began dating Austin, she said if I ever needed any mass messaging or pointers for how to deal with the press to let her know. I think she left out what I'd need when we broke up. Even if she had that in mind with her offering, Elle didn't mention it. But she was the second person I thought of as my world was on a fast descent Thursday into Friday. I finally called her last night, leaving a superbly detailed message. She'd been trying to return my call all day.

Now, for the final call…

I sighed, shoulders caving as the weight of what I was about to do crashed on me. "I can't take him back after this shit, Elle. Cheating? And then on top of that, you're fucking Brielle? I'm licking the wounds on my damn ego now."

"I'm sorry, Shi-Shi. Really, I am." Her tone was magically soothing. "If you want to sleep on this another night, I can hold off until then."

It sounded like a logical idea.

Whatever decision you make, go into it with the confidence of knowing who you are, owning your actions, and know what you want versus what you need versus what you deserve. Jas' haunting wisdom rumbled into my psyche as though they were fresh off his lips.

Inexplicably, my head bounced in small increments before I declared, "Let's do it. I'm done with Austin."

My heavy eyes fluttered open at the alarming sound of Ines opening my bedroom door. "The phone's for you."

What?

The moment I thought to ask myself who could be calling at this ungodly hour, his name flashed in my brain.

"Did I wake you up?"

"A bigger question: why in the hell are *you* up?"

I could hear his cool scoff, "Man, I been up. I'm always up early."

My face wrinkled. "Doing what?"

"Praise and worship...working out. Were you sleep?"

"No. Just trying to get my shit together to leave the bed."

"Leaving the bed to resume life, I hope?"

That damn chirp in his apartment sounded, fueling my morning grumpiness. "It's five thirty-seven in the morning. Have you no mercy?"

"I do." He chuckled, morning vocals velvety and almost indecent. "And remember your mercies and grace have been renewed, too. Know that when you leave your crib for work and whatever the hell else you chicks do in the course of your days."

"Right now, I'm going to pee. Then I'm going to therapy. That'll be followed by work and more work at the studio." Rubbing my tight nose, I was dismissing him.

Again, Jas laughed throatily. "I'm glad you're going back. My appointment's this afternoon. Enjoy your day, Witherspoon."

I yawned. "Yeah. Yeah. Yeah. Tone down that morning cheer, guy."

"Bye, Witherspoon."

Disconnecting the call, I tossed the cordless to the other side of my bed.

My head bobbed and shoulders rolled to Cheryl Lynn's *"Encore"* as I leaned over the counter. The song always lit a fire in me, even if low key because my mother loved it when I was coming up.

"You must dance in your sleep." Peach shook her head, snickering.

I didn't realize it was that noticeable. Winking at her, I swung my ass before dropping down eagle style and gyrating with one hand in the air. It garnered a deeper chuckle from her.

Corinne laughed. "Don't get her ass started. The bitch dances more than she talks."

"It's communication in a way, and I love it," Peach approved.

I stood, taking a deep breath. It wasn't beyond me that I looked better than I really felt. Coming to Corinne's adult store tonight was supposed to break up the monotony of my schedule these past two weeks of therapy, work, and the studio. I'd been antsy, laying low since the announcement of Austin and my breakup went public. I hadn't been to the club or on vacation. I buried myself in the mono-chromaticity of the life I'd been working on enhancing. Boy, had that come to a halt.

"Just like I love y'all for stopping by randomly," Corinne cooed in a voice mimicking a baby. "It's always heartfelt. Especially you, Peach."

"Especially her?" I cried. "I brought *Niña's Sweet Cakes!*"

Corinne's head fell to the side. "You know she's America's next pope and you wanna compare cupcakes to that sacrifice."

"Do you know how long I stood in line in one hundred-twenty millimeter *So Kates* for them?"

Her smile was wicked. "You stand and twerk in them effortlessly.

Just a brilliant talent you are, girl!" I playfully narrowed my eyes at her. "You know Peach has an image to uphold. Each time she comes in to support me, she's telling those closed-minded, blue-ball, Bible-thumpers to kiss her ass."

"This is true!" With poked lips and hiked brows, I nodded.

Opening an adult store had been Corinne's dream since I could remember. She worked hard to pay off her student loans early—not that she had a lot to begin with as her mother was a welfare recipient, qualifying her for more grants than loans in the state of New Jersey—to free up her credit for this. She planned out everything and was able to open this place a year ago. Of course, we stopped in every once in a while. We had to show her love. The shit was inspiring.

Peach rolled her eyes at Corinne's description of her cohorts. "That's a new bronzer, Shi-Shi?"

I nodded, attention snatched at the sound of the chime when two white women walked inside. They began snickering the second their big eyes took in the entrance laid out with mannequins dressed in simple female maid and male biker costumes. It wasn't until you passed to the rear of them you'd see the thong on them both. One of the women wore a trench coat, relaxed blue jeans, and dirty ass sneakers. The other clutched her *Coach* bag close to her belly. Their hairstyles seemed to be a revisit of the nineties era.

"A Thursday night in Lodi," I sighed.

"Hey…" Peach laughed. "If those married women wanna spice up their sex lives, I'm all for it."

"I got something to spice up your sex life." Corinne hit Peach with the tiger growl. She left from behind the counter and picked up a small box from a display not too far away. "This." She handed it to Peach.

"The *Calla Lilly*," Peach read the box.

"Is that like the *Rose* thingy?" I asked. Corinne, with a beam, nodded. "I heard that *Rose* is the truth! What's the difference?"

"The *Calla Lilly* provides anal stimulation, if that's what you're into."

I elbowed Peach. "You like anal play, girl?"

"Shut up, Shi-Shi!" Peach rolled her eyes, flushed. "You into anal play?"

"I'm into it all, darling!" Corinne flipped her imaginary hair. "As long as one of us is getting off, I'm down."

I winked wickedly. "What if there are three of you, but only two of them getting off?"

Corinne shrugged. "As long as I'm next or was first, I'm game. I had this Italian nigga at my head and a Russian behind me, girl, and was going the fuck off so good! When I tell you they both shot out at the same time, twisting my size eighteen ass like a fucking rag."

"Ewwww!" Peach cringed.

"No ewww!" Corinne corrected her. "The reward for that will have your dead head spinning. I came so many times that morning, I thought you'd be doing my eulogy the next damn day!"

I fell out on the glass counter, laughing my ass off.

"Corinne!" Peach admonished.

"Peach!" Corinne's brows were peaked in warning. "Your body is like a canvas and can be used for art. Look at what *Basso* did for his summer line. He painted Pixie's naked body. Did you see the details in the flowers he added in her pelvis?"

"Gorgeous," I agreed.

"People use their body for beautiful things all the time. If we all received pleasure, what's the harm?"

"I'm not going there." Peach dismissed the start of a potential argument and I was glad.

"Someone told me that once."

"What?" Corinne asked me.

"That my body—my dancing—was tasteful art."

"Who?" Corinne wanted to know. "Sergio?"

Smiling, I rolled my eyes. "He's been so far up my ass since…" I bobbed my head.

"Say it," Corinne pushed.

"Yeah," Peach agreed. "We can give that thing power by bypassing it. Say the words, Shi-Shi."

"Since breaking up with Austin," I enunciated each word. No, I didn't like saying it. The shit was fire on my tongue. Nonetheless, it was a decision I still hadn't regretted. "He's been trying to come by."

"Red flag!" Corinne blurted.

"For real. I'm like, 'can a bitch get dinner and flowers before you try to stick your dick in me?' Sad thing is, Serge is cool. He's even offered to help me open a club."

"He owns *Club Sin?*" Peach asked.

"I don't think so. I just learned recently he has a boss."

"He's been there for a few years," Corinne noted. "It's good to know people in high places. I can't wait to find me a man with deep pockets."

"I want a man who's a student of the universe God has created," Peach added.

I snorted, "I don't exactly want a man right now, but the first thing on my list would be fidelity. The second, third, and fourth would be wealth—he's gotta have his own—incredible sex, and…" I thought for a minute. "Some moral base. His values have to be on point."

"So, it matters that he can fuck." Corinne lifted her palm for a hi-five and I automatically reciprocated. "That's my girl."

"I didn't think that was important before, but now?" I did the Gammy *Red Table Talk* index finger erecting while licking my lips. "I may be able to settle with Super Dick and be over finding my knight in shining armor."

As Corinne cheered me on, Peach sighed. "No, Ashira. Don't you want a family?"

My lips poked into the air. "I can get a dog."

"Or a cat," Corinne suggested.

"I'm allergic to those things." I shook my head with closed eyes. Cats were irritants.

"Okay." Peach shrugged with her lips. "Then let Super Dick accidentally drip a baby in you and I bet you'd suddenly miss your knight in shining armor. Super Dicks don't make for good community dwellers. At the end of the day, it's about community."

I cringed. "You sound like someone I know with that community shit."

"Who?"

"Who dat?" Corinne jeered.

I laughed. "Jas."

"Who's Jas?" Peach wanted to know.

My hand thrashed in the air as I tried to think of her name. "The guy I served at the singles event the church had." Then it came. "Cynthia's boyfriend."

"Who's Cynthia?" Corinne asked just as she caught the attention of customers needing help. "Excuse me for a minute."

"Oh," Peach chirped. "You know him, know him?"

I shrugged. I mean, how could I answer that? I didn't know, know Jas, but had spoken to him just about every day since he left my apartment over two weeks ago. It was mostly through text because we hadn't run into each other in the mornings for therapy but for two times, which was last week. Jas had still been an enigma. Our texts' length and depth varied. Some days, I'd check in with him or Jas would send a text asking if I was 'good,' and that would be the extent of the conversation. Others were more revealing. I learned last week Jas didn't belong to an actual church, per se. He regularly watched Pastor Carmichael's sermons and would, on occasion, attend Bible study. He preferred the latter because Jas felt it was less formal and not as well-attended as Sunday services.

"He said you're a prolific preacher?" My grin was filled with pride.

"Who?"

"Jas."

"Oh, so you do know him?"

I shrugged. "We attend the same therapist."

"As in sessions together?"

"No. We run into each other at a coffee shop across the street. Sometimes, he's gracious enough to hold conversations. Other days, he's a closed book."

"I heard he was locked up for a while. I couldn't tell by his mannerisms."

"How can you tell?"

Peach shook her head. "I don't know. Long-term incarcerators typically have a dimness to them. They also have a huge adjustment period…acclimating to technology, gaining a job, and few are able to have full-blown careers. The few who are successful are self-employed."

"I thought that was weird, too."

"What?"

"The fact that Jas has the same laborer's job he's had since being released. In my line of work, they bounce around." I knew he mentioned wanting to have his own builder's firm. "Maybe he's that passionate about construction."

"Or home building. Cynthia mentioned him frequently sharing pictures of his projects."

My face folded. "He's never shared any projects with me. Maybe because I'm the competition." I shrugged, finding that plausible.

"You're also not his girlfriend." Peach didn't look at me when she stated the obvious. In fact, she didn't look at me for seconds after.

"I didn't say I was." Being melodramatic, I blinked excessively. "Why would you mention the obvious?"

Her eyes rolled up. "I think I'm being extra-cautious. I just don't want this to become a complicated scenario, seeing Cynthia is a parishioner at my church and you're my best friend."

I leaned away from her. "Nobody's taking your tithe-payer's boyfriend, Peach!"

Peach scoffed. "Stop it, Shi-Shi."

"No. You stop it. I'm insulted."

"Don't be." She finally met my affronted gaze. "I saw you two that night. I saw your chemistry. I'm not accusing you of anything. I just…"

"Just what?" I demanded.

She shook her head. "I'm just being extra. I'm bugging, Shi-Shi." Her jaw tightened. "And I'm sorry. I know you better than that."

I honestly didn't know what to say.

Chapter Twelve

MARCH | PRESENT DAY

"MY BAD?" I BLINKED AT THE AUDACITY, HOLDING THE OFFICE phone to my ear.

"Witherspoon, it was an oversight."

"Oversight my ass, Ms. Miller. You were told of your mistake two weeks ago—no," I skimmed through the pages of notes for the project, "it was, in fact, eighteen days ago. That means it's only been three days shy of three weeks, Ms. Miller."

"They haven't moved in yet. It'll be another three weeks. It's on my schedule to correct. My old man said your father never made a big deal about the time as long as I got it done."

The hell?

I leaned closer over my desk. "My father ain't here, Miller, but yours still is. He hasn't quite retired from the business and left it completely to you. And you know what else your father has never done, that I'm aware of, after working with him all these years? Made the egregious error of placing builder's grade cabinets in a home requesting custom-built ones. The Gonzaleses bring family and friends there at least twice a week to show off the progress. The wife's a lawyer. Do you want to know what her tone is like each time she asks when the cabinets will be fixed?"

I was seething at this point. I liked Shawn Miller, I really did. But I didn't like incompetence, laziness, or comparisons of my father and me. And with her being groomed to take over her father's cabinetry outfit within the next year, she shouldn't either. Our firm had contracted with Donald Miller for a quarter of a century now. I'd had to disrupt the trust and good practices that had been built year after year.

Shawn Miller sighed. "I'll try my best to get someone over there this week."

"I didn't ask for your best, Shawn. I asked you to get it done."

"Fine!"

I hung up the phone and slammed the folder shut. Inside my office was an inferno, thanks to the nasty calls I'd been making virtually since walking through the door. The urge to comb my face with my palms came, but I remembered my makeup, so I rolled my neck instead. The tension there couldn't be ignored. I'd have to schedule a massage soon.

But first, work...

Just as I was reaching for another file, I caught a woman meandering past my office door, expression fixed into a dark scowl. She was light-skinned, a full head of salt and pepper curls, wrinkled skin in her face, and dark half-moons beneath her narrowed eyes silently brushing over me. A tendril of fear ran my spine. But even amid that was darkness to her aura.

"Can I help you?" someone had the sense to ask when I didn't.

The woman turned in her overalls and construction boots. And when she spun, I caught the glaring scar of her left cheek.

Patty…

"Hey. Yeah," she grumbled. "Somebody said I needed to come back to sign the rest of my tax paperwork."

"Oh." I recognized April's voice. "That's in human resources. This way."

Patty followed her without another word. Her presence reminded me of the new hires. I'd been getting feedback on all of them over the past three weeks and, so far, they'd been working out.

The phone buzzed, followed by Marge-Jean's voice cracking through the speaker. "Line two's for you. Troy Johnson."

Suddenly, my cell phone rang. Jas' name populated on the screen.

"Tell Troy I'm on a call. The permits have all been submitted. I'll call him tomorrow when I hear more."

"Okay…" she sang in a forbidden way, something she was in an annoying habit of doing.

"Hey," I answered, going into my email to forward Troy Johnson the email about the permits for his client's new property.

"Yo," his subterranean chords always struck me over the phone. "Whaddup?"

"Just working." When I heard the annoying ass chirp from his smoke detector, internally, I rolled my eyes. "Are you still home?"

"Yeah. Am I holding you up?"

"Never." I hit send. "What's going on?"

If it was about another blog post regarding Austin and my breakup or Austin and Brielle being sighted together or Austin being recorded crying to his mother about the breakup at *Urban Grind* in *Blackwood* while visiting his best friend, I had no interest in hearing it. Since I'd announced our breakup on all social media platforms, thanks to Elle's team, the spotlight had been on the both of us. I was sure life had been easier for me because I had a regular-smegular life that didn't consist of red carpets or interviews. Still, I'd been bombarded with calls and texts about the latest speculation as to why we'd broken up. None, thankfully, included the truth—well, all but one.

Months before the breakup, when the movie project was

announced, *Spilling That Hot Tea* posted an ominous write-up about me being careful with Brielle working with Austin. I ignored it, as I did lots of their "reporting" because while they were often on point, most of their gossip was hurtful to its subjects. And lately, I'd been the subject...along with Austin's stupid ass.

"I need...*ummmm*." Jas cleared his throat. "I need some friendly advice."

A scoff escaped my throat. "We're friends?"

"What you think we were?"

"Fellow-patients of a psychiatric doctor."

He chuckled. "Oh. You in joke mode, I see."

I could sure use it after the morning I'd been having.

"It's the least I could do."

"Cute. But *ahhhh*... Nah. I legit need your take as a woman."

"Shoot."

"So... Ol', girl. We were kicking it the other day and she brought up a comment her mom and cousin made about her... breasts."

My eyes rolled from the left of their sockets, up toward the ceiling, then to the right. "Ol' girl being..." Then it clicked. *Big boobs.* "Cynthia. Right. Okay." Cynthia was a big girl. She had to be well in the triple letters.

"Yeah. So they said some shit that's making her feel even more self-conscious about her body. Naturally, I 'on't like it and wanna help."

"Okay. That sounds reasonable."

"Here's the thing: I don't know if it's appropriate, though."

"What?"

"I was thinking about buying her a few bras."

I was so grateful this was a telephone conversation and not *FaceTime* because my face was contorted indecently.

"I don't get it."

"Don't get what?"

"Why it would be inappropriate? Women—myself included— love to see our men...lovers appreciate our bodies enough to gift us intimate apparel. It's a major turn-on. But more than that: if you're fucking, what would make buying underwear inappropriate? I mean, it's not like you're asking if you should forego rubbers for the pill or something." Jas got quiet on me. For a while. I jerked my neck, flicked my free wrist as though he could see me motion him to continue. "You still there?"

"Yeah." He exhaled into the phone. That damn chirping grated on my nerves. *Throw the whole damn smoke detector away!* "You know I keep my personal shit to the chest, but I guess because I brought this up I gotta mention the rest." *What?* "We ain't fuckin.'"

"Okay. I'm sure she wants to as much as you,"—*Although I don't know why you would...*—"so, I would say it's still cool." Jas went quiet on me again. "Okay. If we're going to play the breathing game, can we save it for my lunch hour?"

"My bad." He groaned. "You're right. Thanks."

"For what? I don't feel like I've done anything."

"You did. I'm not gonna get her the bras."

"Why not, Jas?"

"Because it won't be appropriate."

I fell back in my chair. "You're not fucking her."

After a spell, Jas sighed, "Nah."

"And you're not planning to?"

What the fuck, Jas?

"No time soon."

"Why?"

"Say less, Witherspoon," he growled lowly, Harlem accent thick as shit.

Jas was closing up on me, and for some ridiculous reason, I didn't want him to. This Black, former gun-dealing goon saw a therapist and was asking me, a suburbanite, for advice. Jas needed to be supported, not badgered.

"Why are you home at close to ten o'clock in the morning anyway?" I changed the course of the discussion.

"I gotta check in this morning. Don't make no sense to hit my sites then come back this way to see parole." *Then you had time to replace the battery in that damn smoke detector.* "Plus, I woke up this morning feeling off. Like I'm fighting a bug or some shit."

My forehead stretched and finger stopped scrolling the page on the desktop monitor via the mouse. "You're sick?"

"Probably not. Just wanted to chill, take an extra few minutes to see what my body's telling me."

"If it's like a cold or something, Ines has this potion soup. It's famous. Will knock any cold out your system with the garlic, turmeric, and whatever else she puts in there. If you have time, stop by tonight. She'll make you a pot if I tell her now her crush is sick." I laughed silently.

"Cut that shit out." I could tell Jas found that funny, too. "That lady's probably old enough to be my mother: you never know with Black women."

"Nope and it shouldn't matter. I'll call her. She'd love to cook for you again."

"Nah—"

A tapping at my door broke my thoughts of my next call. "There she is!" Cecil was in my doorframe with a stack of folders clutched to his chest, standing on one leg as the other was folded in the air in a cheerleader's pose. Batting his non-existent long lashes, he waited expectantly for me to acknowledge him. Only three people could pop up at my office door and disrupt what I had going on: my father, Marge-Jean, and Cecil Brown. The latter, I would cuss out sideways and only bruise his feelings for a hot three minutes before he'd recover and be ready for the next round.

"Hang on one sec, Jas," I murmured into the phone. Then I shook my head, though Cecil knew I was humored. "I'm sorry. As you can see, I'm on a call," I softly admonished.

jas

"You know what Wednesday is, don't you, Ms. Wealthy?" Dude was not only gay, he was flaming. "I just want to be sure you show proper respect."

I could hear Ashira exhale. "That could have waited until after my call, Cecil."

"It's only a question, girlfriend." He must have stepped closer to her because I could hear him even clearer now. "Plus, I can tell the call is personal."

"How?"

"Because of your posture, Ms. Wealthy. You're a flaming bitch when working, but a wannabe Stony from "*Set It Off*" during off hours."

I could hear Ashira's quiet laughter. She cracked the hell up and he did, too, only louder than her.

Finally breathing, she assured him, "I've got you, Cecil."

"Bitch, God got me; you tolerate me. How?" His delivery was dramatic as hell.

Snickering, Ashira repeated, "Again, Cecil, I'm on the phone. But since you can't wait, I have tickets to see Young Lord—"

"*Ahhhhhh!*" he screamed. "Ms. Wealthy! Oh, how I love thee!" This nigga was, for sure, theatrical. "You know I think I'm from Paterson and married to Austin Seers. Right, bitch?"

"Oh, god," Ashira groaned.

"Well, that was until he got me *fockt* up with that Grammy bitch, bitch!" His voice gained conviction at that point. I blinked at his distinct pronunciation of "fucked." "But for real? We going to see Young live?"

"Yup. Next week, Wednesday in the City. We'll be out on your actual birthday."

I steeled in place.

Next Wednesday. Young Lord?

That was the concert I was expected to be at next week. My crew had planned to pull up.

Fuck...

The last person I wanted there was her. I had no idea why I cared if she knew me, the real me. But for some reason, I didn't want her to. I knew the Ashira Witherspoon type and they weren't built for me. I wasn't for them either. Shit. I'd been surprised we'd been hitting it off like we had this past month.

That's because she don't know…

I was convinced of it. The last thing I needed in my life was someone who didn't matter, viewing me as extraterrestrial. Yeah, we were different. Completely. Yes, I had my shit with me being a felon. But trying to mix worlds with a woman like Witherspoon could potentially fuck with me in the long run. She'd never see past my record and lack of life experience even before me doing time. I had might as well suit back up in *FED*dy's gear, including their jewelry. *Can't forget the cuffs.*

Irritation bubbled in my chest. Why did I call her? Why couldn't I just fall back from Witherspoon? We didn't work together and based on our schedules these past two weeks, we could clearly avoid running into each other for therapy. I knew it was stupid for me to call her.

"You're *wealthy!*" he sang.

"And busy. Please close my door. Thanks!" She was sincere with that last word. "You there?"

"Yeah."

"I'm sorry. Like I was saying: Ines can have it ready for you to pick up on your way back to Harlem this evening."

"And I told you I didn't need her soup."

"Well, damn. I was just thinking of a way to help you and give her something to do."

"Did I ask for help, Witherspoon?" I closed my eyes, pinching the bridge of my nose as I performed, snapping on her again. "Don't you think I could ask my moms to make me soup if I'm sick?"

"I guess. Again, I was thinking—"

"I keep telling you, I don't need you for anything."

"Well, *you* called *me*, *needing* advice if my memory serves me correctly."

I breathed out. "Big fuckin' mistake."

There was a break in time before she grated, "Look. I don't need this shit."

Then the call was disconnected.

I hung my head, feeling like shit.

God, why am I this way?

"She strikes chords with you."

"Who?"

My therapist's head rolled to the side. "Witherspoon."

I scoffed, rearranging myself in my seat. She recited the girl's name as though Witherspoon wasn't her client, too.

"I 'on't know if I'll say all that."

"You said it yourself; you halfway want to be friends with her."

A brow shot up as my face screwed. "I ain't say nothing about being friends. I'm too old to care about new friends."

Her smile was faint, but humor obvious when she corrected herself. "Associated with her. I apologize."

Yeah. *That's more like it…*

I shrugged, feeling irritated all over again. "Yeah. And every time I say to just chill and let shortie fade away, some shit pop up and we're in touch again."

She tabbed into her device. "I think it's a good thing—not you feeling like you can't disassociate with someone you feel is best," she cleared up. "But what you did the other day when you called her."

"What do you mean?"

"Last month, I told you, you need to expand your circle of influence, or rather external influence. I think you calling her demonstrated that."

"All I did was ask her about bras," I explained. "Cynthia's a woman. Witherspoon's a woman—a stylish woman. I just figured she'd know something about how women would feel about a dude they're dating buying them bras." Using my hands to demonstrate two women on each side of me, I went further. "One woman was having self-esteem issues about her size and how she looked in bras." My arms went to the right side of me while seated in the chair. "The other woman's got confidence for days, so I went to her for some knowledge to help ol' girl."

She nodded. "Then you flipped on her."

It was my turn to nod in agreement. "I flipped."

"Can we verbalize why?"

My eyes fell and I scratched my nose. Collecting the thoughts didn't take long, and verbalizing them was even easier. "Because I know her kind, and don't fuckin' trust her."

The therapist didn't react as usual, just sat across the coffee table, eyeing me with no fucking emotion at all.

ashira

"Shit..." I exhaled the second I caught the sight of the enormous floral arrangement crowding my apartment door. "The hell?"

Ines, who'd just exited the elevator with me, froze mid-stride, too. "Did you know about this?"

"I mean... Security called and asked if I'd accept the delivery, but I didn't know it would be all of this." I stepped closer to count the number of vases, it filled the entire entrance of my unit. Roses, lilies, tulips—which were my favorite—and orchids. Red, yellow, blue, orange—too many colors to name. There were several large balloons, too. "This is so unnecessary."

"You think?" she hissed, trying to walk through the maze of flowers.

My head jerked back. "You think I wanted this?"

"You just said you gave security the go-ahead."

"I've not spoken to him in almost four weeks! He's been blocked every way I can think of. I've even blocked his parents! I didn't think a 'little' delivery would end up being a damn nursery, Ines."

"It's what you like."

My neck swung her way. "Excuse me?"

"The grand gestures, the luxury…high expense. You may have broken up with him, but this is what comes with the type of guys you like." She clutched the two paper grocery bags against her chest.

I put one of the two I carried down to get my keys. "So, I'm wrong for dating a guy with money?"

"You don't need to have that be the focus. I know you can't understand that because of how you grew up, but there's more to life and men than money."

"I was right. You *do* fault me for wanting a man who has a life-style mirroring mine."

"No. I'm concerned of your need for all of this instead of simplicity." She swung her head to gesture the wild arrangement.

"I don't just live off my father. I work hard and earn well annually. I'm one hundred percent independent. There's nothing wrong with me wanting a man at my financial level or higher. These bills don't pay themselves. My endeavors aren't free, Ines. There's nothing complicated about that." I found my keys and approached the door with Ines behind me. "What's simplicity to you? Oh, yeah. You gotta soft on for that guy, Jas." I turned to her once I managed the door open. "Is that simplicity to you?"

Ines' eyes rolled away. "I don't know him."

"You're right you don't. You didn't know he's a convicted

felon. Have no clue he used to be a guns dealer. Did ten years in federal prison." My brows plucked into the air. "But simplicity for you is just a good-looking guy who appreciates a home cooked meal? You let him in here. How do we know he won't rob us? Or worse, kill us? He could be a murderer for all we know, but we don't care. All we want is 'simplicity' for Ashira." I scoffed, reaching for the grocery bag I abandoned for my keys. "Ines, I may not be perfect. My lifestyle may irritate you because you can't relate, but I'm secure in the woman I am. I like me. I've always had people try to pick me apart or make me feel shame for my privileged childhood and/or comfortable lifestyle. Please don't make me feel I have to be concerned about that in my own home."

With that, I went inside the apartment to call maintenance. I wanted each petal and balloon thrown in the trash.

"Be my whooooooooore!" we sang along with Ragee as he closed his song.

After many of us belted the famous line with him against others cheering him on, the place went hysterical. Cecil, Shizu, Carlton, Corinne, and I were no different. My free arm shot in the air as I hooted toward the stage. Carlton, Cecil's best friend, clutched his chest with his big palms, eyes passionately closed tight.

"My fucking god!" Cecil screamed, jogging in place. "My fucking god! That nigga is just fucking perfect, bitch! Just perfect. I love when he performs with Lord!" he squealed, high off the charged atmosphere at *Club Sin*.

The place was packed, though arranged differently than it was on regular club nights. It was set up like a concert with chairs lining the dance floor. We had a section in the lounge area. The view was better up here, just slightly elevated from the main floor.

"Bitch, you love Raj by hisself, too!" Carlton corrected Cecil.

We all knew he was for everybody. Cecil loved life and celebrities. We all knew that, too.

"Be careful, Ce," I warned, laughing my ass off. "Your crown is going to fall off."

"This crown!" He clasped it over his head, marking his inebriation. "Raj can have it. Look at that nigga's chest, Shi-Shi!"

It was a marvel. Raj was on that stage sweaty and swollen. His body was on point, and so was Young's next to him, only Young was slightly more slender than Raj's teddy bear frame. Cecil was not alone in lust tonight. The show was coming to a close and boy, had this been the best idea. Young brought out Wally, Alana, and Ragee. Wally was from Paterson, and I'd heard Ragee lived in New Jersey, so their presence in Harlem wasn't a stretch, but Alana was a blue-eyed soul girl from London. She was a complete surprise considering her star level. It went to show Young Lord was an influential artist, pulling off the impossible on stage.

"I would drink a gallon of their combined sweat just to get a chance at one of them!" Corinne shouted to us over the hyped crowd.

Shizu fell into me, laughing. I lifted my cup into the air and used my left hand to whistle to the stage.

"That's all you got for them, Raj," Young Lord asked, teasing the audience.

"That's gotta be all." Ragee's dark eyes beneath his fitted cap deeply gazed the audience. "I see some ladies tonight that's reminding me I need to carry my hungry ass home." He grabbed his crotch, intensifying the curls of his pecs, and Cecil damn near fainted.

"Take me!" he trilled. "Fucking take me now!" Falling back on the sofa, he placed his hand on his forehead.

Carlton fanned him with his hand.

"Get your ass up, birthday boy!" Corinne barked.

Shizu and I couldn't stop laughing.

"God bless, Harlem!" Raj bade into the microphone, lifting one chiseled arm into the air and dropping his chin toward his chest. Then he dapped it up with Young before leaving the stage.

"Harleeeeeeem," Young sang. "We fucked it up tonight." The crowd roared in agreement. The show was everything. "And you know where the fuck we at. Right?" He pretended to look for an answer. Even still, we all applauded. "Yo, check this out. Not only are we in Harlem World, we in the home of one of the realest soldiers to ever do it." The place exploded again. Maybe I was two drinks past my limit because I felt like the only one in the place who didn't know where he was going with the next song. But I decided I didn't care, the atmosphere was that stimulated, so I cheered, too.

Young laughed, leaving one side of the stage for the next. He rested a leg onto a speaker box, leaning into the crowd, topless and glistening. The infamous *I'll Never Love Another Sunset* tattoo was starkly visible, running across his sculpted ribcage. "I'm a Silk City nigga, schooled by the great Supreme Body, you feel me?" The audience hooted, and Cecil and I did, too, as though we knew Supreme. I guessed every Lord fan thought they did. Through his music, we understood his reverence for the deceased street general. "And I was taught when you go to someone's house, you pay homage to the soldier feeding the hood." Amongst the whoops and yowls, Young asked, "Y'all mind if I pay a little respect to that Harlem legend?"

"You betta, Lord!" Cecil demanded as though he wasn't from Teaneck, New Jersey.

Born and raised…

Still, I was all in. I now knew where Young Lord was going. A hit from his latest album called *"Homage"* had been a favorite. The deejay began the track and Young resumed working the stage, seamlessly recited the rhymes we sang along to, sounding just as he did on wax. His energy bounced from the stage and onto the crowd of adoring fans. His stamina exceeded his physical appearance. Young looked as though he could go on for hours more.

We sang along to the song clearly expressing Young Lord's feelings of an immoral industry. But when it got to my favorite part of the track, I performed as though I was an act on the marquee.

"Y'all niggas thinks it's sweet…

Industry niggas be weak.
Too scared to stand on ya on feet.
Y'all niggas with the wave…
Ha! The agenda.
Nah, chill. I'mma behave.
Let a bunch of empty-melanin suits tell you how to move…
They tell ya what to say, what to do…just be smooth.
Fuck that. I got my Ms standing on the industry neck…
Pop my shit then run my mafuckin' check.
Raised by the streets with real block soldiers…
Cut that coke, jack that rope, pay cash for them motors.
Real hustlers, big hammers, salty baby mothers.
Y'all look up to skirt-wearing men…
I pay homage to that gangsta, properly named SIN.
Took out them Polack niggas…"

I swayed my shoulders, swung my arm in the air with my index finger in lead as I screwed my face hard.

"Missed the charges then ate the FED's pen.
Sat quiet, never a rat."

I sliced my arm through the air, super convicted. Cecil and Shizu both turned to me, rapping just as hard.

"Nigga 'bout to hit the streets.
Ran the cellies…now ready to spin the block…
Fuck y'all niggas, jerkin industry cock."

Jumping in my *Saint Laurent* over-the-knee heels, I was hyped. This was my shit!

jaz

Her and her friends, down there mimicking thug niggas…

It was almost laughable. Leave it to Witherspoon to make coming out tonight worth it. Young Lord's people requested me to be in attendance tonight. The nigga always showed love. He understood street codes and ethics, though I didn't need the attention. He was the illest rapper out now. Supreme, a former buyer of mine, would be proud. In a culture now filled with rappers—some good, others not so—influencing the masses, but none living the shit they purport through their lyrics, Young was a real one.

Young put in work before getting into the industry. The nigga could not only still go back home, but he made sure he could visit other hoods and be welcomed with open arms like tonight. Tonight, we had real O.G.s in the building: old school Harlem Pride, lieutenants from Brooklyn, sharks from the Bronx, and killer dogs from Queens. I'd already caught up with them before the show. Up here in the lounge near the office, Man had a feast laid with top-shelf liquor and the loudest weed on the streets. Although I didn't indulge, I had a blast catching up with the goons.

Super O.G., Double E Bags, was in the building earlier. He kicked off the feast with a toast, surprisingly to me, and saluted Young Lord for taking my legacy to pop culture. That was hilarious to me. At least ninety-eight percent of the people listening to "*Homage*" had no idea what or who Young was referring to. Some may have even felt he was being creative and making up a parable.

I snorted, attention still below on Witherspoon and her crew. They were cute, likely drunk and having the time of their lives with no worries. Not one had a clue of the vicious goons in this place, congregated yet strapped and on go for whatever could pop off. Of course, as the "host" of this venue, I had to have shit in place to assure the safety of every patron. Nonetheless, I observed the freedom in which Witherspoon and her friends could thrive in and...envied it. How different my world had been from hers coming up. What she had was exactly the naivety and liberty I wanted for my own children: to live animatedly amongst hidden wolves and remain unscathed.

Young pointed up this way when closing the song had me backing away from the railing. Once out of the spotlight, I saluted him, knowing he could still see me.

Chapter Thirteen

MARCH | PRESENT DAY

ashira

WE TRAVERSED THE PACKED PARKING LOT ON OUR WAY TO THE truck. The show was every bit of spectacular. I didn't want it to end, neither did Cecil. They'd been cutting up since leaving our section in the club. Shizu and I had to pee and that took some time. Now, I was hungry and craving a *B-Way Burger* all the way. Cecil said he wanted the cheesesteak with gravy and Corinne mentioned their loaded fries. Shizu made the call final when she told us she had coupons. That's where we were headed once we navigated out of the busy lot.

We clowned the whole way out of the club and now, being able to breathe fresh, albeit cold air, I was turned up. I ground my hips to the beat Cecil set while Carlton rapped Young Lord's "*Sun Showers*."

"Your mouth open, tongue pushing between your teeth...
My lips moving to your cave, the button underneath.
Tight, growin', and swollen...
Flick-flick-flick BOOM!
Showers of your pleasure sproutin' from my hairline, drippin' down my chin.
Your thighs don't stop shakin' anytime soon.
Showers for days...
Tongue swiping through the liquid haze.
My lips stained from your nectar...
Baby, from here it only gets better..."

I stumbled at the recognition of his wide stance. Long legs over a fresh pair of *Timberland* boots, thighs spread a mile apart, chest broad even beneath a black sweater and open bubble vest. Jas' hands were buried into the pockets of his jeans and his piercing gaze on me was dark, intimately familiar, and unapologetically intentional. A sudden delicious puissance jolted my recently emptied bladder at the mere sight of him.

His smile, like his nod in acknowledgment of me, was perceptive yet soft.

"Have me," Corinne murmured loud enough for me to hear.

"Take me now," Cecil followed up with.

"Clean my fucking account, baby," Carlton didn't skip a beat.

That forced me to roll my eyes from Jas to my friends. When my annoyed gaze landed on Shizu, her naturally slanted eyes watered as she whispered, "I want it."

You've got to be kidding me...

I turned back to Jas and a delayed realization dawned on me. He wasn't alone. To the right, far off, Juggy leaned against a truck. His head came up from his phone and he offered me a salute with his hand. To the left of Jas an even bigger guy stood in all black sporting a harsh scowl, causing me to blink hard and quickly look away. Then, not too far from Juggy, standing in front of the truck was another guy, short and stocky, with his hand cupped over the other.

"Paparazzi lurking quietly," Jas' baritone vocals had my attention returning to him as he approached me. "Them pictures're gonna pop up tomorrow like mosquito bites."

"I don't care," I argued without conviction, because I did. "I'm living my life."

He scoffed, "My G." A subtle beam of approval lifted on one cheek.

"Isn't it a bit late for you to be out? I thought you hated the club scene."

"Juggy likes Ragee."

"Shit," Cecil squealed. "Me, too!"

I closed my eyes, licking my mildly dry lips. I knew he'd been waiting on a reason to speak to Jas.

"Juggy," I called out with closed eyes.

"Yuuurp!" Juggy replied.

"Get him home safely. It's late."

At the sound of Juggy's laughter, I peered around Jas. "True that, boss."

Jas, just a couple of feet in front of me chuckled. Then he whispered, "Sorry."

It took a moment for me to realize what the private apology was for. "An apology?" I hiked a brow. "Who do I have to thank for that?"

"The head doctor," he murmured then advanced past my line of sight, behind me. "*Brown Barista?*"

He was asking if I'd see him at therapy tomorrow. My soused mind was able to understand that, too.

When Jas turned back to catch my answer, two guys walked between our line of vision. I waited for them to pass before nodding. I did have an appointment in the morning, but I hadn't seen Jas at the coffee shop in so long, it was no longer an expectation.

After giving me a long, indecipherable once-over, Jas slowly took off. "Happy birthday, Cecil," he called out, never looking back.

"My fucking god!" Cecil groaned, then pretended to faint against Carlton—*or did he?*

Struggling to hold himself and Cecil's six foot two inch giant frame alone, Carlton cried, "That man smelled like he taste like myrrh!" He sucked his tongue against the inside of his top lip, making the sound of a lapping dog.

"Cee!" I went to grab Cecil, ignoring Carlton.

"Bitch, what was up with those whispered words!" Corinne demanded, throwing her zaftig figure my way. "I know code talk when I see it."

"You know him?" Shizu croaked.

They didn't even let Jas and his entourage give four feet of distance before howling like thirsty bitches.

jas

I watched the stories in her *IG* profile. Her friends had been recording themselves all night and tagging her. Witherspoon shared their stories in her own. They were lit all night, singing—or rapping—laughing and drinking.

She's cute...

I didn't know if Witherspoon was putting on for the public, showing them that she was living the "rock star" life after her breakup or trying to show her ex that. Neither did I know if this was who she naturally was when off work, letting her shit hang with her friends. Either way, she was cute, reminding me of the girl I saw when I was sixteen, trying to do right by my pops and interning with a builder in Jersey for the summer. That was an experience I never forgot yet rarely recalled. It was lowkey the moment I knew I wanted shit from life that didn't invoke high risks and illegal deeds.

Seeing her like this made her...real. She looked younger and carefree—even better than she did from a distance when I was eye-hustling them earlier during the concert. Could she ever be that "free" around me? Did I want her to? I honestly didn't know if I gave a fuck.

But I wanted to.

I think...

"Aye, Sin," Juggy called me from behind. He had a bottle girl from the club wrapped around him, all teeth and a humming pussy. "I'mma be in the back room. I won't be long. Then we can roll out when you ready."

Nodding, I dismissed him. We were on the third floor of the club, chilling after it had cleared out from the show. I'd respectfully seen all of my private guests off, releasing them to their varied after-parties, seeing I needed to be getting home soon. It was well past my curfew, something I abided by with ease. I knew tonight, because of the politics of the event, I'd have to violate the rules. And now that the ordeal was over, I could breathe easy and my stupid ass was stalking on *Instagram*.

Witherspoon and her crew left over thirty minutes ago. I didn't need to run up on her in the parking lot, but couldn't help myself. I also didn't think she was safe out in Harlem with her ex being a high profile dud nigga. Man told me about paparazzi lurking solely because she frequented the club over the years. Ol' girl needed to lay low or get some security. She and her crew were visibly intoxicated, leaving them vulnerable.

I heard a door slam, snatching me from my thoughts, and glanced around the empty room. Man had his girl in his office, waiting for the counting to be complete in the basement by his staff. The new security outfit was posted down there, the new place they counted every night since I suggested to Man to switch shit up. That left me alone in the conference room which was transformed into a mini lounge from the pre-party festivities.

My phone rang, Roberto Perez's name lit up the screen.

"Whaddup," I answered.

"Sin, I know it's late. I didn't think you'd answer." I could hear salsa tunes flowing in the background. "I was planning to leave a message." He laughed.

"Oh, yeah? What about?" I was much more comfortable discussing business than lurking on ol' girl's social media. That was some *dud* nigga shit for the nigga she'd supposedly cut off for plugging Brielle. "We need you down here, man," he implored with his thick accent. "Listen, it's not like you've gotta pay for anything. I just need you to see the estate, shake hands, experience the operations face-to-face. Pure politics, I know, but here in Cuba, businesses are respected when owners respect the land. I mean…"

I scratched my head. "Perez, I think we both know I don't need to have a trip to Cuba expensed. It ain't that at all. It's just that I got my hands steep in some shit here in the States that'll trip me up if I just up and leave."

"The coño gordos will make up for any losses of their kind back home, my friend."

"The what?"

"The *ahh*…fat pussies. The whores are supreme here!"

I chuckled. "Trust me." I shook my head, wishing it was that simple. "That ain't a problem for me."

Perez cracked the hell up. "Good. Then you tell me when and I'll take care of the rest. Bring your team. I'll be hospitable."

Biting my lip, I tried to calculate my situation. "Let me talk to a few people, see what I can come up with. I'll hit you when I have something about it."

"Okay, bro. In the meantime, those distributors you brought on were a boost in revenue. And the *Ellis International* account was masterful. We're shipping more product and faster!"

"Good. I'm glad it's been working out. Sadik promised better service than what we had. He's a trusted source—"

I felt the nudge at the back of my head from a hard object. Acute memory kicked in immediately, informing me of what it was.

"Hang the fuck up and run the cash, bitch," was the command from behind.

Shit…

I was right. There was a barrel at the back of my head. Soon, another shooter moved into my periphery, but not close enough for me to catch his face. Thinking quickly, I disconnected the call from Perez and dropped the phone on the miniature bar.

"The fuck're we doing here, fellas?"

"Nigga, you know what this is. Run the cash or eat gunpowder." He cocked the pistol from behind.

The threat tickled a minefield of my temperament I'd left dormant for years. The energy emanating from what was clearly a robbery flipped a switch in the recesses of my brain. Heated adrenaline swept through me, igniting every cell along the way. My heart began to bang to a techno beat familiar to my survival arsenal.

"Come the fuck on, bro!" one screamed hurried, belying his anxiousness. His façade of fear.

They were young, at least the one to my right. I could hear it in his expressive message. At least early twenties if not his late teens.

Shit...

Young hoppers could be more dangerous because they couldn't discern danger if it announced itself. They'd jump off a damn cliff without knowing what was beneath it.

My tongue swiped dry lips. "What exactly do you want?"

Boop!

The barrel was rammed into the back of my head and before I could think, I swiveled around, leaping off the stool, and bumrushed the one from behind. He was a big ass nigga, I identified right away, determining the direction of my actions. Pushing his arms above his head, I swung his big ass around to face his friend, at the same time taking inventory of how many niggas was on me. I only saw the young hopper, rocking a stocking cap over his face. I kneed his ass in the sac with power speed and forceful impact, taking his big ass down.

"*Ahhhh!*" his bitch ass screamed as I yanked the heavy ass *Beretta APX* from his loose grip.

Just touching a gun brought back acute memories of a world I denounced years ago. It tied my stomach into knots, loosened my lungs, and tickled my groin.

I kneed him in the face, blood splattering everywhere before he barreled down to the floor, groaning in pain. His ass may have been big—three inches taller and fifty pounds heavier than me—but he was fucking weak, collapsing. Angered by his fucking audacity, I kicked his ass in the face.

"Move, bitch!" The perceptive sound of a gun cocking snapped my attention.

The young guy…

I turned to find him posting me up with a semi-auto. They say just before you die, your life flashes before you. That wasn't exactly my experience. It was the barrage of thoughts firing across my brain like rapid synapses.

I've never had a home.

I've never been called Daddy.

I've never worn a ring.

I've never fucked a woman or laid in bed with one without clothes.

I've never been loved.

I've never made love.

My brows shot to my forehead. "A fucking *Saint Vik*," I swallowed, out of breath. "Two-two-three REM and five point fifty-six millimeter NATO." I smiled at his veiled face, mouth salivating like a motherfucker, pulse dancing, veins on fire from flaming blood shooting through, and dick inflating in my pants. "I've seen lots of guns—shot lots of them shits. You know what you're holding, my G?" I could see his hands shaking as he struggled to steady the gun. Smelled his fear permeating the room.

"Just go get the money and you won't end up with a hole in you," he grated.

"Made by *Springfield Armory*. Weighs 'bout…" I seesawed my head from left to right. "Sixteen pounds. Got about thirty rounds in *her*—"

"Shit!" the fat fuck beneath me squealed. "It's him, D! That's the nigga, Sin!"

The youngin' accosting me glanced down at his partner then back away from me. But it was too late. Man slid through the front door of the room behind him, *Glock* stocked and ready. Behind me, a cocking of a gun sounded, likely Juggy approaching.

"Yo, money," Man warned the kid. "You know both of y'all ain't walkin' out a'here. Right? Don't be stupid."

Security that was in the basement for the night's count bolted through the doors. Immediately, guns were drawn when weapons and a man down were noticed. The club's manager was next, creeping inside, deathly shook. His eyes were wide and ghosted, pulse hammering through his neck.

"This fat nigga look familiar to you?" I asked him.

Shaking, he cautiously padded over to the wailing man. His head popped up to me and he nodded. "We hired him right after Thanksgiving last year."

"And here I thought I was 'bout to die alone." I scoffed at his fat ass, telling the truth.

I had never feared death. I'd had nothing to lose. Because I'd never had a home, been called Daddy, worn a ring, fucked a woman or laid in bed with one without clothes, been loved, or made love. There was nothing to leave but the respect of my goons, and I'd done that once before for over ten years. Their lives would go on—had gone on. And so had everyone else's in the world.

I slowly inched up to the kid, seeing his shaking more and more. When I was close enough, I yanked the gun from him on the second pull. Unlike the fat fuck wallowing in a fetal position on the floor, this kid didn't let me take it smoothly. Man snatched the stocking from his head and the second the kid seemed to react by jerking his shoulder, I jabbed him in the mouth with my left. Seamlessly, Juggy, from behind, pulled the gun from my grip, subconsciously freeing up my right hand. That was all I needed.

I beat his ass like he stole something because he almost did. If I'd been another nigga—if my crew hadn't been just rooms away—if these niggas were real killers—I'd be dead.

God's words would have never come to be. His mercy, grace, and promises would have never materialized.

"You thought you was gonna run up on us and get us again?" Man demanded from the fat fuck when Jug was able to peel me off the kid's ass. He didn't reply so Man kicked him so hard on the back, the sound reverberated around the room. "Who you think we is, muthafucka? You seen them bosses posted up in here earlier! You think they came for the drinks, bitch?" Man stomped on his face.

I knew then, the night was far from over for us.

"It's been a stressful time for you," my therapist offered matter-of-factly yet in a gentle tone.

I was out with my crew until two this morning, leaving me less than five hours of sleep before I had to be here for this appointment. Stress could sometimes be self-incurred.

"For real."

"Time in the valley is often filled with rainy days."

"When it rains, it pours," I murmured, agreeing. "And I didn't understand why Ines couldn't see that. I know she's never liked Austin, but to be so insensitive as I'm separating from him. She could have waited." My right leg bounced, crossed over the other on the white leather sofa. "I don't bother people. I don't judge how people conduct themselves in their personal lives. The whole world gets to judge me, though! And that, I can tolerate. But to have that shit in my home grates my damn nerves." I scoffed, "And then the hypocrisy of it all!"

"How so?"

"She lets a strange man she knows nothing about in my apartment. Several times! She cooked for him and gave him full reign, at least twice."

Her forehead creases. "Who?"

I rolled my eyes. "Jas."

"Oh." I wondered, with that one syllable, if she was judging me. He was her client, too. "But you hosted him in your home, too."

"I did, but knowing he has a record. Knowing why he went to prison." Then I thought. "Or at least, what he wants me to know. He's not very forthcoming."

"Why do you think he isn't?"

"Because he shuts down any questions I have; some personal, some just generic."

"When Ines let him into your apartment, what was it for?"

I laughed. "Because I took a timeout to nurse my feelings after finding out my boyfriend of three years cheated on me with pop music's empress. I kinda think she crushes on him. She must've thought he was cute when I had him over the first time to discuss business."

"Has she said she's attracted to him?"

This time, I laughed harder. "No. Ines would never."

"Is she known to be attracted to guys you bring around?"

"I don't know what Ines likes. I'm being cynical, trying to justify her interest in Jas. Her ease in having him in our home. She used him to snap me out of my sulking." My eyes fell to my lap.

And it worked…

I felt suckered by his random act of kindness a few weeks back. It seemed as though Jas gave me access to a deeper side of him that Sunday when he took me to the safe house. The same when he called me about his pseudo-girlfriend's bra situation. But then he snapped on me about Ines making him soup. And then, today. When he told me last night he'd meet me at the coffee shop, Jas stood me up this morning.

"Did it work?" the therapist asked.

I thought about that for a minute. "I guess it did, but she also tried to imply I should try dating a 'simple' guy instead of wealthy ones. I'm pretty sure she had Jas in mind." I couldn't help my spit of laughter.

"What's wrong with Jas?"

My eyes cast into the corner of the room and I shrugged, knowing the obvious answer. "He's a laborer with a sordid past." I shook my head. "I know what men like that think when they see women like me. They see a ride. They see a different species unrelated to them. What could he offer me? A few words of encouragement when my 'trivial, privileged' life is in shambles gets tiresome after a while. He won't truly respect me or see me as an equal. Quite frankly, he doesn't now." This time, I shrugged with my mouth. "So let the laborers labor with their own kind. I love who I am, and will not allow anyone to think of or treat me less than I deserve."

And that's on that...

12:43 PM
Me: HEY
12:57 PM
Witherspoon: *FIRST YOU SNAP ON ME OVER SOUP. THEN YOU STAND ME UP (AGAIN). LOSE MY NUMBER.*
Me: OUCH.
Witherspoon: *BLOCKED*
Me: *I HAD A RUFF NIGHT. SOME UNEXPECTED SHIT I HAD TO HANDLE. I CANCELED MY APPT WITH HER THIS MORNING.*
3:02 PM
Me: YO. DID YOU REALLY BLOCK ME?
3:41 PM
Witherspoon: *NO. I'M JUST BUSY WITH WORK. BUT I SHOULD HAVE.*
Me: CAN I EXPLAIN? I CAN MEET YOU LATER.
Witherspoon: *I'M BUSY ALL DAY.*
Me: WHAT ABOUT TONIGHT?
Witherspoon: *I'M AT THE DANCE STUDIO WORKING.*
Me: WHAT'S THE ADDRESS? MAYBE I CAN PULL UP.

ashira

Miesha struggled with embodiment. She knew her choreography, but didn't sell us on the story told via Whitney Houston's "*Why Does it Hurt So Bad*," a historical piece for a twenty-four year old. But I enjoyed the track and appreciated her attempt at originality.

When the song ended, the room applauded Miesha as they should. Hers was a thoughtful attempt. I clapped along with them while traversing to the center of the studio to her side.

"C'mon, Jennifer," I called for the next dancer en route. "I love the song selection," I explained to Miesha. "It took research and pure intention to take it on. What I need for you to work on is expression. I didn't believe you were distraught. I didn't feel you were betrayed, tired, exhausted from trying to move on." Miesha, out of breath, nodded in acknowledgment. "I want to see that again, but with more conviction."

I loved dancing. Performing, teaching, and mentoring. When I was at the dance studio, very few negative factors attacking my life permeated. I was charged in here, inspired, creative, and invigorated. Proof of that was me critiquing expressive dance tonight. With only getting four-plus hours of sleep after last night's concert, I knew I'd regret not canceling. On my way here, I learned Cecil and Shizu had just awakened for the day and were still recovering: I called Shizu and Cecil had texted me. But the moment I changed into my cropped sweats and high-heeled dance shoes after arriving, unbelievable inspiration energized my mind and body.

Jennifer came in hard with *"Morning"* by Teyana Taylor. Her moves were eager and on top of the beat. She even dressed the part, exposing her waist in a black sheer bodysuit. It was a dope idea considering her hard hip wind component against Teyana's syllables throughout the song.

At the conclusion, she had even my respect. "Incredible." I hi-fived her. "One thing: please don't chew gum unless it's a part of the act. I couldn't stop looking at your mouth even with those dope ass hip twists with your winding." I mimicked her and was rewarded with the class laughing. "Good stuff, Jen." I slapped her ass while we parted ways.

Just as I was about to call Evelyn, the next dancer, men began trickling into the studio with long, inspective gazes. It took seconds for the girls to catch on. The first guy I didn't recognize, but the second guy provided the revelation of who these guests were. My guests. I sighed internally, regretting sending Jas the address. I'd bitten off more than I could chew this morning in my session with the therapist. After explaining why I would never date a guy like Jas, our conversation somehow wandered into the gray area of whether or not I found him attractive. After attempting to answer with a complicated *no*, I'd been pondering who guided us down into that rabbit hole: her or me.

Why do I make my life more complicated than it naturally is?

But I wouldn't express that outwardly. Instead, as the dancers in the room lost focus, reacting to the new virile presence in the studio, I clapped my hands to get their attention. Immediately deciding to ignore them felt like the absolute right thing to do. Women looked stupid lusting after Jas. If only they knew he hadn't been a free man for two years yet and the ten before it, he lived in shackles. There must be a glow about men recently released from prison. A potion of delusion stupid women were poisoned by. Not me.

"Evelyn, let's see what you've got!" I gave the cue for her to get ready to begin.

Just as Leah cued the music, my eyes brushed past Jas. He stood against the wall on the opposite side, leaning against the mounted ballet barre coolly. His posture was relaxed but eyes alert as he nodded, acknowledging me. I returned the nod before turning my attention back to Evelyn. Her selection was Aaliyah's "*4 Page Letter.*" I knew Leah and Kaz, another instructor here, had been working with her on an audition she has for a music video. Immediately, I looked forward to being impressed, though this wasn't the routine for the video.

Evelyn was one of the more tenured dancers on our roster. She left Atlanta for Jersey when she caught a lick, dating someone from Joe Budden's camp. When that ended, she got a gig as a video girl for a rap group. She found my studio through dancers from around the way. Evelyn was good; versatile and confident in her craft. She reminded me so much of myself when dancing.

She respected the heavy drum breaks and double and triple beats in the track. Evelyn had fun with it—until she freestyled. She went off the reservation when gyrating across the room to entertain our guests. Evelyn made it clear her attention was narrowly on Jas. *Of course!* She ran her index finger down his chest mouthing, "I'm writing you a love letter tonight." Jas' impassive eyes were on her in their close proximity. Then she returned to the center and closed the performance.

It was okay at best.

We all applauded her in good sportsman-like behavior. The room was alive from people shouting Evelyn out, as she was one of our best undoubtedly. In that moment, I realized Evelyn was proud of herself, too. She accepted her praise with winks and tongue flashes. My prized pupil also couldn't keep her eyes from Jas. I waited, standing still, unspeaking, and observed it all. The guy with Jas whom I didn't know was raptly fixated on the dancers and so was Juggy. Jas, on the other hand, was in his phone. He brought it up to make a call.

See!

Weird.

"Alright! Okay!" I shouted, clapping my hands to quiet the room. It took longer than usual, I was sure, because of our guests. "That was good. I appreciate the detour from the choreography, too. We had impromptu guests: you included them in the choreography unplanned." My and Evelyn's palms met in a hi-five. "Tonight, I saw better planning than execution. As I've told many of you, you're telling a story just as much as the lyrics. Get in there and do the work," I explained to the class, specifically Evelyn, "You have to sell him with your seduction. I'll show you."

I whistled across the room to Jas then jerked my neck, summoning him. Before I knew if he'd obey, I got a chair from the corner and returned it to the center of the floor. Reasonably, Jas was headed my way and as I considered the song, I motioned for him to have a seat. Quietly, he did, and with him came his signature musk: sandalwood and sage. It was striking and agreeable.

Maybe it was his scent or overall presence, but a dizzying revelation hit me in a split second. Jas wanted to see me. He apologized and even ignored the bullets of coldness I shot him earlier in our text message. Also, he didn't embarrass me by declining to be put on the spot in front of strangers. That wasn't Jas. Our eyes locked and congruent to the dark edge of him was a softness in his eyes. That, too, was unusual. Was he okay? I'd have to deal with that later because right now, I had a session to close.

And that's when it hit me.

"Wale!" I instructed Leah, controlling the music. "*Bad*."

Jas

On her way over to the wall of mirrors, Witherspoon glanced over to ol' girl controlling the music. "The original, not the remix."

She then turned her back to me, dropping down into a squat, sitting on the back of her ankles. She stayed there when the track started, the intro was some talking. I didn't focus on the voice, too intrigued by her stature. When the first three beats hit, Witherspoon remained in place. But when the subsequent three came through, she kicked her leg, swung her body around to face me, and lifted from the other leg.

And she could move. I couldn't believe what I saw from bar to bar of the lyrics. Witherspoon had a hidden rhythm on par with the bass of the track. Her face was blank, but body said a lot when she dropped her torso backward, head meeting high heels. Then quickly on a thrust of her hips, the woman shot upright then talentedly dropped into a twerk where only her ass moved.

When the hook came through again, Witherspoon, at the top of the room near the mirror, seductively runway-walked toward me, mouthing the lyrics, "Baby, I never made love." But when "she" conveyed she could fuck, my dick twitched. It felt like a whispered promise. Her acting was on point for sure. The class cheered her on, applauding her creativity. I couldn't really hear or see anything but what Witherspoon wanted me to.

This particular Wale album dropped while I was new in *FPC Montgomery*. Still settling in from the violence, the ego, the anger. But I recalled it. I had no damn appreciation of what it conveyed. An unattainable "bad" girl. Was that Witherspoon? I doubted it. But watching her rocking in an eagle's position, ass inches above the floor, I second-guessed. The woman jumped from the squat, and went into somersault motion, stopping midway and pushing back in reverse on her two heeled feet.

What the fuck…

I could never show her my excitement, definitely not in a room full of people. But Ashira Witherspoon had impressed me. She totally transformed into an entirely different being. She twirled to me, spiking my pulse. Witherpoon disappeared behind my chair. Her long leg appeared, then thigh. The bottom of her shoe planted on my thigh as her pussy swiped the back of my head in an entirely different manner than the barrel of the *Beretta APX* last night. I watched her watch us through the mirrors ahead.

She took me roughly at the top of my head and chin and mouthed, "Yeah, I'll be good in bed, but I'll be bad for you."

Then she was gone, from around me, but not my sight. Again, I was locked down when this track touched down. I'd never picked up the sound of the mattress springs in the background. That was until Witherspoon was directly in front of my widened thighs emulating fucking on top, springing from the base of her feet. She was simulating riding my cock, disturbing the mattress.

Shit…

She was dangerous. A bad bitch with an alpha appetite. She stayed in character, earning the hoots and applause of her class. Witherspoon's face didn't move an inch as she crawled to me like a cat at the closing of the song. The lyrics were done, no mouthing needed. Just her sensual energy teasing the repressed monster I had in restraints. I wanted her. Had flashes of bruising her pussy, tenderizing her nipples, and tearing her vocal chords.

But in an instant, I was sobered, believing her. Ashira Witherspoon was bad for me. She wasn't on my checklist.

When the song was over, Witherspoon resumed the squat position, but leaned over on her hands, out of breath as her class jumped all around hyped up.

I leaned toward her, "You think you've 'sold' me?"

ashira

"I think I've done worse," I panted, inches away from his beautiful face.

My heart flipping and sex throbbing as I squatted beneath his open body. Jas was ultra-masculine, sitting unbothered throughout my whole freestyle in everything but his eyes. Beneath them was the same storm I'd seen weeks ago, at my apartment. The vortex of seductive wickedness, arrogance, and unrepentant pride. Jas didn't hide: he veiled it for a warning.

His eyes busily caressed my parted lips. "What's that?"

"I think I've sold myself."

I was attracted to Jas, and had been for some time. Wildly.

I straightened from his thick frame and walked away.

Chapter Fourteen

MARCH | PRESENT DAY

ashira

I LAUGHED MY ASS OFF. LIKE…WAS CURLED OVER, MOUTH HANGING open, eyes closed, and stomach squeezing type of cracking up!

"You pulled off?"

"Hell yeah," Jas chuckled, plopping a fry into his mouth. "I had to get out of there. The nigga was fuckin' around."

I sat up on the couch then leaned over my crossed legs to place my glass on the coffee table.

"I don't know strip club etiquette for men, but for women, we're ready to go after watching all that skin and meat. I guess Juggy couldn't wait." I howled all over again.

"He couldn't wait?" Jas scoffed, eyes lit with humor. "I just got out the box from a ten-year bid. Juggy could've held that shit for later or blew it before picking me up from the airport. It was my first night out."

"What were you in such a rush to do?"

"The same thing every nigga coming home needs to do. I had to get my shit out the dirt."

"Huhn?" I didn't get it.

His eyes bounced between my two then swept down my torso with a pinched brow. Then he sighed, looked away, and shook his head. "Say less. No need to go there—"

"Noooo. No! You said you wanted to talk tonight so you can apologize for shutting down on me once again." This was why I didn't fuck with thugs. Their communication skills were so limited and they penalized me for wanting more. I was more convinced of his need for therapy. "You cannot apologize then turn around and do the same shit." I pointed to the flowers on the side table to remind him.

Once I dismissed my class, Jas and I agreed to have a late dinner together and that he'd meet me at my place. On my way home, I called and ordered burgers to be delivered from a restaurant in my development. I was truly tired after missed sleep last night and a long day today. While waiting on Jas to arrive, I quickly showered, changed into loose sweats, a tank, and a robe, and opened a bottle of wine. Boy, was I surprised when he sauntered into my apartment with a beautiful bouquet of flowers.

He grumbled something beneath his breath before biting his bottom lip in irritation. But his tone was gentle when he shared, "Getting your dick out the dirt is a metaphor—*euphemism*—for having sex for the first time after being locked down."

"Oh." My face folded. "Who was the lucky lady?"

"Witherspoon!" he whined, eyes closing adorably in torture.

"What? It's not like I know her." Then I thought. "Unless she's in construction. Is she in construction?"

"No, man!" he groaned. "Nobody special. Just a check off my list."

"Someone you always wanted to bang?" I winked.

That earned me a laugh from Jas. "Nah. Not like that at all."

"You gave me the impression you take that list very seriously."

He nodded. "Always have."

"Then if she wasn't a trophy fuck, how did she make the list?"

"Because she got bagged by an associate of mine before I made it to a year behind bars." His mouth twisted.

"Your girlfriend cheated on you?"

"She wasn't my girl, but it was understood. I was taking care of her and her grandmother for like two and half years before I cut her off."

"Damn. That's tough," I breathed. "So, it was revenge pussy."

Jas nodded. "Samona ended up helping out with my time in the end after all. Anyway, can we change the subject?"

"Yeah." I wiped my mouth. "Let's, because I can't see you doing that, especially with how convicted you've been about your spirituality."

"Now you know how I earned my name."

"Like the club. Right?" I laughed.

Jas didn't.

"Awww, come on! I'm sure you share these stories with your rotating women."

"Nah," he exhaled softly. Shaking his head, he explained, "I don't."

"Your other female friends?"

"I ain't got many of those. At least, none I have time to kick it with. Since being home, I've honestly been working, making up for lost time."

My smile was suspended when Jas' gaze on me dimmed. His nostrils spread, lips parted then the muscles around his eyes relaxed. I didn't understand.

Confused, my expression sobered. "Are you in my home insulting me?"

Jas didn't move, energy didn't let up. "Yet another example." His voice was raw, guttural.

Then his eyes fell to my mouth. My ears began ringing, pulse banged in my neck, and my belly turned over. Did he want to kiss me?

Jas?

I considered it. Quickly, I tried to think of ways it could go wrong or right.

Only there were more wrong ways than right.

His phone rang, causing Jas to snap out of his heated gaze with a deep blinking of his eyes. He exhaled before answering by way of *FaceTime* and I leaned away.

"Hey…"

"Hey, cuzzo! You look cute!"

He really did.

Jas scoffed. "Whaddup with you?"

"Just hung up with Alvin. I think we should give Sean a birthday party this year. He's all the way down in Delaware now, and I feel like we need to send a message to him, his new boo, and her peeps that Sean belongs to a clan."

With pouted lips, Jas' soft nod was perceptible. "Uh!"

She smacked her teeth. "Is that all you've got to say? I know it's two minutes past your bedtime and all."

I swallowed back a snicker.

"What do you need from me?" he groaned.

"The crab legs. You know he loves those things."

"Hold up." Jas' brows met. "Ain't his birthday in April?"

"The third. Yup. So, in two weeks."

"A'ight. Anything else?"

"I'm gonna ask Aunt Charmagne to make some greens and lasagna." She paused and Jas waited patiently while I busied myself with cold onion rings. "You bringing Cynthia?"

He shrugged at the screen with his lips. "I'm not sure what her schedule is. *Nah.* On second thought, she's got class."

"Too bad. I know you said you liked her macaroni salad. I was going to tell you to see if she could bring that. You think you could take a stab?"

At that, I did cackle.

"Is that her?"

Jas looked at me with a deadpan expression. I'd interrupted his conversation. Did I blow his cover? We weren't creeping.

And I couldn't stop laughing.

"Who's that, Jas?"

I laughed so hard my shoulder twitched as I leaned on the opposite side. When I opened my eyes, trying to stop, Jas had turned the face of the phone my way.

"Who is that?"

I couldn't quite recognize her face from squinted, teary eyes. Why I found Jas talking to his cousin about regular smegular shit funny, I had no idea. And that made it funnier.

"I'm not her," I answered, still cracking up.

"Oop!" the cousin gasped.

"Nah, Chels. I'm with Tiffany Haddish over here," Jas jeered dryly.

Of course, that intensified my tickles. Crazy thing was, I wasn't drunk or tipsy. Just found him funny.

"No," I tried catching my breath. "Let me stop." I sat up and wiped my eyes. "Oh! Hey!" I waved, trying to recall her name.

Her face lit up. "Shi-Shi!" Then her expression fell, almost in realization.

The cousin from the "*Wonder*" play. "Chelsea! Hey!" Her name finally came to me.

Jas retracted the screen, putting it back on himself. "Before you start assuming, no." His eyes flashed animatedly. "Say less."

"What do you mean?" Chelsea giggled. "Don't be accusing me of nothing. All I said was hi."

"Actually, you didn't. And, if you did, I know what was behind that hi. Witherspoon's cool."

"Yeah," I shouted their way. "The lil' homie." I swiveled my 'hang loose' hand signal in the air.

Jas cracked a chuckle. "Don't be corny, Witherspoon."

"Why I gotta be corny? Ain't that what you called me?"

Jas shook his head, feigning ignoring me. "What time?"

"What?" Chelsea asked. "Oh! The party. If he drives up, we need to give him time to. So, I figured around two o'clock would be good. Then he can leave when he decides to go for the ride. Back to Shi-Shi: did you hear Christina C. Jones may be signing off on having her first series adapted into film like her other projects?"

Oh. "No, I didn't." Jas swiveled the phone. "I don't think I read her earlier stuff, though. Should I read the series?" I had no time to read these days.

"It's such an easy read. She keeps her books at a palpable length. Not too short to cheat you and not too long to bore you or hold up your *Goodreads* annual goal."

Chelsea gave me those same warm Black girl vibes she had last month. That spurred a thought.

"I make a mean macaroni salad. It's my plus-one at all my family events. I can send the salad with Jas. If you like it, I can give you the recipe."

"Or you could bring it yourself." *BOOM!* I could have shimmied in my seat at how easy that finesse was.

My face bloomed. "Really?" I tossed a questioning gaze to Jas, who gave nothing away.

"Yeah. Why *not*—unless, cousin, you…"

"I'm about to fall asleep. I can't even tell you what just happened here. First the food then Christina P. Body, then recipe—"

Both Chelsea and I corrected him, "Christina C. Jones."

"It's C. Jones," Chelsea finished last.

"Whatever, man. Count me in. I'll clear my schedule." Jas yawned. "'Xcuse me."

"What about Shi-Shi?"

My doorbell rang, and I swiftly sprang to my feet. It was likely the maintenance guy. Ines told me about the garbage disposal going out. When I made it to the door and peered out of the peephole, I was surprised to see Noelle.

I couldn't unlock and open the door fast enough. "What the entire hell, Noelle? It's almost midnight!"

Her shoulders were low and face long as she inhaled deeply. "My mom."

"What about her? Did she drop you off?"

"No," she answered petulantly. "She put me out again."

Lattice, her mother, never actually made her stay away for more than a day or two, depending on the situation. While I thought it was foul, making her think she's kicked out, I also understood Noelle's teenaged-tempered mouth.

"What did you do? Where's your bag?"

"I'm not coming from home."

"Where are you coming from, Noelle Witherspoon?"

"From a party in Fair Lawn."

I cocked my head to the side. "On a school night?" She lifted her shoulders in a shrug, holding them suspended like a child would. "The fuck, little girl!" I groaned, moving to the side, letting her in.

"I would've been home at a decent hour, but Mindy's car broke down and when I called home to ask my mom for a ride, she flipped out." Her moue was one I wish I'd caught on camera to later clown her about.

Closing the door, I sighed. "How did you get all the way out here from Fair Lawn?"

Those heavy shoulders lifted again. "Your *Uber*?"

"Okaaaaay," I sang. "Nice." My head bounced. "I suppose that was the right thing to do. It is why I added you to my account." She followed me into the living room as I asked, "Were you drinking?"

When Noelle didn't reply in sequence, I turned to find her frozen in place, mouth hanging open while gazing ahead. Following her line of vision, I found her source of wonderment. Jas was up on his feet, deeply stretching his arms into the air, balancing on his toes. That length made his shirt deficient in coverage, exposing the lower portion of his belly. It was bubbled, in accordance with a fit man. His happy trail leading to the forest was pleasing—*no*—teasing to the eyes. Or whatever.

"Yeah," Noelle finally answered me, "*but I'm totally intoxicated now.*"

My head whipped back to her. "Girl!" I shrilled, face balling with fury. "If you don't show some dignity!"

Noelle whispered, "How can I? That nigga's thick."

"The hell!"

"Who's this?" Jas' voice box was in expiration mode. It was clear the hour was late and he was tired.

I rolled my eyes away from my sister and to Jas. "Seems I've got a pop-up visit from another Witherspoon. Meet Noelle."

Jas smiled kindly. "Your cousin? Y'all look alike. Same little nose and thick eyebrows."

I grinned hard, still reeling from Noelle's behavior—all of it. "Sisters."

"Oh, word!" He moved closer, coming into the vestibule. "You did mention a sister." He extended his hand to Noelle. "But you ain't say she was prettier than you, though."

Noelle's face squeezed tightly and leg kicked back in delight, her little tongue protruding as she met his shake.

I mumbled, "The charmer, this guy."

"Everyone in the family knows," Noelle continued with the joke. "We made a pact to not remind her." She playfully waved off the notion.

"Aww. Cute." Jas smiled at her adoringly.

I saw the moment he recognized my sister's gaze in return was filled with pubertal thirst. His beam shrunk and the foyer grew awkwardly silent.

Thanks, Noelle!

Jas broke the moment, peering my way. "I'm gonna go. Jug's downstairs."

"Give Harlem my regards." I tried lightening the moment, but not even I believed me. "Juggy, too,"

He grabbed his coat from the rack near the door. "Nice meeting you, Noelle. I'll fall in line with the family about that."

Her giggle provoked my rage. Moving away from her, I grabbed the door for Jas.

"Thanks for dinner." He turned to face me after crossing the threshold. His posture, the tender cocking of his head, and the softness in his eyes made me feel there was more to be said. I wouldn't be the one to say it, though, because I couldn't quite articulate it, halfway understanding.

Did Jas realize I would have kissed him tonight? Did he know about my revelation of being attracted to him? I didn't know if I wanted him to. We were different people, having completely polar life experiences. "Thanks for letting me apologize, too," his tone was softer, lower as though he didn't want my sister to hear.

Swallowing back the lump in my throat, I shook my head softly as my eyes fell away. "Don't make me do it again."

Jas' head tossed back and he hooted. "Say less, Witherspoon!" He turned, taking off for the elevator.

I laughed, too, but mine was lodged beneath all the other emotions I couldn't speak.

"He's a blue-blood," Ezra explained, eyes toward the ceiling while into his storytime, something I continued to find captivating, "extensive education, Rhodes Scholar—"

"Like you?" I asked.

He shook his head. "I sat amongst them, but my academic pursuits were an ambiguous, opaque path I'd created for myself. There's no distinction in my body of work. Till this day, I wonder why I hadn't gone for my doctorate degree while single and without dependents." His attention went down to his plate, I was sure, trying to shake the detour I'd caused with that question. "Rothenberg is well-spoken, unimaginable rangy lexicon—"

One of my phones rang on the table, disrupting him. It was Cynthia calling and I didn't want to leave this story. I could hit her later. So, I tapped to silence the ringing, though it still rang until reaching my voicemail. When my attention lifted to Ezra, his eyes were on the screen.

I tossed my chin toward him. "What about his vocabulary?"

"Superbly immense," Ezra continued, voice even raspier. "He was the only one I had to be concerned about in our debate class. And he almost held the advantage this one time the topic was public policy, as that was his field of study. However, I was able to successfully interweave sociology into my argument as it relates to politicians' superlative breeding—"

My phone rang again. This time, it was from an unlikely and unusual caller. I hadn't heard from her since leaving her place last week.

"I'm sorry," I offered Ezra. "You mind if I take this right quick?"

"Of course." His attention went to his plate.

I accepted the *FaceTime*, expecting the crisp view of the main object, not her background. Under the loud, Caribbean music was a dude with only a thong and body makeup on, dancing on a chick in a chair. Other chicks watched on, cheering the two in the middle of the room.

The fuck?

Witherspoon flipped the camera, face wide with sloppy happiness. It was clear she was leaving out of the room where the action was taking place. "Just wanted to share my night with you." She bit her lip, mascara-stained eyes low and heavy.

Witherspoon had tossed back a few.

Confused, I asked, "Where are you?"

"Cayman Islands. My girlfriend's bachelorette party."

She was map-hopping again. Damn.

"Looks like you're having a good time. Enjoy and be responsible." I was prepared to end the call.

"Wait. I'm not done sharing my night."

I squinted. "Okay…"

"After the stripper's done, I'm going back to my room to get my shit out the mud."

Ezra's head popped up.

"Get your what where?"

She winked. "Get my shit out of the mud." Her eyes blinked over and over while Witherspoon swung her head to the side, prompting me to think.

Then it fucking hit me. I almost choked, laughing my damn head off. "You're saying it wrong. It's 'out the dirt' and the object is more vulgar than I want to say in mixed company. Either way, I don't think you have that problem." I tried to control my volume, catching Ezra's curious eyes on me.

Then her expression turned shocked. "Oh, yeah! Get my shit out the dirt. Damn, I told Corinne the wrong phrase!"

"You sharing jailhouse talk with ya girls, Witherspoon?" I tried sounding offended.

"No. Just trying to season my suburban sophistication." She pouted, looking so damn adorable, being silly. And the beach behind her was gorgeous. It was dark out, but for the tiki torches and white string lights. Shit. The view was amazing. "Where are you?"

"Having dinner with a friend."

A cat-who-ate-the-canary smile opened on her pretty face. "Where?"

I glanced around at the empty spot: Juggy at the counter with his crossword puzzle and Ezra's driver, Carlos, at a table near the back door on his phone. "At the tea shop."

Witherspoon laughed. "Eating what? Tacos?"

I chuckled at her silliness. My eyes went to Ezra's plate.

"Nah. Tonight's special is grouper."

I had Frankie buy it fresh earlier today for Ezra.

"Grouper!" She swirled her neck. "*Ooooh!* Fancy tonight. Can't wait to come back—wait. With who?"

Even though I couldn't help my smile, I wrinkled my forehead. "I told you with a friend. And I'm being rude."

"Oh." A flip had switched in Witherspoon's eyes, but she caught herself and tried to smile again. "Is *Sin* with his *Cyn?*"

I snorted, "Nah."

Her head snapped back dramatically. "Then with who?"

"My pastor."

"Who?" Her red-stained lips formed an *O*.

"Bishop Carmichael."

"The pastor I met with his wife at the safe house?" I forked a steamed carrot and bit off the tip. "The one and only."

Witherspoon laughed. "Bullshit. If you wanna get off the phone, just say that."

I really needed to end this call. It was crazy rude. So I took the asshole route, flipping the camera on the *FaceTime* so she could see my tablemate.

Ezra's head lifted when he caught on. When I flipped the camera back to me, Witherspoon looked ghosted as hell. Eyes wide and mouth hanging open.

"Oh, *my*—Okay. Bye!" She ended the call.

I couldn't help cracking the hell up, forking more of my fish. "My bad, Bishop."

"No. No," he rasped coolly. "No affront here." We continued to eat, and I wondered how long she would be out there—*I ain't even know she was going*. Witherspoon sure lived the moneyed life. This was her second vacation in six weeks. I didn't know many chicks who did that. Did she start that when dating ol' boy or had she always lived high-class? It could have gone either way for her. Shit. I couldn't even get down to Cuba to see about my business, but Witherspoon jet-setted to celebrate engagements and weddings. *And how many of her friends getting married this year?* "But I *am* struck with a thought."

My head lifted, his rasp breaking my idle mind. "What's up?"

"Cynthia called seconds before your occupational contemporary. You ignored her call, but when your colleague rang, you answered without thought." He sat back, grinning behind his beard. "I'm no mathematician, but something in this equation is off."

"C'mon, man. You know my path is unique." I referred to looking for my wife. "My vision is sharp."

"Yeah. Yeah," he murmured defenselessly. "I'm familiar with that vivid vision of yours without prejudice." His head bobbed as he peered out of the bay window we sat in front of.

Snorting while chewing, I prompted, "But…"

Ezra returned to his food, shaking his head, forehead stretched. "No. I was just thinking how long I waited on my wife. How many years, how many admirers, how many rejections on my behalf, and many times I questioned my steadfastness." His index finger rose in the air. "But when Jehovah Jireh delivered her—literally to my feet—there was no waiting for me. No indecision, no tarrying, and certainly no interviewing process. I knew."

Shit...

"Did she know?"

"Alexis thought I was maniacal—*still does*, I'm convinced. But she knows I'm committed to our covenant, have been since the first time I laid eyes on her."

I sat back and exhaled, peeping his undertones. "I wish my journey was that black and white. But hey, the race isn't given to the swift."

"But time and chance," he murmured, lifting his glass in the air, "happeneth to them all."

ashira

"Gosh, this view is to die for," Becky wistfully confessed. "I can't say thanks enough for this, Shi-Shi. A bachelorette party in the damn Caymans."

I brought the cigar to my mouth, pulling in deeply before blowing it out and nodding my head. The view of the Caribbean Sea was hypnotizing. Either that or it had been serving as the perfect focal point to help with my running thoughts.

"You're worth it, babe." And I meant it. Becky and I had been best friends forever. It was only right to fly a few of us out to celebrate her last few weeks as a single woman. And I couldn't leave out Shizu and Corinne. "I'd do it a thousand times over."

"Can you believe one of us is getting married?" Becky asked the group.

"Shizu's ass is next," Corinne mumbled, deeply concentrating on rolling a fat one.

Shizu laughed. "I always thought Shi-Shi would be first."

Becky lowered her sunglasses with her index finger, peering curiously over to Shizu. "Why?"

"Because. She had all the guys after her."

I rolled my eyes over to her at that lie. "I've never had to pursue a man, but I ain't ever have to evade a line of them at my front door either."

Becky murmured, "I thought Austin was the one."

"He called me again," Corinne shared.

"Feel free to block his number," I exhaled, releasing smoke.

"I heard he just bought a new house," Shizu shared over a yawn.

"Happy for him," my energy dry.

"Maybe we shouldn't talk about him—or me," Becky suggested. "This is a hard time for Shi-Shi."

"Nah." I waved off the notion. "I've faced tougher battles. Even this shit with my dad's firm is biting my ass."

"But even with considering the merger, I'm sure a future with Austin was in that plan."

My brows furrowed and lips pursed. "I'm not sure it was."

"Come on, Shi-Shi!" Corinne challenged. "You loved that guy!"

"With all my heart. And if things would have remained solid, I'm sure we would have considered getting married at some point, but I'm a more 'in the moment' kind of girl. And especially lately with realizing just how delayed my dreams are. I feel like I haven't launched yet. Corinne, you got your adult store, a major goal of yours. Becky, you opened your bakery, something you claimed in tenth grade. Plus, you lived in Croatia for two years before coming back to the States and settling your life. Another life mission accomplished. And Shizu, your travel agency has grown steadily over the past seven years. You used to have us come up with places we wanted to visit and you'd map them out, using travel websites all the time in high school. What have I talked about?" My eyes were to the mesmerizing water. "What have I done?"

"But, Shi-Shi, we all know you out-earn all of us." Becky laughed.

I wasn't impressed. "Money ain't always the most important factor for quality of life."

"Always stated by people who have it," Shizu jeered.

I pulled from my stick again. "And I bet those people understand that life's not about the accumulation of anything like it is experiences and memories."

"You have good memories with Austin. Right?" Becky questioned.

"Yeah. But I'm over relationships for now. I need something... less intense. Something that would allow me to focus on my dreams." I smiled. "And learning new cultures and lifestyles while at it."

"You wanna eat coochie then go back to dick, then say that shit, Shi-Shi," Corinne hissed. Becky, Shizu, and I spit riotous laughs so fast, she had to chuckle herself. "Damn, girl! Can I get high first?"

"I'm not over bats, Corinne. I said I was over relationships. Trust me, that ain't it."

"Then what is it, Shi-Shi?" Shizu's head dropped to the side.

"Spill it, bitch!" Becky demanded.

Slowly, I dragged from the cigar, holding it for a second as I gathered my words, then let it out. "You ever wanna T-Pain a nigga?"

Corinne's spine jolted. "What's that?"

"The tell that nigga 'let's get drunk and forget what we did' type of T-Pain."

Simultaneously, Becky and Shizu sucked in salted air.

"You're really over Austin!" Shizu surmised.

"Then, *shit*. I been T-Pain'ing all my life!" Corinne theorized. "That's why I've been telling y'all bitches to fuck outside of relationships. It's so liberating." Corinne stood from her lounge chair, blunt rolled and ready. She shook her head and took off for our unit to smoke by the pool.

"Who is he? Will he be your plus-one at my wedding?"

I returned my gaze to the water, feeling helplessly off. I couldn't be crushing on Jas; he wasn't my type. What in the hell did I look like dating a damn brick-layer? My father would never approve and his respect for me would wane more than it was shaping up to with me leaving the firm.

"I doubt it. He's...different."

"What do you mean?" Shizu seemed anxious to know.

"Promise to keep this here?" I dropped my sunglasses and tossed them both a glare. "Like...especially not Peach. I don't need her down my ass."

Becky laughed. "Peach is hardly judgmental. She doesn't condone and she doesn't judge."

"You wanna talk about Peach or this?"

Becky's narrow, orange-stained lips constricted. "Fucking go already, Shi-Shi!"

"Okay!" I flipped on my back again. "He's fine as fuck—thick and cut. Sunbaked brown casing. He's rough—street guy for sure, but his impressive aptitude sneaks up on me often. He's smart...calculating, and way more reserved than I prefer. He's too damn spiritual, too, something I'm trying to understand about him. The life experience doesn't match the convictions." I shrugged. "He makes me...curious."

"About what?" Becky asked before her bracelet vibrated. "I have to walk. Burn some of these calories to get into the gown. But about what?"

I smiled, more at my pitiful self than anything. "About him. His culture. If his convictions are true."

"But no relationship?" Shizu seemed to need clarification.

I sputtered a laugh. "Absolutely not. But I'd be curious to know how much of his dick fits into my mouth."

The girls laughed at my crassness.

"And on that, I'm off." Becky left her chair.

"I need to pee." Shizu stood and stretched her arms in the air. "Then maybe have some of Corinne's indo."

I was left alone to my *Por el Amor del Amor* and stupid thoughts. I'd hyped up my ambition of Jas to my friends more than I had the heart to execute. But I didn't lie about being attracted to him. That, I could no longer deny. I wondered, though, if the feeling was mutual. We'd only known each other for hardly two months.

After twenty minutes of racking my brain about my feelings—or lust—or curiosity for this guy, I decided to call him. My behavior during our last *FaceTime* still weighed on me. I would never speak that way in front of a pastor.

On the third ring, an image opened up and Jas appeared. His head was hung.

"I'm starting to believe you only calling to post up."

"What are you doing?" He looked to be in an office.

"Working. In a meeting, actually."

"Oh."

Finally, he lifted his head, a soft yet perceptive smile playing at his mouth. "Oh."

Sitting up on the beach lounger, I felt uneasy. "Well, this shouldn't take too long."

"I'll remind you of that when you come back to forty-eight degree weather and you're in the middle of your workday."

I rolled my eyes. "I just wanted to apologize for my language last night in front of the pastor. I really thought you were playing around."

"I don't lie, Witherspoon. I may say less, but I'm an honest one."

"I see. I see." I played affront. "My bad. I hope he won't hold it against me."

"Dude's like Jesus; he digs hanging around sinners. You ain't special, girl."

My eyes blossomed. "Oh."

"Oh." There was that flash of wickedness in his eye.

Smiling pathetically, I asked, "Could you send me the address for Saturday? I'm flying back home tomorrow and have a ton of running around to do, including get the ingredients for that macaroni salad."

"Oh, damn. I forgot all about that." His brows furrowed. "You really pulling up?"

My eyes rolled to the side as my face wrinkled. "Yeah. I was invited."

"Oh."

"Oh." I echoed his cheekiness earlier. "Anyway, I'll let you get back to—"

Jas' face hardened and he seemed to point below. "The formatting on this report is different than the old ones, Divine."

"Indeed." A man's rumble in the background sounded eerily familiar. "There's been a system upgrade. It's one of the things I wanted to point out to you before you hopped on your *urgent* call."

Oops...

"Ashira," he began, referring to me unusually by my first name. "I really have to go."

"Divine?" I called myself whispering. "Do I know him?" I was curious.

"I doubt it. We don't run in the same circles."

"You don't know my circle."

Jas laughed. "And you damn sure don't know mine."

"Prove it."

Without further provocation, Jas, once again, flipped the camera of the *FaceTime* call. Immediately, an intimidatingly familiar figure came into view. It was Azmir Jacobs, also referred to as Divine, in a dress shirt and tie, looking over paperwork. It took him some time, but he eventually caught on and peered up. His forehead wrinkled, eyes squinting, making me swallow involuntarily.

"Shi-Shi?"

But it was too late. Jas had already switched the camera. He appeared annoyed now. "Got me acting really bitchy, Witherspoon. Have a safe flight."

"Hold up," Azmir called out. "I know her."

I fixed my face to express Jas was wrong about me not knowing anyone from "his world."

"Hi, Azmir."

"How are you, Shi-Shi?"

I sort of figured he was referring to my breakup with Austin. "I've seen worse days. Rayna texted me a few days ago."

"Yeah. She said she would reach out...hopefully catch dinner with you when she flies out tomorrow. She's going to be in town for the weekend then head up to Montreal for a few days."

"Oh, that's *this* weekend? When I got her message, I was boarding my flight. Okay. Well, I have plans on Saturday."

"We're here until Monday morning. Dinner Sunday? In fact, you should come through, too. My lawyers can have this shit settled by then and we can toast and explore how you know Shi-Shi."

Jas reserved his silence and I quickly considered it. Saturday, I'd be with Jas and Sunday, I planned on being at the studio to catch up on a few choreographies. Peering straight into Jas' face as his attention was on whatever task that brought these two unlikely figures together, I saw the benefit.

"I'm down." Finally, I accepted. "I'll text Rayna for the details. Jas, I'll let you finish your meeting. I'm sorry." Jas' eyes finally returned to me, but empty. I didn't think he was happy with the arrangement. Ironically, for me, it was my first time looking forward to dining with Azmir Jacobs instead of being so intimidated by the man. Rayna would be there, but Jas would, too. "Good day, fellas." I winked before disconnecting the call.

Chapter Fifteen

MARCH | PRESENT DAY

Jaz

"You gotta put me on with a job, cousin. Child support been eating my ass!"

"That's because *you* like eating ass," Man chuckled at my cousin, Myron.

We all had to laugh at that. Myron was the pretty boy kid growing up. All the girls chased his ass and, apparently, he'd taken advantage of it over the years. Two days before turning myself in, I'd just attended his third baby shower. A month before my release, Chelsea told me about having gone to his seventh baby shower. One thing was for sure: this family supported his over-seeding the earth.

"For real, cousin," Myron returned to me, holding a *Diet Coke* in his hands. "Give me something. Anything."

"You still at *Home Depot?*" I asked.

"Yeah, but they threatening to cut hours over there. I can't afford that shit. I'mma pick up a night job somewhere."

"Ya big ass should apply for something at a gym where you can burn some calories, bruh!" Man wouldn't lay off his ass.

And the small group that seemed to have assembled since I arrived at my cousin, Sean's, birthday party was relentless with their laughing at Myron's expense. He was a big nigga. Not only had he expanded his family during my lockdown, the nigga did the same with his waistline. His weight had ballooned.

"C'mon, bruh," Myron hissed, waving him off. "What a nigga look like sizing up another nigga, my guy?"

"You ain't a nigga, nigga. You's a whale, nigga."

I hung my head, not being able to help the explosion of laughter from my belly. Man needed to relax. Myron was sensitive as hell.

"This nigga," my cousin murmured then took off.

"We about to eat!" My cousin, Tanya, shouted from the back door of the house.

It was just under sixty degrees out; not warm, but not a freezing temperature preventing us from using Tanya's backyard for the festivities.

"I told him he know you gonna put him D, fam," Sean, the birthday boy, shared. It was him who encouraged Myron to ask me for help. "Sounds like he really hurting."

I unscrewed my water bottle for a sip. "I got him."

"Incoming," Juggy choked out, walking up on us.

Before turning, I knew what he was referring to. Having Wither-spoon here required some pre-gaming. She was still a stranger as far as I was concerned.

I turned to find her leggy physique coming through the yard with a powerful and confident gait. Her legs were bare. An oversized BSU hoodie, short shorts, and pine green *Air Jordan 1 Retro High OGs*. Her long hair was pulled back into a ponytail revealing big ass diamond studs, which had to be five carats. She carried a big aluminum pan with her, locking my lazy attention to her thighs then ass as she took the stairs for the back of the house.

Stranger, danger…

"Shit…" Juggy took off in her direction, and I fully understood his sentiment.

I invited Witherspoon, once again having to spend time with her, but couldn't pursue her because she was trouble—but not my type. *He* had to be with her while she was here at the party, but couldn't pursue her because of me.

A few minutes later, I sat under a large party tent, kicking it with my cousins and their friends from around the way. I hated the attention and adoration for my reputation because it reminded me of the old me, made me feel smaller than their legend of me and, most importantly, didn't allow me to chill in the cut and observe Witherspoon's confounding ass.

Nonetheless, she found me. Cutting through the cypher of niggas surrounding me, she appeared with my cousin just a few steps behind her.

"Hey."

I saluted her with a hand to my head. "Hey."

"You gonna break this weird ass vibe and introduce me to everybody?" It was weird as hell having everyone in our mouths.

I found that funny. "You think I know everybody here, Witherspoon?"

She readjusted her weight on one hip. "I do."

Ignoring her sass, I pointed to my cousin. "Here's the birthday boy. Sean, this is Wither—"

"Shi-Shi," Witherspoon corrected me.

"I think my girlfriend follows you on *Instagram*." Sean extended his hand for a shake.

Witherspoon accepted it. "She sounds smart."

A few in the small group found it funny. Those who didn't laugh were caught in a trance by her thighs, height, and heavy presence. Witherspoon carried a celebrity-like energy I didn't realize until this moment.

"Come on, girl." Chelsea tapped Witherspoon's arm. "I'll introduce you to everybody. Plus, it's time to eat."

"Please tell me the hot dogs are done."

"Yup. What do you want on it?"

"Onions. Lots of raw onions," Witherspoon emphasized.

"Damn!" Sharkie, a neighborhood cat, sang. "All 'em onions for a pretty girl like you?"

Witherspoon's face went tight and she shrugged. "It ain't like I've got anybody to kiss at the end of the night." She scoffed and took off with Chels.

As soon as we started for the food area in the modest-sized yard, a woman holding a tray of shots announced, "Hold up! Before we eat, we need to toast the birthday boy. Let's kick this shit off proper!"

"Oooh!" I elbowed Chelsea. "Shots! I like you people already."

She laughed at my wink. "That's my sister, Tanya. This is her and her husband's home."

"Oh, nice!"

We collected our shots and somehow gathered almost in the center of the yard, holding them in the air. I found Jas, who was receiving a water bottle.

Prude...

I threaded the small group for his side. His sharp gaze was on me before I made it.

"You couldn't have one for your cousin?" I whispered. "Just one?"

Jas scoffed in his cool guy manner. "I'll live vicariously through you, Witherspoon."

"Tisk. Tisk. You'd have far more fun living *with* me." I winked. "The benefits of that arrangement would change your life."

Jas' face dropped before catching himself. That or before Chelsea began the toast.

"Sean, we're proud of you. There are days we miss you. But here's to you never forgetting this place called home. The place you can always return to for something familiar, to open arms——"

"To call Sin and get the gat!" a guy shouted, causing a rip of laughter.

I didn't get it, but felt the unity.

Snickering, Chelsea continued, "to support and to feel a part and at home. Happy birthday!"

Several people shouted happy birthday out of sync, including Jas. He even gulped back a bottle of water as we chugged tequila. It was cheap, but I didn't care. I was happy to be here. So happy, I couldn't help ramming my hip into Jas.

"Loosen up, my guy. Issa celebration." I laughed.

"Come, Shi-Shi!" Chelsea called me. "I'm starved."

"Coming!"

Hiding behind his cheeks was Jas' humor, too. "Be easy and have fun, Witherspoon."

On our way to the table, I saw we moved too slow. So many people had flocked over there and the complaints of jumping the line and women going before men had begun.

"Leo, come take these ribs over there," an older, hickory-hued slender woman croaked while struggling with a large aluminum pan.

Without thinking, I relieved her of the pan that was rather heavy and hot. I didn't even think to wait for whoever Leo was; I charged my way to the table, calling folks to clear a path while en route. I was happy as hell when I reached the table.

"Over here, sweetheart," a woman instructed, pointing to an empty chafing dish rack.

Immediately, I complied.

"Oh, shit!" some kid trilled. "That's you, Shi-Shi!"

"Ohhhhhh!" someone else followed with. "That is her!"

"Yoooooo!"

That's when I became uneasy. I didn't want to be Shi-Shi from the *Gram* here. I wanted to be Shi-Shi the builder who fit in.

"What you doin' here, ma?" a young girl who looked as though she'd beat my ass asked.

"She's celebrating Sean like everybody else, Toya." The chastisement in Chelsea's tone couldn't be ignored.

"I'm just saying," a kid taller than me chimed in. "Can I get a pic, Shi-Shi?"

"Word." A thick, chunky light-skinned guy smiled slickly. "Let's make that nigga jealous. Let 'im know you with a Harlem Pride nigga."

They found themselves funny and before I could reply, Juggy appeared out of nowhere, ambling down the line. "Guest of the Big Homie."

With just those few words, the catcalling stopped.

"And here you go." Chelsea was back at my side, handing me a plate with two hot dogs, mounted with onions. My stomach cried at the sight of them. "Let's get a beer and down these babies. By the time we're done, the line should have disappeared."

A few minutes later, Chelsea and I were swigging down beers and munching on delicious ass hot dogs while discussing Black romance authors who write all white characters when I noticed two things. Juggy stood from the table and approached a woman for taking pictures of me. That's when I realized people, even from a distance, kept eye-hustling me. I hadn't noticed before, so caught up in dialogue with Chelsea, who had been confirmed in my mind. I really liked her. She wasn't Harlem like her cousin. She was educated, open-minded, big-hearted, and down to earth. Conversation with her was easy, so I wasn't aware of the unwanted attention.

"Damn, Jug!" the woman shrieked, grinning with embarrassment, it seemed. "Ain't like I was gonna post it or some shit."

I couldn't make out Juggy's words to her, but I was convinced they weren't nice. My attention went across the tent to Jas. He was in the same corner, almost centered with people around him. However, his attention was on me—or Juggy. A woman handing him a plate had him turning away.

"What's up with King Jaffe Joffer over there?" I murmured to Chelsea.

She laughed, covering her mouth with her hand as I took another bite of my hotdog. "Jas? He's perfectly Jas. I'm happy he came today. We all need to be together."

"Is he a recluse?"

"Not really. Just working so hard, and all the time. The *Wonder* play? You wouldn't believe how hard I worked to get him there."

"That's so sweet. You two close, huhn?"

She nodded, wiping her mouth. "I try to be. He's my favorite, but don't want to admit I'm his, too."

Really?

"What makes him so special?"

Peering his way, Chelsea shrugged her shoulders. "He's never not held me down. Jas is a really good guy. Never changed."

"Did you go visit him?"

She shook her head. "I wanted to so bad, but I was struggling, trying to finish school. He didn't want me stressing about the cost of the flight and hotel stay. So, I wrote him regularly. He schooled me through letters. We talked about everything: guys, papers I wrote, his walk into Christianity—"

"His girlfriends?" I tried softening my inquisition with a snicker.

Chelsea didn't buy it. She leaned into the table and whispered, "You two…" Her brows raised.

I shook my head. "Purely colleagues…and not even that. He doesn't work for me or…we don't share an office. We're just…" I shrugged, picking up my beer, "both in the same line of work."

There was a spark of wisdom in Chelsea's eyes followed by killing the conversation. She knew something, but judging by her self-proclaimed allegiance to her cousin, Chelsea wouldn't tell me anyway.

"Oh! Look who's here? 'Bout time, bitch," Tanya, Chelsea's sister, shouted to a woman walking into the yard holding a toddler.

The girl smiled in a fitted green and pink *Gucci* sweat suit with matching colored *Asè Garb* sneakers. Her body... Damn. She was stacked. Big *Gucci* bag on her childless arm.

Black people still buying Gucci? Or are they like me and only wear what I bought before their racial hiccup a couple of years ago?

"Bitch, please." The girl ambled over to Tanya, who was near our table. "You got my message about Lisa's hair?"

And she was...beautiful! Rough around the edges—likely Harlem bred—but damn beautiful. Big pretty white teeth, mild makeup enhancing her toasted walnut skin. Her lashes were tastefully long and her coffin-shaped nails were intricately designed and colored. Her jet-black hair was boy short, tapered in the back and on the sides with a long, blunt cut bang in the front. She was stylish—urban flair, but very much in touch with fashion.

"Yeah, but I've been busy doing this. You see him?" she tried to whisper.

The girl twisted and turned, struggling to hang on to her baby. "Oh. Over there with Man and 'em." The girl laughed, Tanya tried keeping cool. "I ain't see that muthafucka since he came home. That nigga came home different."

"I know. I thought y'all was gonna get back together."

The girl shook her head. "That nigga came home just to play in my face—litera-*fuckin*-ly—and told me to have a nice life." Judging by the grin on her face, I couldn't tell she was heartbroken.

Then Tanya whispered something I couldn't hear, but the girl's eyes traveled until they landed on me. My nosy ass couldn't look away to play it off. She tried to size me up when she registered my presence, but it was impossible considering I was sitting at a table. As Tanya continued to talk, the girl looked at me again with new eyes. Then Tanya turned to face me, catching me eye-hustling her. Smoothly, Tanya took off in one direction.

"Whaddup, Juggy," the girl greeted him at the end of my table. Juggy sat alone with a crossword puzzle book.

He saluted her with his hand, but that was all he gave, and the girl walked off.

"Who is that?" I asked Chelsea.

When she turned to me, I motioned the girl sauntering off with her baby at her side.

"Samona? That's my sister's best friend."

It was her, Jas' ex-girlfriend who abandoned him and cheated with a friend of his while he was away. I was never a proponent of dating men in prison, even if he was yours at the time of incarceration, but hearing it from Jas made me feel bad for him.

"Is that her baby?"

"Mmmhmm." Chelsea confirmed.

And this chick was bad! Nice round ass, hardly moving in its wake, and a non-existent waistline considering she'd recently had the small child.

"I'm on a different journey now, Witherspoon." His words played in my mind. *"Shit that used to appeal to me, gives me pause now."*

Interesting...

jaz

"Big homies." My cousin, Jonathan, wore a wicked ass beam stepping up to our table as we played cards. "And ladies. In case you're in need"—He yanked open a black trench coat, outfitted with clear plastic pouches.—"I got some loud, xans, purple haze, mollies, percs, brownies, and even some gummies today." He winked at Witherspoon. "For you, I've got some yummy hard candy."

Studying my hand to try and end this game victoriously, I asked, "Jon?"

"Yeah, boss?"

"How's school going?"

"It's cool." He couldn't remove his sloppy eyes from With-erspoon.

"Chemistry classes, too?"

That's when his face fell and he turned to me. "I took a break from those this semester and I'm knocking out electives. They were bustin' my balls."

"It's what career training and prep is like." I played my hand. "The fuck else is there for a twenty-one year old?"

He mumbled something beneath his breath and walked away. Jonathan had so much potential and was crazy bright but, like his peers, was easily distracted by fast living. His mother stayed worried about him and had even mentioned it to me earlier when I'd arrived. His older brother was killed five years ago, devastating her. I wanted more for the kid and wished he wanted more, too.

"Boom!" Witherspoon made a show of laying her cards on the table, declaring her the winner.

"Oh, shit!" my cousin, Greg, cried.

"Damn!" Chelsea joined in. "No biggie. It's getting cold out here anyway. I feel like I need another shot to warm my bones." She left for the house.

"Bring me one!" Witherspoon ordered to her back.

The whole group, including those who were just bystanders, broke the cypher, going to various places in the yard, some even in the house. The temperature had dropped out here. Doing a back-yard party in March was a bold idea. They were lucky we got no rain today, but nature would never be outdone. It was nearing brick out here.

Witherspoon brought her chair closer to me. "Told you all I do is win in life."

"Oh, yeah?" I stretched back in my chair.

"Jas, you want another plate?" my mother shouted from the door.

"Nah. No thanks."

"I'm making something to take home. You want me to make you something, too?"

"Nah. You got it."

"Awwwww!" Witherspoon teased. "Ain't that cute?"

"What?"

"Your mom making sure you have food for later."

I shrugged. My mother had been on good behavior today. She didn't drink too much, and I even saw her dancing earlier when her brother, Earl, hooked up his deejay set and spun some tunes. The family got down dancing, but really loved when Witherspoon got out there with them. She even tried teaching my mother how to twerk. Of course, it was my mother's idea. But Witherspoon was all too accommodating, wearing those little ass shorts she had to be freezing in now.

"You know what can't be cute?" I dodged her joke about me living with my mother.

"What?"

"How you gotta be freezing your ass off in those shorts."

"I've got sweats in the car. You can get them for me when I need them."

"Oh, yeah?"

"Yup. And you can't send Juggy. He has to be tired of babysitting me for the day." I chuckled at her being able to peep that. "I mean, how necessary was that?"

"You don't know these people. Plus, you're like a little celebrity and I figured having all that attention from people could be crazy, seeing you don't know nobody. Plus, my cousins—a few of them— may look unassuming, but they're stickup girls. All they know is confrontation."

"Who? Teea and the one with the red hoodie?"

"Yup. And Tiny over there with the yellow coat. And Gina with the army fatigue jacket at the drinks table." They were known to terrorize hustlers from Jamaica Queens to Crown Heights in Brooklyn. I couldn't count the times I had to intervene when shit fell back on them. They were all around my age, most older, and had been spinning the block as long as I had. It was like the pot calling the kettle black. We pledged our souls to the streets, thrilled by near-misses with death and imprisonment.

"That's how she got that scar from her forehead down to her neck?"

"Nah. Teea got that fighting Tiny one night. They were drinking too much and shit got out of hand."

"Damn," Witherspoon breathed, eyes wild on my cousins. "And by the way, I'm no celebrity; my ex is. I get the connection and misperception and just roll with it."

I nodded. "You did a good job at it today. Just wanted to be sure you didn't get hit with my family's lack of hospitality. Jug helped out with it."

"Why Juggy? Why not you?"

"Because I knew my family would come around me with shit that would bore you." That was as close to the truth as I could explain. I'd gotten all types of grievances and requests for bailouts in the past few hours. Witherspoon being around for all of that would have given her the crumbs to figure out my old world. I didn't want that. "A pretty girl like you don't need to be without protection."

"You think I'm pretty, Jas?" I felt her turn toward me in the dimness of the yard.

Ignoring that trap, I admitted, "I ain't think you'd stay this long."

"I had a good time. Interesting time, too."

"Oh, brother." I exhaled. "Here we go with the discoveries."

Witherspoon chuckled. "I guess you're learning me."

"Been. What is it? My uncle, Earl, spinning the twos with one leg? My lil' cousin, Myra, walking around here with a black eye and busted lip?"—something I had Man handling as we spoke—"Jonathan, who's supposed to be studying pharmacy, wanting to skip the school part and do it from his coat? What?"

"No. None of those. My family ain't perfect either."

"Then what?"

"Your ex over there with Tanya?"

I searched the yard, finding Samona helping Tanya clean up the serving table.

"What about her?"

"She's very pretty—by even my standards."

"Very." I nodded in agreement.

"She seems fashionable, too—I mean, providing nothing she's wearing is counterfeit."

"I doubt it. Mona makes a decent living, owning a salon." *I paid for...* "Been doing hair, nails, and other things out of there for almost fifteen years."

"So I am right: she's a baddie. A little hood, but definitely a boss bitch, as you've labeled me."

I eyed Witherspoon with caution. "Okay?"

She shrugged. "Just observing how your current concubines are a great departure from that bad bitch over there."

"My—" When I caught on to the joke, I snickered. "Concubines. Really?"

"You're not answering the question, Mr. Jas."

"What're you even asking?"

"I know *of* Cynthia. Have been seeing her around for years because of my best friend. She's...dry at best. The picture you showed me last month of the..." She snapped her fingers to recall. "Marie—no. Maria. You showed me a picture of her and she seems to be like Cynthia."

"And what's that?"

"Dry. Rather large."

"You got something against thick women, Witherspoon?"

"Not stylish at all." She ignored me, continuing with her point. "My question is, when did your taste change?"

It didn't take long for me to answer. "When I learned bad bitches came with unfair, one-sided expectations, high price tags, and expiration dates. I know I'm selective on the shit I share, but one thing's for sure about me: I've done a lot of work on myself, Witherspoon. Long-term imprisonment'll do that to any level-headed person.

"It's how I was able to come up with that checklist of how I would take over the world. And I'm no dummy: there's no way a man can build an empire with a partner who's more concerned with surface-level shit than building what we need to build. I can't have a woman unsettled in her heart, worshipping shit that adds no value to our foundation. I'm on 'go' right now. A beautiful woman ain't specifically a size six, hourglass body with perfect teeth, and in the latest *Asè Garb* gear.

"Beauty is a woman who could stand beside me and build this empire without ego, ulterior motives, or the latest *Chanel* bag. I need a woman with a common belief system and set of morals. I want a woman who wants to be a wife to build and not to floss."

"Okay. And what about sexual chemistry and her taking pride in her presentation?" Witherspoon pushed.

I shrugged. "I can learn to fuck you right. Just give me time. And who's to say Cynthia or Maria don't take pride in their appearances? That's subjective, Witherspoon. Shallow as hell, too." It was time to go and I was done with this conversation, so I stood. "I got a curfew to make, plus a few errands to run before turning in."

"You're ready to leave?"

I tossed with my head, shrugging. "The life of a parolee. Let me walk you to your car."

"But Chelsea's bringing me another shot."

"And you can't be drinking and driving, so you're good." When Juggy dropped down the stairs from the house with bags of food to go, a thought occurred. "I can drive you home."

"And what about my car?"

"I can ride with you or drive you and have Jug follow to bring me home."

Her face was tight with disappointment. "Do you have a driver's license?"

"The insults have no chill with you, do they?" She waited for an answer. "I do have a legal driver's license, Witherspoon," I answered with pure honesty.

"Then why don't you drive anywhere?"

"Because Juggy likes to." I shrugged, trying to come up with an answer, no matter how weak it was. "Making up for lost times, maybe." When that didn't seem to satisfy her, I thought of a compromise. "Okay. Have your shot with Chels—have two—then I drive you home to make sure you get there safely. That'll make me feel better. You've hung out with my family all these hours and pretended we were normal. It's the least I can do."

Her discontent, the way she expressed it identified something supple inside of me. The shit annoyed me, but I wouldn't show it.

After a few seconds of shooting me rocks with those pretty eyes I could get lost in if not careful, Witherspoon swiveled on a huff and strutted to the house in search of my big mouth cousin.

I know it was Chels who told her about Samona...

ashira

Jas pulled smoothly into one of my designated parking spaces in the garage. Juggy, in their beat-up white work van, wasn't too far behind. I explained to security at the gate he'd be following. He cut the engine, but the car's system was still very much alive. As he inspected the bells and whistles of the interior of my car, I snapped the release of the seatbelt, turning to him.

"You like?" I grinned, feeling myself.

After a while, Jas murmured. "Shit is nice. A good friend of mine got one in black. I've seen him pull up in it a lot, but never rode in it."

"Or driven it, I see."

"True that. *Mercedes AMG GT Coupe*. This shit is nice, Witherspoon." I actually believed Jas was impressed.

"Any sports cars on your 'empire' checklist?"

"I'm more of an SUV type of guy than sports."

I rolled my eyes. "Yeah. For the impending family and all. Yeah. Heard it all before."

His head rolled up. "You shittin' on my dreams, Witherspoon?"

"No." I feigned being shaken. Then I laughed, bringing my legs up for my knees to meet my chest. "But I can't wait for reality to hit you, though."

"How?"

My shoulders lifted, belying my alleged liquid courage. "This checklist." I stalled. "You taking all those trade courses in hopes of becoming a builder." I swallowed, trying to think of all the bullshit. "Your method of dating. You not fucking Cynthia—*and I can see why*—but I'm sure you've bagged one of her sister-wives. But what confuses me is why you haven't fucked Cynthia. Based on what I've seen of your women, they're all built like her and are her level of dry. Newsflash: you don't even know what your type is, my guy."

I scoffed, feeling the consequences of that third shot I'd snuck in with Chelsea as Jas waited outside by my car. Juggy caught me, though. "Shit. For the right price, I'll help you look for a bad bitch with good credit." I shrugged. "I can always use gas money."

"I 'on't need a chick with good credit—"

"You know what?" I shook my head. "Never mind. You're too weird. You don't even look at me like that. Imagine that. You were locked up for more than ten years, meet me, nurse me through a breakup, and not once tried to get a lick. You don't find *me* attractive, what makes me think you'd find a woman with good credit and willing to relent to your empire-chasing ass checklist?"

Jas' head cocked to the side, a blank expression darkening his face. "Say less, Witherspoon. You're walking a fine line; I'm not a toy or a boy."

I laughed. "But you're a guy who dates two women at a time. One who's cautioning *me*? Let me ask you this. How do you decide which one to use condoms with—full warning: trick question here."

He hesitated, eyes bouncing around the windshield. "Look..." His tongue crept out, gliding against the lower portion of his top lip. "I don't kick it to nobody—*well*, maybe one confidant about this, but not in specific terms—but since you're back on your judgmental bullshit again, I'mma let you know." Jas' lips puckered then rubbed together. "I don't own rubbers because I'm not fuckin' anybody."

My damn back collapsed against the seat, head dropping hard on the rest.

Oh, my god...

My stomach turned over. Shit, I was going to vomit in my *GT*.

"You're gay?"

How did I miss this?

Undeniable anger flashed in his eyes, thick brows knitted, and fist tightened on the wheel. I'd hit a nerve. "I'mma let you fuck around and find out." His growl reverberated around the car. "But last I heard, gay people use condoms, too. You gotta stop drawing those fucked up conclusions. All I'm trying to say is *chill*. I'm a man, Witherspoon, and I've been doing good, holding my shit. Maybe in your lil' mind, I'm just a rabid curiosity; the shit you don't have in your comfortable universe you wanna experiment with. But I'm a man, trying to do shit the right way and secure my own universe. You're gorgeous...fucking out of this world beauty foreign to me, too. But I'm not reckless anymore. I know my lane and I'm comfortable in it."

"With the Cynthias and Marias of the world?"

He scoffed, eyes ahead. "Yeah, if that's the way you wanna put it. I'm just a simple man. I don't want any trouble. I gave up the fast lane, high risk/high rewards lifestyle years ago. Simplicity is my new obsession."

I pursed my lips out while staring into the distance at nothing at all then shook my head. "All I'm saying is what you said about women like Samona and me back at Tanya's was harsh."

His eyes closed, head shook faintly. "I'm so confused. Is this why you went on a fuckin' diatribe claiming I'll never have my own business and diagnosing my ass with the need of a chick with good credit?"

I wouldn't look at him because I honestly didn't know what I was saying. It all just felt fucked up. "Why can't we like nice things and still have the fortitude to hold a man down? You may be clear on what you want in a woman." I peered his way. "But I'm clear on what I want in a guy once I date again. Just like I shouldn't discriminate against your civilian status, you don't get to judge women who don't want to be shopping with our kids in fucking *Sam's Club*."

Jas' neck twisted even more, eyes narrowed tightly. "I'm starting to think you want me, Witherspoon. You're weaving here too much, though."

Annoyed as fuck, I pushed the passenger side door open and hissed. "Don't think too hard. Hurry up and put the alarm on. I've gotta pee." Leaving the car, I slammed the door behind me.

Seconds later, Jas appeared. He locked the doors and tossed me the keys.

"Night, Witherspoon," he offered to my back.

"Yeah. Yeah." I was on my way to the lobby door. "Safe trip back over to the City."

Fucking dummy…

Chapter Sixteen

MARCH | PRESENT DAY

Jas

"Final-*fuckin*-ly..." Juggy grunted from behind the wheel as the van began to pick up speed on Route 4.

Traffic was unbelievable tonight. We had to have passed three accidents within a seven-mile radius. The inconvenience matched my already shitty day. It was enough I didn't sleep well last night, waking up after two fucking bad dreams. That led to a weak worship session this morning from being so tired. Then the delays on two work sites and three of my trades calling out, causing more delays. That meant Juggy and me had to chip in on top of what our own schedules called for today.

"Jas?" her voice was laced with concern.

"Ye—yeah." I swallowed, scrubbing my face with my hand. *"I'm sorry to*

bother you. I know it's Sunday and… I still work on Sundays, I guess because…my lifestyle. My bad if this is your day off—"

"It's okay. Totally fine. I gave you this number for emergencies. For the first time, you're using it. What's wrong, Jas?"

"I had two nightmares last night—this morning." I squeezed my eyes, hating how bitchy it all sounded. "One this morning…technically."

"Were you in a prison setting?"

I licked my lips, mouth desert-ass dry. "The first one. It was the usual: nighttime check."

"Tell me about the second one."

"I was here—home—and I woke up and went to the kitchen for something to drink. These random ass kids were crying in the chairs babies sit in to eat?"

"High chairs?"

"Yeah. Them. There were two and even a baby kinda crawling on the floor. Then there's this chick over the stove with a big ass house dress on with no bra." Her shits almost reached the floor. "She was stirring a pot and smiling at me. That's when it hit me…hard as hell."

"What?"

"She was my wife. Those were my…kids. Like I knew it from that moment in the dream. But deep inside…I wasn't connected to them. They didn't feel like what I think about when…"

"When you think of the family you want to have?"

I nodded my head before admitting, "Yeah."

After a few seconds, she took a deep breath. "This sounds like it could be self-conscious. Like…maybe thoughts you took to bed with you?"

"This shit may sound petty to you, but it felt so real and…scary as hell for me."

"I understand. Could you have possibly talked or thought about any of the elements of the dreams yesterday or the day before? Anything about a family, small children…marriage?"

I thought about that for a minute. "I guess."

That's when I knew what set off an insecurity in my subconscious.

All day, I worked hard, trying to ignore the disappointing fact that I let this chick in my head. For what? *Fuck her!* That was it. For real, for real. I had to stop chilling with her. Tonight would be the last time.

Having missed lunch to cover the sites, I was starved. I'd only had the time to go home, shower, and change for this dinner I didn't want to be at. Could have picked up some *B-Way Burger* and been content with that.

Now this bullshit…

"Here we go," Jug announced as we pulled into the parking lot of *DiFillippo's* next to *River Square Mall* in Hackensack. "I'm running to pick up a couple of burgers and a new book." Crossword puzzle books. He bought them shits daily. They were his tool for peace of mind.

When he stopped in front of the restaurant, I grabbed my coat and hopped out. I reached the double doors as an older couple of Asian descent did. He jumped ahead of her to open one of the doors for her. I grabbed the door above his grip and found myself eye-hustling them as he walked her down the steps. Why simple shit like that appealed to a vulnerable side of me, I could never understand.

Moving from the small waiting area and inside another set of doors for the lobby, I immediately caught eyes with one of the guys behind the reception bar.

"Can I take your coat, sir?"

I handed it over, realizing how useless it was seeing I carried it inside instead of wearing it. Then I felt a pulling of energy to the left of me. Turning, I saw her standing from the bench, beauty taking my fucking breath away with each inch she grew, standing to her feet. Witherspoon's hair was pushed back into a ponytail. She wore a casual, black sweatshirt with one side exposing her smooth espresso shoulder, cropped leather joggers, and black leather, high heel booties. Readjusting the strap of her *Chanel* bag, I noticed how large her eyes were. Witherspoon rocked a little bit of makeup, nothing too loud or distasteful. Mostly a bronzy highlight. Then again, I would never expect "distasteful" or "clownish" from Ashira Witherspoon. She pushed her hands into the pockets of her leather pants as she approached me.

There wasn't an ounce of joy in her face when she murmured, "You mind if we speak alone before we go back there?"

Feeling defensive, I found myself eyeing her up and down, wondering if I trusted that. But I consented with a nod.

She walked past me and, like a stupid fuck, I followed. When she opened a door behind the concierge bar, I didn't think twice. The room was small, some kind of storage with chairs and vacuum cleaners.

The door closed behind and Witherspoon turned to face me, her whole body tense to the point of popping. I was so close to telling her to go fuck herself and to stay the fuck from around me. I couldn't take any more of her schizophrenic, snobbish ass ways.

Her face was low, index finger beneath her nose, then she exhaled, finally looking up to me. Those dark lined eyes marked with a different bitch she gave when being the CEO at *Witherspoon Homes* or the head choreographer at the studio she owned. And it wasn't looking good for her because I wasn't in the mood to deal with a *bitch* at all tonight. A bitch is who fucked up my sleep last night.

"I'm sorry, Jas." Her face was toward mine, but her eyes faltered for a bit. "You're probably tired of my apologies, and to be honest, so am I. It's just our chemistry. It seems to bring out the worst in me—"

"So, your shit is my fault—"

"*and* a thrill I don't think I've ever felt." *Shit.* "One second, I resent you for not sharing—you won't even tell me your real name—then the next, you're using your spirituality to help me out of my shit. I'm inspired by you, I'm frustrated by you. I want to kiss you then I want to break you down to size to project how you make me feel when you reject me. When you don't open to me, it..." She sighed, eyes closed tight. "...it exasperates my inse-curities."

My chin dipped and eyes blew the hell up.

Witherspoon nodded, picking up my shock. "Yeah. The privi-leged girl from Millburn has insecurities. And you, the felon from Harlem, irritate them." She took a deep breath. "But this isn't your problem to deal with. I understand it's mine—and I will manage it. I just don't want..." She swung her head away from me. This shit was hard for her to cop to. "...I don't want you to lose patience with me."

"Why do you give a fuck if I lose patience, Witherspoon? It's all good if we go back to not knowing each other."

"Because I don't want to. Just because we don't have much in common doesn't mean we can't be cool. I still think you need a person like me to socialize you." She fought off a grin. Then she jerked her head and widened her eyes. "We'd be good for each other, dude."

I scoffed, shaking my head. "Whatever you say, Witherspoon." I just didn't want the bullshit anymore.

She opened her arms. "Hug it out?" The humility in her voice was cute. It was something that should be protected.

Bitch aside, Witherspoon was still a woman, had a lot going on for herself. She shouldn't be dangling out there for assholes to exploit.

Shit...

Was I about to do this? Didn't I *just* say fuck this chick?

I did, but couldn't.

Quickly, I reached down and ducked into her flowery personal space for a hug. I didn't allow myself to measure just how soft her dope ass body was and made the hug quick.

"You good, Witherspoon. I ain't trippin.'"

"Whew!" she sighed then laughed at herself as we broke apart. "Eliminated one obstacle, now let me endure the other." She rolled her eyes, passing me for the door.

"What're you talking about?"

"Azmir."

"What about him?"

"Aside from the fact he's my ex-boyfriend's Hollywood plug, the guy's always intimidated the shit out of me."

"Oh, word?"

She nodded. "Rayna's cool, but even with her, it's weird because they know Austin from him dating her sister. But Rayna and I kind of bonded over dancing. She's cool, but it's always felt weird to me because of how we were connected."

That's when I vaguely recalled Divine telling me about the "next Denzel Washington," or some shit during his last visit to me in Montgomery.

Damn. The world was really small. Who'd have thought that same kid from Milwaukee would blow up in less than two years?

And I'd be standing here with the girl he fucked up with...

"Seems to me she still wants to be connected."

"You know her?"

"Not really. They linked up when I was locked down. I'm talking about what Divine said when you *FaceTime'd* me. He made it seem like everything's all good."

Divine didn't say much about Witherspoon when I hung up with her outside of asking how we knew each other.

"How do you know him?"

"Divine?" I took a deep breath. "I've known dude since I was a pup." I shrugged. "To be honest with you, I don't remember a time when I didn't know that nigga."

"Here we go with the 'say less' vibe without saying it." She rolled her eyes. "Whatever." Witherspoon opened the door then turned back my way. "Oh. And I won't say shit about your 'girl-friends in waiting' anymore."

"In waiting? What that mean?"

"Lady in waiting, or me not breaking your balls about them?" I just stared at her. Witherspoon rolled her eyes again. "Lady in waiting. A common role of ancient times. The women who were assigned to royal queens, princesses, or other noble women. They helped them dress, get up in the morning, with their hair—basically, a personal assistant in the most intimate ways."

"So how do *I* have them?"

"Because, Jas, these women ain't doing nothing but preparing you for the woman you'll eventually marry without all the tryouts. I respect you for having a process, but chemistry ain't all that complicated." She swung her head, telling me it was time to go.

ashira

"They had a place out there in mind, but when Launz had the building inspected, the shit that came up was wild," Azmir explained. "So, they're considering switching gears now."

"They can ask for a cheaper price," Jas suggested. "Spend the back dough on the needed upgrades. Or…" He shrugged, gathering the last of his eggplant parm. "They can find a new spot. Build fresh."

"I think the problem with new construction is this is just a pet project for them," Azmir explained. "A passion piece. They may be on it for five to seven years then move on to something else. So the time to shop for land, bending to new regulations." He shook his head.

I tossed my napkin in my plate, deciding to stop trying. I didn't have an appetite. Having Jas here really took the load off. I'd never seen Azmir so talkative and animated as I had tonight. He and Jas talked nonstop. Austin never had a flow with Azmir like this. I tried hiding in conversations with Rayna as Austin and Azmir talked. Tonight, I couldn't help being intrigued by his topics with Jas. And especially now, since the topic had turned into one I greatly understood.

"Yeah, zoning can be a headache," Jas agreed. "Have him give me a call if he wants me to come out and take a look. My firm is suited with all trades—in house."

I reached back for my purse. "Or you can have him call me. I'm sure I can equip them with whatever information or issues they may incur."

Jas chuckled, wiping his mouth as he sat back. "The Launz guy is Divine's friend. I'm Divine's connect. Who invited you, girl?"

Rayna sputtered a laugh and I couldn't help my own, but I was dead serious about the job. I could help.

"From what I understand, Azmir's friend needs help in an arena I've spent my career mastering and dominating. I can help. Plus," I addressed Azmir specifically, "We're Black-owned and operated. His boss runs the most colorless ship over at plantation *Rizzo Custom Homes & Developers.*"

Jas shook his head, humor in his eyes, though. "I told you that's been changing. But I'mma let you hold on to that ancient truth that's turning into a lie." I handed Azmir my business card. "I guess your boy'll have options."

"Awwwww!" Rayna cooed. "He's conceding."

"No the hell he ain't," Azmir scoffed, tucking my card into his wallet. "The nigga's being calculating. I've known him too long."

Jas chuckling quietly made me wonder if Azmir was right. Was his calm, defenseless mien telling of him being conniving?

"How long?" Rayna's eyes narrowed in the same curiosity I'd had.

Jas, a laborer, knows mega-mogul, Azmir Jacobs? In what universe?

Azmir tossed his napkin into his plate as well. The waiter assigned to our private room took his cue and began cleaning our table. Dinner was over. "Since he was a teenager, for sure." Azmir's gaze on Jas was fixed, almost as if he was asking for help, remembering. Jas shrugged with his lips, agreeing. "He was a fuckin'… vulture as a kid, tearing up the damn streets. I wasn't working on the East Coast much at the time, but my ear is always to the streets. An associate of mine had been throwing this young kid from Harlem work that he'd been eating up without a trace."

What exactly does that mean?

I mean…

I knew Jas grew up in the streets so the context of this conversation had to be illegal, but I was desperate to devour each morsel and was gobbling too slowly.

And Azmir Jacobs? I knew he was a resourceful and influential man. But it was becoming clearer and clearer he had some street ties at some point in his life. A point where it intersected with Jas. I'd need more time to stew on that. Either way, clearly those days of illegal running were over, seeing the vast difference in their lifestyles. Azmir was a millionaire, Jas a construction laborer. I knew who'd be paying for this lavish dining tonight.

Azmir nodded before continuing. "I was chilling one year, making a stop out this way and the kid who'd earned this reputation so happened to be at the friend's...job." It was clear Azmir was using code words, which I didn't understand, but was so desperate for more information, I wouldn't dare dwell on that fact right now. "The thing was, I didn't know the kid was a *for real* ass kid. I thought he was maybe in his early twenties. I never liked that shit, but anyway." He waved off the thought. "Over the years, I'd see him when out this way and I was able to watch him. I liked what I saw." Azmir swallowed back the last of his brandy.

"Which was?" Rayna asked as the table was still being cleared. *Thank you!*

"A lot, really. There are some cats that wear the streets like a second skin. It's in the way they walk, talk, and the company they keep. It wasn't that way with him. He was unassuming. I'd seen him talk shop like a goon from BedStuy *and* articulate his way out of a ticket like a *Princeton* student. He could always speak to the occasion. That ability is rare and I knew it. Jas was and still is like a prism: multidimensional...symmetrical structure.

"Meaning from the bottom—his foundation—he's solid at his base. And at the top he was sharp. No matter how you flipped him, he'd land on a two and still be sharp as hell at the top." He nodded reflectively. "Still is. Even as a kid he was calculating. His eyes moved fast and mouth stayed closed. He didn't run with a gang of niggas, at most three. Everybody knew their role—*as kids*—and he was their leader." He pointed across the table to Jas. "A beam of light and it shocked me that all the O.G.s in your presence never picked up on it. Well…one did."

Both men shared an inside chuckle.

"Anyway." Azmir lifted his glass of *Mauve*. "Here's to the kid who took bullshit in and shot out light with it, who reflects light, is the light."

Jas pushed his crystal glass filled with water above the table. Rayna was next, lifting her drink in the air, which was the same as her husband's. Azmir followed, meeting his empty tumbler with theirs. Finally, and obligatorily, I raised my *Château Blevin*.

Jas shared, "A friend of mine—weirdo at the time—said something similar, referring to a prism. Crazy." He nodded humbly. "Cheers."

"Cheers." Rayna and I offered at the same time.

The waiter returned to the room holding menus. "Care to see our selection of desserts?"

"I don't need to see, Angel," Rayna addressed the older man. "You know what I need."

The waiter beamed professionally. "Crème brûlée for the Mrs. Ahh!" He addressed Azmir. "And for you, sir?"

"I'll just have some of hers. I'm good."

Then Angel turned to Jas and me. "And for this lovely pair?"

Jas' attention was on me, offering me to go. I didn't want dessert. I had no appetite, mind preoccupied at a capacity I wasn't used to.

"I'm going to pass."

"Don't insult the pastry chef," Azmir teased.

"The tiramisu is to die for." Rayna blew a chef's kiss.

I didn't know which I hated more: being pressured or being rude. These were the Jacobs', for crying out loud. How many could say they had a casual dinner in Jersey with Azmir and his wife? But I had warring matters on my mind.

Stretching a wide smile, I muttered, "Maybe to go?"

Azmir gave Angel a nod, to which the waiter returned. "And you?" he asked Jas.

"I'm good."

"Very well. I'll get that right out to you."

Rayna clapped her hands, bouncing in her seat. It was clear she was anticipating her dessert.

"Really, Brimm?" Azmir asked, challenging her.

"Mmmmhmmm!" Her head bobbed up and down. Then she reached over, pulling his tall torso to her for a kiss. A kiss Azmir did not hesitate on for a second.

I cleared my throat, tossing a cursory glance over to Jas. "Little girls room for me. Be back."

jas

Rayna was getting busy on her dessert and Witherspoon's was packed up in a small *DiFillippo's* logo paper shopping bag when the waiter popped up at the table.

"Is there anything else I can get for you tonight?"

Divine shook his head while into his phone. "That'll be all. The check is fine."

Rayna elbowed him and, without looking, he leaned over toward her and opened his mouth for more of her food.

These two…

The waiter pulled the leather portfolio from his vest pocket. "Thank you very much. Mr. and Mrs. Jacobs and friends. It has been a pleasure serving you this evening."

I grabbed the check while Divine and Rayna returned his pleasantries. Before he could take off, I slipped my credit card into the portfolio and handed it to him. I glanced behind me near the door of the private room for Witherspoon. She'd been gone a while.

"You got something you wanna tell me?" I turned to Divine at the sound of his inquiry.

It took a few seconds, but I knew what he was hinting at.

"Yeah. Thanks for not going farther than you did." I turned back for the door again, hearing him laugh.

"Anything more?"

I turned back to the couple and caught the glimmer in Rayna's eyes. She was on it, too.

"Say less, Jacobs. We're just colleagues."

"Oh, word? I've been around Shi-Shi enough to know she ain't never burn a hole in the side of Austin's face like she did yours tonight."

"And still, he fucked her over for the queen of pop," I mumbled. "Ain't that what they're calling her?"

"He's in an alternate universe. No one's loyal to no one. Not even to family or their kids. No different from the streets. Some ain't loyal to themselves."

I turned back to Divine whose attention had disappeared into his phone and pointed over my shoulder. "Lemme go make sure this is okay."

"Indeed," he replied without his eyes.

Leaving the room, I cut a left into the hall leading to the restrooms. There was no line because this was the private side of the restaurant, which made the shit so weird. So, I waited.

And waited.

Waiting was bullshit. I'd been out of the game for a minute—maybe I'd never been in the game at all, really. But I didn't recall chicks taking so long in the fucking bathroom. I stepped forward then detracted my foot, hesitating. Because... *Damn.* I wasn't about to go into the ladies' room or knock. I knew little about etiquette, but understood that was a no-no for me. So, my worrying ass stepped back and posted up against the wall across from the door.

Was this normal?

For Witherspoon, *hell nah*. Was she sick? Was something said back at the table to make her wanna hit the mad dash and haul ass out of here? Just as I was about to say *fuck it* and go inside, the door of the restroom opened and Ashira ambled out, fluffing her hair, eyes blinking nervously. That was until she noticed me just five feet away.

I cocked my head to the side as she approached me, trying to zip past a server. She grabbled for the flap of her purse to close it.

"The hell, Witherspoon?"

"What?" Her eyes still bright and anxious—making *me* anxious. *This fucking girl…* "What did I do?"

"I thought you bounced on us. Checked out."

"Me? Why would I do that?"

"Why did you take so long in the bathroom?" Then I thought. "Something not agree with you?"

She glanced down, catching on to my question. "Oh, no!" Then her eyes chased mine. "Did I really take that long?"

"If I'm here, about to come in to check up on you, what do you think?" I shook my head, eyes closing. "What were you even doing in there? You still ain't answered that."

That's when I noticed the white dollop near her chin. Using my thumb, I swiped it. She rolled her eyes when I licked to taste what I had quickly assumed was toothpaste.

My brows met when I asked, "You washed your mouth?"

"I brushed my teeth." She tried looking away.

"For what?" I quickly thought about the times we'd been out together and not once did Witherspoon give me a reason to believe she brushed her teeth after a meal. "Since when?"

Her dark eyes rolled again. Sudden and undeniable embarrassment coated her mahogany features. Her strong confidence had cracked, and she mumbled, "I didn't want to be talking with specks of food in my teeth."

What?

"I would've hooked you up if that was the case. I wouldn't let you go down like that. You sure that's the reason?"

Again, I'd eaten out with this woman too many times to believe these were real issues for her.

Her eyes cut back to me. "People—who truly care about their appearance—brush their teeth after eating, Jas. You never know what occasion may arise. It could be food, a lingering odor from the meal, or maybe an unexpected kiss at the end of the night."

Huhn?

Two busboys carrying trays of dishes charged up the hall, forcing her closer to me.

"Who you kissing tonight?" I wondered out loud, not under-standing her. Witherspoon, inches away, dropped her eyes to my mouth. I smelled the mint of her breath and the sweet fragrance of her perfume and hair. Then, I was breathing her air and she had to be breathing me in. Ashira Witherspoon. This was her, inching up near my mouth with parted lips. Stupidly, fumbling the "cool" bag, I grumbled again, this time from my throat, "Who?"

Her eyes rolled slowly then long lashes clapped at the last centimeter to my mouth. She fucking kissed me. And when I was about to let it go, she leaned into my body then pushed up again, bringing our mouths together again. *Shit.* I was instantly weakened. Like my whole fucking body felt unstable, it didn't matter that I was holding her weight. My belly rolled and damn knees shuddered. Then her tongue slipped into my mouth, boobs pushing into my chest.

The fuck...

Witherspoon's lips were anxious, but her tongue was hesitant. I tasted her, sensing the mint as much as I did her nervousness. *What the hell is this?* I asked myself while enjoying her softness. Un-fucking-mistakable femininity I hadn't felt in years, if at all. It seemed like I'd felt her over, beneath, and against me. I was covered in her warm-ness and hunger unlike anything I'd ever felt from her. I wanted to second-guess what was happening. No way Ashira Witherspoon would be up on me, kissing me part timidly and hella intentional.

In the short instance, my tongue rolled against hers, lips caressed the flavored determination in hers. And immediately, I felt dominant. Witherspoon had shrank—all things about her I'd been perceiving to be out of my league or elements I'd thought I wasn't cut for had withered in this moment. While against this wall, caught up in the heat of the unexpected, Witherspoon was potential prey. I could devour her—I *wanted* to devour her.

So caught up, I didn't even give a damn who watched us. And at the same damn time, I felt stripped, dangerously vulnerable as a motherfucker. Weakened. She'd done it. Witherspoon had fucked up this thing we'd had going. And I let her. As she continued to roll her tongue around in my mouth, I took her at the back of her head and plunged mine into hers, needing to burn her feminine flavor into the meninges of my fucking mind. She tasted good. Felt good. Unable to help myself, I fucked her mouth with my tongue. Witherspoon's little hands grabbed up my shirt and she moaned, swallowing me. I'd be a liar if I didn't cop to this very thing being a feature in my fantasies.

That was until she pulled away from me, breathing out of control. My eyes opened tightly, suddenly disturbed the audacity of our reality. A waitress whizzed past us, tossing a wink. Her colleague, approaching from the opposite direction, gave me a nod of approval. My mind was so fucked up, I didn't acknowledge him. Witherspoon and I locked eyes, a torrent of ruthlessness heating behind our gazes.

Why was I so damn angry?

I didn't know, but couldn't shake my feelings of betrayal. Kissing a man like me, knowing the sensitivity of my situation. Witherspoon was toying with me. Why the fuck had she put me in this situation?

I turned for the private dining room. "C'mon, man. Let's go."

There was no need to look back to see if she followed me. Lowkey, I wanted to leave this whole night behind. I'd already been exhausted then this shit happened, fucking up my head.

"We thought y'all ran into some issues back there." Rayna was collecting her things from the table, wearing a smirk.

Divine tapped on the leather jacket of the bill, letting me know my card had been returned. While Rayna and Witherspoon hugged out their goodbyes, I quickly snatched up my card, wrote in a generous tip, and scribbled my initials on the receipt.

"Rayna." I lifted my arms as she approached me. "It's been real as always."

"You gotta come out to the West Coast."

"You already know. The minute I can, I'll be there."

"Good! Can't wait."

We all made it out of the room and to the front of the restaurant, where Divine and I said our goodbyes. As we waited for our coats, I sent Jug a text telling him we were coming out.

"I'll walk you to your car." Those words to Witherspoon didn't come out in the most pleasant way, but it was the best I could do.

I don't think Witherspoon cared. She couldn't look me in the face, just chirped okay. We passed the Jacobs' East Coast ride, the *Maybach GLS 600*. Then it dawned on me, Witherspoon didn't have her ride valeted. She should have, considering the luxury of it. Plus, Witherspoon didn't need to be roaming around alone with no protection. I was surprised not to see paparazzi. They lurked at this spot. Nonetheless, I followed her as she clutched her *Chanel* in one arm and the dessert bag in the other hand.

"I'm right here," she instructed then popped her trunk. Juggy pulled up just behind me. When Witherspoon slammed it close, she walked up to me. "You're mad at me. Don't be." I didn't know what to say and hated it. I was sure the type of guys she liked, talked all the time. But how could I speak after what she'd just done? My dick was still half awake. "We're friends, right?"

"I 'on't know what kinda friends you got, but my friends—"

Witherspoon's feathery laugh shot over my words. "Stop it, Jas." She was at my chest again. My body was hot all over again. "One last request."

"What?"

"Invite me over to your place?"

"My place?"

She nodded, a V forming in her forehead. "What's the big deal? You've been to my house lots."

"I know, but—"

"And don't give me shit about you still living with your mom or you living in the projects." *Oh shit!* "I don't care. I'm turning off my snobbish ways to get to know you. Can you make that happen?"

I groaned, thinking about the impossibility. "Why?"

"I told you why—wait! You don't have roaches, do you? Because I can't—"

"Say less, Witherspoon!" I rubbed my face with my palms. "My mom don't play with bugs or rodents. Don't offend her in the same breath of asking to visit her crib."

Witherspoon sucked in a playful breath and bit her lips together. "My bad." Then she reached up from her toes and kissed me again. This time, it was a simple a peck. But even that wasn't simple to me because Ashira Witherspoon was in my personal space and I was smelling her *this* close. "Can we make this happen?"

The anxiousness of it all hit me again. "When are we talking?"

"Soon. I leave for Savannah this weekend."

"You're traveling again?"

She nodded. "My best friend's getting married."

"The Peach girl?"

Witherspoon shook her head. "Becky. They're getting married on her family's property down there. My dad and sister are going."

"When?"

"We leave Friday morning. She's having a dinner that night. So why don't I come by on Thursday night? I heard your mom's a good cook."

By who?

Of course, I didn't ask. The idea of having her at my moms' crested every thought.

"Jas!"

"Okay!" I snapped out of it. "Thursday. Let me just run it past her. Make sure she'll be there and up to cooking."

"And if she isn't, you can still have company. Right?" She walked away after winking. "I promise I won't disrespect her home in the absence of her supervision."

"*Witherspoo—*"

"I know." She made it to the driver's side. "I know. I'm saying less. Call me when you get in. It's after your curfew, kid."

She was cute. So fucking cute, it drove me crazy watching her take off.

"Aye!" She turned to me. "Don't have me fuck up my checklist."

"What do you mean?"

"I told you. I got a checklist for my life. Don't put me in a damn jam. Don't fuck it up, Witherspoon."

She twisted her mouth, eyes swiping left and right. Miraculously, Witherspoon didn't utter another word before dipping into the *AMG GT Coupe*.

Fucking Ashira Witherspoon. She kissed me. And I could tell by the kiss, she wanted more. That shit woke up a hunger in me I'd been able to successfully keep under control for thirteen years.

After watching her take off, I pulled out my phone as I walked over to the van. By the time I was inside, Man answered.

"Yo, I need something done."

"Shoot."

"My mom's crib."

"Yeah?"

"I need my old shit cleaned out. Bring in a new bed and pillows. I need some clothes in there, too."

"The fuck, bruh." He laughed. "You moving back to the buildings?"

"For Thursday night, I will be."

"Reed?" Jug inquired from the left of me.

All I could do was shake my head.

Why the fuck couldn't I just say no?

Chapter Seventeen

APRIL | PRESENT DAY

Jas

"JAS, I SWEAR TO YOU, I SPOKE TO THE OLD MAN TWICE. THE second time, it got so ugly it upset my mom." Danny Lewinski found that statement funny.

His boys were a choir around him.

I knew what this was. Danny Lew was backing out on the deal we made. We agreed on a partnership after the acquisitions of the firms he'd been collecting under his father's reign. The night I met with him in February, we talked for over an hour about merging firms to dominate the industry.

And now this?

I snorted, swiping my nose with my thumb. Danny Lew wanted to be a class clown, it was clear to me. First indicator was him avoiding my calls. Then it was to meet in the back of the bar instead of inside, which meant these cats were likely prepared for a brawl. Violence hadn't been my companion in years. I'd separated with that bitch at *FPC Montgomery*, and divorced her the day I was released. On this new journey with Christ, I decided I didn't need her. That bitch brought too much attention to my life. Too much trouble.

But Dan wants a passionate reunion...

I felt anger stirring from the bowels of me. But I swallowed back the steam rising. This was my legacy we were talking about. This merge could mean the difference of me being able to pay college tuition to my family spending Thanksgivings in Croatia and Christmases in *Saint Justin* when we wanted.

"Danny Lew—"

"That's my name. Don't wear it out, motherfucker!" he joked, sticking out his tongue and waggling his index finger.

And, again, his choir of four cats found that corny shit funny.

"I feel like you're being disrespectful here, Danny Lew. First, you give me the runaround, then you have me and my niggas out here at night, in the cold. I'mma street nigga, D, and under all these conditions, I'm feeling disrespected and threatened here."

We were five deep to his four. I had my cousin, Quan, stay back on the street in case something went crazy—like Danny Lew reneging and being disrespectful about it.

"Come on, bro! I get it." He raised his palms in the air. "I totally get it. But we ain't bunkies no more in the *Green Monster*." He laughed. "I know what you wanna do and I tried. Sorry."

"Sorry?" I took a step closer to him. "Is that all you got for *me*? You fuckin' tried?"

"Listen, dude! I don't owe you shit. The rules in lockdown don't apply out here..."

juggy

He playing Sin…

The white boy and his white ass pussy friends was all fucking us around. I knew I shouldn't care so much. Knew this was Sin's business and my role was to support and protect him. That last assignment was some shit I took seriously. I would die for Sin, and right now, I felt like letting somebody else go first.

Chill, Jug. We ain't on that wave no more. We can live a better, risk-free life. We can be legitimate now. Just give me a few years. You won't go hungry.

Those was his words to me before he came home. Man, hell yeah, I trusted him. Especially because I was the reason he was locked up in the first place. I never made the drop the day Newark PD came looking for him for the Bartinickis. If I'd taken care of my business instead of getting necked by Stacy Peterson from Lennox Ave, my nigga would've never been locked down. Or if he'd let me fall on my foul judgment, he could have been freed and I would've been down in the pen. But the nigga ate the charges and lost years on the streets.

That was Sin: always about the people he loved. Even as a kid, the nigga was solid. When he found out my moms' boyfriend was beating the shit out of us, the nigga taught and showed me I had power. I went from pissing my shits at night, waiting for him to finish on my moms and start beating my ass to pissing on his corpse, thanks to my nigga, Sin. It changed my life. He changed my fucking world.

So right now, when he was trying to make moves legally and shit, and this clown ass coke head wanted to play Sin, I couldn't do it. Nah. Sin been doing the right thing, keeping his nose clean. He ain't deserve to get played in front of these meth-heads. These bitches was tweaking in our faces.

"You're right, Danny. Those rules don't apply out here, but a deal is a deal. You said we were partners and assured me you'd take care of the minor detail of your pops. And now you're saying...?"

"It ain't work out!" he screamed so loud, lines bulged out of his neck.

Fuck that...

I charged the big, fat ass motherfucker in front of me, pulling out my Glock. Then I slapped the butt against his head. Bodies moved around me until I heard the cocking of a gun followed by Man's warning. When fat boy stumbled, I cracked him in the forehead then in the nose. Feeling his blood splatter over me, I jammed the barrel of my shit in his mouth. He cried like a bitch in pain. And when I knew he wasn't going to be a problem, I swung my head to peep Sin.

I saw it in his eyes—all of it. I was out of pocket, going this route. He ain't want violence. The nigga only wanted Jesus and all that goodwill shit. But another thing I caught in his eyes was the fucking lust of it all. We was fucking Vikings. Nothing could change that. We got off on violence. The sight of blood made us merciless.

My confirmation was Sin stepping to white boy Danny, shoulders flexing and nose wide. "Danny Lew." His damn voice was deeper, words carried longer. "Talk to the old man again or..." He shrugged. "don't mention my name again until you control the majority of the firm. But we will resume our original agreement—"

"I gotchu, Sin!" the white boy cried, pushing his hands in the air defenselessly. "I swear on my unborn kids, we'll do it. I was just fucking around—we were just fucking around. I'm sorry. I'm an asshole." He walked over to the fat fuck I had pinned down. "You didn't knock out his teeth, did you? Jesus, Bobby, are you okay?"

I stood from his big ass belly, tossing all the pussies now shaking in their boots a final message from my eyes.

I may have needed this more than anything to satisfy the craving for the high I got from this shit. The fight at *Club Sin* last month wasn't enough. Once I came down, I would pledge a life of straight and narrow to my nigga again.

I fucking swear it…

ashira

"I'm pulling in," I spoke through my *Bluetooth* when hanging a right into the black metal fence. There were people milling about or squatting all around. Music played in the distance and children ran and yelled in between moving vehicles. That made me nervous and extra vigilant. This was Harlem, home of… *Jas.*

Shit!

I still didn't know the man's name but found myself pulling into his home in the projects like a damn fool. What in the hell was wrong with me? Was this desperation masked by curiosity? Had I really been so hurt and affected by Austin's betrayal that I would do something so dangerous as putting myself…my vehicle in danger like this?

I'll only stay an hour…

"I see you," his thick vocals assured, making me pliant deep down and pathetically. "Keep to your right. Past the cement barrels and come around the circle. I'm at the end."

I did as he instructed, going slow to be watchful for carefree children and trying not to stare at the junkie to the left of me, dozing off on his feet.

"You see me?"

Blinking snatched my attention from the teenagers throwing rocks at each other for fun, and I saw Jas' large frame, holding one phone to his ear while thumbing into the second one with his other hand. In the sixty-one degree weather, he wore a midnight blue long john shirt, blue jeans hanging a tad bit low and...

Slippers?

I couldn't confirm that. He was now directing me into a parking space it seemed he'd been holding. It was in the front row. Once I was in and cut my engine, I took a deep breath and grabbed my bag. When I stepped out, I placed the bag around my head and shoulder then locked the car.

Jas stood at the hood, eyeing me from head to toe with humor gleaming from his eyes and spasming in his cheeks. "You got the *Louis V Bumbag* across ya chest, the army fatigue cargo jacket, joggers, and motorcycle boots on? You dressed for war or a trip to Harlem, girl?"

Suddenly irritated and slightly embarrassed, I rolled my eyes. "Whatever." I glanced around, noticing the unsavory stares around. "Is my car going to be okay?" I tried whispering.

It was my plan to switch cars with Cecil. He loved to cruise Linden with my ride and lie about it. But I couldn't wait for him to be done with his pedicure appointment. I didn't want to be late today and more than that, I didn't want to get here after the sun fell. It was setting now.

"For sure." He reached for my hand. "T-Ski!"

"I'm on it, Sin." A burly-looking guy in need of a cut in a major way tossed a wave from a makeshift card table that was nothing more than a single serving tray with legs. He looked scary curled over the tiny thing, sitting across from an older gentleman with a weathered trench coat and a cigarette wedged behind his ear. "Ain't nothing."

Sin...

That nickname tickled me. By large measure, Jas was a nice guy. I had no idea of his past, but foolishly believed I knew his spirit. It felt gentle. Reliable and consistent.

"This way, lady." Jas led me into the building.

Right away, I noticed the constant double-glances, ballooned eyes, and momentarily frozen stares. And *damn!* I smelled a bit of urine. It wasn't bad at first because my focus was on the reaction to people passing in the lobby or those standing near the mailboxes or windows. Everyone was staring. Jas pressed for the elevator, hand still sealed over mine.

"Aye, yo," a kid no taller than my hip pointed. "You that fine ass Shi-Shi, the dancer. Ain't you?"

It was my turn to freeze. I glanced over to Jas then back to the kid.

"Yo, who's ya moms?" Jas asked in a manner not so friendly.

The kid tossed his little chin. "Brenda from the second floor. Why?"

"Because I'mma have to tell Brenda to teach her son when to curve his damn mouth."

His tiny face tightened and he hissed. "Who the fuck is you to tell my moms shit? Why don't you tell yours to suck on my nuts, bi —" The little boy was yanked up by an older man with sunglasses and a blanket expression. He kicked little legs fruitlessly in the air while being carried away.

Jas tugged at my arm, getting my attention. "C'mon."

I noticed when we stepped onto the elevator, everyone else waiting parted like the Red Sea, allowing us on first. Then the doors were closing before they could get on. *They don't want to, Shi-Shi...* They didn't even try, just continued to mutedly gape at us, at him. Is this what Cynthia and the rest of the harem experienced coming here?

And fuck!

Urine was for real the winner of the elevator ride. I glanced over to Jas. His brows lifted and lips curled in response. I didn't know if he knew what was going on in my head. Of course, he didn't. He lived here. When you're used to a scent, you no longer experience it. I just prayed this aromatic excursion wasn't indicative of his apartment.

We made it to his floor and before the elevator door slid open, I heard ruckus. Jas didn't take my hand this time, but I followed him when he hung a right. Behind us were several guys in a huddle with fixed attention and animated responses. By the time I ripped my eyes from them, we were entering his apartment.

It was…small. Not to claustrophobic levels, but smelled freshly cleaned by way of bleach and lemon. Beyond that, the scent of comfort foods diffused the closed air. It made sense when I realized the first room we made it to was the kitchen.

"Ma!" Jas barked.

"She here?"

Jas didn't answer as I followed him into the kitchen. It was busy with just his mother, but food everywhere: simmering on the stove, vegetables chopped on the countertop and some in a strainer over the sink, and some still in the grocery bag on the table.

"Witherspoon, you remember my mom, Charmagne. Right?" He snapped a carrot between his teeth."

"Hey, girl! You that dancer from Sean's party. Right?"

I was embarrassed. Yup. *That's me: Shi-Shi, the twerker amongst strangers.*

I smiled. "Ashira. It's nice to see you again. Thanks for inviting me into your home."

"Pleasure is all mine, child."

"She ain't know what you eat. She made a whole bunch of…" He peered around. "What's all this, Ma?"

"Stew fish, fried chicken, meatballs soaked in barbeque sauce, greens—with smoke turkey—mac-n-cheese, white rice, beans, cabbage, and…" She looked around herself. "…cornbread. It's just that y'all kids eat so different nowadays. You know when he came home, he was… What is it?" she asked him. "Vegetari—"

"Vegan."

"Yeah. That." She waved her hand in the air. "Guess how long that lasted?" Charmagne balled her mouth. "The nigga was cut and swole the hell up, but got sick. Them doctors said his numbers was all fucked up. You know why? No smothered pork chops, fried chicken, barbeque ribs…none of that." She snapped her fingers. "Damn! I made potato salad, too. Made that shit last night." She took a quick sip of her *Corona* before making a one hundred-eighty-degree spin for the fridge and pulling out a large plastic container.

"Look at her thighs. Witherspoon eat everything, Ma."

"It's Ashira, and everything that's good." I cut my eyes at him. "I heard your potato salad is legendary. I think I'm in for a treat."

Jas shrugged, introducing me to a more relaxed side of his persona. "I tried to tell you."

"I was just being sure. You said you wanted her fed." Charmagne shook her head. "You ready to eat, baby? This shit just about done."

Sucking in a deep breath and holding it with wide eyes on her son, I didn't know what to say. Truthfully, I needed a moment to gather myself in this new environment before doing anything. I needed to be sure there were no roaches or furry residents in the place.

"I'mma kick it with Witherspoon before we chow," he told his mother. "You want something to drink?" Jas asked me. "I got your fancy ass *Château Blevin* on the way home from work."

Why?

Not knowing whether to laugh or roll my eyes, I shrugged. "I'll have what the lady of the house is having."

Jas went for a cabinet door. "In a glass. Right?"

"No. No." I shook my head, clearing my throat. "The bottle is fine."

"Oh, shit!" Charmagne snapped her finger. "She my speed, Jas. Ain't no damn holy-roller. She ain't stuck up like you said. She boughetto! Hey!"

I cocked my head to the side, shooting the hardest glare to Jas. Stuck up. *Really?*

Chuckling, he popped the lid off the *Corona*. "C'mon, lil' homie. I need to shower before I eat."

My plate was loaded, I was on my second beer, and feeling far more relaxed than I did pulling up to the building.

"You were really vegan?"

Jas forked stewed fish when he nodded while chewing. "For about seven years."

"Why?"

"Just wanted to be clean in and out." He shrugged. "I started the journey to discipline and addressed my diet first."

"Prisons support veganism?"

"For a little while now. Nothing five star, though."

"Like this food?"

"You like it?"

"Your mother's hands are blessed." I meant it. Other than the cornbread not being as sweet and buttery as I preferred and her taking a heavy hand with the salt on the beans, my palate was pleased. Even with that one incidental, they were still tasty. "Why did you stop being vegan?"

"It fucked with my immune system. I was low in Zinc absorption. So when I came home, I got reintroduced to more germs my body couldn't fight like normal people do. Mine was pretty severe. My hemoglobin was low, too." He plopped the fish in his mouth and I watched him chew. "All of that could've been handled with supplements and time. But the doc didn't think I should, and I agreed. I was otherwise healthy. No need to manipulate my diet."

"My girlfriend, Aimee." I took a sip of the *Corona*. "She's a doctor…family doctor at a health clinic in Michigan. She said some patients show with hormonal issues after starting a vegan diet."

"Well." He wiped his mouth. "Thank God that wasn't another issue for me."

"Yeah," I agreed seamlessly. "Because that would account for all these years of successful abstinence. Right?" I tried holding a straight face, but couldn't.

"You got jokes, Witherspoon?"

"I'm just saying." I laughed. "I've been thinking about it. That's insane, dude."

"What choice did I have? I was in prison. Ain't no nut in the world worth the assistance of another man. And there was the one female C.O., but as soon as I got her warmed up, she got transferred. Cute girl, too, from out there in Alabama."

"Awwww! No nunu for Jas."

"Nah." He went back to his plate. "Not at all."

"I'm just messing with you. I have no idea how it affects the hormones."

"Yeah. You just love clownin' me."

"I live for it." I continued to eat.

"Glad I can give you that."

The doorbell rang. Seconds later, Charmagne was out of her bedroom and peering through the peephole. "Can I help you?" she asked after swinging the door open.

I couldn't hear the exchange, but did catch Charmagne pivoting so the guests could be seen. It was an older man standing with the kid from downstairs in the lobby.

"Peace, god," the older man offered stoically.

Jas stood. "Peace. Y'all come in."

He pushed the kid hard at the shoulder, prompting him to come inside. I registered the discomfort of the little guy as he obeyed.

"Sorry to interrupt. The lil' nigga got something to say to you and the lady."

As though he could feel the man's heated gaze searing his little head, the boy mumbled, "Sorry for what I said downstairs."

The guy popped him on the head. "And what else?"

The boy winced. "Sorry to ya moms, and to you, Shi-Shi."

My heart sheared. Nervously, I chuckled before standing myself. "Hey, you." I stood beside Jas. "It's all good. Was actually kind of cool to be recognized. Thanks."

The boy wouldn't look at me, and the guy gave me a quick once-over before breaking his attention to Jas. "Mr. Jenkins told me about what happened, man. I whooped his ass over it. These kids don't get code. My bad. O.G." He placed his fist to his chest.

"Ain't no thing," Jas returned then squatted to get eye-to-eye level with the kid. "Yo, what's ya name?"

His eyes rolled up before shooting down. "Duquan."

"Well, Duquan, now you know me—you still don't know Shi-Shi, but you know me." The way he said my nickname was like the tip of a feather winding down my spine. "And her." He pointed toward the door. "That's my moms. When you see her, you say hello and if she needs help, you make sure she got it. I'll do the same with yours, too. A'ight?" Jas lifted his palm. The boy met it while nodding. "A'ight." When Jas stood, the guy gave a firm nod. "'S'all good, bruh."

"'S'all good, lue,"

With a nod, Jas dismissed them. By the time we sat back down, the door was being closed.

I grabbed my beer. "Was all of that necessary?"

"With him? Maybe."

"Why? And what is lue?"

"Because some kids're that damn disrespectful and only respond to fear and intimidation. Did you hear the mouth on him?" He pushed mac-n-cheese into his mouth, garbling around it, "What's lue?"

"What he referred to you as."

"Oh. Lieutenant. Just a title of respect."

"Oh." I had to remember I was a foreigner in this land. There was so much I didn't know.

We ate in silence for a while, giving me time to absorb my being there. Charmagne's place was efficient, I supposed. Two bedrooms and one carpeted bathroom that would get lost in my bedroom closet. It amazed me how the small, nine-hundred square foot apartment was utilized. There were pictures on the walls of yesteryear. Jas was in some, and others were people I didn't know. But the picture of Jas in a white tank and tan khakis, clearly 'posing' on the yard, caught my attention.

"When was that?"

He peered up into the area I pointed to. "That was in two thousand…" He took time to think. "…fifteen maybe."

"You were big."

"I still am big."

"Not that big."

He nodded. "Witherspoon, I'm actually bigger than that."

"How?"

"More muscle mass now. Less fat, I guess. I 'on't know."

"Are you the only child?"

"For my moms, yeah. My pops got a son. Seventeen."

"Oh. Like me."

Memory lit his eyes. "Your little sister. Right. She's a lil' cutie."

"I won't be telling her you said that. Not even your guy downstairs keeping an eye on my car would be able to keep her away."

"You two have the same father?" I nodded.

"Yup. I'll be meeting them in the morning at the airport. That's if my dad doesn't forget her. He tends to do that." I rolled my eyes internally.

"He can't be that bad."

"Oh, he is," I sang. "She wanted to stay with me to ensure that wouldn't happen, but…" I swung my head side-to-side.

"But you wanted to experience Harlem before jetting off to the wedding."

"I'm a sucker for being led by my curiosity." I wouldn't look at him.

"What are you curious about?"

I shrugged. "Your duplicity, I guess."

Jas sat back on the sofa, stretching his arms and accidentally knocking over the little *Ty* stuffed animals his mother had collected there. "What do you mean? I'm a simple man. Simple life. One past, one path, one future."

"Dude!" I groaned, not wanting to talk about it. "You're ruining good eats."

"Witherspoon, you ran through that big ass plate. You only have like two forkfuls left."

"See! That's one contradiction! Your mouth—your language. You're supposedly a Christian man, Jas."

"I'm working on my presentation, but I'm faster at my heart. You know I was joking."

I do and love it…

"That's not what I mean. *You!* You want your own building firm, but seem content working for one of the most racist ones in town. You claim to want a wife, and to get it, you date two at a time!"

"And you ate more of my moms' food than you did at *DiFillippo's*. You want some more?"

Was he kidding me? That was Jas' way of blowing me off instead of his usual "say less" method.

"I'm done eating. You want me to take this?" I referred to his empty plate.

"Nah. I got it. You're a guest."

"Nope." I scooped up his plate. "I want another beer."

"You don't want wine? I can open for you."

"No. Beer is fine." Then I turned in the kitchen archway. "Unless you wanna tell me your full name."

He snickered, shaking his head. "Jas."

"*Ugh!*" I grunted hard before taking off.

I was beginning to think there was something wrong with me, enjoying this cat and mouse game with him. I wouldn't let Jas know that, though. After placing the plates on the small countertop, I pulled another bottle of *Corona* from the fridge. On my way back to the living room, I saw Jas was on one of his phones. But what surprised me was the game console I spotted on the wall unit, near the DVD player.

"Oh, shit!" I stopped in the middle of the floor. "Is that a *Wii?*"

Jas mumbled something about his mother asking for it years ago. I was too far gone at this point, figuring out how to fire it up.

"*Just Dance 4*! Oh, my bum-bums. I'm about to kill this!"

Jas scoffed, "She still got that shit? I remember when she asked me for it when I was locked down in Montgomery, saying she needed to work out."

"For what? Your mother's like a size four."

He shrugged. "She said her stomach was getting too big."

Within minutes, I was warming up at a beginner's level. This was perfect to work off the food I'd just inhaled. By the time I accelerated, Jas was still into both his phones.

"Dude!" I shouted at him. "You're not a CEO or a drug lord. Get off your ass! I'm killing this routine. Come join me!"

Of course, he didn't drop his phones and acquiesce. A mild smirk warmed his face, his attention fixed on the "tasks" at hand. That was until I stopped and pulled one phone from his thigh.

"C'mon, Witherspoon," he warned.

"Dance with me. Show me what you're working with." I laughed, spun around then slipped the phone into the back pocket of my joggers. "Let's go! Do what he's doing and don't embarrass me."

For several seconds, Jas stood there with his big hands at his waist and face to the floor. Then his head began to bob. When he started to incorporate his arms, I knew he was a good time. A new facet of his personality was deposited into the game of getting to know "Jas" better. Not only that, but he was now speaking my language. Dance was a communication I was highly fluent in.

Within five minutes, Jas was committed and focused on exacting the moves precisely. His shoulders were flexible, and pelvis…impressively agile. When he wouldn't smile or laugh with me, I worried he wasn't enjoying it. But then it dawned on me, perhaps Jas was fine. That when faced with a task, he locked in. He was doing this for me. I, Ashira Chivon Witherspoon, had a thug from Harlem and a convicted guns dealer dancing in the middle of his mother's tiny living room. Life could get no better for me.

As I laughed my head off while keeping up with the sequences, he barked, "This why you wanted to pull up to my moms' crib?"

"It's been a fantasy, for sure!" I laughed even harder. Jas was adorable.

"Let me know more of your fantasies so I won't fall for the okie doke no more."

Ah…

That proposition sobered me just enough to be honest. I swallowed, eyes unbiddenly locking to the small television screen. "To fuck you totally naked in front of mirrors."

Within seconds, Jas stopped and my heart dropped from my chest. I didn't turn to him at first, just watched through my peripheral.

Nice, Ashira…

"Jas…" I didn't know what to say. I couldn't lie. I did want to fuck him and watch myself do it. But I didn't want his typical rejection either. "I just…"

"Nah. Ain't nothing." He scoffed. "*Taking Tips from Tynisha*'s on." He pointed his thumb over his shoulder. "I'll let you finish this while I go get into that. I missed last week's episode."

Oh, shit!

He turned on his heel, and I shouted, "No! I'm coming, too!" I began frantically looking for the remotes. "I haven't seen the last two episodes. Wait, Jas! *Damn it!*"

Not only did I have to shut down the console, but I needed to return Charmagne's entertainment system back to the state I found it in.

Chapter Eighteen

APRIL | PRESENT DAY

Witherspoon yawned at the top of the bed. "I can't believe Alton Jr. said that to his mother."

"What? That he wants a wife like her one day?"

"Mmhmm." She wiped her tight eyes and tried to flash them wide as though to wake herself up.

We'd just caught up on the last three episodes of *Taking Tips from Tynisha*. I even watched an extra one she'd missed.

"What's so unbelievable about that? Sons should want to have women like their mothers if their mothers are good women. They should want to treat them better than their fathers if their fathers treat the mother like shit."

"You want a woman like Charmagne?"

I shook my head, not going there. "You're tired. You gonna need for me to drive you home? I can call Jug and have him follow us."

"Don't you have a curfew?" I nodded. "I won't risk that for you." Then she shot up. "You think that T-Ski guy left my car?"

"Yeah. For about an hour to eat and shit. Mikey took over. He's back out there now."

"But for how long?"

"Probably for another five hours. T-Ski's life is that game table. He'll play by himself. He's..." I used my index finger to circle my ear. "...different. Nobody fucks with him. If he says not to fuck with him, someone else, or some*thing*, the whole hood know to listen. Even the cops try to stay out of T-Ski way and not be the cause of his ass having a fit."

"What's having a fit?"

"The nigga go ape."

She nodded, possibly understanding. T-Ski cracked Man's uncle's skull with his bare hands when we were pups. He went to the crazy house for two years for that. Before then, he spent fifteen years in the pen for manslaughter. I didn't want that in Witherspoon's head.

I crawled up to the top of the bed and lay on the opposite side of her.

"I can drive myself." She picked up the remote.

"No. You can't."

"Why not?"

"It's damn near midnight. You're not leaving me at this hour and going home by yourself. I'll make sure you get there safely."

She turned the channel. "And what's going to happen to me alone?"

"You'll never know on my watch, Witherspoon."

"What do you think happened before I knew you?"

"Not my problem."

"You think your mother minds I'm here this late?"

I opened my eyes at that odd question. "I'm grown, Witherspoon."

"But it's her place."

The place and belongings I've paid for. "She's good. Let me know when you're ready to go. Jug's on standby."

"Ooooooh," she breathed. *"Cold Case*! I loved this show back in the day. You know I visited the set in L.A. back in two thousand… seven or eight?" My eyes broke open again. Two thousand-eight was the year my life had changed drastically. The year that set the loss of freedom into motion for me. "It was so cool! I wish they still did those studio lot tours."

My eyes opened to silvery darkness. The pole light from the parking lot shone into the window. I'd forgotten how my room didn't get dark at night unless I went up to the roof and shot it, busting the bulb. That would get me a few months of darkness at night because the public housing authority took their time with repairs here.

Damn…

I was back here. My old room, but with a mopped floor, a new bed, and television with cable. I could hear the sirens blasting in the distance against the crackheads fighting. The car alarms going off added to the soundtrack of home. None of this shit was new. I loved this place, enjoyed the people, worshipped the streets.

What was new was the heat emanating from the opposite side of the bed and the light snoring that likely woke me up. She must have turned the television off at some point. Did she try to wake me? I wasn't a heavy sleeper at all. It was never safe to be for me back in the day on the grind or in the pen. I checked my phones to see if I missed anything from Jug.

Nothing. Just the usual call-outs and chicks I had no plans on entertaining. But there was one from her.

Witherspoon: G*UESS WHO'S SPEN'N DA NIGHT IN* H*ARLEM* YO! Y*OU OWE ME.* Y*OU CAN PAY BY RIDING WITH ME HOME IN THE* MORNING.

My damn belly warmed at those words. I wasn't new to chicks

wanting my time. I wasn't a "ladies man" before getting locked down and didn't want to be now. But I'd always had chicks wanting to be my girl or just to fuck or to get in my head—like what Witherspoon here wanted. Yeah. She said she wanted to fuck earlier, but I felt what she wanted was what she'd probably never had. She wanted the thrill of a real nigga. I didn't like the idea of it because I was a real man on a real journey that could get derailed by fucking with a woman like Witherspoon. She'd have her fun, get bored, then go back to Austin Seers-type niggas where she belonged.

Her ass had me dancing…

That was some shit I ain't do in years. But it made sense for her to do it. Witherspoon may have been a bitch at work and when dancing, but outside of those environments, I realized she was silly as hell. And sexy. *And so damn cute…*

The bitch.

The bitch only lived in a few aspects of her life. Those facets where she was gullible like when she was dancing in my mother's living room earlier. She thought I was busy into my phones. I used them to disguise my watching her body move. Those long thick thighs and just enough of a sloppy ass were just as dangerous as her big, silly persona. No bitch. All lil' homie—

Her eyes opened directly to me as she lay on her back. Then a faint smile formed. "Was I snoring?" she whispered.

I snorted, "Blame it on the *Corona*."

"Beer does that shit to me every time."

"And you downed it the one time you sleep with me," I joked.

"I was not touching that wine, man." She rubbed her tight eyes. "Why?"

"Because." She yawned. "I would've gotten too comfortable and did some crazy shit." I loved her soft, scratchy voice. "Charmagne would've thrown my ass out for…dry humping you or something." She laughed at herself. It was a dull, sad one. Witherspoon shook her head.

"Please don't dry hump me, Witherspoon." The visual was funny, but I wasn't smiling.

"I'm *jokin*—"

I reached down and kissed her. She didn't see it coming and neither did I. I felt it, though. She was too cute, too tempting, and even though Witherspoon weakened me, I felt good around her. There was only so much resisting I could do. So much ignoring the rage in my groin or the ache in my chest for her body, silliness, or cuteness.

Her soft hands grabbed the back of my head, fingertips pressed into my scalp. I lifted to kiss her more, pushing my tongue deeper to taste the musk of the beer, the vulnerability to our chemistry. The sounds of our tongues smacking lit a fire in my chest, a hunger in my belly. I left her mouth and kissed her chin, then licked the pulse of her neck. Hearing her breathing getting louder made me want to taste more.

I crawled over her warm body, straddling her. When I took her hand and softly pulled her up, Witherspoon sat up and kissed me again. My hands roved up the back of her shirt, feeling the softness of her skin. My need to feel more—taste more—had me feeling free to touch her. I didn't think to ask, I'd passed a point of control. My hands reached her bra strap and my damn pulse jumped to my throat. My hands shook as I unhooked it, but more than I was afraid to explore, I was scared as hell to lose so much fucking control. It was never who I was.

Then I was fucked. She lifted her shirt over her head, staring me dead in the eyes. I was steel all over watching her chest rise. The only thing keeping me from seeing her breasts was a loose bra. Witherspoon knew it, too. Her eyes dropped down to what had held my attention. Then those tight eyes swung back up to me. I pulled down the right strap then left, unleashing the prettiest, brown, swollen boobs.

Swallowing hard, I decided I wanted to see more. To see it all. To taste it all. So I did. She helped me with her pants and panties. Her shoes had been off since laying on the bed earlier. I wanted her socks off, too, and made it happen. When that was done, I had a shivering and breathless Ashira Witherspoon on the bed, and damn, was she beautiful as fuck! She was more than I imagined her to be this way. Ass naked. I could say so much, but had more to do.

I kissed her again, Witherspoon was ready, meeting my slow pace, holding me to her face. I started up top, worked the tip of my tongue over her chin, then licked her neck again. She smelled soft, flowery, and bad ass at the same time. My tongue traced down the center of her tits and I couldn't tell if this was reality or my frequent prison fantasies. I was so excited, I felt dizzy. She had to feel my jitters. Fuck, I hoped she hadn't. But my nervousness and rustiness were damn sure real. I wasn't so sure when I kissed her left nipple and Witherspoon's whole body shivered. Then when I put my palms over them and stroked, her eyes closed as I pushed them into my hands.

Damn.

I'd been missing out on this.

For years…

Pulling them shits together, I didn't have to choose which nipple I'd taste first. I just let my tongue roll over them slowly then fast, feeling her legs move beneath me. Witherspoon made a sucking sound between her teeth and that shit drove me wild. My mouth left her boobs, but my greedy ass hands didn't want to. I pushed down, kissing her flat belly, rimming her navel with the tip of my tongue.

That's when her agile fucking legs broke from beneath me. The scent of pussy hit my nose, and I swear on everything I love, I almost passed the fuck out. This was too rich, too surreal. I'd smelled pussy more recently than I licked boobs, but I'd never smelled anything that made me lightheaded in need. I didn't think. Couldn't. My hands went to the back of her thighs where I kissed the bottom of her ass, working my way up. When I made it to her ankle, I went to the other cheek and tasted my way up.

When I was done, Witherspoon's face was contorted, her breathing was desperate and I was still hungry. I pushed her thighs apart and dove in between and kissed her there.

"*Uhn…*" she panted.

I didn't hear much after that, but did know I was at a damn precipice. I'd been here before: the first time I'd shot a gun, the first body I dropped, the first payout for a gun sale, my first arrest, my first conviction, my first encounter with the Holy Spirit.

I'd fucked up.

Staring down the barrel of no return, I pushed my tongue into her pussy, plunging into the canal over and over again. Coming out, I flapped my wide tongue up her whole slit, lathering what was caught inside between her fat lips. I swirled through them, high as hell from her deep berry scent mixed with musk and fucking gold. I was like a dog on table food, licking all over. But when I settled on the swollen bulb up top, her little hands hit the back of my head, holding me in place. Lifting her until her ass was in the air, I knew not to move from there until she let go of me first.

It was like scrapping with a nigga and putting him in a choke-hold. You stayed right there with the same strength and intensity until he tapped out by going loose. I did that, flicking my tongue and seeing her boobs heave from this angle. Her hips began to move harshly with urgency in short movements and fingertips pressed hard into my scalp. Then a glow opened on her face and Wither-spoon let out the most feminine cry with her eyes rolling to the back of her head. And I kept licking.

This.

This is what I was keeping myself from losing control over. This was a distraction for a man like me. It was dangerous. Feeling her go limp around my head as her body jerked was my fucking leap from the forbidden edge of my control.

And when she was done, I wasn't. I was just getting started. When Witherspoon's breathing came down, I flipped her ass onto her stomach and buried my face between her cheeks, swiping until the fat of her ass vibrated against my face.

I wasn't done there either. In fact, I wasn't done until she cried, "Ohmigosh! No moree…" during her last orgasm hours later.

That.

That was why I didn't want to give the "bitch" the time of fucking day back in January in *Brown Baristas*.

I'd slip and she'd show no mercy.

I watched as the car pulled into the terminal at Newark airport. I leaned against the door, fist holding my chin.

"Ms. Witherspoon, I just got word your nine-seventeen flight to Savannah is on time. The aircraft is fifteen minutes out, and your father's car just pulled into the terminal."

"Do you know if he's alone?"

"I do not," the driver in the front seat answered.

Then she grumbled to herself, "I hope he didn't forget this girl."

My phone chirped.

Jug: *We got a problem in w caldwell Houston and I got pulled over last night when I made a bway burger run DAMN*

Shit...

I was late. Knew I'd be when five-thirty rolled around this morning and Witherspoon had to leave. She wasn't joking when she said she expected me to drive her home this morning. But she damn sure remixed her proposition when she added me riding with her to the airport. But before that could happen, she had to shower, finish packing her "toiletry bag," and get dressed. I didn't fight her on it: I couldn't. I was here, doing what she wanted.

Me: *I'll be there soon*

I sent Juggy ahead of me when Witherspoon offered to have "her car" drop me off on my worksite after.

"And here we are," the driver announced, pulling over to the busy curb. "I'll quickly get your things."

I felt her eyes on me, so I turned to her.

"You okay?"

I nodded. "I'm good."

A shy smile opened on her face and eyes fell. "Tired, I bet." I nodded. She cleared her throat. "Look..." She was able to look at me again. "I got you something—well, it came last night when I was with—you know. When we were hanging out. I don't want you to freak out or anything. I just thought it'd be something you'll like. In fact, I'm sure you'll like it; you said so."

She opened her *Asè Garb* duffle and pulled out a small shopping bag.

"What's this?"

"Something for you." I took the bag from her and nodded again. The driver knocked on the door. Witherspoon had to go. "I want to kiss you."

I didn't want her to. For one, if she did, I probably wouldn't let her go. And then because I wanted to punish her for leaving. The truth was, I needed her to go. I needed my time to myself. I had some shit to sort. Needed time on the ride to West Caldwell to pray. My morning routine hadn't happened, but last night into this morning did.

And I knew what she meant by wanting to kiss me but not trying. Witherspoon didn't want me to reject her, probably feeling like I had last night by not fucking her. I couldn't. I'd already lost too much control.

So, I grabbed her hand. "Safe travels, Witherspoon. Enjoy ya bestie's wedding, lil' homie."

A hesitant smile contracted on her beautifully naked face. "Say less, Jas."

Her eyes fell again before she turned and left the car.

"Shi-Shi!" a girl called her.

It was her sister. She ran up to Witherspoon, did some silly dance then hugged her. As we pulled off, it became clear her father was the big guy in the camel wool coat. The last thing I saw was him pulling her into a hug with one arm.

"And we're off to West Caldwell," the driver announced.

Sighing, I looked down at the bag. Deciding to go for it, I lifted a box from the bag and peeped the *Moments & Measures* leather box inside.

No, you didn't, Witherspoon…

Inside the bulky box was a hunter rubber strap with a blacked out, rectangular face. It was the watch she wore the first time I pulled up to her crib. Inside was a black metal dog tag with Ambrose McNeil's signature. This timepiece ran a few Gs.

Shit…

She did.

love *belvin*

ashira

I cut out of the massive, and very festive barn and into the perfectly green savanna. The night was chilled after a mild and sunny day. The sunset brought a dip in temperature, but it still beat the one back at home.

Home…

I smiled, admiring the beautiful white lights roped around the tall trees. The white cloth cocktail tables mounted with candles really gave the best romantic ambiance. Becky and Connor's wedding was beautiful. Great atmosphere, thoughtful décor, and delicious food. And no one seemed to have balked at the amount of color and culture amongst their guests. Connor seemed to have more non-white friends than Becky. It had been fun. But now that the event was winding down, I was restless, wanting to leave.

Tightening my shawl, I pulled my phone up to make a *FaceTime* call. There were a few rings before his face popped up on my screen. I was upset right away because like me, he was under a light, and from that angle, his features were dark. And it didn't help that he wore a baseball cap.

"Where are you?"

"Outside." His natural timbre in that one word heated my sex.

I felt dizzy with stupid and very juvenile excitement. "Where?" I bit my lip.

"Where are you?"

"Outside."

"Looks nice."

I glanced around, taking it in. It was gorgeous out here. "You didn't answer my question."

"What was that?"

"Where are you?"

"I 'on't want to say."

My brows met in sharp reaction. "Why?"

"'Cause I'm mad at you."

I couldn't help my giggle, even tossed my head back. "Why?"

"Because it's been over twenty-four hours since I've heard from you."

Oh...

"I'm sorry. I slept as soon as we checked in yesterday because, as you can imagine, I was tired as hell. But that bliss wasn't long enough because Becky called my room, hyperventilating about *Neiman Marcus* mailing the wrong shoe to her. So, I had to go out and find a suitable shoe in her size with the rest of our friends. We showed up at the rehearsal dinner so late and barely got instructions for the ceremony." I laughed, feeling silly. "And then you know we got wasted because...that's what the fuck we're supposed to do. Right?"

Jas laughed with me. "Sounds like that's why you were asked to be a bridesmaid."

"Well, I *am* a good time. Nobody throws a good party like me or brings out the party in other folks." I clicked my teeth and winked. "You should ask about me, bud."

"No need. I've had enough to know."

My nipples flashed hard and pulse raced. Jas didn't smile. He didn't laugh it off or try to change the subject. He was putting himself out there and it thrilled me.

"You miss me?"

"Say more."

My eyes flashed wide. "Why do you miss me?"

He didn't speak at first. Jas wanted the moment to linger, his feelings to permeate the quiet space. "I don't know why. You insult me every chance you get. Then you let me taste you and I officially hate when you leave town."

My lungs seized. "Jas…"

"Say less, Witherspoon. Just get your ass home. I wanna take you out."

"Out?"

"Yeah. Like on a lil' date; make you laugh, and kick it with you about some shit."

"Kick it as in…" I peered around to be sure no one was following this conversation. "Going further than you did two nights ago."

"Nah. Kick it as in…say more."

I nodded, understanding his lingo. "We can kick it about doing more, too, Jas. I know you want to."

"I do."

"Then…" I angled my head. "…do."

"Let's hang out, Witherspoon."

That offer made me happier than I should have been. But I wouldn't be me if I didn't find a way to bust his chops. "You know…" I licked my lips. "I'd love to get to a place where you don't call me my father's name."

"Whatchu want me to call you?"

I shrugged. "My name. Anything that makes you feel you know me past work or therapy."

Jas sat back, allowing the street light to fall on him, exposing his handsome features. His top teeth peeked when he licked his lips, his beam was that perceived. "Get home, Witherspoon."

I didn't want to hang up, but I could tell Jas did. There was so much hanging in the balance of our grins and snorts, but I'd follow his lead and leave it there.

"Night, Jas."

A deep nod sent the gesture back to me. Simultaneously, I sensed a presence rounding me.

"Shit, Peach!" I whispered, leaping inches off the ground.

She leaned onto the table directly across from me, sporting a curious gape. "That anybody I know?"

I shook my head, so much going on with my damn pulse and my belly being invaded by butterflies. And Peach wouldn't stop looking at me like the momma who'd caught her kid's hand in the cookie jar. "I didn't know you were out here."

"I didn't announce it." She shrugged.

"Yeah. I guess not."

I pulled the shawl closer around my shoulders, feeling chilled and naked now. Cold water had just been doused on me, thanks to my best friend creeping up on me.

"You know," she began. "While you guys were out shopping for shoes for Becky, I got a call from Neveah. You remember her. Right?"

"The one whose house got burned down two years ago?"

She shook her head. "That was Maddie. Neveah is the one going for fire chief in Newark."

"Oh." I recalled vaguely.

"She called me about the smoke detector inspection at the church then hit me with a sidebar."

"Oh, yeah." I pulled my lip gloss from my strapless bra. "What's that?" I was always entertained by the wild stories Peach confided in me.

"That apparently Cynthia is single again."

"Cynthia?"

Peach dropped her chin. "Cynthia, the one our age who goes to my church. The one dating the felon you know."

"Jas?" Him being a felon felt foreign in that moment. The guy was so much bigger than that stain on his civilian status.

"Yes, Jas. Isn't that who you just bade a goodnight to, girl?" My eyes blew the hell up and Peach's expression mocked mine.

"Damn." My eyes fell to the table. "I didn't know that."

"Oh, ya didn't?"

"No. I swear."

"I believe you. Now answer this: would it have anything to do with you?"

"I doubt it. I'm not even his type." This was true.

"Then who is?"

"Cynthia and most of the women in your singles ministry."

Peach shook her head. "I don't even know what that means."

"I'm too worldly. Too high maintenance, or some shit like that." I shrugged. "I don't care, though. There are plenty of willing bachelors after ya girl. Ha!" I flashed my tongue.

"Ha!" Peach mimicked me, tongue and all. Then she rolled her eyes, standing straight from the table. "You be careful, Ashira."

Damn. Ashira? Not Shi-Shi?

"What is that supposed to mean?"

She turned toward me. "One who is faithful in a very little is also faithful in much, and one who is dishonest in a very little is also dishonest in much."

My mouth dropped. "Are we quoting scripture now? Is it that serious, Peach? They're not married or even engaged. Did you know he 'dates' two women at a time? Do you see me participating in bullshit like that—with a damn laborer, no less?" She folded her arms against her chest. "I'm not in their world. I have nothing to do with their situation. Sorry it didn't work out for Cynthia, but I tried to tell you that back in February. They're not compatible."

"You think I care if Cynthia marries this man, Shi-Shi? You think it's my business or place to make that happen?"

"Then why are you on my back?"

"Because I saw something between you two, and I don't know if you're in denial, lying to yourself, or you're trying to keep it from me. Either way, all I'm saying is steer clear of any crooked roads. We single women find our way into these suspect circumstances and take chances in relationships, all for the thrill of having companionship—"

"He ain't my companion type, woman!" Why couldn't she understand that?

Peach knew me better than most. My ideal man wouldn't be interested in *thrift shop Cynthia*!

Her palms raised into the night air. "I'm not going to win this one tonight, I see. So, I'll be the dramatic preacher friend and leave you with this. Proverbs twenty and seven. I wish women would apply that principle to their 'love' pursuits."

She walked away, leaving me so damn confused.

Again…

love belvin

There they are…

The day was gorgeous. As I pulled up to a park just outside *Turner's Park*, I knew the day would be perfect. I'd waited all damn week for this. It was just a fair, I knew. But more than that, it was our first official date. The stars and moon seemed to have aligned with Saturday being the perfect day of the week and the weather being great with clear skies and the temperature mild enough for me to wear a dress with cute new booties.

Jas and Juggy were standing near a tree talking. Well, Juggy appeared to be talking to Jas, and Jas' eyes were on my car. As I parked, they crossed the street to me.

"Aye there, Shi-Shi!" Juggy greeted me rather friendly.

I guess we were past that point now.

"Hey, Jug!" I closed the door and straightened my dress. "You got a fresh lineup, I see."

He patted his head smoothly, walking over to check himself out in a random side mirror. "You see that shit, huhn!" I laughed, never seeing him this open. "Now, tell your girls to come one by one; we overdue."

"Ohhhh!" I eyed Jas. "So, he finally did it?"

"What?" Jug asked.

"Asked for me to hook you up."

"Oh." He smirked. "I was just tryna give you some time to get to know me. You know. Let you figure this shit out." He patted his head again then thumbed his cheek.

Jas shook his head. "Give him your keys. He's gonna drop your car off at our final destination.

Oh...

I went into my bag for the keys I'd just dumped in there. "Final destination." I handed them over to Juggy. "Then how are we getting there?"

"You'll see." He reached for my hand. "You eat already?"

"I can't remember." It was true. I was too busy preparing for today.

I ran into Jas once this week at therapy. We had coffee together —him tea—and we found ourselves planning to see each other today. It wasn't until midweek I realized I didn't like not seeing and speaking to him every day. I didn't like not having hours of the day carved out just to hang. That's why today was so promising. I would be the lil' homie.

"How was your week?" he asked as we left Juggy behind.

"Bland. We got three new accounts that drained me. I had major negotiations and even terminations to handle."

"I had two of them shits myself—on the same day."

I looked up his way. "You fire people?"

Jas didn't speak at first, and I was used to this response. "I do now. I got another promotion."

"That's great! To what?"

We walked under the great metal banner of the park. Beneath was a cloth banner with the fair's name in bold print. Big colorful balloons hung from the antique light posts aside it. These fairs were legendary. They happened every year, attracting residents, their neighbors, and quality vendors alike. It was cute, small town vibes.

Jas led me over to the admittance table where he presented our tickets. He must have paid for them while waiting for me. This was adorable. Him taking me on an actual date, a modest and practical one.

"I could have paid for those," I murmured when we entered the park.

"I didn't need you to. They're ten-dollar tickets, Witherspoon."

I rolled my eyes. "Back to chastising, I see. Anyway, tell me about the promotion."

"I'll explain more later, but Rizzo knows my plans of having my own firm and has been helping me learn all the areas of building. So, I've been floating. My last role was floating foreman. I was oversee—"

"I know. A number of sites...troubleshooting trade issues... etcetera, etcetera."

I pointed to the clowns we walked past. One was sad, plucking flower petals, the other happy juggling balls.

"This one is more administrative: reading writeups, listening in on review panels, sitting in on—or in this week's case—giving the separation news, and shit."

"You don't like that part, huhn?" I broke from his grasp and stopped at a beads table.

Jas joined me. "Nah. I don't. But it's a part of the gig. Right?"

"Yup." I called over to the girl behind the table with her back to me. "Hey! These are five apiece?" When she nodded, I requested twenty and left her to pack them up.

I turned to Jas. "I try to stay away from all that shit. I did it for like eight months and decided to hire human resource professionals. Utilizing the skills of that profession separates the bosses from the trades from day one. You get hired"—I shrugged.—"it's on you. You get fired. Guess what?"—I shrugged again.—"that's on you, too. There's nothing personal." Jas nodded his understanding and I turned for the table. The girl had finished bagging the beaded chains I'd give to the dancers at the studio. They'd love the cute accessory.

"That'll be—" Jas cut the girl off by handing her a crisp one hundred dollar bill.

I immediately felt uncomfortable. He took the bag from the girl, too, then my hand, and we walked off.

"You know you didn't have to do that. Those are for the dancers at the studio."

"Yeah. I didn't exactly think you'd wear twenty bead necklaces at the same time, Witherspoon."

I laughed, enjoying the soft breeze and pleasant presence of the bright sun warming the chill still left in winter's wake. Spring could take a while to warm up the East Coast some years.

"First of all, they're waist beads, not necklaces. And dude, I wouldn't even let my boyfriend pay for something like that for them bitches."

"We know I ain't that, but…" He turned in front of me to stop my stroll. "For the rest of the day—shit, from now until you decide you don't wanna fuck with me no more—I pay. Okay?"

My face tightened with confusion. "Why? Jas, you know I can't do that. I'm not the high maintenance snob with fantasies of you treating me to *DiFillippo's* several times a week at the whim of my cravings." I needed him to understand this. "If it's something you can't do, I'll be glad to do it. I want to do it. I want to be cool with you."

The hardness in his features slowly smoothed out and Jas nodded. "That's cool to hear, Witherspoon. It really is." My chest began loosening, too. This wasn't rocket science. We were just hanging out, trying to enjoy each other. "But my rules stand. You won't be spending a dime today or…" He stalled. "…moving forward. We're only at a fair. How much can you buy? Let's just chill and enjoy this corny, peaceful shit."

We started walking again and I hooted a threatening laugh. "Oh, you have no idea how much shit I can buy from here. My mom loved fairs and festivals. She'd bring shopping carts and buy the most random shit our housekeeper would end up selling in our neighborhood's yard sales. How did you hear of this place anyway?"

"I'm a little familiar with the neighborhood."

"From work. Yeah. Did you know on the other side of this entrance is a gorgeous lake? I think people park their boats there…" Then I thought. "…or they have boat shows on that side? Something."

He chuckled, "Well, let's get through the vendors and see."

Chapter Nineteen

APRIL | PRESENT DAY

Ashira

ALMOST THREE HOURS LATER, WE WERE FINISHING UP ON HOT DOGS and loaded fries.

Jas reached over the table with a napkin and wiped my mouth. "Cheese," he explained with humor in his eyes.

Damn, he was sexy. Even being zapped from hours of walking, talking, laughing, and shopping, the man was fine. And I wanted him.

"Stop it."

"What?" I hissed, cranky from swollen feet.

"You're lusting."

Chewing, I tossed my fork into the fry basket. "I'm too tired to deny it."

Jas found that funny. "How could you be tired and horny at the same damn *ti*—never mind." He shook his head. "Don't answer that. I should know better."

"Finally, we have another adult on the other end of this conversation."

"I'm always an adult, Witherspoon."

"Then why am I afraid to mention last Thursday, at your place?"

"What about it?" His expression placid as he sipped lemonade through a straw.

My face dropped, eyes pinned to him. "In your bedroom…the place where I think I lost my mind because I ain't seen that shit since."

He chuckled. "Oh, that."

"That," I confirmed. *Fuck it…* I decided to go for it. The man spent over three hundred dollars today, thanks to my fair compulsions. There was but so much rejection he could do after that. "Like… Have you thought about it? Brought it up in therapy? Kicked it with Juggy about it?" I scratched my head, twisting my mouth. "Wanna do it again?"

Jas studied my face, an energy dancing in his eyes. "I do."

I broke a suspended breath I wasn't aware of. "When?"

He shrugged, pushing around fries with his fork. "Whenever you're ready."

Arousal blazed through me and I could feel my nipples hardening into pebbles. It was so intense, I forced my attention elsewhere. Boats. On the other side of the gate were the boats on the lake. "I see we're done with the first part of our date. Please don't tell me we have to walk back to the east entrance for Juggy's van. My feet will blister." I turned my nose and lips up at the thought of that painful prospect.

"Nobody told you to wear heels to the park."

"I was trying to be the adult in this. I was trying to be sexy," I groaned. "So what's the plan?"

"Did you pack your bag?"

"Yeah. But it's in my trunk."

"Cool."

"Then how are we going to get it? Or get to where we're spending the rest of the day and night. With all this crap I bought in tow?" I hoped we were going straight there. My damn panties were embarrassingly wet.

Jas chuckled. "Chill, Witherspoon. We're right there." He pointed to the marina.

"A boat?" That answered my lack of memory about what happens on this side. "We're going on a boat."

"Yup." He stood and began collecting our trash. "You're done. Right?"

My attention was to the water. "*Ye*—yeah…"

I didn't see this coming. Suddenly, I was reminded of Jas sharing his interest in boats. I guess this was proof of it. I followed him with sore feet to the marina as he carted the two hefty bags of useless shit I just had to have. When he turned back, he must have registered my flummoxed state or that of my discomfort.

"Stay right here, girl. *Damn*." He continued on.

My head swung back, begging his damn pardon. I was a dancer, could function in foot pain. It was the mystery of this date that had me off my game.

I watched Jas being greeted by security, on his way to a boat. He dumped the bags on one of the bigger ones then jogged back my way, making my face burn in a smile.

"What is this——"

He swooped me into his arms, carrying me past the security gate where the guy on duty laughed. Jas didn't let me down until I was at the open stern near the bags.

"You need help taking those off?"

I glanced around the wooden floors, the cabin door, the white padded benches, shiny wooden paneling, contemporary lounge area…this was a damn boat. Tugging at my feet alerted me to Jas making the call for me. We made a workout of removing the booties from my swollen feet. I took a deep breath once out of them then followed Jas up the steps to the cabin. He placed the bags and booties near the door before going to the dashboard. I felt the boat come alive beneath my feet. The engine ignited and a motor came alive beneath us.

"Have a great day, sir!" The security guard was unraveling a rope.

"You got it!" Jas returned to him in a shout. His volume was lower when he requested, "Come here, Witherspoon."

I leaped at his command, turning to amble further into the cabin. He opened a small refrigerator, pulling out a bottle of champagne. Then he turned to pluck a bottle of *Château Blevin*.

"Whoa! We've got wine and bubbly?"

"Which?" He held them higher in the air.

"You rented a boat! We've gotta go with the champagne, dog!"

Jas shook his head, I was sure, laughing at me. I didn't care. This was all so thoughtful, and unpredictable, and perfect: just like his weird ass. The cork popped and I was thrilled. Jas handed me a flute of champagne, of which I knew I'd enjoy alone.

"Have a seat." He pulled out of his vest, attention to the dashboard.

I was taking my first sip when a revelation hit. "Wait. *You're* driving us?"

He turned to me with an expression between shocked and confused. Jas nodded.

I blinked hard and successively. "Okay…"

And he did. Within seconds, we were taking off on the lake. I'd never taken such a ride, creating waves, and charting nature from the other side. I was used to the highways and runways from flying, *but boating?* It hit right immediately; the vibe. Jas was like a maestro standing at the steering wheel.

"Is this what you do to wow them church girls?" I leaned into his sturdy frame.

He snorted, shaking his head. "No, Witherspoon. You want something to nibble on? There's some cheese and crackers in there."

"No. I'm still full from the hot dogs and loaded fries. Speaking of which, why did you cut Cynthia off?"

His brows met, and I knew I switched gears too fast. "Who said that?"

I dropped my head to the side. "And you did do it before I left for Becky's wedding. Why?"

"Because you kissed me."

What?

"And?"

"And I liked it."

Shit...

"And?"

"And I ain't feel right being...not being honest with her."

"About what? It was just a kiss."

Jas pulled his big hands up to rub down his face and groaned, "It's been two months, and if I kissed somebody I ain't even dating, obviously I need to regroup shit."

Shit... I didn't know what to say to that.

"I feel bad. Maybe you should call her and check in."

"I plan to."

Jealousy struck. "Why?"

"Because if it got to her pastor, it must've hit her hard. I'm not in this shit to hurt or get hurt."

"Who said anything about Peach?"

Jas adorably smacked his teeth. "Y'all got any other mutual friends?"

I rolled my eyes away, watching the passing trees. This was amazing. "I can't believe you boat."

"There's a lot of shit about me you don't know."

"Because you won't share."

Jas had no comeback for that because I was right: he didn't open up to me. Sometimes, it felt like a tool to keep me intrigued. Most times, it was frustrating as hell. Either way, I felt good in the moment. He felt good. That's all I needed. This was a distraction from Austin, the blogs, gossip television shows, my selfish father, and demanding work. Playing this game with Jas was my escape from it all. When this fizzled, I'd be strong enough to take on those elements of my world that were harder to simply remove. Austin had still been trying to call...along with his mother and assistant *and* best friend. I wasn't ready, and didn't care to be considerate. What I wanted to do was what I was doing now. Escape.

We drove out to the Hudson into the state of New York, passing tiny islands, ports, and various sizes of ferries. I drank champagne and Jas enjoyed bottled water and *Blow Pops*. The man loved those lollipops. He sucked down four as we cruised. I wondered how he'd maintain good oral care, consuming all that sugar. That aside, it was great to see him do what he said he liked to do for fun. It made Jas believable. And hot. He didn't lie when describing enjoying the grip of the stern. Looked to me that he'd mastered it.

By the time we made it back to Jersey and turned into a creek which eventually opened to a river, Jas explained, the sun was retiring. I took it all in, snuggled in a blanket he handed me when the temperatures plummeted. He turned on the heat in the cabin, too. The boat was beautiful, a social vessel with dining space, a lounge for a small party, and even a deck above the cabin for laying out, according to Jas. I didn't venture much, just appreciated the ride and tonight's captain.

"These homes are beautiful," I observed out loud, not recalling ever seeing a boating neighborhood in Jersey.

I'd seen them in Florida, Oregon, and even in other countries… islands, but never here. These were luxury homes, too, opulent with docks and boat garages. Jas tapped on the beautifully lit dashboard and glanced up. I followed his line of vision to the right and noticed one of the garage doors opening. From this distance, the retracting wall seemed small, but as he slowed down, hitting other "gear commands," it was clear we'd reached a destination.

He tapped my shoulder. "You see that? Around the house?"

Squinting, I peered in between two massive properties and saw my car, parked in a circular driveway.

"Oh…" I guessed we were really here, our *final* destination of the night. "Shit, Jas. How much did this set you back for the night?"

He snorted. "Would you chill, Witherspoon?"

That quickly, my attention went to the extravagant lighting of the back of the estate. Slate, basalt, and copper exterior colonial-style structure. An infinity pool was just above the boat garage we were motoring into, and a lounge area and cabana directly over us.

"This place is remarkable," I breathed as Jas turned down the volume of the stereo.

Like a pro, Jas parked the boat, tabbing and clicking controls on the dashboard. The garage door closed behind us and when he was done, he pulled the blanket from around me.

"You ready?" Using his head, he gestured to the champagne flute I'd been using. "You can bring your bubbly. I've got more in the house if you want it."

I nodded, shocked at the vibe he'd created by going to lengths to impress me. It was a successful task: I was blown away. Following him to the back, Jas grabbed the bags and my booties, then helped me out.

The garage door led into a long hallway with dark wooden floors and velvety gray walls with stunning white trimming and wainscoting illuminated by white candles and white flower petals. I was stunned into silence at the image against the soft sounds of Switch singing *"There'll Never Be,"* an old school track my parents loved and would sing to each other.

"Shit," he mumbled, stopping abruptly. Then Jas chuckled, almost nervously. "If I track shit in the house with these boots, Consuela's gonna have my ass," he mumbled, reaching down to remove his *Timberlands*.

An unwelcoming feeling of guilt began to snake around my heart as my groin churned, so turned the hell on.

"Look.. Jas..." I swallowed. "I appreciate—"

His face darkened in the glow of the candles and head collapsed backward in frustration. "If you're about to mention cost or money...or whatever shit you're calculating in your head—"

"No!" I pushed my palms into the air. "Well, not exactly like that. I was just going to say, I appreciate the thoughtfulness incorporated into today. I don't think I've been this wowed since I was sixteen and my crush, Joshua, brought me a little *Tiffany's* bracelet to ask me to be his girlfriend. I just..." I straightened, eyes rolling to the ceiling.

"Just what, Witherspoon? I'm not the kind of guy who's gonna make you do anything you don't want to do. I hope you know that."

I snapped my fingers and pointed my index one his way. "Actually, you do. You're the first guy I wanted to '*let's get drunk and forget what we did*' and you've made me hold it alone because of your religious beliefs."

"Spiritual?" He mildly corrected.

"Okay. Spiritual." I bit my lip. "Back to my point. I feel like I'm the cause of a lot of your rules being broken. Like last week at your place, when I asked to come over, it wasn't to spend the night—"

"It's all good, Witherspoon—"

"But I damn sure was happy I did. I figured I could help you out with your skills eventually—fantasized about it, really. But damn…" I shook my head with squeezed eyes at the memory. "I didn't know you were so passionate and *extremely* attentive. You watched me come in your mouth…a lot." Jas' head cocked to the side, and I knew I was overloading him with too much emotion and not enough context again. "I thought you'd require lots of coaching and then all this shit between us would eventually fizzle out, but…"

His head shook faintly, forehead wrinkled. "If you don't want to—"

"That's the problem: I do! I want to see you naked and find out if I'm right about the size of your dick. I want to be the first to see —" A thought struck. "Wait. For clarity: you haven't had sex in…"

He sighed. "The last time I had pussy was the morning I turned myself in, back in 2008."

Wait… "But I thought you said…Samona."

"That was the plan when I got there, but it ain't turn out that way."

"What happened?"

"Witherspoon," he whined, rubbing his face.

"Just tell me."

"It didn't feel right. She ain't feel right." He shrugged. "After I let her blow me, I let her go. Let all the shit go. I needed to be at peace with the betrayal." Another shrug. "And I moved on."

Each muscle in my face fell. My shoulders dropped, breasts

hiked, and nipples stung in need. "I'm going to bust your cherry." My brow peaked with arrogance.

A snort left his chest as Jas rolled his eyes adorably, his fingers pinching the bridge of his nose. "Fuck you, Witherspoon."

A smile broke out on my face. "I'm about to."

"Is that what this dramatic babble was about? You being the first since…?"

"About me taking your virginity." I nodded. "I just hate that you had to spend all this money. I didn't need it. I would've paid for it."

Jas shook his head, unamused by my joke and continued down the hall, wide back swaying sexily. "Fuck you, *Wither*—"

I jumped on his back, causing him to struggle for his balance. Then I lowered myself to the floor to circle his thick frame, feeling the bulge of his muscles from my sudden impulsion. I captured his face between my palms and kissed him. His soft, full lips were sweet and tongue ready, moving with purpose against mine. And Jas deliciously grunted when I began to climb him. His palms were rightfully possessive on my ass, gripping and lifting me as I tried lowering to find his cock to grind against. I hardly felt us walking.

The next thing I knew, he leaned over, sitting me against a hard cool surface. I opened my eyes to find a stainless steel below zero fridge faintly lit with glass doors ahead of me. My eyes closed again when his mouth traveled down to my neck and his big hands pushed up my dress. Heat exploded in my groin from anticipation. He pulled my thong down to my ankle where it dangled and Jas' big hand lifted my other leg, tracing kisses down to my valley.

My back gave out and arms flayed, hitting paper bags filled with something warm. I retracted them and tried catching my breath and controlling the excitable cells bouncing all over my body at his touch. Then his mouth hit my cleft and his tongue stroked broadly. My hands flew to the back of his head and I rocked my hips, creating a rhythm Jas understood right away. The restraint of my bra and dress frustrated me, I wanted to be naked and have my nipples stroked even if only by the air.

"Shit…" I cried, feeling the pads of my feet heat in pleasure.

He was fucking me with his tongue, pushing stiffly inside of me.

With each plunge, I was dizzied with pleasure. His tongue stabbed in and hooked upward coming out, massaging a bed of nerves he found buried inside me last week. Jas didn't stop until my hips twisted with fury and I exploded, crying out intensely. I didn't hold back, unveiling my vulnerability.

Beneath my heaving breaths and burning lungs, Jas rose to his feet, expression stoic, body broad and intimidating. He pulled my torso from the counter and kissed me hard and long. We didn't stop, didn't feel like I wanted to, though I knew my lungs were on fire from not breathing, lips swollen from the pressure.

But Jas stopped first. Above the soft music still floating in the air were our desperate breaths and the heat from them, and our charged bodies.

"Ashira," he heaved. *He called me Ashira.* "I want you so *fuckin—*" He whipped his head away as though pained by the admission. Then Jas gripped the ledge of the marble countertop, head dropped between his shoulders, inches away from my heavy breasts. "You need to eat...use the bathroom, or something? I didn't give you a chance."

I shook my head, though he couldn't see me. Hell no! I didn't need anything but him.

Shakily, my hand went to the back of his bowed head and fingered softly. "Did you..." I licked my swollen lips and swallowed nothing. "...remember the condoms?"

Jas' head swung up, eyes expressively wide. "You still...you want to?"

I nodded. Profusely, I nodded. Of course, I wanted this. "I do."

He studied my eyes for seconds long before nodding. "Okay. Okay. It's just that I'm outta practice with the consent step."

"You have it." I was breathless with need.

"Now?"

"*Boy!*"

He scooped me up, eyes locked on me as we traveled through the empty, slow jams-filled halls. In our trail were candles and flower petals. Ahead of us was the "finally" of our curiosities—at least mine. He stopped and I could hear and feel him opening a door beneath my ass. Once inside, he let me down and prompted me with his eyes to look around. I could make out more candles from my peripheral immediately. Hesitantly, I broke my sight of him and peered around. Music still flowed and—*oh my*...

Mirrors...everywhere. Giant mirrors, too. They were secured by wooden bases and all encompassing a single tufted leather bench.

"Jas," I breathed. "This is..."

"You said you wanted to fuck me in front of mirrors—that was before you copped to wanting to take my virginity. I figured I'd watch, too." He glanced around again.

I took a few steps, right away enjoying the feel of silk petals beneath my feet. This had to be the dining room of the house. It was immense, but I couldn't see much beyond the gigantic mirrors because of the reflection of the candles. He did all of this because I talked shit to him? I couldn't help but to think about the expense. Whose house was it? Well, an *Airbnb*, of course, but... Were there any penalties to moving furniture and possibly setting a fire? Because having all these candles lit—even if he had help from Juggy somewhere here in the house—was a huge risk. When I turned to ask, my damn lungs seized.

Jas was stripping. His thermal shirt was on the floor and tank t-shirt was being pulled over his head. His eyes were dark and hungry on me, making me decide in that very moment. I'd assume any financial risk posed here today. Jas was ready, and so was I. My jacket went first, Then I began fisting the sides of my dress, gathering it in my palms until I reached the hem. Next, I pulled it over my head, being kissed by the air in just my bra and thigh-high stockings.

Jas worked at a moderate pace, now down to his boxers and socks. He peeled them off one by one, dumping them over flower petals. I swallowed, admiring every cut, swollen bump, and flex of his muscular being. When Jas paused, I reached back and unsnapped the bra from my back. With soft tugs at the straps, it fell down my chest then to the floor. But he'd seen me naked before. Jas had tasted just about every inch of me last week, something no man ever had.

It was now time for me to see all of him. And so far, I was treated by each body part except the featured guest of the night.

I licked my lips. "Ready?"

"Been." His chest flexed at that one syllable.

Then I nodded in his direction. "Time's up for those."

Jas chuckled then reached for the waistband of his boxers and pushed them down his roped thighs in one swoop. His torso sprang upright revealing the king's jewels. Suddenly, he was too far and I needed a close-up. Slowly, I toed over to him, eyes to his, requesting permission. When he nodded, my heavy arms lifted and brushed against the silk of him with the tips of my fingers. Jas grunted softly over my head. I peered up and found his eyes closed. Then I grabbed him, a palmful, stroking him upward. Quickly, I decided on two palms to capture the thick ridges and explore the full length of him. He was thick, well-endowed…a fucking secret treasure.

I was proud of him. Impressed by his ability to keep this a secret. If I were a man with all of this, I'd tell everyone to suck it with confidence.

Just me, though…

But Jas wasn't me. He was otherworldly, a box of treats and treasures, and apparently humble.

Slowly stroking him in my hands, I softly asked, "What's your name?"

Jas' eyes rolled close. Shit. I didn't want him shutting down on me. This wasn't supposed to be a day of combat. Just exploration. Annoyed by his guard, I reached up on my toes, found his mouth, and kissed him. This time, it took Jas a few seconds to warm into it. I accepted it and stayed at him. Sucking on his bottom lip then caressing his tongue. I worked my way to rhythmic strokes and sucks on his tongue. The combination so smooth, Jas moaned.

Holy shit…

His face contorted into a helpless expression. That act of satisfaction propelled my work and I continued, enjoying the small act of intimacy by way of exploration. Jas was beautiful and giving me control the others in his harem had never had. That realization made me so damn hot. *He* was hot, and I could do this all night.

It all stopped when Jas covered my hands, halting my rhythm. "You forget how long it's been since I've busted with a woman touching me?"

"Oh…" I mouthed, loosening my grip. "I got excited. You're beautiful."

"And so are you."

I smiled, eyes tight with lust. "Thanks." I turned from him, searching the room. "Where are the condoms?"

He tossed his chin toward the bench. Toeing over, I found them on the opposite end. A brand new box. In the mirror, I saw Jas remained exactly where I left him.

"Sit down," I invited him, opening the box. Jas sat on the bench and I took to my knees in between his thighs, handing him a single condom. "You remember how to put one on or should I try?"

Shaking his head softly, Jas ripped open the packet with his teeth as I sat on my knees, inhaling his scent. Manly. That's all I smelled was a man, and that enhanced my excitement. Once he had the condom on and adjusted, I reached up for his face. Jas quickly grabbed me off the floor and I straddled him.

"Look… *Wither*—Ashira," he whispered over a heaving chest. "I can't promise… At first—*this* first…"

"*Shhhhh*… I get it. You're not going to last." I smiled at his vulnerability. It literally reversed the age of his facial features. "I'm actually looking forward to clowning you tomorrow." I pecked his lips. "And next week." I kissed him again. "And hopefully next month at *Brown Barista*."

"Fuck…" he whispered to himself, anxiety blasting through his pores.

It emboldened my touch, gathering him to rub between my already wet and swollen lips to lather him. A warm gripping palm clasped onto my left cheek and his other on my breast. Jas' hungry mouth found mine and tongued me with heavy breaths as I steadied his shaft and lowered myself onto him. Lubricated and all, I still needed to rock my way down the sequoia. The thick root was a destination, but not my goal *this* time.

I felt the boy in Jas, a twittering mess beneath me, bracing himself.

"Baby..." I held him at the back of the head, peering into his eyes. "Relax. It's just us...together. Look," I whispered, turning to the mirror on the right.

He was beautiful, thick long thighs spread wide for me. Bulky arms roped around me for anchoring. His chest swollen and spine straight. I took my time, working my way down, enduring the pressure of his thickness. It wasn't too bad, remembering what was at stake helped. I was his first. First in a long time, yeah. But I believed Jas' particular ass had not had sex in all this time. There was no need to lie. I saw the way women reacted to his being. It was predictable. He could have any woman he wanted—shit, he was having me.

The last type of guy *I* was into was a felon laborer, but Jas was different. Different enough to have fun with. And that's what this was: fun for the both of us. His thick appendage, my wet suctioning pussy, warming deeply, and acquainting finally. We looked good together, the mirrors confirmed it.

"Fuck..." he grunted, arms crushing me as I stroked over him as fast as his pulsing breadth would allow. I rocked and rocked, forgetting the discomfort, or maybe it disappeared.

Leaning into his ear, I whispered, "You're a blessed man." I moaned at his grip on my ass, his vibrating pelvis. "Thanks for this."

Jas' deep groans inspired my ride. I stretched my pelvis more, thrust against him harder and faster, loving his girth, vulnerability, and every muscle of his virile frame. I felt everything, including him growing even thicker inside my walls.

When air shot from his lungs and Jas tossed his head back, I knew he'd come. But I only slowed when his brutal grip on me loosened. I stopped when I felt him shrinking inside. Jas and I sat there, collecting our breaths again. I was in no hurry to speak or move, immediately wondering what he thought of it.

Breathing harshly, his chest rumbled, "I'm waiting for you to laugh."

"You lasted longer than I thought. I'm starting to wonder if the joke's on me," I spoke into his shoulder. "Was that... Okay? Was I okay?"

He smacked my ass. "You were perfect. Tight, wet as hell, and perfect."

His face glided down my cheek, lips trying to reach my lips against his shoulder. I gave it to him. Let him kiss me lazily but with the passion Jas kept hidden but for a kiss.

"*Ohhhh...*" the sounds of her cries were still foreign to me, but so good.

Ashira's hand reached back, gripping the back of my head, keeping me in place. I flicked my tongue harder, feeling the saltiness of her cum fall on my tongue. The squeezing of her ass cheeks against my face drove me wild, making me think I was in the middle of a porn flick. Maybe I was. But I had rather not think too much into it. Ashira wasn't my girl or my wife, but I knew from the first time she let me taste her pussy, she was the best lover I would ever have. Crazy shit, but true. Earlier, down in the family room, when she worked her way onto my cock, I knew there wasn't a woman on the planet with a better pussy, at least for me. *I just knew it.*

Now, having her cum on my face as she leaned onto the shower walls, I knew I was addicted. Rushing into sex wasn't my speed. It wasn't something I was into because of the many risks I didn't want to take. I knew when I was released from prison I had to work hard to protect myself from anything capable of blocking the focus of my plan. My list. One risk was having my vision blurred by the distraction of women. *Or* thinking just any set of legs were golden.

As I reached for the condom on the bench, watching her small back rise and fall, *I knew* I'd fucked up. My hot blood was rushing in one direction, giving me a high. I was open as hell, and so soon. I knew from the moment I tasted her a week ago, I'd fucked up. Then when the tight walls of her pussy strained to fit around me earlier, *I knew* I was—*that damn quickly*—addicted. *I knew* I'd make sure she wouldn't feel another man's hands, mouth, or cock again as long as I breathed. Insanity, *I knew.*

"Jas!" she cried, seductively sucking in air as I slid into her from behind. I froze. "You're still…new to me." Her face lay against the glass wall and right hand flexed over my ass cheek encouragingly. "Go slow…work your way in."

Understanding, I moved slowly, working my way deep inside her. Ashira was warm, soft, and cushiony. She was wet and flexible, and made it painfully clear she wanted this. My eyes fluttered closed, a chill of violent lust rippled through my chest. It was familiar, but never experienced through sex. This excitement existed when I was a damn raging animal, ready to kill or to be killed. The speed of my heart only happened when I felt danger and imposed it.

"*Oh…*" Ashira panted, head collapsing backward as I fucked her at a steady pace.

The sounds of her milky pussy flexing around me; the realization of fucking with no clothes on was a first for me today; the anticipation of having her naked in bed tonight all had my head saturated in a pool of fucking lust. Addictive. *I knew* already I'd hit a moment of no return. It was a deal I made with God. I wouldn't fuck around, wasting my time with meaningless sex. Instead, I'd been circumventing the bullshit and putting in work for the real thing.

A wife.

"*Baby!*" she moaned.

Ashira Witherspoon's moans and cries while my dick stroked her were tablespoons of poison to my mind and body. It was like heroin:

potent and addictive. I didn't do addiction, though. It was why I didn't drink or do drugs. It was why I stayed planted in my Word and laid low. This was what I had been avoiding for almost two years. I spent years praying about this, fighting for self-control.

Because when I exploded, it was hard, possessive, and life-altering. The weight of my body bounced on my toes, ass squeezed, and balls warmed as I jetted hard.

"*Jas...*" she cried again, encouraging my fall into the snare again.

Then she reached for the back of my head, pulling it down to her opened mouth. Ashira sucked the cries of ecstasy from my soul with a long kiss. I'd never felt this, never had so much passion and expression when fucking.

Feeling my heart pounding in my chest and head swimming in fucking bliss, I knew I wouldn't recover from this fall. As my body buzzed in a hard ass orgasm, an alarm rang out in my head. Completely fucking caught up, I was a fallen man.

God, have mercy on me. Don't let me lay in this trap...

ashira

The bed creaked at each thrust spent into my core. Beneath me was soft, fluffy bedding as Jas' strappy arms draped around my arms and down my back, cupping my ass. His big hands held me to his sweaty torso, hard chest squeezed into mine, tight skin teasing my nipples. My pelvis met every thrust as we rocked into each other.

Our tongues circled and caressed hungrily. My hands pressed into his hard dewy ass, wanting to feel each muscle of him as the most dominant one pelted into my pussy, filling me to the hilt. I'd finally fit him all the way in. It didn't happen in the shower after our first time downstairs where he took me from behind with shallow thrusts. I waited through a toe-curling orgasm from his mouth in the bathroom and another here in this bed.

Third time's a charm.

And so was patience. Jas and I had been unhurried since running to get naked earlier. We'd been slow and graceful, and ego-free—equally again. We were also on the same wavelength about respecting each other's desire to explore one another. Everything had been slow, organic, smooth, and generous.

Maybe that's why he had me spread wide and cupping me missionary style. I wasn't expecting this proximity to his chest or the commitment of his pelvis and determination. His chest was to mine, face to mine, lips on mine. This wasn't fucking. Jas didn't understand that. He didn't understand this position was reserved for people making love.

And maybe I wanted to get lost in naivety with him, because my legs were locked around his waist, heels stabbing his ass as my groin began to churn with deep pleasure. My hips moved harder as I squeezed around his dick. My fingertips pressed further into his hard back.

I moaned deeply, biting my lip. Then I tensed my core muscles, tilted my ass, and exploded beneath the unrelenting horsepower he drove into me. He stroked and stroked, using each muscle group to form a missile, shooting through my core.

"*Fuck, Jas!*" I mewled hard as my body shook, not caring who'd hear.

Soft lips and prickly hair ends tickled the back of my thigh. An unexpected sigh pushed through my nostrils.

"Ashira," his well-deep chords beseeched. "Time to get up."

"*Mmmmm!*" I cried, not wanting to move. Not only was I comfortable, but I smelled him all over the pillow, sheet, and comforter.

I could literally die here.

"C'mon. I've got something for you to eat."

That's when my head lifted from the pillow and neck whipped to find him. He stood over me shirtless and ripped with low-hanging lounge pants. Jas' hands were in his pockets, posture casual. Through my mental fog, it was still possible for me to realize one thing: *All of that.* I'd had all of that man in, over, beneath, and behind me last night and this morning.

Finally.

I rubbed my eyes then licked my lips as I sat up in bed. "What's your full name?"

His chin dropped to his chest. "You wanna eat or what?"

Seeing him standing over me as I lay in bed felt domesticated in ways I'd never considered with him. This was a new dimension of Jas that I could use to stave off my deep curiosities of his full identity a little while longer. He was opening to me even more, which was far more addictive than any drug I could explore.

"You're still not done?"

Jas' eyes narrowed. "Done?"

"You took me out on the most fun, blissful, yet casual date yesterday. Then drive me on a boat appearing out of nowhere up the Hudson, then to this beautiful rental—" My face fell. "By the way, I had no idea this was a rental. Thought it was privately owned by some asshole who didn't want to do anything with it." Neither did I expect for it to be so contemporary inside.

I watched Jas' eyes narrow ever so slightly. His tone was so gentle when he advised, "We need to talk, Ashira. Go get showered, and I'll work on breakfast."

I exhaled, stretching out over the bed. "Just give me a minute." I patted my chest. "My heart is about to explode. I've never been in this place before, Jas." Yes, I'd just tipped my hand. I didn't care. All of this was so damn intense. "This is a lot."

I took a few deep breaths before opening my eyes. Jas nodded in a way that made me feel supported in my vulnerable state. Then he padded off, out of the room, the grooves in his sinewy back rolled rhythmically with each step away from me he took.

I exhaled again. *"Come on, Shi-Shi,"* I chided myself in a groan before wiggling my naked frame out of the bed.

I held the towel against my dewy skin while bending over, brushing my teeth. The bathroom was amazing during the day; white porcelain marble walls, heated floors, all-glass walls shower, built-in bench, separate under-mounting whirlpool tub, his and hers vanities, fireplace, and private toilet room.

Which agency manages this place?

I rinsed my mouth and dried my clean face with a towel. Leaning against the vanity, I froze when two things happened: I realized how sore my pelvis area was and I heard a familiar irritating chirp. My gaze circled the room. The source of the sound wasn't in the bathroom. Dropping the hand towel, I toed into the bedroom. The area was sparsely furnished with a king-sized mattress, dresser, bureau, and a mounted television on one wall and a set of security monitors on another. Their views were of the perimeter of the property: the sides of the house, the front porch extending to the street, and the backyard, which included the empty pool, outdoor kitchen, veranda, boat driveway, and the massive lake I saw last night.

Lake...

I turned to the live view of *Lake Sha'Ron*. It dawned on me: I'd heard about this very private and exclusive neighborhood it ran through a while ago. Its homes were valued in the seven-figure range, consistently exceeding the million-dollar price point. The neighborhood was a highlight in the real estate community because of its reputation of rarely having properties for sale and never having one on the market for long at all. Except for one. There was a bidding war over one property in particular. It was some years ago, so the details of it were a bit fuzzy now.

A knock sounded outside. "Hello?" a woman called. "Hello in there!"

I tightened the towel around my body and toed out into the bedroom.

"Hi, there. Jas couldn't remember if he added extra towels in there." It was her. The short, funny looking woman from the tea house in Harlem. She was as short as a middle schooler, but with big glasses and a warped face. "Sorry about the noise. Jas had a guy over for the past two days, trying to fix the wiring for the smoke detectors. He thought he had it taken care yesterday. They used to chirp all day and night. Now…" She shrugged. "…it's back. The electrician just pulled up."

Swallowing hard, I couldn't begin to understand the clusterfuck unfolding now.

"*Tha*—Thank you." I took the towels and backed away to close the door in her face.

"*There's the house along Lake Sha'ron. You know that exclusive row of big houses? Well, her crazy idea was to squat the house for a day. This house on Lake Sha'Ron had been vacant for years. None of the houses in that neighborhood make it to a listing. She looked up that place on our lunch one day and we saw it was sold. An internet search led to a name, but she still didn't believe it. Homegirl had been plotting on this house for years—it had been allegedly vacant that long. So, we drove all the way there one day and saw this old, white lady with jet black hair pulling up weeds in the front yard.*" Kema's voice on the beach back in January played in my mind.

"*You know who she favored? The old, white short woman from that old movie, 'She-Devil.'*"

I blinked, an ache growing in my chest.

"*The old white lady. Short…with the 'Matilda' blunt cut bob with the bang?*"

"*The old woman from Kindergarten Cop!*"

"Linda Hunt. All you had to do was say the lil' old lady from NCIS – Los Angeles."

My head swung to the door and the fresh folded towels hit the floor.

This morning was all kinds of fucked up.

I made it back to the room, unhooking the knob to find her slipping on her last boot. It was all etched in her pretty face.

"Witherspoon—"

"Where are my keys?"

Shit...

"Hold up for a minute." My ass actually started to panic for real. "Just hang on a minute. I woke you up so we could talk."

"Then you should have let my ass sleep. Maybe I would've missed this annoying ass chirp. Or maybe Linda Hunt out there would've remembered she's the tea-maker in Harlem!"

I nodded, understanding how all this shit must have seemed. "Ashira, listen—"

"*WITHERSPOON!* To you, a lying ass, gaming ass, fronting ass laborer, I am Witherspoon!" She choked on shock as she realized she was tearing up.

I was fucking shocked. It wasn't supposed to go down like this.

Twisting my lips, I took a deep breath, understanding I was responsible her reaction. "A'ight. I deserve that."

"No! *Don't!* You don't deserve shit. *I* deserve the truth. Who are you? Is this where you've been living all this time?"

"That's what I wanted to explain—I knew I was going to explain. Yesterday, I told you I was going to explain it."

"Explain what? That this isn't a rental?"

"Yes." I gave a nod, finding it so hard to look at her pretty face when it was soaked in tears.

"Who owns this place? Her?"

I whispered, "No."

"Then who?"

I swiped my nose, changing my stance. "I do, Witherspoon. Frankie's name is on the deed, but I had her buy it for me a few years back."

She sucked in a breath. I tried reaching for her, but she yanked her body away. "And whose apartment was that, that I slept in last week?"

"My mother's." That was the truth.

"And you don't live with her?" I shook my head. She didn't speak for a while, trying to control the tears. "And the boat. It's yours." That wasn't a question.

"It is. Is there any way we can talk about this?" I was fucking begging. "If you can give me twenty minutes to handle these people…" I pointed to the open door.

The knocking had my head whipping over my shoulder. Jug's big ass eyes craned his head inside the door. He peeped what was going down and nervously reminded me. "Reed's bitchin' the fuck out down there."

I turned to Ashira. "Ten minutes," I begged.

"Give me my keys!" she howled, chords pushing out her damn neck.

I motioned to Jug. He pulled her keys from his pocket and handed them over to her. Ashira snatched them out of his hands then grabbed her coat and purse I was able to bring up here before the shit exploded this morning.

When she clamped out of my room like a woman on fire, for a quick second, I debated it but couldn't let it ride.

"Witherspoon, wait!" I followed her, a few feet back as she rushed through the circular hall to the stairway.

At the start of the stairs, I could see one of the electricians drilling on a high ladder and Reed pacing with a clipboard in his arm.

By the time we were in the center of the stairway, he glanced up from the candles and petals on the floor, spotting me. "Aye! What are we doing here?"

I ain't have time for his ass. "Mr. Reed, I just need a minute."

"A minute to tell me why your ass didn't answer my call here last Thursday?" His arms shot in the air. "How the fuck did a ticket issued to your damn vehicle in Harlem that same night after your curfew pop up in the system?"

Seconds after his "questions," Ashira stopped and turned to look at him. Then she looked at me.

"You alright, young lady?" Reed registered the tears on her face, the swelling of her eyes...*her mouth.*

Fuck!

The last thing I needed Ashira Witherspoon to see was my parole officer, tying me to the thug she thought I was. The broke nigga, living off pennies earned as a low laborer, trying to chase a dream with a dollar, only a Rizzo-printed dollar.

Nope.

Seems like the only dream I'm chasing is you...

Witherspoon finally turned and left out of the open door for her ride. That's where the chasing stopped. I watched her pull off in her *AMG GT Coupe* like a bat out of hell.

grace.

the prism series : two.

~Love Acknowledges

Visuals: __Indelible Images__ — Mae, once again, your professionalism was impressive. Your patience and diligence saved us in the ninth inning. Thanks so much! Leo Watkins — You were a true save in the eleventh hour! Thanks for opening your mind and participating in my madness. LOL! Eriel Davis — It was you on sight! Ashira was officially personified by your beauty. My best to you both in all your endeavors!

Beta Reader: — Yorubia, aka Uncle GWORL, you think you be editing (and I love it)! Teehee! Thankyuh! #YouSTILLGone-LoseYoJob

Research: Special thanks to Adrienne G. and her A.G. for helping me with Jas' background. I appreciate it more than you know!

Christina C. Jones aka CCJ — You got that good-good, girl. *#Pause* Hahahaha! Love to love you much, momma!

Interior Artist: Cedeara Ardell McCollum — Thanks, baby girl, for the imagery you've designed for my books! Love you always!

Proof Reader: Tina V. Young — I know I stretched your immense brain with the timeline! But you came through as always.

Thanks so much for your constant dedication to #TeamLove. #SecretWeapon

Editors: Zakiya Walden of ***I've Got Something to Say!*** — Although I made it easy on you with the submission of this project, I guess I made it difficult with the selection of my clients. LOL!! Thanks so much for your professionalism, flexibility, and enthusiasm.

Santisha Taylor of ***AccuProse Editing Services*** — I did it, Joe. I did it! I DID IT! Crown me! Thanks so much for cleaning and organizing my mess.

MDT: We're still climbing. Next level soon come!

Master, my ***Jireh***, my ***Rohi***, Psalms 85:10 (NKJV) "Mercy and truth have met together; Righteousness and peace have kissed." *Thank you, Father, for my peace of mind.*

~Jas & Shi-Shi

See visuals from the series here on my website – http://www.love-

~Jas & Shi-Shi

belvin.com/Projects/Prism

~Other Books by Love Belvin

Love's Improbable Possibility **series**:

Love Lost, *Love UnExpected*, *Love UnCharted* & *Love Redeemed*

Waiting to Breathe **series**:

Love Delayed & *Love Delivered*

Love's Inconvenient Truth (Standalone)

Love Unaccounted **series**:
In Covenant with Ezra, In Love with Ezra & Bonded with Ezra

The Connecticut Kings **series**:

Love in the Red Zone, *Love on the Highlight Reel, *Determining Possession, End Zone Love, Love's Ineligible Receiver, *Pass Interference, Love's Encroachment, & *Offensive Formations (*by Christina C. Jones)

Wayward Love series:

The Left of Love, The Low of Love & The Right of Love

Love in Rhythm & Blues series

The Rhythm of Blues & The Rhyme of Love

LOVE IN RHYTHM & BLUES series

The Sadik series

He Who Is a Friend, He Who Is a Lover & He Who Is a Protector

The Muted Hopelessness series:

My Muted Love, Our Muted Recklessness, & Our Reckless Hope

The Prism series:

Mercy, *Grace*, & *The Promise*

Low Love, Low Fidelity (Standalone)

~Extra

You can find Love Belvin at www.LoveBelvin.com
Facebook @ Author - Love Belvin
Twitter @LoveBelvin
Goodreads: Love Belvin
and on Instagram @LoveBelvin

*Join the #TeamLove mailing list on my website to keep up
with the happenings!*

Click here (with WiFi) to join!

Made in United States
Cleveland, OH
28 November 2025

26920273R00236